POSSESSED BY PASSION

"Are you afraid now?" he asked, his lips against hers.

"No." She was, but she feared he might stop. "Kiss me, McKaid. A real kiss."

"If I kiss you the way I want to, I won't be able to stop. Do you understand?"

A wild, wanton flame of desire leaped to life at his seductive words. She didn't want to stop, she knew that. For the first time in her life she didn't want to consider what was proper, reasonable, right or wrong. She wanted this moment. She wanted McKaid.

"Don't stop," she answered. "I don't want you to stop."

"Why?"

More soft kisses rained over her face, down her neck. "I want to belong to you."

"Why?"

He wanted all of her, she realized. He wanted the words that would remove the last of her protection. He wanted absolute possession, complete surrender.

"I love you," she confessed honestly. She closed her eyes as his fingers trailed over her body. This was no dream. He was going to make love to her. It was shamelessly erotic, this power of the flesh. Erotic and beautiful, and with McKaid it was so right . . .

LOVE'S WILD FRONTIER

Jeanne E. Hansen

ZEBRA BOOKS
KENSINGTON PUBLISHING CORP.

To the men who make my life an adventure,
my husband Kraig
and
my sons Eric and Drew.

ZEBRA BOOKS

are published by

Kensington Publishing Corp.
475 Park Avenue South
New York, NY 10016

First printing: April, 1989

Printed in the United States of America

Prologue

Sophie stretched over the sink in the kitchen area of their small house and peered out the window to catch sight of the children as they played under the solitary cottonwood tree. Jack's eyes were drawn immediately to her slender and shapely backside. She straightened again, glanced at him, and grinned knowingly at that familiar glint in his eyes.

She wiped her soapy hands on the cotton towel, but before she had finished, Jack had his arms around her waist and was pulling her back against his hard chest and abdomen.

"You excite me as much as when we first met," he murmured against the side of her neck.

She shivered in sensual delight and turned in his arms, offering her lips to his. He kissed her for a long time, and very thoroughly.

Outside, Ruthie, just turned seven, yelped as her brother, two years older, dangled a small lizard in front of her face. She jumped up and ran toward the house, James in close pursuit. They reached the kitchen window together.

"Wait," James whispered, grabbing her arm to restrain her. He shook his head. "They're kissing again." Ruthie stretched to see, too, and smiled at her parents' antics.

"Ugh," James said quietly. "Let's go." Forgetting the lizard, which had successfully wriggled away, they ran around to the back of the house to play in the trickle of water in the creek. Ruthie glanced back at the house, her heart secretly glad to see

5

her very much loved father and mother hugging and kissing each other. It gave her a very warm feeling inside.

Riding north through Texas, the Corbett gang skirted to the west of Forth Worth. Fort Worth was full of lawmen who would know about the bank they'd robbed in Waco and the three men they had shot, and who would be on the lookout for them.

"What good is all this money, if we starve out here?" Wes complained to his older brother Dink.

"We'll get us some supplies, just not in town. I don't fancy a noose around my neck, kid."

"Where, then? Dammit, I'm hungry."

"We could all use some grub, and a good stiff drink," Lefty said, mopping his brow with his shirt sleeve.

Lefty was the middle of the three brothers, and the most cold-blooded. He had killed over twenty men in the last three years. Two other men rode with them, men who had been in the same jail when the Corbetts broke out of confinement in Fort Dodge, Kansas. The five men who made up the Corbett gang had been pursued throughout all of Kansas and Oklahoma, and were now adding to the work of the Texas Rangers and their law enforcement friends.

"There's a small ranch not far from here," Dink said. "We can stop in there and take what we need to last us into the next territory."

"That's fine by me," one of the others, a man called Gordo, said. "I'd just as soon keep away from those Rangers. I've had too many friends killed or locked up by them to want to hang around in Texas."

"You worry too much," Lefty chided. "They bleed just like everyone else. They ain't immune to bullets, much as they'd like you to think they are."

"No? Well, I heard tell there's one who can't be stopped."

"McKaid," Dink said, the name falling with a mixture of awe and frustration from his parched lips. "He's damned good, I'll give him that."

"I heard he can hypnotize with those eyes of his so's you can't draw down on him," young Wes said. "That true?"

"I never came to a showdown with him, but I've seen into those eyes."

6

"And?" Wes demanded. Wes was enthralled by the thought of facing McKaid. He was young and as foolish as most gunslingers who thought they were good. And he wanted desperately to prove himself to his older brothers.

"And what?" Dink snapped, irritated by his kid brother's questions. McKaid's name always left him feeling churned up inside. McKaid had foiled his plans more times than any other man on earth. McKaid had cost him thousands of dollars. McKaid was responsible for the chunk of lead that still remained in his shoulder and caused him pain when he rode for long stretches, as he just had. "Let's get going. We ain't gettin' no closer to food sittin' here jawin' about some legend that may or may not be true." No one argued as they followed Dink toward the Brazos River.

Three more men rode west out of Fort Worth. Tex Donner and Biff Story—both in their fifties, both old-timers in the Texas Rangers, both still commanding a great deal of respect and admiration for their skill and daring—rode alongside the legendary Dash McKaid.

"You sure now, young feller, that Jack's missus won't mind us two taggin' along with you?" Biff asked.

"Sophie? Heck, no. She'd welcome you anytime you're of a mind to stop. And Jack would love to catch up on what's happening with the Rangers."

"He don't miss the life?" Tex asked

"Oh, yeah. He misses it," McKaid answered. "But he was right to resign. He never did like the thought of leaving Sophie and the kids alone without his protection. And when he was almost killed, he decided enough was enough. Besides, his leg was badly damaged. It gives him trouble even now."

"How's he like ranching?" Tex asked. "Always did think that when I retired, I'd like to go back to that."

"Back?" Biff asked. "You had a ranch once?"

"I didn't *have* one. I worked on one up in Kansas."

"You were a cowpoke?" Biff croaked, stroking his gray stubbly whiskers.

"What's wrong with that? It's a dad-gum sight better'n swabbing decks on some Mississippi rat boat."

"Hey, now, I never touched a mop. And it was the *Mississippi Princess*, not no cargo barge. That was the good life. Not many

7

lads seen as much of the world as I had at sixteen."

A spark of humor lit McKaid's eyes. He knew the two men who rode at his side, and knew them well. But he was sure no one else knew that one had been a greenhorn cowboy and the other a lowly cabin boy. But then no one would ever guess that he'd been hoping to be a physician either. How odd it was that one little decision could change the entire course of history. His life had been turned around, and the lives of hundreds of people he'd touched over the years, because his father decided to take his mother on that one, as it turned out, fatal trip.

Alone at eighteen and with no financial support, he headed westward, as many folks did at that time. He crossed the country with the wagon trains twice before a man who appreciated his skills with a horse and a gun approached him and persuaded him to join the Texas Rangers. He worked hard at his job, made a reputation for himself, then spent three years with a special Ranger contingent during the war, before returning to Texas to again take up his duties as keeper of law and order.

He never learned how to heal the sick, to ease pain, to prevent disease, but it seemed that all his adult life had been spent in protecting innocent people from a plague and a scourge of a different kind—men who lived as parasites, taking and killing at will, with no care at all for the carnage left behind. The major difference, and one that never ceased to disturb him, was that in doing so, he himself had to take life, and take it often. More and more that thought crossed his restless mind. Maybe he should think about giving it up, too.

"Hey, McKaid. You ain't heard a word we been sayin' to you. Something on your mind?"

McKaid gave one of his brief and all too infrequent grins. "No. Just thinking, that's all. The past sometimes has a way of catching up with me when I'm out here riding."

"Yeah. I know what you mean."

"Hey, did you hear that?" Biff interrupted.

"Gunfire," Tex said laconically. "Your friend a huntin' man, McKaid?"

"Not usually. Let's go. The Corbetts are headed up this way from Waco, and as good as Jack Warren is, he can't take on all five of them."

*　　*　　*

8

Jack Warren saw the five riders approaching and sent the children indoors with Sophie. It was always wise to be cautious. He fired one shot in the air. "Who comes?" he shouted. "State your business."

The five men split up and circled around the ranch house. Jack, knowing trouble had come to visit, backed toward the front door. Only one other hand was on the ranch that day, since the others had taken Warren's small herd to join the drovers heading north. Jack was about to call out to him to warn him when Old Joe ran out of the barn and into a barrage of bullets. Jack knew his friend was dead before he hit the ground.

He turned and raced into the house. He had a battle on his hands. Sophie, holding the two children against her breast, stared at him in horror.

"Get down in the root cellar," he told her grimly, and she wasted no time in moving the table, sliding the rug aside, and lifting the trapdoor. She climbed down into the cool, cramped hole, pungent with the odor of musty ground, vinegar, and smoked meat, and lit a lantern for the children. They followed her down, and she hid them between the pickle barrel and the lard vat under some empty burlap flour sacks.

"Who are they, Mom?" James asked, as scared as his little sister, but trying to be brave.

"I don't know, but they shot Old Joe. You stay here and be absolutely quiet, no matter what you hear upstairs," she warned them.

"Stay with us, Mommy," Ruthie cried, grabbing for Sophie's hand.

"I can't, baby. Your father needs my help. James, hold on to her and keep her quiet. I'm counting on you now."

She left them and went up the ladder, shutting the door behind her. James remembered her last words when the shooting began. Ruthie screamed, and he pulled her against his shoulder and held her tight, tears running down his own face and into her pale blond hair.

The three Rangers rode at full speed when they heard the shots. A tight knot of fear formed in McKaid's stomach, and turned to cold rage when he crested the hill and saw the barn in flames, a man's body lying nearby, and one of the attackers throwing a torch through the back window of the house. With guns blazing, he and his two friends rode toward the house.

The Corbetts were surprised by the Rangers and fled, but not before McKaid's bullets caught one of them, and Tex winged another. McKaid, reaching the house first, jumped from his horse and raced inside.

"Jack," he called as he burst through the door. "It's McKaid."

Jack didn't answer. He was bent over Sophie's body, weeping as his own blood mixed with hers.

"Oh, God," McKaid groaned, feeling sick, sicker than he had ever felt. "Jack?" he asked quietly.

Jack looked up, and all the pain in the world was in his drenched eyes. Sophie was gone. He sputtered and coughed, his face twisted in pain.

Jack was also hit, and McKaid placed a hand on his shoulder. "Let me see, Jack. How bad are you hurt?" He tried to pull Jack away from Sophie, but Jack wouldn't let her go.

"No, McKaid. It's no good. Let us die together." He coughed again and was seized by a wrenching stab of pain. "McKaid, the children. Root cellar. You'll take care of them for us? Promise me, McKaid."

"Let me help you, Jack, for God's sake."

"Too late. McKaid!" he cried out as more pain clutched at him. "Promise me."

'I promise, Jack. I promise. Oh, God," he groaned and wiped the tears from his own eyes. "Hold on, Jack. Please hold on," he whispered, but as if he'd been released by McKaid's promise, Jack gripped his wife's body, released his last breath, and slipped away.

"McKaid," Tex said softly from the doorway, "the house is burning. We better get their bodies out unless . . ."

McKaid stood slowly, never taking his eyes from the peaceful faces of his dearest friends. "You and Biff take them out by the cottonwood. I have to get the children."

James and Ruthie were standing in each other's arms when McKaid opened the door and stepped down the ladder.

"They're dead, aren't they?" James said, trying his best to keep his tight voice from wobbling. Ruthie was biting her lip and clutching at James as she waited for McKaid to bring their world crashing down around them.

McKaid took a long breath and let it out slowly. "Yes," he said simply, and cleared his restricted throat. "You'll be

10

coming with me now."

Ruthie launched herself into his arms, and he scooped her up and held her tight as she sobbed her heart out. McKaid looked over at James and held out his other arm. James went to him. How could this have happened? How could good decent folks die when men like the Corbetts lived. When men like himself lived, men who lived by taking the lives of others. There might have been a line of distinction between him and the Corbetts, but at the moment he couldn't see it. Jack and Sophie Warren were dead.

A couple hours later three markers stood under the tree where earlier a young boy and girl had played. Behind the three men and the two children, who stood in prayer, were the smouldering remains of the ranch house and the barn.

Tex looked up at McKaid. The younger man's eyes were staring at the graves, unseeing, and burning like hot ice. Tex didn't need to ask what Ranger McKaid was thinking. McKaid wouldn't stop till every one of those murderers was dead.

"McKaid," he said lowly, bringing McKaid's frozen glare to meet his own sympathetic eyes. "It's time to go. The children."

McKaid nodded once, and his eyes softened. "Yeah," he said hoarsely.

"What will you do now?" Tex asked, knowing McKaid wanted to ride after the Corbetts then and there, but would have to wait until he had the two kiddies settled somewhere first. He'd heard the promise McKaid made, and McKaid was good for his word.

"My uncle has a ranch outside of Santa Fe. I'll take James and Ruthie there."

Biff handed Ruthie up to McKaid and helped James mount his own horse, one of the two they'd been able to save before the barn roof collapsed. The second horse was packed with the few articles they could salvage from the burning house, the children's clothes, blankets, a diary, a Bible, Jack's watch, mementos for the children to keep.

"Mr. McKaid," Ruthie asked, turning her head to look up at her father's best friend. "Daddy's with Mommy, isn't he? She gets so afraid when Daddy's not with her."

"Yes, sweetheart. They're together."

"Forever? With God, like she said would happen? And they're happy? And we'll see them again someday?"

11

McKaid blinked his eyes to clear away the moisture. He wondered what it was like to love someone so much that dying only meant that you'd be together forever. That's how it was with Jack and Sophie. That was one of the reasons he was so drawn to them. He loved them both. Just being near their love for each other and for their family helped fill a gaping hole in his own life, where that didn't and probably never would exist.

"Mr. McKaid?" Ruthie prompted.

"Yes, doll. It's just as your mother said."

Chapter One

Williamsburg, Virginia

The brass bell chimed over the door of the West End Book Shop. Elizabeth glanced up from her bookkeeping chores to see the delivery man from one of the publishing companies push a loaded dolly through the door. She laid her pen aside and with a smile stood and rounded her desk.

"Afternoon, Miss Hepplewhite," the tall, thin man said, holding out his log for her signature. "You're missing a beautiful day out there."

"So I see. And now you've just insured that I'll miss the rest of it."

"Well, I could skip this store and take your merchandise back. I'll tell them you weren't open."

"I've already signed for them. It's too late," she teased back. "Anyway, I'm anxious to see what you brought."

As soon as she waved the man good-bye, she tore the cartons open and rifled through the books. This was the best part of her job, setting out the new releases, putting up advertising in the store window, reading the books that especially appealed to her. She sat down on the floor and began to scan through them.

Micah Hepplewhite found her that way a few minutes later. He opened the door, walked in, and gave a bark of laughter.

"Oh, my gosh," Elizabeth exclaimed, jumping to her feet and dusting off her skirt. "Oh, Dad. It's only you. You gave me a fright."

"It's only me? What a way to greet your father."

She hugged him and gave his cheek a quick kiss. "There. Is that better?"

13

"Infinitely. How late are you going to work today? I thought we could go out to dinner."

"To celebrate? You got it!" she enthused.

"I did. You are now looking at the new chairman of the Department of English and Literature."

"Was Wooly very disappointed?" she asked, concerned. Wooly was a dear man and a frequent guest of theirs. He had also been considered for the same position at the college as her father had.

"That was strange. I got the impression that Wooly was more relieved than anything else. I think he's just as happy to teach his classes and then go off to read his journals. Responsibility is not one of his *fortes*. Velda wanted the prestige of his position more than he did."

"That woman. She's always basking in her husand's glory. She should go do something on her own."

"So, I've asked Caroline to have dinner with me, and now I'm asking you."

"Caroline? Oh, Dad, you don't want me tagging along with the two of you."

"I most certainly do. It's a special night."

"And all the more reason to keep it dinner for two. Besides, the new books are in. I really do have to work late, and then I plan to curl up and read one of these." She patted the new books stacked on the table.

Micah read the determined set of her jaw and knew she wouldn't be persuaded. His daughter had a definite mind of her own. "Very well. We won't be too late. Wait up for me and we'll have some bedtime cocoa."

"Sounds wonderful." She kissed him again and sent him on his way. He was still a very good-looking man, and much too vital to be a widower for as long as he had been. He might have had his share of lady friends over the past eight years, but no one he really fancied until now. She had her fingers crossed that Caroline, a widow herself, would be the one to capture her father's elusive heart. Caroline was a very special lady.

Not long after her father left, the bell sounded again. She finished her column of figures, tallied the sum, and closed her book. Only then did she look up to see who had entered the shop. It was late, she realized, and she should have put the closed sign at the door, but she'd forgotten. She'd never get to

14

the new book display at this rate.

"May I be of assistance?" she asked, looking up at last. "Derrek. How nice to see you again." She really should have put the sign in the door.

"Hello, Miss Hepplewhite," Derrek said nervously. "Wasn't it a beautiful day today?"

"I really didn't see much of it, I'm afraid. And you must call me Elizabeth. I insist."

He began to fidget with his coat buttons. "As you wish then, Elizabeth. I was wondering if you had a collection of Lord Byron's works on hand."

"Why, yes. I believe we do, Derrek. It's quite costly though."

"That's of no matter. It's for my mother's birthday."

"I see. This way then."

"Are you still angry with me, Elizabeth? I know you were terribly offended."

"I was never angry with you," she answered, hiding her dismay. "It is nothing to do with you that your mother's viewpoints on life and mine don't coincide."

"It's just that she puts so much importance on good blood lines. When she learned that you were . . ."

"Adopted, Derrek. It's not a word I could ever be ashamed of. The day the Hepplewhites adopted me was the happiest day of my life."

"Yes, yes. I'm sure. I only wanted you to understand that I—ah—don't think less of you for it. Only Mother can't bring herself to . . ."

"Never mind, Derrek. You don't have to explain. We all must do what we must do." And Derrek must always bow to his mother's dictates. And she must get him out of the shop before she broke down and laughed out loud at his sputtering attempt at an apology.

"I did enjoy our evenings at the opera, Elizabeth. I wish things could have been different."

"Here you are. I'll put that on your acount?"

"Yes. That's fine. Well, goodnight then. If ever you would like to go . . ."

"Goodnight, Derrek."

"Yes. Goodnight."

She closed the door, breathed a sigh of relief, and hung up

15

the closed sign. Why had she ever accepted his invitations to begin with? Was she getting that desperate? "Take care, Elizabeth," she scolded herself aloud. Just because she had overheard a woman referring to her as a spinster, just because she wasn't married at the age of twenty-six, didn't mean she had to grab at the likes of Derrek Pommelroy.

She checked her appearance in the little mirror she kept in her desk. She supposed she could have her hair cut, or curled, or styled in rolls and poufs, but that would take so much time to fix each day, and by the end of the day it would be a wreck anyway. Far better to keep it pulled back into an easy and neat twist.

"Nonsense," she muttered, pushing her gold-rimmed glasses up her straight nose. What did she care? When—and only when—a man loved her for herself and not her hair, her clothes, or something as ridiculous as her bloodlines, would she think about marriage. Marriage to her meant a union and partnership with someone she could talk to, really talk to, someone who could be counted on to consider her point of view, and with whom she could work side by side through everything life threw at them. To be tied to someone who thought her an ornament, or a prize, or an inferior species to be coddled and protected from the world, was abhorrent to her. In short, she wanted a marriage like her parents had had.

Two hours passed before Elizabeth was satisfied with her new window display. She locked the store, knowing that the owner would be pleased with her efforts, and walked the short distance to the little red brick house that had been her home for so long. The grass, newly cut, smelled fresh and clean. The boy who kept the lawn and gardens had also trimmed some of the ivy back from the windows, she noted. It looked nice.

Inside, she went directly to the kitchen and put the kettle on for tea. Micah had left her a slow burning fire to which she added more wood. She put some sliced ham and leftover potatoes in the oven to warm while she went upstairs to wash and change into her nightgown and robe. She took her glasses off, cleaned her face and hands, then unpinned her light brown hair and brushed out its thick length to hang freely down her back.

Captured by an urge, she lifted her hair onto the top of her head and turned her face from side to side to see the effect. She

16

could be pretty if she tried. Her father always said she had a pretty face, but didn't all fathers say the same to their daughters? Her wide honey-colored eyes, darkly fringed with thick lashes, and her nicely formed nose were her best features, at least they were when they weren't hidden behind her glasses. Maybe she should throw them away. Maybe she should change her simple style, do something with herself. Maybe she should. . . .

What was she thinking? She tossed her hairbrush down and swung away from the mirror. Hadn't she been through all that before. And what did it get her then but a bunch of insufferable boors who thought her world should revolve around theirs and who were mortified by her outspoken opinions.

"You lure them in with your flirtations, and then you threaten their pride and masculinity with your assertions," her father had once told her. "They don't know what to make of you."

"That's balderdash," she had returned. "Paul had no trouble with my beliefs. It wouldn't have mattered to him if I owned property and kept it after marriage, or if I helped select the members of Congress, or if I became a doctor or a lawyer."

"I'll grant you Paul was an exceptional man," her father lamented.

"Yes, he was. He had vision. He could see the way things were and the way they had to become. He said that eventually my viewpoints would become more and more common and people would be forced to listen."

"You miss him, don't you? I think Paul is your problem, sweetheart. You love Paul's memory, and no one has yet to match it. It may be a long time till you find someone who does."

"Then I'll wait," she had said staunchly. And she had waited—for years. Only she had stopped flirting and trying to attract men, had actually discouraged most relationships from deepening, because she was able to see from the start that she wouldn't be happy with those men.

Only on two occasions since Paul died had she come close to becoming seriously involved, and in both those relationships she'd received proposals for marriage from the gentlemen. But when it came to making that final commitment, she hadn't been able to do it. That oneness she had felt with Paul had

17

always been missing. Or maybe it was love and respect that hadn't been there.

She opened her bureau and took out her scrapbook. She looked again at the articles written about the work Paul had been doing at the hospitals during the war. There were no letters to read for she had worked at his side then, sharing the triumphs, the heartbreak, the exhaustion of wartime medicine. It was such a senseless waste that a man with so much to offer should be killed, but war was like that.

She replaced the past and went downstairs. She'd have her dinner, curl up in her favorite chair, and see what this new author had to say about life on the wild frontier. She'd selected to read one of the new novels about the West. They were the rage at the present. Dime novels, pulp novels, inexpensive, printed on inferior paper, and cranked out by the thousands. Oddly, they were selling. She wanted to see why.

A couple hours later when Micah Hepplewhite quietly let himself in the front door, Elizabeth was still reading. He stood for some minutes at the archway to the parlor watching the enraptured expression on Elizabeth's face. It must be some book to bring on such a reaction in his stolid daughter. Her mother used to laugh out loud, or become furious, or cry her eyes out as she read, but never Elizabeth. The most he'd ever received from her was a dry literary critique. Not so now. She was caught up in this story, whatever it was. He cleared his throat.

"Oh, hello, Daddy. I didn't hear you come in."

"No. Must be a good book," he said, raising a sandy-gray brow as he saw her eyes dart down to read a few more lines.

"What? Oh, it's—" She was stopped by the look of amusement on her father's face. "It's entertaining," she said noncommittally, marking her place and setting the book aside. She directed her full attention to him. "How was your evening?"

"Entertaining," he returned, still smirking.

Her rosy lips tightened at the corners. "Very funny."

"Tell me about it," he said, coming to sit across from her.

"What? The book?" she asked, seeing his eyes move to the table at her side. "It's nothing," she replied dismissively. "It's rather a lot of silliness actually, but I imagine some would be taken in by it. Quite a few as it seems."

18

"But not you?"

"Certainly not. Why, the whole thing is absurd, really. Here. Listen to this," she said, grabbing the book and leafing back a few pages from where she'd marked it. She read dramatically: "*Thunder cracked ominously overhead, making the ground shudder beneath him, and lightning flashed its deadly spears of light all around, threatening to lance his very soul. His horse reared up in fright and fought to be free to escape the terrifying violence of the sky, but Colt Sterling tightened his control and rode on into the gnashing teeth of the storm. No risk was too great if he could save the lovely Penelope, his heart, his love, from the vile and sinister Snake Durham.*"

Micah gave a hearty laugh. "Sounds good, only it'll never be the same unless you read it aloud to me. You've a flair for the dramatic, dear."

"Don't be silly," she huffed, snapping the book shut. "It's the writing that's dramatic, not I. I mean who can credit a name like Colt Sterling. Can the man possibly be anything but virile, handsome, fast with a gun, and touched by God, Himself. And contrarily, we all know the kind of man Snake is. I mean this stuff is pure . . . pure . . ."

"Entertainment?" Micah suggested.

"Drivel!"

"Come on, now. Admit you were entranced by it."

"I was not."

"Elizabeth, I know you've lost your romance, your imagination, and your sense of adventure, but please don't lose your honesty."

"Father," she protested, "that's unkind, as well as being untrue."

"Okay. If you say so. You probably don't want to finish that piece of literary nonsense, so why don't I take it to bed with me. I'm most curious to see what happens to the lovely Penelope."

She snatched the book up. "Never mind, you old goat. All right. I want to finish it," she said sheepishly. "And you can rest easy. He rescues the fair damsel once again."

"Again?"

"Sure. The first time he chases down the runaway stage and grabs her out just before the carriage tongue breaks and the stage plunges over a cliff. The second time he crashes through

19

the door of a mine shack, where she's tied up, and throws the stick of dynamite out the door seconds before it explodes. The third time . . ."

"I get the picture," Micah chuckled. "How about that hot cocoa now? Then you can get back to your dashing hero."

They had their drink, and when Micah Hepplewhite kissed his daughter goodnight, he couldn't help wishing she'd find herself a man who could make her face light up as her storybook character had. He touched her cheek softly. "Don't read too late, and pleasant dreams."

"Sleep well, Daddy. I love you."

"You, too, kitten."

Territory of New Mexico—April 1868

Clint Colfax scratched his head and raked his fingers through his gray hair. "Emma, are you sure they aren't in the house somewhere?"

"I've looked everywhere, Mr. Colfax," replied the distraught housekeeper. "They've run off again. What gets into them two, I just don't know."

"Relax, Em. We'll find them. You have to realize they're still in shock over losing their parents so violently. It'll take some time for them to come to grips with their loss and accept this place as home. And they always get restless when McKaid is gone."

"I just don't know what to do anymore," Emma burst out, trying unsuccessfully to hold back her tears of frustration. "I can't get through to them. I can't spend the time with them to do that and still keep up with all my other duties. It's wearing me out, Mr. C."

"I know, Emma," he said, taking her shoulders and giving her a light squeeze. "I can see that now. Don't worry. You get back to your baking, and I'll get a few men to help me search the ranch. We'll find them."

"Thanks, Mr. C. I feel real bad about this."

"No need. No need at all."

Clint and three of his ranch hands spent two hours searching the immediate area of the Circle K. When they finally met back at the house, no one had found the children.

Russ Packard, the foreman, scratched his head of unruly auburn curls. "How can two little kids just disappear? I swear I've searched every single building, every square inch here."

"And I checked all around those caves on the ridge and a good distance either side of them," reported another hand.

"They have to be here," Clint said in exasperation. "Where can they go?"

"When did they leave?" Russ asked.

"I can't be sure, but Emma seems to think it must have been at dawn. They never came down to breakfast, and when she went up to check on them, they were gone."

"That's four hours now."

"How far can they get on foot? Little kids like that? Dammit, I wish McKaid were back. We've got a round-up to get organized."

"Four hours," Russ repeated. "It would take us all day to search an area around the distance they could go in that time. And then we only find them if they want to be found."

"Hell!"

"Hey, boss, I don't think we'll have to go out again. McKaid's coming, and it looks like he's found them."

All four men turned to watch as McKaid rode across the valley floor. Little Ruthie was in his lap and James was holding on behind the saddle.

"I'll be damned," Clint cursed.

McKaid rode up to the men and in turn handed each of the children down. Clint started to say something, but McKaid stopped him with a look.

"You two go up to your room and wait for me there," McKaid addressed the children. "I want to talk to both of you."

Ruthie and James looked at each other, crestfallen to be spoken to so sharply by McKaid, then somberly agreed and walked hand in hand to the porch. McKaid watched them until they disappeared into the house, a worried frown etched into his brow.

"We've been searching for hours," Clint explained. "Where did you find them?"

"They were over halfway to Lenore's ranch when I spotted them. James said they left before sunup."

"Why?" Russ asked.

21

"They clammed up on me, but it's my guess they feel some sort of need to be around Lenore. She must remind them of Sophie."

Lenore, the widow of Jacques Beaumont, still oversaw the running of the Bar M Ranch to the southeast of the Circle K. Though she didn't really resemble Sopie, Lenore was still a young woman. And very pretty. Maybe that's what drew the children to her. Or maybe her manner was like Sophie's. Or maybe they weren't going there at all.

"Hell, how am I supposed to know?" McKaid snapped. "I gave Jack my word I'd look after them, but I don't know the first thing about what goes on in the mind of a kid."

"Well, let's leave it for now," Clint said. "We've got a lot of work to get done today if the men are to get started on the round-up. Talk to them, McKaid, and see if you can get to the bottom of it. Let's get busy, men."

McKaid watched them walk off as they led their horses and his to the corral. Clint was annoyed, and had every right to be. This was the third time in a month that those kids had run off. And unfortunately, each time it happened, McKaid had been gone. Maybe that was it, he thought. Maybe they felt deserted when he left. Well, he was going to find out. And damned quick.

He didn't find out that morning, though, because the minute he walked into the children's bedroom, Ruthie threw her arms around his legs and began to cry. He scooped her up and sat down on the rocking chair in the corner, with the little girl clinging to his neck.

"Don't be angry with us, please don't, Mr. McKaid," she pleaded brokenly.

McKaid looked over at James and saw his downbent head and his dejected pose as he sat on the edge of the bed. He had fully intended to give them a sound tongue-lashing, but he just couldn't. They were so unhappy.

"I'm not angry, sweetheart," he crooned, his heart melting. "Not at all. We're all just very concerned about you, and sometimes that looks like we're angry. We're also very confused. I thought you'd be happy here. I wanted this to be your home."

"It doesn't feel like home when you go away all the time," James said quietly. "We're in the way."

"No, you're not, but everyone needs time to adjust to changes." And everyone was so busy at the Circle K. Nobody had time to let the boy tag along and learn about the ranch. Emma was far too busy to take Ruthie under her wing. And none of them had ever had children of their own.

"Where were you going?" McKaid asked quietly. Ruthie sobbed once, and he tightened his arms around her.

"Nowhere, in particular," James said. "We were just going."

"Would you do me a big favor then, and stay for a while. We can work everything out. You're not helping anything by making the men chase after you. And you could very well get yourselves into trouble. What would Ruthie do if you got bit by a snake, or fell and broke a leg?" he asked James.

James looked horrified. "I didn't think of that."

"Perhaps you better the next time you decide to run off."

"Yes, sir."

Something occurred to him then that he hadn't considered before. "What did you do for schooling before your parents died?"

"Ma taught us," James answered. "She got the books in town, and each morning we had lessons. She could read and write real good, and she was teaching me to figure, too."

"I see." An idea began to form in his mind, but it was one that required some thought and a conference with Clint and Emma. Emma needed some help, and the kids needed some concentrated attention. If he could find the right person . . .

Ruthie was sound asleep, and he gently laid her on her bed and covered her. The poor little mite had walked miles. "Why don't you come with me, James, and help us get provisions set out for the round-up. I'm sure Clint could use another hand."

"Okay," James said, brightening. "I could help real good."

It was late that night before McKaid had a chance to talk to Clint alone. They each poured a drink and sat in the library beside the low fire that crackled in the hearth. "Everything ready for the round-up?" McKaid asked.

"We'll be ready to leave day after tomorrow. What happened in Sante Fe? Did you see the marshal?"

"Yep. You're looking at a fully sworn-in deputy marshal of the Territory of New Mexico. He was relieved to see me, actually. It seems some fracas down south at the border

23

requires his personal attention, so he's turning Ramirez and his gang over to me."

"Thought you were going after the Corbetts."

"I am. I'm betting that eventually the Corbetts as well as the Dawsons will join up with Ramirez."

"That makes a helluva gang then."

"Over twenty, as I figure."

Clint whistled through his teeth. "And they're in the area?"

"Close enough. And I'm the man who's going to bring them in."

"Don't let your personal feelings get in the way of your better judgment, now. Men get dead that way."

"They're not going to get away with murdering Jack and Sophie. That was a big mistake, and I intend to see they pay for it." Implacable determination reflected from every feature of his face, especially those ice-blue eyes.

Twenty men, Clint thought. It was a damned army of outlaws. How did McKaid think he could take them on single-handedly. He'd get himself killed for sure.

McKaid took a long drink and winced as the liquid burned his throat. He closed his eyes for a few seconds, and when he opened them again he seemed to have shaken off his disturbing thoughts.

"I want to discuss another idea with you, Clint, about the children. I think we ought to hire a governess, or teacher, or nanny, whatever those ladies call themselves."

Clint was about to raise his glass to his lips, but his hand stopped midway, and he stared wide-eyed at his nephew. "Governess?"

"Well, teacher then. A live-in teacher who could look after the kids, see to their schooling, as well as lend Emma a hand now and then."

Clint's brows shot upward and his lips pursed as he gave the idea some thought. "It would have to be the right person. Emma wouldn't take to some bossy snippet coming in to take over running the household."

"I'm sure she wouldn't, but surely we can find someone in all of the Southwest who's pleasant and biddable, yet interesting enough for the children."

"But can we find someone with all those qualities who'd be willing to bury herself all the way out here?"

24

"There are dozens of young men around, way out here."

"That could be another problem altogether. We could find ourselves with a passel of in-house fighting over the only available female. Of course, she'll probably fall straight in love with you anyway. Most do."

"Then she'd leave, broken-hearted, because I have no intention of getting involved, or having some moon-eyed miss pining around after me."

"And that wouldn't be good for the children. They need stability, someone they can depend on to stay. Why don't you want to get involved? I thought you liked women. I've even wondered a time or two why you never took a shine to Lenore. That would be the perfect answer. Get married and adopt those kids. Give them a proper home."

"Don't start with me again, Clint. Aside from all the reasons I've already given you—a dozen times, I might add—what woman would want to start married life with a ready-made family?"

"Lots, if that family came with you included, I'd think. Okay, okay," he said hurriedly, seeing McKaid's temper rising. "We could run an ad in the local papers, even go as far as advertising in, say, Kansas City."

"At least we'd stand more of a chance of finding someone with adequate training that way. We could speak to those who respond to the ad, and be very certain that the lady we choose understands that she is to refrain from flirtations of any kind, either with the men, or with, God forbid, me."

"Wait a minute," Clint exclaimed, jumping up and pacing in front of the fireplace. "I've never heard that she married. Surely Micah would have notified me. Good Lord, yes. She'd be perfect. And she's family."

"Who? What in blue blazes are you talking about?"

"Elizabeth," he stated, laughing at the blank expression on McKaid's face. "Elizabeth Hepplewhite."

"Never heard of her."

"She's your cousin, only from the other side of the family. She and her father live in Virginia."

"How old is she, this cousin of mine?"

"I don't know," he said. One brow dropped as he calculated. "She was fifteen when last I saw her. Shoot, she must be somewhere around twenty-six or seven."

"She's never married?" McKaid asked, his interest piqued.

"Not to my knowledge."

She must be homely, he thought. That was good. "Educated?"

"Very highly educated. Her father teaches at William and Mary."

"What does she do? Is she already employed as a teacher?"

"That I don't know. When I saw her last, she was a kid and had her nose in a book all the time. That was a couple of years before her mother died. After that I lost track. Micah was never one to write."

"Her mother was your . . ."

"My sister. What a lovely woman she was, too. She was madly in love with Micah, and sailed right off with him. No one could stop her, though none of us tried very hard, except my father. Micah was a terrific fellow, and he loved her as much as she loved him. Elizabeth will have known a very happy homelife. She can help give that to James and Ruthie."

"What does she look like?" McKaid persisted.

"It's been over ten years. Gangly young girls do grow up. I don't know what she looks like."

"But she's a spinster."

"Well, I guess you could call her that."

"And she likes to read, so your library should be enough to keep her content. Do you think she'll be willing to give it a go?"

"I can only ask. I'll write to her father and explain the situation. We'll have to wait and see."

McKaid went to bed with a load off his mind that night. He would tell James and Ruthie that he'd hired a lady to be their teacher and companion. That should keep them at home. Yes, it was the perfect solution. Elizabeth may not be pretty, not like Sophie, but kids tended to overlook flaws once they learned to love someone. They'd take to Elizabeth, he was sure, especially if they knew it was what he wanted, and certainly when they learned that Elizabeth was family.

McKaid realized how badly he wanted this. He needed a free mind to do his work. He needed to know James and Ruthie were receiving the best of care. God, what if she refused? Or what if she turned out to be a real bitch? He couldn't think like that. He had to hope for the best.

What would his cousin be like? He found he was curious about her, and not because of anything to do with the children.

26

She would be thin, maybe too thin. And terribly retiring. That would explain the absence of men in her life. He could imagine how her eyes would drop and how she'd cower whenever he spoke to her. And she probably had mousy brown hair, and maybe crooked teeth. She would surely wear glasses. A poor little sparrow who would be terrified by a man like himself, but who would be oh, so grateful to him for giving her a chance to do something useful with her life.

He fell asleep, grinning.

Chapter Two

"Are you ready, Elizabeth?" Micah Hepplewhite called up the stairs to his daughter. She was surely taking longer than usual to get herself dressed and primped tonight.

"A couple more minutes, Dad. We aren't late, are we?" She smoothed some rosy lip gloss on her lips and added just a touch of color to her cheeks. Why she was fussing she didn't know. She'd been to the symphony a half-dozen times with Arnold. Why start caring about her looks now? She parted her hair neatly down the center and smoothed it back, twisting it into its usual tidy chignon. At the last minute, her hand went to the cloisonne combs her mother had left her. She carefully secured them so that they added a touch of color to her rather neutral hair. She stood at last and turned to go downstairs.

"You look lovely, my dear," Micah said, holding her wrap for her. "What is it that you've done? Oh, yes. You aren't wearing your glasses. Could it be that you're actually trying to impress this young man, Elizabeth? Might I expect to hear wedding bells in the near future?"

"Daddy, don't you ever stop? I am not interested in the holy state of matrimony. I agree wholeheartedly with Mr. Samuel May. He writes that women should not rush into wedlock just to avoid the disgrace and cruel taunts directed at them by men because they remain unmarried, taunts at which the most strong-minded of your gender would quail, only to end up in an alliance that is so ill-matched as to cause only sorrow, regret, and pain to both parties. And as long as I am capable of maintaining my own life, I am pleased to do so."

"Are you going to start quoting that stuff and nonsense at me again?" he asked, his eyes twinkling at her flushed and indignant countenance.

"Are you going to keep on about my finding a suitable husband?"

"Suitable is a good choice of words," he said placatingly. "You know I wouldn't wish any other husband for you but one who suited you."

"Then please allow me to be the judge of that," she said more calmly. "Excuse me, I'm going to get my spectacles."

Micah grinned as she stormed back up the stairs. He was used to teasing her. Usually she took it in her stride, content to volley back some piece of her mind. He had never, though, seen her bristle as she had just done. His grin disappeared as he wondered if someone had insulted her or hurt her earlier in the day to make her so sensitive. That would account for why she had been so meticulous with her appearance. He was sorry that he'd teased her. He was even sorrier when she returned, her face scrubbed clean, the lovely combs removed from her hair, and her glasses perched on her dainty nose.

"I apologize, kitten," he said sincerely.

"That's all right. Let's just go. Arnold and Caroline will be waiting for us."

As an evening on the town went, it was a very pleasant few hours. Elizabeth always enjoyed talking with Caroline and watching the interaction between her and her father. Caroline didn't let him get by with his terrible teasing any more than she did. Arnold was a different matter. Though impeccably polite, almost to being obsequious, and though a passable conversationalist, he irritated her. He always left her with the disquieting feeling that he, a man, was doing her, a woman, a great kindness by escorting her to some function. As if she couldn't, and didn't, on many occasions, go on her own if she felt like it. Although she had to admit that those outings had been made most uncomfortable for her by those who snickered and stared at her "single" status. Nevertheless . . .

"I noticed your new display in the shop window last week when I happened by the store. It is very creative. Did you do it by yourself?" Arnold asked dubiously. They sat in a small café near the concert hall enjoying a late evening dessert.

"Of course. Even I am capable of rounding up a pair of boots, a stetson, and six-shooters if the occasion demands."

"It is a delightful touch for showcasing the new books on the West," Caroline said, sensing Elizabeth's annoyance and

30

attempting to divert trouble.

"Yes," Arnold said quickly. "I meant it only as a compliment."

"I'm surprised, though," Micah couldn't resist teasing, "considering how you disliked the novel you read."

"To say I disliked it is a bit strong. I thought it fatuous. And I'm sure you'll agree that my likes and dislikes don't enter into promoting elevated sales for the shop. I do work on a commission basis. What's good for sales is good for me."

Her father laughed heartily. "Ever the practical one," he said.

"When will McArthur return from his trip?" Arnold asked. "You must be anxious for him to get back to take over the store again."

Elizabeth bit her tongue. They were in a public place after all. She knew Arnold, a manager at the National Bank, was surprised that McArthur would turn his business over to her while he went away for a month. Arnold believed she had misunderstood when she first told him. McArthur had a son who Arnold thought would surely take over. She smiled at him, mentally gritting her teeth as she did so.

"I'll be happy to see him again, yes. I'm very fond of Mr. McArthur. But I did write and tell him I was managing very well, and that if he wished to extend his stay, I would be happy to continue on as I have been."

"Really? I'd have thought you'd be ready to be done with all the bookkeeping and the arduous details attendant to running a business."

"Why? Are you, by some chance, thinking of giving up your job, Arnold? Don't you like what you do?"

"Me? Sure, I do. I was talking about you."

"What's the difference? Oh," she said, feigning the dawning light. "You mean because I'm merely an employee, and a woman at that."

He leaned back in his chair and smiled ruefully, suspecting accurately that he'd made the situation worse. He just couldn't get used to her being so strong-willed and independent.

"Elizabeth," her father warned softly.

She laughed then. It really was funny when it didn't make her blood boil. "Don't worry, Dad. I shan't embarrass you."

"I didn't mean to be condescending, Elizabeth. I find it difficult to remember you're not as scatterbrained as my sister.

31

Again, I'm sorry."

"My ego is really taking a beating tonight," she said wryly. "But I do accept your apology."

That night when Micah kissed her goodnight, he gave her an extra hug. "You are a very nice person, Elizabeth. I know you wanted to fly into Arnold with both fists tonight for what he said, but you acted with admirable restraint."

"And I'm exhausted because of it," she said, leaning with exaggerated weariness against her door frame. "How long do you think I could endure marriage to him? Or he to me?"

Micah chuckled softly, then turned serious. "It's difficult for you, isn't it? It's a man's world, and you have to fight to find a place for yourself."

"Yes, it's a man's world. Because you all made it that way. What is there for us apart from being a housebound slave to a man's whims." She straightened from the door. "To own property is made untenable by taxation, determined by men; to marry is to lose it anyway, a scheme also concocted by a man, I believe. A woman makes a fraction of the salary a man makes, when she's lucky enough to be awarded a position; she isn't *allowed,* and I abhor that word, any voice in how the business is managed, or her own country, never mind that women make up half the population and have given life to the other half; and we can't get a foot in the door to change anything because the clubhouse has a big sign that reads Men Only."

"Go to bed, kitten. You can't change the world tonight, and everything will look better when you've had some rest."

She sighed and grinned weakly. "You must get sick of my rantings. I don't blame you. I'll see you in the morning. Goodnight, Dad."

Micah stood staring at her door after she'd closed it behind her. She was right about what she'd said. Women did get a bad deal. He had to admit he would rather have Elizabeth deciding policy and legislature than most of the men he knew, but he didn't know what else he could do about it. He'd already discussed most of Elizabeth's complaints with their congressmen, none of whom wanted to stick his neck out and rock the boat. He was afraid it would take the women, themselves, to finally get fed up enough to rise up in protest and put on the pressure. Unfortunately, aside from a handful of crusaders like Elizabeth, women were either satisfied with the state of affairs or too afraid to risk voicing dissent.

Micah loved his daughter wholeheartedly. She meant the world to him, and he wanted to see her as happy as her mother had been. But where her gentle mother had viewed the world differently and accepted with equanimity what she couldn't change, Elizabeth was like a caged lioness fighting constantly her unjust confinement. And who could blame her. It was as much his fault as anyone's. He'd been the one who introduced her to literature, philosophy, history. He'd been the one who'd taught her that many world rulers had been women. He'd been the one who'd seen that she got admitted to the university and passed her courses with the highest of marks.

But he hadn't been able to secure her those two teaching positions when her competitors had been men. He hadn't been able to prevent her losing her employment at the bank to a man who had only half her experience.

Her keen mind and fighting spirit were enchained in Virginia where so many eager young male graduates were blazing new trails into business. She needed a new frontier of her own to conquer. His shoulders slumped and he bowed his head. It was time for him to let her go. He made the decision then to show her the letter he'd received from his brother-in-law. He hadn't intended to show her the letter at all. He didn't want her to leave, but maybe it was her only chance. He went to bed with a heavy heart.

Micah took his lunch with Elizabeth the next day, and after their meal in the small park across from the bookstore, he handed her the letter.

She took it and looked at him curiously. Silently she opened the envelope and pulled out the folded sheet of paper. She looked at him again, wondering at his somber expression. "Daddy—"

"Read it, my dear. We'll discuss it then."

She did so, and the more she read, the more her stomach began to tighten. Why, she wasn't entirely certain.

"Well?" Micah asked when she'd quietly folded the missive and slipped it back into the envelope.

"I remember Uncle Clint. He came to visit us before the war."

"Yes," was all Micah said.

"I can't possibly go. Who would take care of you?" Elizabeth said, tamping down the small bud of excitement that had begun to grow in her breast.

33

"You're not to think of me. Besides, I have . . ." He hesitated, unsure of what her reaction would be, but decided to plunge ahead with the rest of his decision. "I have made up my mind to ask Caroline to marry me. So, you see, I'll be fine."

"Oh, Dad. That's wonderful news," she said, excited all the more.

"You don't mind?"

"Mind? I think she's terrific. I couldn't be more pleased."

"I wasn't sure how you'd feel about my remarrying."

"Mom's been gone for nearly nine years. Actually, I expected you to find someone else long ago. You haven't been holding back because of me, have you?"

"No, no. Not at all. Caroline's the first woman I've met whom I've really felt . . . well, good about."

"Do you think I should go, Dad?"

He watched as her eyes took on a faraway stare. He could see the questions in them, and the eagerness for a new challenge. What he looked for, and found not the slightest hint of, was doubt. He was right. She needed this. And she wanted it.

"I can't make that decision for you, darling. I will miss you terribly, but I sense you need something in your life right now that you're not going to get here."

She pulled the letter out again and reread it. "Two orphaned children," she said wistfully. "It would give me a chance to repay in a small way all the love you and Mother showered on me." She looked up and met her father's misty eyes.

He loved her more at that moment than ever before. "It won't be easy, Elizabeth, but you'll see a new world, one just beginning to grow, and you'll be able to be a part of that. You'll even be able to get back to those horses you used to love at sixteen."

She laughed. "I doubt that it will be the same. I don't believe fox hunts are a big event out there."

Micah laughed with her, then grew serious. "He's your mother's brother, princess, and he needs your help right now. I wouldn't even have shown you the letter, for purely selfish reasons, except that I could see this may be the answer to your restlessness. And I know Clinton will take good care of you. My only fear is that you'll meet some tall, dark, hero like your Colt Sterling, and he'll keep you there for good. But I could even accept that, if he makes your face light up as your Colt Sterling did."

34

"Oh, Dad," she sputtered, blushing, remembering that she'd read that book twice. "Colt Sterling is a figment of someone's overactive imagination, probably some little runt who wishes he were like that."

"You never know. He may be out there, waiting for someone like you to step into his life so he can ride off into the sunset with you."

"What nonsense! Do be serious."

"As you say," he answered teasingly. "You think about it. We'll discuss it tonight. Oh, by the way, I'm bringing Caroline home for dinner."

"I'll get something special on my way home from work. I won't be late tonight."

A week later, though rushed to get everything done, Elizabeth had turned the bookstore over to its owner, had seen her father married, and had packed one large trunk and a traveling satchel for her trip. She was standing at the train station with her father and Caroline, still wondering how they'd managed to accomplish everything so quickly.

"I still think you should wait a week until my sister can accompany you," Caroline said, worrying. "It's not right or proper for you to travel so far by yourself."

"Don't fret about it," Elizabeth said. "I am perfectly capable of taking care of myself, and I would only worry the entire trip about Amelia's comfort and safety. Besides, she needs to be near you. You're all she has left."

"She's right," Micah said to his new wife. "We've checked with the station master. The train will be perfectly safe for her. You saw the maps. There's only a short distance she'll have to travel by coach, and that, if necessary, under military protection. She'll be fine." His words were brave because Elizabeth wanted to travel alone, but he was worried too.

"Be sure to wire us when you arrive," he added, knowing he would be unable to rest without that assurance.

"I promise." The conductor gave the signal for the passengers to board, and Elizabeth kissed her father and her new stepmother. "I have to go. You two be happy together. I love you both."

The train pulled out of the station, and Elizabeth sat back in her seat. Quite without volition her hand went to the novel she carried in the satchel on her lap. She ran a finger over the stamped lettering on the cover. *Desert Sunset.* "Colt Sterling," she said to herself, "let's see how much of a fabrication your world really is."

Six days later she arrived in Abilene, Kansas, and a less impressive town she had yet to see. Its name, taken from the Bible, meant "city of the plains"; Abilene was the terminus for the Kansas Pacific Railroad. It was also, she learned, the terminus for the cattle drives up the Chisholm Trail. Several large herds had already reached the cattle pens adjacent to the depot, and the sounds and smells emanating from there were overwhelming as she stood on the platform awaiting her trunk.

"We don't get many young ladies through these parts," the porter said, claiming her trunk for her. "You staying in town?"

"I'm going to Santa Fe," she explained.

"You'll be wanting a room at the hotel then for the night. Hey Pete, Ty, come on over here," he yelled to two scruffy young men who were leaning against the railing. "Show this lady over to the hotel and tote her trunk for her. Stage leaves at ten sharp," he said to her. "If you're not ready, Amos'll leave without you."

"Thank you, sir. I'll be ready."

The two young men greeted her effusively. Pete, the taller of the two, hefted up her trunk; at least he tried to.

"Holy sh-shucks," he exclaimed. "What you got in here?"

"Gone soft, have ya?" Ty mocked, laughing. He took one handle while Pete took the other. At the weight, Ty, too, turned and raised a brow at her.

"Books," she said, grinning. "Are you gentlemen cowboys?" she asked, taking in their leather chaps, the spurs on their muddy boots, their sweat-stained and dusty clothes and stetsons.

"Yes, ma'am," Pete declared. "I sure am. Ty, here, he's just a *plain* cowboy. There ain't nothing gentleman about him."

"Don't pay him no mind, ma'am. He's been out in the sun too long, livin' off loco weeds."

"You a shool marm, or somethin'?" Pete asked, guiding her around a patch of pungent mud. "Watch where you're going now. We had some steers get loose in town last night. Had a hell—heck of a time gettin' them rounded up again."

She laughed, a light merry sound that left both cowboys with an arrested expression on their faces. These boys, for they

36

couldn't yet have reached their twentieth birthdays, were right out of the book. And so, indeed, was the whole town.

"Here's the hotel," Ty said. "It ain't grand or nothin', but it's clean."

"Are you gonna be stayin' in Abilene?" Pete asked again hopefully. "To teach, or something?"

"I'm going on to Sante Fe in the morning," she said. "To teach, or something." She could stand to be flattered like this more often.

Pete looked disappointed. "None of the nice ones stay, or if they do, they got daddies meaner'n sin."

"Do you want us to carry your trunk up to your room?" Ty asked.

"I don't think anyone will run off with it if you put it down there."

"You can say that again," Pete groused.

"Thank you very much. It was a pleasure to meet you both."

Her room was small but neat, and the pitcher on the washstand was filled with tepid but clean water. She undressed quickly and washed, changing into fresh clothes from her full trunk. Refreshed, though her clothes were somewhat wrinkled, she went downstairs to find a restaurant. She was starved. But as hungry as she was, she was hard-pressed to do justice to the huge platter of steak, eggs, fried potatoes, and biscuits set before her. And then there followed apple pie, which was the best she'd ever eaten.

She asked the clerk at the hotel to make sure she awoke early, then went to bed and slept soundly through another rowdy, drunken night in Abilene. The next morning she was up and dressed when the clerk knocked at her door.

"I was beginning to worry," he said. "Didn't want you to miss your stage. Maude serves a good breakfast across the street. You best eat hearty as there ain't much 'atween here and where you'll stop tonight. I'll see to your trunk."

"Thank you. You're very kind."

"Not at all, ma'am. You travelin' alone?" he asked.

"Yes."

He shook his head. "Well, don't guess there's too much to worry about," he said as he escorted her downstairs. "I'll tell Amos to take care of you. He'll see you safely to Santa Fe. He's the best stage driver around, and he always takes Bert to ride shotgun."

"Shotgun?" she asked, wondering if Shotgun was a horse. A strange name for a horse.

"Guard."

"Oh," she said, mentally laughing at her own stupidity. "Well, thanks again."

Maude served up a huge bowl of porridge, covered with milk and honey, and a steaming cup of black coffee. "You eat that, honey," she ordered brusquely, having already miraculously learned of Elizabeth's destination. "You'll be glad you did down the road."

Elizabeth ate. She was beginning to wonder what she'd gotten herself into. Her trepidation grew when Pete and Ty met her at the stage depot. Pete handed her a small bag of apples, and Ty presented her with a shiny canteen.

"Filled with spring water," he said, blushing.

She leaned up and gave each of them a swift kiss on their clean and shaven cheeks. "You are truly gentlemen. I hope all the rest of the cowboys I meet are as nice as you."

"Go on. Away with you two, now," the driver scolded. "We're already late. Amos is my name, miss. You watch your step now," he said, helping her up into the coach. He slammed the door and turned with no nonsense to his job. As the horses lurched forward, Elizabeth leaned out the window and bade the two young men good-bye.

She was jolted back in her seat as the team found their stride. Elizabeth had copied the few ladies she'd seen in Abilene and dressed simply in a plain white blouse and brown and black Basque over her tailored brown skirt. And she was minus two of her three petticoats. Alone in the stage, she swiftly rid herself of her jacket and the hat perched on her head, and made herself comfortable.

"Five days or so," the driver had said when she had asked how long their trip would take. "Barring anything unforeseen." She couldn't help wondering what "unforeseen" meant. "Oh, floods, a breakdown, bandits, Injuns. You know," he replied flippantly when she asked.

She didn't know. No one had mentioned Indians to her. Well, for better or worse, she was committed. That is if she wasn't shaken apart before the day was out.

They spent the first night in Great Bend, named for the sharp twist that the Arkansas River took at that point, and the

38

second in Dodge City, or rather Fort Dodge, where Amos insisted she stay.

"There's womenfolk there who can see to your needs. Nobody but trail hands and ruffians outside the fort," he said by way of explanation. He didn't think she needed to know that the small town outside the fort was filled with vermin of all sorts who wouldn't blink an eye at robbin' a woman of her virtue.

And so she met Major Wheeler and his wife Lila, who saw that she had a nice hot bath and that her dusty and soiled clothes were cleaned by the women who took care of those chores at the fort. She spent a very pleasant evening with the Wheelers and learned to her surprise that Major Wheeler had once met Paul. Paul's name was Wheeler also, and the major remembered him because of that.

"We tried very hard to decide if we were related," the major reminisced. "We couldnt' find one relative in common. I'm sorry to hear he was killed. How did it happen?"

"There was an explosion at the officers' quarters," she said simply.

"Such a shame," Lila said sympathetically. "What takes you to Santa Fe?"

"I'm going to be teaching two young orphan children, and taking care of them for my uncle at his ranch."

"Oh, you're a teacher, then?" she asked. "Not a nurse?"

"Yes. By way of any profession, I guess. I only worked with Paul because we were to be married, and he needed my help."

Lila nodded. "Those were very trying times, as I remember." She looked at the ornate clock on the side table. "Goodness, look at the time. You must be exhausted, dear. And reveille comes early."

"I am tired. Thank you both so much. You've been very gracious to me to let me come into your home like this."

"It's the least we can do, being Virginians too," Lila said, walking with Elizabeth to a small room at the rear of their quarters. "And it's been wonderful to have someone to talk to from back home."

"Lila," Elizabeth said hesitantly at her door, "the driver said something about Indians . . ."

"Oh, fiddle-faddle. They've been quiet for a couple months now. No one's even seen them along the trail. He's probably trying to frighten you. Amos does that to newcomers. One of these days he'll get his comeuppance."

"Not soon, I hope," Elizabeth laughed, relieved. "Goodnight, Lila."

Her fears were laid to rest for the night; however the next morning they were back with a vengeance when she saw a troop of cavalrymen mounted up and ready to escort them to the next fort along the Santa Fe trail.

"Why are they coming?" she asked Major Wheeler.

"It's been a routine we've adopted lately. The chances are slim that they will be needed, but it's always better to be prepared when crossing Comanche and Kiowa territory. Besides, we're sending two freight wagons along with you to Fort Union. You'll be very safe, I assure you."

The caravan took the Cimmaron Cutoff, shaving a hundred miles off their journey, but in so doing had to cross sixty miles of arid desert. After two more grueling days on the barren and scorching trail and two more nights lying exhausted yet unable to sleep in suffocating, boxlike rooms or in the stagecoach itself, they were finally on the last leg of their trip to Santa Fe. The military contingent left them at Fort Union in New Mexico, from that point on was deemed safe from Indian attack. Morning passed uneventfully, as well as their brief stop for lunch and a fresh team of six mules. The mousy little man, Phinneas Whitney, who had ridden across from her since Dodge City, had lapsed into a sullen silence. For two whole days she had listened to his non-stop bragging about his faultless education, his wonderful tour of Europe, his successful ventures into the world of high finance, and the important position he had accepted in the politics of Santa Fe and the new territory. Or else his whining complaints about his discomfort.

"You are a very boring woman," he finally snapped in frustration, unable to elicit even a spark of interest or sympathy from Elizabeth.

"Really?" she replied and turned the last page of her book. After a few minutes she closed it and slipped it into her satchel. She'd read *Desert Sunset* for the third time. She'd never read any book more than once in her life. But then . . .

The mysterious little smile that played at the corners of her lips disappeared when a loud whip-cracking snap and a spine-tingling "Haaghh" resounded from above the carriage. In

40

the next second Elizabeth was thrown back against the seat, and her frustrated admirer was sprawled out with his knees on the floor, one hand firmly clutching her thigh, and his shoulder in her rib cage.

"Good grief!" she cried. "What's going on?"

"I'm sorry, I meant nothing by it," Phinneas Whitney said, mortified. He grabbed his hand away, trying to regain his balance in the rocking stage.

"Not that, you dolt," she ground out, shoving him away. "Oh, do get off me."

"I'm sorry. You mustn't think I was being forward. You see . . ."

"Oh, forget it," she snapped, peering out the window. "We seem to have trouble here. I think we're about to be robbed by a band of outlaws."

Just then a bullet ripped into the wood directly beside her head. She jerked herself back onto her seat, staring at the jagged, splintered door frame. "Good Lord," she breathed. "I almost got shot." She turned to look at Phinneas and found him as white as a sheet and staring sightlessly through her.

"Mr. Whitney," she said, and watched the intrepid world traveler slowly slump to his seat in a dead faint. Any dim and dubious hopes of a rescue coming from him were soundly laid to rest. She stared at him as he slowly rolled off the seat to lie in a heap at her feet.

"Oh, for pity's sake," she grumbled. She couldn't leave him there. His head would be a mass of contusions. Struggling with his dead weight and the bouncing and jarring of their rough ride, she managed to hoist his body to her seat where the forward momentum of the coach would keep him in place. She grabbed hold of his thighs and shoved his hips back against the backrest, tucked his knees up, and secured his dangling arms against his chest with her satchel. At least she was doing something. There was so much gunfire outside.

Just then a masked man threw open the stage door and swung his body inside, and Elizabeth was staring down the barrel of a wicked-looking gun.

The bandit looked at her huge eyes, grunted, then turned away from her and began searching the man on the seat.

"Yeah," he grunted, finding a wallet full of bills. "Where's your money, lady?" he finally addressed Elizabeth.

41

"Money?" she asked. "Why should I carry any money? He had it all," she said, thinking rapidly that it would be a shame for them both to be robbed. Besides, she'd have to lift her skirts to retrieve her money from the pockets she'd sewn into her undergarments, and she had no desire to further provoke this beastly man to more violence.

"I don't believe you, lady," the bandit said, pressing his big dirty hand to her throat and stabbing his long gray gun into her side. "Let's have it."

"Okay," she squeaked, terrified, and began to pull up her skirts.

There was another loud crash, and another man burst into the crowded space of the stage. The bandit pivoted around, releasing her, and in an instant the newcomer kicked the gun from his hand. The two men, scuffling with each other amidst loud cursing and a good many swinging fists, headed in her direction. Quckly she shot from the corner where she had tried to hide herself to the other seat, pressing against the sleeping Phinneas. She saw the bandit go to the floor on his hands and knees, saw him grab his gun and swing his body around. A loud report almost split her ears, and she saw the bandit drop his gun and clutch his chest. In a flash, the second man shoved open the door and booted the bandit out.

She stared, aghast, as his body tumbled out, flipped twice, then was gone from view. Only then did she turn to look at the second man. She gasped audibly.

"Everything will be all right now, ma'am," he said reassuringly, but she didn't really hear him. She was staring straight into the sky-blue eyes of Colt Sterling. If she'd made him up herself, he couldn't have been more perfect. Dark sable hair, curling just slightly at his collar, strong nose, a little crooked maybe, square jaw covered with a stubble of dark whiskers, long legs that were far too long to straighten out in the stage, and shoulders that took up half the seat. She could only stare. Her voice had deserted her, her wits had vanished. He was the most beautiful man she'd ever seen, and her heart set up a crazy rhythm in her tight chest.

"Excuse me," he told the speechless, gape-eyed female in front of him. "I have to stop the stage before we go into the river."

She watched as Colt swung out the door and pulled himself to the top of the stage. She slumped, feeling very winded, against the back of the seat, and slowly began to recover her senses. Stop the stage? Before we go into the river? And then she knew. She started laughing and couldn't stop. Lord, it was just like her father to do this. He probably plotted the whole escapade with Uncle Clint, right down to the Colt Sterling look-alike. She laughed until the tears came to her eyes.

Chapter Three

The stage slowed and came to a stop. She smothered another giggle. She wasn't about to let her father get away with this. He'd never let her live it down if he thought he'd been able to dupe her into reacting in a totally emotional, female way—as he'd often lamented that she never did. She'd have to be sure he learned differently. She hastened to straighten her disheveled clothing and to smooth her hair into place. She shoved her glasses higher on her nose and, not wanting the men outside to think she was hiding away, pushed open the door and stepped down.

No one was in sight. Her heart did a little jump. Perhaps he had been hurt in his daring rescue. And where was Amos? And Bert? She walked around the back of the stage. "Amos?" she called.

She stopped mid-step when she saw Amos and Bert sitting on the ground, leaning against the wheel. And beside them, down on his haunches, was the other man. At the sound of her voice he turned his head and looked at her. Their eyes met, and she felt again that same light-headedness and an odd twisting in the region of her stomach. The man's head tilted to the side as he studied her thoroughly from head to toe and back again. His brows cocked curiously. When she only stood there, speechless again and feeling an absolute fool because of it, he dared to smirk at her. Not many men got away with mocking her. Her indignant pride came to her rescue, bringing with it her heretofore faulty voice.

"Excuse me," she said firmly, "but if this sideshow is over now, could we possibly be on our way again?"

The big man slowly stood and turned his entire body to face

her, and she was shaken to her toes anew by how utterly devastating he was. Her body felt as though she had received a shock, going hot and cold by turns, and her stomach was performing in an oddly bizarre way. Nervous that he might see how his overwhelming presence was making her heart thump and her breathing grow shallow and uncontrolled, she rushed into speech again.

"That was a truly fine exhibition, I'm sure, though somewhat overdramatized on your part; but as you can see, I'm hardly the sort of woman who's likely to be impressed by such obvious theatrics. There is a man in the stage, however, who was mortified to the point of actually fainting by all of these amusing theatrics. Perhaps in the future you should consider that all men are not as constitutionally fit as yourself. And I'm certain Mr. Whitney would appreciate the return of his money, though no amount could make up for the broken bones your poor friend must have suffered in tossing himself with the help of your boot out of the moving stage."

The man glared at her, his eyes chilling as he raked up and down her rigidly held body. "You impertinent little brat," he said, his voice even colder than his silver-blue eyes. "You should be on your knees thanking me instead of flinging insults like a damned shrew."

He turned then and stooped down to talk quietly to Amos. Apparently satisfied by Amos's answer, he stood and glared again at her, daring her to open her mouth and utter even one more word.

She shivered slightly, but wasn't about to be cowed. She gave a light lilting laugh, though she felt no humor at the moment. "Don't be offended, mister. I'm quite certain you'll still be paid, even though your little charade didn't produce the intended results."

He muttered something under his breath and took two long strides that brought him very close to her. Pure defensive reflex made her step backwards.

His strong hands shot out and grabbed her shoulders, giving her a brief shake. All at once her body was molded to his and his mouth was on hers, grinding her lips forcefully against her own teeth. She struggled, pushing against those hard, muscular shoulders of his, but she couldn't fight his strength. He held her effortlessly, and she stopped fighting, deciding to simply wait him out. He probably liked conquering a fighting woman.

46

She wouldn't give him the satisfaction of even that much response.

Gradually his kiss changed. Gone was the pain of his lips pinching hers against her teeth, the rough abrasion of his whiskers against her tender skin. His lips softened, molding themselves to hers, moving persuasively against her mouth. His right hand went to her throat, stroking and cupping her jaw. With the slightest of pressure he opened her mouth and took total possession.

Elizabeth felt her heart thumping against her ribs and she was frightened by the sudden changes in her body. She'd never been kissed like this before. Even Paul, a man she would have married, hadn't been so familiar with her. And still she didn't try to push away. She was caught by the power of it, the magic.

His bold tongue found the delicate tissue of her lips, explored the sensitive roof of her mouth, finally sought her own tongue. Sensations altogether new to her spiraled through her body, making her tingle and ache inside. His arms tightened around her, holding her head still beneath his masterful lips and her yielding body tight against his hard, demanding thighs. She could feel his desire for her pressed against her lower abdomen, and felt a shocking surge of recriprocal desire flare in her own body.

Her fear subsided and drifted away as she was borne up on arms that left her floating in thoughtless sensation, yearning for more. She had no idea that she was clinging to him, digging her nails into his hard shoulders, or that her body had become pliant, begging for him to continue, or that she was kissing him back with an ardor that would have shocked her had she realized. She no longer waited for him to be done with her; she wanted him never to stop.

All in all, it couldn't have been more than a handful of seconds that she'd been in his arms, but an eternity had passed for her, time enough for her to know she would never be able to forget this man and his kiss. And then he was abruptly pushing her away. She was gasping for breath and her legs nearly buckled beneath her. With one hand she grabbed behind her for the rough wood and cold iron of the wheel to steady herself, and with the other she wonderingly touched her fingertips to her sensitized lips.

She stared at him, and he returned her gaze coldly, his lips curling smugly. "At least that made an impression on you," he

47

remarked cynically and turned away.

"You'll be all right?" he asked Amos.

Amos, his stunned gaze moving between the tall man and the dazed woman, only nodded.

"I'll see if I can track down the rest of the gang and retrieve the stolen money then."

Elizabeth could only stare as he smoothly swung himself onto his horse and rode away. She felt a great wave of disappointment and regret. He hadn't meant anything by that kiss which had affected her so much, except to humiliate and punish her for daring to attack his pride. Her vision blurred, and she swiftly wiped at her eyes, too embarrassed even to look at Amos when he called her name.

"Don't weep, now," he said. "He don't mean no harm. You jest got him riled, that's all. You shouldn't ought to have said all those things."

"But, I thought . . . Amos! You're bleeding."

"Course I'm bleeding. I usually do when I get in the way of a bullet."

"I thought this was all an act. A practical joke. Here, let me help you."

"I can assure you I don't make it a practice to get myself shot for the entertainment of passengers."

"No. I can see that you wouldn't. Then that man?" she asked, looking toward where he'd ridden.

"He's the real McCoy. McKaid, actually."

"I beg your pardon?"

"McKaid. His name is McKaid. Dash McKaid. Texas Ranger. Toughest man in the Southwest."

"Texas Ranger?" she asked, incredulous. "Then that other man back there was . . ."

"One of the Corbett gang. Real mean, too. He would have kilt you for sure."

"He's dead?"

"If McKaid shot him, he's dead."

"And did McKaid really stop the stage?"

Amos looked sheepish at that question. "I dropped the reins when Corbett shot me. McKaid climbed over onto the wheeler horse and pulled him up."

She stared at him, dumbfounded. "He can really do that?" she finally managed.

"Missy, he did it. That's all I know. Now about that help."

48

"Yes, of course. Let me see your arm."

"Not me. We got to get Bert into town to the doc. He took one in his shoulder and one in his leg."

At that moment Bert stirred, moaning in pain. Elizabeth moved to his side and inspected his wounds. Frowning at all the blood he was losing, she rushed to the back of the stage and found her trunk. She took out her cleanest petticoat and secured the luggage compartment again. Tearing the snowy white garment into strips, she cleaned and bound Bert's wounds. She did the same with Amos, though he grumbled at her for it.

"If you can help me, we'll put Bert in the stage with Mr. Whitney," she said. "He'll be more comfortable if we can get his leg elevated. It'll also slow that bleeding."

"What happened to Whitney?" Amos asked. "He shot?"

"Passed out. Let him sleep. Believe, me, it's for the best."

Amos laughed, new respect forming for the girl who'd lit into McKaid and got herself kissed for the trouble. "Where are you gonna ride?" he asked when both seats were taken up with recumbent bodies.

"I'll ride shotgun," she said and laughed at herself. Dash McKaid? This just couldn't be happening.

Wes Corbett paced the camp like a raging bull, tension in every muscle of his body. Every now and again he'd draw his gun in a lightning quick motion, pretending to gun down his imaginary opponent.

"Sit down, Wes. You're making me nervous," Gordo said.

"I got to go back and get Lefty," he argued. "I ain't leavin' him like we left Dink. I have to give him a proper burial. He was my brother, dammit."

"He's past caring, kid, and me and Tomlin ain't 'bout to risk our necks for no dead man. That Ranger'll be trackin' us for sure."

"Yeah," Tomlin added to the argument. "Ya wanna hand yourself over to him nice and freelike?"

"I want him dead. That's what I want. And I'm gonna kill the son of a bitch if it's the last thing I do. He better be watching over his shoulder all the time, cause one of these days, I'm gonna be there."

"We'll get him in time, boy. Now sit down," Tomlin

ordered. "We got business to discuss."

"You thinkin' about joinin' up with Ramirez again?" Gordo asked, lounging back against his saddle.

"With Lefty and Dink out of the picture, we're gonna have to. Dink was the only one with any smarts in this crowd. We ain't no good by ourselves. Even Lefty weren't smart enough to hightail it when McKaid showed up. To my way of thinking, Ramirez is our only hope."

"Then we don't need you to think," Wes argued. "We don't need Ramirez either. Besides he ain't keen on lettin' people back into his group what once left. And Dik made him damn mad, sleeping with his woman like he did."

Tomlin shook his head and waved that aside. "Ramirez, as rumor goes, is getting together an army of his own. He wants to own this area. He thinks it belongs to him. My guess is he'll take anyone who can shoot. Can't hurt to try, Corbett."

"I ain't going with you. Not until I kill McKaid."

"Hell, boy, you can't take McKaid," Gordo said, indolently licking the edge of a cigarette paper and rolling it into a slender tube. "Nobody can take McKaid. At least not alone." He lit the cylinder and inhaled the strong smoke. "Ramirez wants McKaid as much as you do. Not only does he think there's gold on McKaid's ranch, but McKaid killed his kid brother and his nephew a few years back over in Texas. Ramirez has sworn to kill him, and to get that gold. He don't 'specially like to lose out on his quests for vengeance."

"He'll have to this time. McKaid is mine."

"Ramirez may decide to kill you then. Ever thought of that?"

"I'm a Corbett, and I say we stick together, the three of us."

"Being a Corbett don't mean nothin' now, kid. What's your vote, Gordo?" Tomlin asked.

"I say we join up with Ramirez."

"Me, too. Looks like you're on your own, boy."

"That's fine by me," Corbett grumbled peevishly, and went off to sit by himself. He was a Corbett, and he could go it alone if they wanted out. And he would get McKaid, Ramirez be damned. He sat for a long time thinking about what he'd do to McKaid when he next met him. He'd make his brothers proud of him. When Gordo took over the watch, Corbett went back to his bedroll and slept fitfully till dawn.

Tomlin looked down at the young man sleeping on the

ground. He knew he was hurting, losing both brothers like that, and both to McKaid's guns. He was alone, desperate to get even, and too hot-headed to be able to handle all those feelings. He'd go the way of most young boys who thought they were indestructible once they got a gun in their hands. He'd get himself killed. Tomlin didn't want to see that happen. He owed it to Dink and Lefty to look after the kid.

"We're movin' out now, Wes," he said, shaking the younger man's shoulder. "You better think twice about going after McKaid alone. He's dangerous. Wouldn't it be better to come with us and let Ramirez do all the work. He'll draw McKaid out into the open. That way you have us at your back to protect you, and you still get your shot at McKaid."

Wes thought a minute. He didn't really like the idea of being alone. He'd never been alone before. "You think Ramirez is really planning to go after McKaid?"

"Sure. He hates the man. My guess is he's here in these hills only because McKaid's living at his ranch now. Ramirez can get everything he wants in one move."

"Maybe there's something to what you say. But if the chance comes up before we find Ramirez, McKaid's mine."

"Sure. Come on, kid. Pack up your stuff. Let's move out."

The stage rolled into Santa Fe several hours later. Its first stop was at Doc Mason's office on the south side of town. Mr. Whitney had long since awakened, and he and Amos helped Bert into the doctor's house. After a thorough examination, the doctor informed them that Bert would be fine after the bullets were removed, although very sore for a few weeks, and he praised Elizabeth on what she had done to stem the flow of blood. He tended the flesh wound on Amos's arm, cleaned it, and put a few stitches in it, after which Amos decided it was time to get the stage to the depot.

In the center of the quaint, lazy Spanish town, Elizabeth stepped down from the stage and looked around. Newer buildings were tucked in around the older adobe structures, and tall trees shaded the streets and verandas. The aroma of spicy food met her nostrils, and her stomach grumbled in protest at not having been fed since their rather inedible lunch earlier.

"Someone meeting you, Miss Hepplewhite?" Amos asked,

hoisting her trunk down from the luggage rack with a loud grunt.

"Let me help you with that," she said, taking one handle and assisting in getting her book-laden trunk to the boarded sidewalk. "My uncle is supposed to meet me, but not until tomorrow. I'll need to find a room for tonight."

"There's a hotel down the street on the right. You'll find a room there. I'll see your trunk is brought down later. And miss, thanks for helping with Bert. I'm sorry you had such a bad first look at our country. Where'd that Whitney feller go?"

"I don't know. I think he was embarrassed. He didn't say two words after the bandits attacked."

"Heh-heh," Amos laughed, twirling his long gray moustache. "He sure had enough to say afore that."

Elizabeth grinned wryly. "You should have arranged for your Texas friend to put on his little exhibition a couple days earlier. It would have spared me the entire story of Mr. Whitney's illustrous life."

"Hey, speak of the devil and he do appear," Amos quoted in his own fashion.

Elizabeth turned to follow Amos's gaze. Sauntering down the sidewalk with his thumbs under his gun-belt was not Whitney as she expected, but none other than Dash McKaid, Texas Ranger, hero extraordinaire. She groaned and turned to pick up her satchel and her jacket, but her stomach did that funny little dance again, remembering his kiss. She also remembered why he had kissed her.

"Well, howdy, ma'am," the Ranger drawled. "I see you arrived safely. No more sideshows along the way?"

Her back stiffened and her chin rose a fraction. She spun around to face him, and even her dusty spectacles couldn't conceal the anger flashing in her eyes.

"No further mishaps, Ranger McKaid," she said succinctly. "I admit I made a mistake about you, and I apologize for the unkind remarks I made. And I thank you for your timely assistance. But you keep away from me. I don't care to be subjected to a repeat of your brute masculine force."

McKaid chuckled, and Amos hid a grin as he watched the sparks fly. "I could have sworn that for a moment there you enjoyed my brute force," he drawled maddeningly.

"My response was intended to convince you to release me.

And if memory serves, it worked." The little white lie rolled easily off her tongue.

"Perhaps we should test it again," he growled, annoyed all over again by her snippishness.

She felt a thrill rush through her body at the thought of being in his arms again, and knew she had to stop him. Her response this time would be just as violent and uncontrollable as last time, and she would never be able to hide it from him or the half-dozen onlookers.

"You could try, I'm sure. You are physically capable of doing so. Keep in mind, however, for the benefit of our audience," she retorted, glancing at the assembled curious eyes, "that brute force is only superior in a totally barbarian society, and those of limited mentality who resort to such force have obviously run out of more logical ideas to solve their difficulties. And God alone knows what your problem is. It certainly has nothing to do with me."

"Why you little . . . ." He took a step toward her, ready to wipe that supercilious smirk off her face, then brought himself up short. He'd prove her right if he did what he wanted to do to her. And he hadn't run out of ideas. Not by a long shot. He knew his appeal for the opposite sex. He knew he'd left broken hearts behind all over Texas and other territories of the West, however unwittingly done. He grinned down at her. She was such a shrew she must be starved for a man's attentions. She'd be easy to seduce into admitting she wanted his kisses. No, he hadn't run out of ideas to take her down a peg or two at all. And it would be fun to see how quickly he could do it.

Elizabeth thought for a terrifying second that he was going to do it, to kiss her again in front of all these people. Then, to her relief, he stopped. But the slow grin that followed left her even more unsettled than before. She couldn't tell what was going on in his devious mind, but she could sense it meant her no good.

"If you'll excuse me, please," she said icily and brushed past him with all the chilly aplomb she could muster.

Amos laughed at McKaid's dark frown. "She git the better of ya, did she?" he laughed.

McKaid glowered, then caught the guffaws and jeers of the rest of the men. He had to admit she had stopped him in his tracks. Most *men* were intimidated by him, but not her. She was some lady. He chuckled then, shaking his head. "She's damned prickly, that's for sure," he answered, looking after her. His eyes narrowed speculatively as he watched her turn into the hotel. "Maybe I'll see if I can't smooth off a few of those thorns. See you 'round, Amos. Gentlemen," he said, nodding to the rest of the men who were still snickering.

"You partial to havin' your eyes scratched out, McKaid?" one of the small crowd yelled to his back.

"He'll tame her," another answered. "He don't mind a rough time. Don't you know that Rangers are so tough they sleep on cactus."

"He oughta be good an' used to it then."

McKaid ignored their jeering. It didn't matter to him what people said or thought. What mattered was finding out who that irritating female was. He'd thought about her all afternoon, so much so that he'd given up his search for the outlaws sooner than usual and hurried back to Santa Fe.

No woman had ever played on his senses in such a way. He convinced himself it was because she had made him so angry, but that didn't account for the fact that he couldn't get that kiss out of his mind. When he grabbed her to give her a good shaking, he hadn't intended to kiss her. It simply happened. Beyond his control. And his own body's response to those soft lips and her pliant body had been instantaneous. He snorted. Maybe he was the one who was starved for female attention. He should do as she said and stay clear of her. She was an Easterner, a snooty one at that, and not at all his type. He liked his women sweet, frilly, adoring, nice and round, and willing. Yes, he'd get on his horse and go back out and look for Corbett. Instead he walked into the hotel.

Elizabeth was signing the register when he leaned his back against the counter and tipped his hat back on his head. She looked up and her whole body jerked in reaction to his presence. He grinned again as she straightened and stiffened her back.

"Go away," she said crossly.

"Now ma'am, I'm sure you'll understand that I'm only doing my job. As a lawman it's my duty to see that no undesirable characters move into town."

"I am not undesirable," she shot back, unthinking.

"No," he replied slowly, scanning her figure briefly. "Strangely enough, you're not."

"Oh . . . ooh . . ." she ground out, clenching her fists, itch-

54

ing to slap his arrogant face.

"Running out of ideas?" he taunted. Without waiting for her answer, he spun the register around and read her neatly written name.

"Hepplewhite?" he roared, jerking himself upright. "You're Elizabeth Hepplewhite?"

His obvious shock alarmed her. "What's the matter? Is something wrong?" She grabbed his arm. "Has something happened to Uncle Clint?" she demanded, not stopping to think he might not know her uncle.

"No, no," he said, stepping away agitatedly. "You're not supposed to be here until tomorrow," he accused angrily.

She shrugged. "So?"

"So?" he yelled. How did he miss this? He should have realized that Amos and Bert were early, but he hadn't stopped to think when he saw the Corbetts attack the stage. And he should have realized that this was Elizabeth. Not that many women traveled to Santa Fe. But she was so different from what he'd imagined Elizabeth would look like. Or act like. And his mind had been on the Corbetts and that damn kiss.

"Is something bothering you, Mr. McKaid?" she demanded. "Have you some problem with my name? Does it not meet with your approval?"

"Or course not," he snapped. "I mean yes, it's fine. It's just that—I—you— Oh, never mind." With that last indecipherable muttering, he pivoted and strode out of the hotel.

Elizabeth's brows rose a notch, and she turned to see the clerk holding her key, a bewildered expression on his face to equal her own.

"What a strange man," she said and accepted the key to her room. "I wonder how he ever got to be a Texas Ranger." All he seemed able to do was kiss and sputter, she thought to herself. And jump through stage doors in the nick of time, don't forget. And shoot bandits and stop runaway stages. She turned toward the stairs. And kiss. She found she was smiling.

So maybe he was good at his profession, she conceded. It still didn't explain his reaction to her name. He was truly upset. Perhaps he knew Uncle Clint, and Clint had mentioned she was coming. Perhaps he was afraid Clint would take offense that he'd kissed her so roughly, or kissed her at all. That could explain it. In fact, that was the only explanation she could think of.

McKaid went directly to the cantina. He purchased a bottle of whiskey and took it to the table in the corner. He downed two shots before he allowed himself to think again. What was he going to do now. This new quirk of fate changed everything. Punishingly he tossed another shot down his throat, wincing at the fire in his stomach.

He'd kissed her, and he had wanted to do it again that second time, and not just to still her razor-sharp tongue either. The whole conversation with Clint passed through his mind again, about not having a woman around who would fall in love with him and make his life miserable. What a laugh Clint would have if it turned out the other way around. And he wasn't sure at the moment if he could be trusted to keep his hands off her.

But she was his damned cousin, for god's sake, even if she didn't know that yet. How could he feel that way for his cousin. He had to get a hold of himself. He had to put a stop to his wayward desires.

She was sure to tell Clint, too. What in the world would Clint say about it. Clint had sent him in good faith to pick her up and deliver her safely to the ranch. Well, god damn, he had kept her safe. He'd saved her lovely neck actually. And if he were to admit the truth, Clint would probably think the whole incident very funny. It was his own pride he was concerned about. How was he going to face Clint's laughter? And how was he going to face Elizabeth in the morning and tell her who he really was.

Well, one kiss wasn't so bad, was it. Some cousins even married, though he could never feel right about that. Still, a kiss wouldn't hurt her. It was probably the only one she'd ever had, poor thing that she was. He took another long drink and shuddered. He was feeling better, so much so that when Amos came in, he called him over to share his bottle.

"Been quite a day, eh?" Amos said, smirking.

"Quite," McKaid laughed.

"Did you see that little lady to her hotel room?"

"No. I left her to fend for herself. You know who she is?"

"Miss Hepplewhite," Amos said with a shrug.

"She's Clint's niece. She's the one we brought here to take care of James and Ruthie Warren."

Amos nodded. "I figured she might be when she explained how she thought you were sent by her daddy and her uncle to play a trick on her, to shake her up a little. It has something to do with some book she read on the West. I guess her daddy thinks she's a mite too set in her ways."

"That's what all that nonsense was about?" McKaid asked, laughing incredulously. "No wonder she lit into me."

"It was a good show you gave her," Amos replied, grinning beneath his shaggy beard.

McKaid's lips curved into a crooked grin and his eyes narrowed thoughtfully. "Maybe, just maybe, I'll keep the show going."

"What you plannin' now, McKaid. You take it easy on her; she's really a nice lady."

"Nice? I bet she's tough as shoe leather. But don't fret. I'm not planning her any harm. Just a little fun, that's all."

"You watch your step, Ranger boy. The last laugh may be on you."

Chapter Four

After a restless night when the bold faces of Colt Sterling and Dash McKaid, so similar to her mind, blended together in a confusing mixture of strange dreams and wild wanton fantasies, Elizabeth awoke, feeling more confused than ever. She'd gone to sleep determined to put that blasted Ranger out of her mind, but he'd stayed persistently rooted, through no fault of her own. Now she felt on tenterhooks, wondering if he'd show up again as surprisingly as he had those two times since she'd arrived in town.

It took her hours the night before to finally admit to herself that she was just a little infatuated with him, but she allowed that it was only because he resembled her fictional hero so much. And that was pure poppycock. Still, she was assailed by the jitters at the thought that, for whatever his reasons, he might seek her out again.

She dressed with extra care that morning, just in case, and went downstairs to find someplace to eat. The clerk jumped to his feet and greeted her enthusiastically, giving her directions to the "best little café in town."

"I'm expecting someone from the Circle K Ranch to come for me today. Would you know if anyone from there has arrived in town yet?"

"Oh, yes, miss." He looked at her curiously. "But didn't you . . . Well, never mind. You go have your breakfast. I'm sure he'll find you when he's ready to leave."

"Thank you, and could you have my trunk brought down for me, please."

She found the café easily enough, but when she stepped through the door, the first person she saw was McKaid. She

59

was about to turn around and find somewhere else to eat when McKaid lifted his gaze from his coffee cup and saw her. He stood immediately.

"Miss Hepplewhite, good morning."

He was so friendly she could only stare in amazement. Her silly heart did a quick pit-a-pat at his open smile. She moved into the restaurant. It would be awfully rude to turn around and leave now that he'd seen her and greeted her. Or so she told herself. Still, she couldn't help wondering where that arrogant and insufferable man of yesterday was.

"Good morning, Ranger McKaid,' she returned with reserve and took a chair at another table across the room, as if she thought that would stop him.

He picked up his coffee cup, strolled casually to her table, and made himself comfortable on the chair across from hers.

"Mr. McKaid," she said, protesting, "I would really prefer . . ."

"Don't go getting on your high horse again," he interrupted. "It's only natural we eat together this morning since we'll be spending a lot of time in each other's company in the future."

"And just what is that supposed to mean? I came out here to work as a teacher. I have no intention of spending any of my time entertaining someone I find obnoxious."

"You find me obnoxious?" he asked, chuckling dryly. "That's interesting. Most women find me irresistible."

"Good for you, Mr. McKaid. Go find one of them to eat with." Of all the nerve.

He laughed aloud. "No. I think I'll stick it out here, Elizabeth. Elizabeth." He said her name again, studying her tightly controlled face and her snapping eyes, hidden behind those awful glasses she wore. "No, that won't do. I mean, it's a lovely name and all, but it doesn't suit you."

"It suits me just fine, and has for quite some time."

"Lizzie. That's it. We'll call you Lizzie."

"I hate the name Lizzie. My name is Elizabeth. Miss Hepplewhite to you. Now go away."

"Sorry. I haven't eaten yet."

The waitress arrived then with two plates, heaped with scrambled eggs, bacon, biscuits, and red-eye gravy. She put one down in front of each of them, then turned her big brown eyes toward McKaid.

"Anything else for you, Mr. McKaid?" she asked, dripping

her sweetness all over him.

He gave the dark-eyed, utterly smitten young girl a brilliant smile and a naughty wink. "This is perfect, Dolores, honey. It looks wonderful. Perhaps you could bring Miss Hepplewhite a cup of your excellent coffee. She gets a little cranky if she doesn't get it first thing in the morning."

"Oh, yes, sir," she answered brightly, not even looking at Elizabeth. "I'll bring you a refill, too," she offered and scurried away to do so.

McKaid turned his cocky gaze on Elizabeth, a gaze that said, "See, they all fall for my charms."

Elizabeth clucked her tongue in annoyance and looked down at her breakfast. "I didn't want this," she said.

"Sure you did. I ordered it especially for you. You need fattening up some."

"Of all the colossal cheek!" she fumed.

"Now simmer down, Lizzie, girl. I'm only looking out for your best interests."

"My name is Elizabeth!" she shot back hotly.

"People are staring. Eat your breakfast. We have a long ride ahead of us."

She glanced around and saw that not a few of the men seated at the other tables were gawking at them with a great deal of interest and amusement. She felt her cheeks grow hot and turned to glare at McKaid. Before she could utter a suitable reprimand, however, Dolores arrived with her coffee and a refill for McKaid.

"Thank you," she felt constrained to say, though she'd suddenly lost her appetite.

"Are you the lady what's come to teach the Warren kids?"

"Yes, that's correct," she answered as Dolores looked from one of them to the other with some thought that obviously disturbed her. She was probably entertaining fantasies of becoming the next mistress for the handsome Dash McKaid, Texas Ranger, and was afraid Elizabeth would interfere. Foolish girl, on both counts.

Elizabeth forced herself to eat, and when the love-bitten Dolores finally took herself off, Elizabeth looked up to meet McKaid's mocking blue eyes.

"Jealous?" he taunted.

"Don't be absurd. I am not jealous, and you should be ashamed. She can't be more than fifteen, and you're going to

61

break her heart. You shouldn't flirt with her. It will only encourage her infatuation."

"Sixteen. And out here that's considered grown up."

"And do you intend to rob her of her youthful innocence just so you can add another name to the many you have *charmed?*"

"Whether I do or not," he answered with a conceited smirk, "is really none of your business."

"You're despicable."

"I think you are jealous. Are you already in love with me?"

She slammed her fork down. "I am not—" she snapped forcefully, then caught herself as she saw all those heads turn to stare at her again. "I am not in love with you, Mr. McKaid," she ground out between her teeth.

"Yet," he said over his coffee cup, his eyes laughing at her. "Eat your breakfast, Lizzie, honey."

"I'll choke on it," she said, so angry she had to keep a tight grip on herself to refrain from dumping her coffee over his damnable head. "And what did you mean by *we* have a long ride?"

"Just that. We. You and me."

"You're taking me to the Circle K?" she squawked.

He leaned over the table conspiratorially. "We'll have almost two hours alone, Lizzie. Alone. Out in the middle of nowhere. Just you and me. Not many women get such a treat."

"Only us fortunate ones, hmm," she returned sarcastically.

"Now, that's the attitude," he said complacently. "Eat up."

Elizabeth ate, and though a hundred thoughts ran through her head, none could find a path to her lips. Perhaps that was just as well, because her emotions were a jumble at the moment. Two hours with McKaid?

She'd never before met a man who infuriated her so, and at the same time left her feeling so highly charged and stimulated. She wanted to slap his pompous face and at the same time laugh at his idiotic tomfoolery.

When she'd gulped all she could manage to eat, she took a last drink of coffee and set her cup down with finality. Only then did she look at McKaid.

"Maybe I should feed you all the time. I actually had several minutes there without having my hide shredded to pieces."

"Count your blessings, Mr. McKaid."

"Why don't you drop the Mister. Call me McKaid, honey.

Everyone does."

"Next you'll want me to call you Dash, darling," she mocked his use of the endearment.

"Dash Darling," he repeated musingly, trying it out. "Might sound good in the dark, but somehow it doesn't fit my reputation in the daylight."

"And we must preserve your reputation, right?" she retorted, rising as he did from the table.

"It's important in my line of work. What outlaw would quake and quail at the name of Ranger Dash Darling?"

She laughed in spite of herself and glanced up to meet the surprise in McKaid's eyes.

"You're very pretty when you laugh, Lizzie, girl," he said, watching as her lovely smile turned back into a scowl. "Oops, there it goes. Oh well, back to the cactus patch," he shrugged.

"What?" she barked.

"Nothing. Come on. We have a stop to make before we leave town." He paid their fare and led her out of the café and down the street a few blocks to the general mercantile. A small fragile-looking man greeted them at the counter.

"Morning, Auggie," McKaid said. "Mr. Colfax would like his niece fitted for some clothes, and I think Miss Hepplewhite would be more comfortable dealing with your wife. Could you ask her to join us, please?"

"Oh, certainly," he said, looking Elizabeth over. "I'll get her."

He hurried away, and Elizabeth rounded on McKaid. "What's this? I don't need any clothes. I've a whole trunk full."

"Are all your shoes like those?"

She looked down at her practical leather slippers. "What's wrong with these?"

"Nothing, if you want to tempt the ankle-hungry rattlers in these parts."

"Rattlers?"

"Snakes. Mean ones. With long, sharp teeth. And you'll have a heck of a time keeping those skirts in order when you climb up on the back of a horse. Or did you think to bring some riding skirts?"

"Eh, no," she admitted, looking down at her plain tailored skirt. "I'll be teaching, not going around punching cows, whatever that is."

63

It was McKaid's turn to laugh. "Maybe, but I want the children to learn to ride, so you may as well learn, too."

"What makes you think I don't ride?"

"Do you?" he challenged.

"As a matter of fact, I do. I took first place at the riding academy several years ago."

"Riding academy?" he hooted. "Lady, out here we sit a horse a bit differently than what you're used to, and we don't much go in for red coats with gold braid and brass buttons or little black caps on our heads."

She tried to picture that and found it made her laugh again. She was still grinning foolishly, she was sure, when a very hearty and robust woman marched through the back door.

"Ah, McKaid," she boomed. "It's good to see you again. I see you ain't got any uglier since you were in here last time."

"I try to maintain my special charms for ladies like yourself,' he boasted immodestly, kissing the woman on the cheek. "Rose Stanhope, meet Lizzie Hepplewhite."

"Elizabeth," Elizabeth corrected him. "It's nice to meet you, Mrs. Stanhope."

"Call me Rosie. You the new teacher? We all been waitin' for you to show up."

"Oh?"

"Clint wants her outfitted for ranch life. Top to bottom. Can you do it?"

Rosie looked her over, top to bottom. "We'll see what we can do, McKaid."

"I'll be back later. I need to pick up the wagon at the feed store. Oh, and here's a list of supplies that Emma wants. Be a good girl, Lizzie, honey, and listen to Rosie." With that he tipped his hat, gave Rosie a roguish wink, and walked out.

"Ooohh," Elizabeth seethed. "How can you fawn over him? He's such a conceited tyrant."

"Got to ya already, has he?" Rosie chuckled.

"No, he has not," Elizabeth insisted. "I'd like to give him a good kick."

"Ah, he ain't bad as all that. At least he's easy on the eye."

"Only when his mouth is shut," Elizabeth mumbled, glaring at the empty doorway.

"Let's get to work, dearie," Rosie said, grinning at Elizabeth's furious face.

Knowing her uncle was probably right, she let herself be

fitted with sturdy riding boots, not unlike those she'd put in the window of the bookstore, a couple of split riding skirts that only needed small alterations to fit her slender waist, a couple of sensible blouses, a leather vest, kid gloves, and a hat to keep the sun off her face. Most of the garments were decorated in some fashion to look feminine, but they still managed to make her feel like a cowboy, and she wasn't sure she liked them.

"I'm going to include a few lengths of wool and this here pattern. It's for a coat. It gets cold here. Anyway, Emma can sew it up for you."

"I can sew, Mrs.—Rosie."

"Here's some heavy thread and some buttons, then. I gotta fill this other order now. You just make yourself at home and look around."

She did as Rosie said and was amazed at the variety of merchandise housed in the one store. She found two slate boards and some chalk, which she hadn't included in her packing. The children would enjoy using them. She took them to the counter and added them to the bundle of clothing Rosie had assembled.

"I'd like a half dozen of those peppermint sticks, please," she said. "And do you think Uncle Clint would like some of those cigars?"

Rosie took down a box. "These are his favorites. Anything else?"

"Maybe something nice for Emma. I'm afraid I don't know what she likes, though."

"She's had her eye on this lavender gingham for some time now. I'm afraid it's rather dear, though," Rosie answered.

"That's all right. Give me a dress length for her." Elizabeth chuckled, running her hand over the fabric. "I don't even know what she looks like. You'll have to judge how much she'll need."

Rosie's hands worked swiftly, measuring out and cutting the fabric. "You gonna give McKaid a present, as well?" she baited Elizabeth good-naturedly.

Elizabeth snorted. "Only the kick I mentioned before. And I think I'll put on those pointed-toed boots first."

"Speak of the devil," Rosie said when McKaid came strolling into the store.

"Was Lizzie here drooling over me again?" he asked Rosie, after which he planted a bold kiss on Elizabeth's cheek.

"The devil is right," Elizabeth snapped, pushing McKaid away and wiping her cheek. "Twice now folks have referred to you that way. They obviously know you well. And keep your kisses to yourself."

"They don't do me any good."

"Me neither," she shot back.

"She's a mean-hearted woman, Rosie. Maybe I should get me some chaps to wear if I have to ride beside her all the way to the Circle K." Rosie laughed.

"Why are *you* taking me? Don't you have some 'rangering' to do somewhere?" she asked disdainfully.

"I could find some, but as it is, I'm the only one Colfax trusts to get you safely to the ranch."

"Surely there are others who—"

"Nope. I'm the best there is, Lizzie, girl."

"That's a pitiful commentary on the West."

Another robust howl of laughter came from Rosie. "Clint's gonna like this girl," she hooted.

"I'm afraid so," McKaid said wryly, his crooked grin lighting up his handsome face. "What's the damage to my bank balance, Rosie?"

"I'll be paying for my own belongings," Elizabeth declared.

"Sorry. Clint insisted," McKaid said, shrugging. "I have my orders. If you want, you can take it up with him."

"I'll do that," Elizabeth said, not wanting to get into another wrangling match with the autocratic Ranger. She did carry her own packages out to the waiting buckboard, though, ignoring his protestations.

"You two be good now," Rosie yelled and waved them on their way. She gave another horsey laugh when McKaid got impatient with Elizabeth's attempt to pull herself up onto the seat and placed his big hand on her backside and shoved.

"That wasn't necessary," she sputtered at him when he jumped up beside her.

He looked laughingly down into her flushed face. "I thought you needed my help."

"Not that kind."

"What *do* you need me for?" he said suggestively.

"I need you to deliver me to Uncle Clint with haste, then disappear into parts unknown."

"Ouch." He slapped the reins, and the buckboard shot forward. "Pricklier and pricklier."

"I am not prickly," she ground out and threw him a fulminating glare.

He laughed. "I'd suggest we start all over again, but shucks, ma'am," he drawled, "it's too much fun watching you spit and sputter."

She took a deep breath and bit her tongue. She would not argue with him. He only did it to make her angry. And then only to amuse himself more. He was a thoroughly exasperating man. All the same she was glad he was beside her. She had to admit, however grudgingly, that she felt safe with him. She leaned back and relaxed, determined to enjoy the crisp air, the bright morning, and the stark beauty of the rugged scenery.

"See that low house over there? That used to belong to one of our resident witches."

"Go on," she played along.

"No, it's true. She finally lost her head over some man, literally, but people swore for decades afterwards that on certain nights, when the moon was right, they could see her head rolling down this very street, hunting for the man who betrayed her."

"Have you got one chasing you?" she asked tartly. He only grinned.

"Why aren't you married, Lizzie?" he asked, settling himself more comfortably on the narrow seat and propping his feet up on the front of the wagon. "Or maybe I shouldn't bother to ask. Those Eastern men are probably too thin-skinned for the likes of you."

"As a matter of fact, I was betrothed, and have had several offers since."

"What happened with your fiancé? Did he betray you?"

"You would think that," she said with asperity. "But he did, in a way. He died."

"Oh. Too bad about that. Did you love him?"

"Yes, I did."

"Did you sleep with him?"

"Mr. McKaid," she gasped. "Even *you* can't be crude enough to expect me to answer that! Though I don't know why not, since you were crude enough to ask it."

His shoulders lifted in a careless shrug. "I guess that's answer enough. What happened to the other gentlemen? Did they die on you, too?"

"Nothing so dramatic. I simply did not wish to marry them."

"I see. Why not?"

"What difference could that possibly make to you?"

"Just curious. What did your father think about that? What's his name again?"

"Micah. And he thought nothing. The gentlemen didn't propose to him."

"Didn't he think you ought to be married?"

"Just for the sake of being married?" she asked deprecatingly. "Why aren't you married then?"

"Women are supposed to get married. It's different with me. I'm a man," he said superiorly.

She snorted inelegantly. "I have news, Mr. McKaid. For every woman who gets married, so must a man."

"I guess we're the odd pair out, then."

Odd was the right word for him, she thought. "Tell me about the children, James and Ruthie," she requested, changing the subject.

He grinned at her tactics but did as she asked, relating the details of Jack's and Sophie's death and the difficulties the children were having at the ranch.

"Emma's not as young as she used to be. So Clint thought you might help us out. We're both grateful you decided to come."

She was nonplussed at the sincerity in his last comment. "So the children are actually your wards, not Clint's?"

"He welcomed them readily enough at the Circle K. That's the kind of man he is."

"That's why you're in this territory instead of Texas then, because of the children? That's why you came for me instead of Clint? Why didn't you explain earlier?" She felt bad about insulting him. If he accepted the children, he must have some decency in him. And that also explained his shock at learning who she really was. She'd wondered about that.

"Yes and no," McKaid answered. "I had to bring James and Ruthie here to live, but I'm also after the Corbett gang who killed Jack and Sophie."

"I see. Well, I'm happy to help the children. It's the least I can do." She didn't explain further when he cocked a questioning brow at her last comment. She didn't intend to tell him she had no idea who her own real parents were. He'd only use it in his campaign to aggravate her.

"Does that make you like me a little more?" he teased. "It

must be painful to have to admit such a thing."

She grimaced. "Yes, it is," she said, not daring to look at him, certain his crooked smirk would be back again.

"If it's any consolation," he went on, "I like you more now, too."

"I can't begin to tell you how relieved I am," she said facetiously.

He chuckled. "Okay, so you're not ready to be friends yet. Tell me, what do you do with yourself when you're not reading?"

"How do you know I read so much?"

"All those books in your trunk. How else? But you needn't have carted them all this way. Clint has a very extensive library."

"All those books, as you put it, are for the children. They are the latest editions in educational material available."

"Oh. I hadn't thought of that. I mean books for the kids."

"As I anticipated. You surely didn't expect me to take on this venture unprepared for the task, did you?"

"Now you sound like a Miss Elizabeth," he said grinning openly.

"Oh, hush. Have they had much schooling?"

"Only a little. Sophie was trying to teach them, but she'd only begun when . . ."

He seemed to drift off into the past for a minute, a very sad past. "I'm sorry about your friends, Mr. McKaid," she said.

His head turned and his gaze met hers and held. "I think you mean that. Is there a tender heart under that tough hide of yours?"

She felt her heart swell and push upward into her throat as she looked into his penetrating blue eyes. She could actually feel him searching her mind, her heart, her soul, and for once in her life, she couldn't prevent it. She couldn't shut him out, and she felt very exposed and vulnerable under his intense gaze. She didn't know what he was looking to find, but she knew then that she wanted him to approve of her, to like what he saw. Contrary to all her ideology, she suddenly wanted to be what a man wanted her to be, and it disturbed and confused her.

Her lashes fluttered down and she turned away, studying her hands in her lap. "I'm not so tough," she said quietly.

"Just strong-minded, determined, resourceful, outspoken,"

he rattled off, sensing her sudden unease and knowing exactly how to diffuse it. "Sharp-tongued, quick of wit, stubborn, cantankerous . . ."

She smiled and relaxed visibly. In this mood, she could handle McKaid. "Thank you very much. And you, Mr. McKaid, are the most arrogant, conceited, overbearing—"

"All with good cause, my dear. And I thought you were going to drop the Mister."

"I can't just call you McKaid. And Dash seems too familiar. Where did you ever get the name Dash? Is it a nickname?" She laughed briefly. "Because you dash in and out of stagecoaches, rescuing fair maidens from peril?"

"So you are still a maiden. I thought so. I don't think you've even been kissed properly yet."

"Your kiss certainly wasn't proper," she snapped back.

"Oh, I do much better than that. Shall I show you?"

"I'll take your word for it," she said, blushing. "Your name?" she reminded him.

He laughed openly at her. "It's short for Dashiel. An old family name I'm doomed to bear."

"It's not so bad. Shall I call you Dashiel then?"

"Why not just McKaid, like everyone else."

"I'll try," she said doubtfully. "How do you know my uncle?"

"He's my mother's brother." He watched Elizabeth's mind put that together.

"He's your uncle, too? You're my cousin?" she asked, puzzled. "My mother never spoke much about her family," she said, trying to excuse her ignorance, but she felt foolish. All this time . . . all her crazy thoughts . . .

"No. Her father wasn't pleased that she ran off with Hepplewhite. He disowned her. As I understand it, Jack Colfax was a very abusive man."

"Oh. So did Uncle Clint leave home also and come out here to ranch?"

"Not at first. The Circle K was built by my Grandpappy McKaid just before he died. That was, oh, eight years ago now. I was too wrapped up in the Rangers, too wild and ready to take on the whole world to run the ranch, and Pappy knew it. He left it to both Clint and me when he died, provided Clint would agree to come out and run it."

70

"What about your father?"

"My parents died when I was eighteen. That's when I came out West."

"I didn't know I had an aunt. My mother never mentioned her."

"My mother died when I was born. Clint said it was her death and Jack's cruelty that finally convinced Hepplewhite to take your mother away. I was raised by a stepmother. She was very good to me, and I loved her dearly."

"You really are my cousin then?" she asked, trying to construct some sort of family tree.

"Sort of, I guess. Does that bother you, Lizzie, girl?"

"No. Not at all. If anything, it'll make you behave."

"We're not that closely related, cuz."

"Whether we are or not, you can mind your manners."

"I'm not too good at taking orders, honey. And I've never had many manners."

"I'll teach you," she stated categorically, ignoring McKaid's loud groan. "I remember meeting Uncle Clint's sons once. Are they at the ranch now?"

"Jim and Cory. No. They died in the war."

"Oh. I'm sorry."

"Yeah. They were good boys."

"So many good men died in that dreadful war," Elizabeth said remorsefully.

"Where were you then?"

"We stayed in Virginia. Daddy wanted me to go to New York, but Paul was in Virginia, and I wanted to stay with him."

"Your fiancé," he said, nodding his understanding. "Was he a soldier?"

"A doctor. We worked together in the hospitals."

McKaid's brows shot up at that, and when he looked at her again, he saw her through new eyes. "That must have been hard work."

"Sometimes."

"How did he die?"

"An explosion. Paul had been working for almost three days straight. He'd gone to the officers' quarters for a few hours' sleep. Someone had planted some dynamite and . . ." Her voice died away.

"What did you do then?"

71

"Continued working. It's what Paul would have done."

They rode on for a ways in silence, each lost in deeper thoughts. McKaid tried to picture that spitting little shrew he'd rescued from the Corbetts as a nurse, holding the hands of dying boys. He had to admit that his younger cousin had him baffled. There were several facets in her personality that he'd already seen, but he wondered how many more there were.

He wondered if there were sides to her nature that she, herself, was unaware of. She was a fighting spirit, a self-reliant woman, not accustomed to leaning on a man for support. He liked that in her. And she was also compassionate. She would not otherwise have dedicated her youth to helping the wounded and dying. Or helping out with two orphaned children who had no relationship whatsoever to her personally.

But he wondered if all that compassion could be turned to equal passion. He couldn't, try as he did, forget that one kiss. He'd felt fire in her then. She'd denied it, of course, and he was sure she kept it safely locked away, but he knew it was there. And cousin or not, the thought of learning for himself just how far he could awaken her to her own femininity was a very enticing challenge indeed.

Elizabeth, likewise, was confused. She didn't normally discuss her past with people she barely knew. Or people she knew well, for that matter. And here she sat, telling it all to McKaid. He was an easy man to talk with. Whether they were fighting, or sparring, or serious, she felt comfortable with him. Except for the times he made her aware that he was a man and she a woman. She didn't know how to handle him then. He had only to look at her in that knowing way and with those devil's own eyes, and her wits flew off and left her stranded to deal with him defenselessly.

"How much longer?" she asked abruptly, not wanting to think anymore.

"You're not enjoying my company?" he asked, feigning bafflement.

"Why should I enjoy it or not enjoy it?" she shrugged indifferently. "I just asked a simple question."

"You're not very good for my ego," he complained.

"Your ego is massive enough as it is," she retorted. "You don't need me to feed it."

"It would be nice, though, if you were as adoring and worshipful as the rest of—"

"The rest of your women?" she suggested sarcastically. "Count me out. I don't intend to be one of your broken hearts."

"Don't be so selfish, Lizzie."

"Selfish?" she exploded. "You're calling me selfish? Why you . . ."

"Now, Lizzie, don't get in an uproar. Out here men like their women docile and malleable."

"Men everywhere like their women docile and malleable. And brainless, and spineless, and blind, deaf, and mute."

Deep, resonant, utterly masculine laughter followed, and it sent her pulse skittering. "I gather you don't agree with that," he remarked.

"For once, you're right," she said scathingly. "And why should I? I'm just as capable as any man of intelligent thought. More than most."

"But you're just a woman," he replied reasonably. "You're supposed to let us stronger types take care of you."

"Take care of us? Is that what you call it?"

"Wouldn't you? We dress you, feed you, put a roof over your heads. And we fight all your battles. You didn't see any women fighting in the war between the states or running off the Indians."

"You didn't see any women in the Congress that decided to start those wars either."

"Ah, now you want to run the country, too?"

"Why not? And women did fight in those wars. Just as much as men. Maybe in a different way, because they were forced to, but all the same . . ."

"Okay, okay," he surrendered momentarily.

But she wouldn't be shushed. "There are women raising families alone who can't make a decent living because men won't give them a chance. Men won't do business with women, they won't pay them fair wages, they won't give them any consideration in how business is conducted."

"Then those women should get married," he said, baiting her further.

"How typical! That's my point exactly. A woman shouldn't have to marry a man she finds odious and repugnant just to survive in the world. What kind of life is that?"

He grinned at her temper. He wished she'd take those silly glasses off so he could see her flashing eyes better. She had

73

pretty eyes. Actually, she wasn't nearly as plain and unappealing as she tried to be.

"Is that why you never married? Do you find all men odious?"

It took her a few seconds to realize he had turned their argument to her personal life again. She glowered at him. "For the most part, yes. Except for my father. He is one of the kindest, wisest men in the world."

"How could you ever leave such a paragon then?" he asked.

"Oh, McKaid, don't be ridiculous. Anyway, he just remarried, and I thought he and Caroline should have the house to themselves."

"So he kicked you out?"

"No, he did no such thing. He didn't want me to come, but he knew I needed something else in my life. 'A purpose, a challenge,' as he said. So he finally decided to show me Uncle Clint's letter."

"Coming out here really appealed to you?" he asked curiously.

"At the time," she said witheringly.

"Have I ruined it all for you, Lizzie, love?"

"I wouldn't give you that much power over me, Dash, darling."

The mocking laughter she'd come to expect from him didn't meet her ears, and she turned to see why.

"Elizabeth," he said sternly, eyes scouring the rocky hills on either side of them. "Climb into the back and lie as flat as you can."

"What's wrong, McKaid?" Something was. He never called her Elizabeth.

"Do as I say, right now. Go!" he barked when still she hesitated.

She went, giving no thought at all to the shapely legs she exposed as she clambered over the back of the seat. She had just stepped into the wagon bed when McKaid gave a loud shout and slapped the reins, sending the team into a fast gallop. Also sending Elizabeth sprawling.

She landed hard, but fortuntely on the bags of flour which sent up a cloud of white dust around her. Then a bushel basket of apples tipped over and cascaded down onto her belly.

"Oooph! McKaid!" she cried.

"Keep down and hang on," he yelled back just before the

first shot rang out.

She couldn't have gotten up if she'd wanted, not the way McKaid was driving the horses. She rolled to her stomach, shoving apples out from under her, and lifted her head to peek over the back of the wagon. Three men were chasing them, at least she could only see three in all the dust. And they were shooting at them. She twisted and saw McKaid slide down in the seat.

"Are you all right?" she shouted, concerned that he may have been shot.

"I'm fine, dammit. Stay the hell down," he shouted back.

"Well," she huffed and buried her head in her folded arms. So much for gallantry. Colt never cussed at Penelope.

Chapter Five

Only moments passed before Elizabeth understood the urgent severity of McKaid's command. The three outlaws were gaining on them, and bullets pinged off the wagon in a steady shower. Elizabeth wriggled her way down between the bags of flour and boxes of ranch supplies, burying her head under her hands. The wagon lurched suddenly and bounced over several deep ruts and rocks, tilting at a crazy angle. It settled to the ground with a sharp jarring bounce that snapped her teeth together and came to a stop. Elizabeth's heart seemed to stop beating, sure McKaid had been shot, or worse, killed.

Before she could tamp down her wild fear and react in McKaid's behalf, strong hands gripped her upper arms and dragged her upright and over the side of the wagon.

"McKaid," she cried and threw her arms around his hard chest. "I thought you were—"

"This isn't the time or place to avow your love, lady," he said curtly, jerking her away and shoving her ahead of him up a rocky hill to an outcropping of boulders.

The three bandits rounded the curve in the dirt road and came to a stop when they saw the wagon. "Take cover," one of them yelled, and more shots rained around McKaid and Elizabeth as the three below them dove for the rocks on the other side of the road.

"I was not avowing my love, McKaid," Elizabeth hissed, jumping as a bullet ricocheted off a rock nearby.

"For God's sake, woman, get your head down," he ordered, pushing her firmly to the ground. "Can you shoot?" he asked.

"Eh, no. I've never even held a real gun," she said, though the guns she put in the store window were real, she supposed.

77

She had never given a thought to the fact that they might have been used to kill someone.

"Why me?" he groaned. He ignored her then as time and again he tried to shoot their way out of trouble.

"Can't you get them?" she asked helplessly.

He glared at her, incredulous. "I'm trying."

"I thought you were so good with a gun," she challenged.

"If I could get a line on them, I would be."

"Well, if you can't see them, they can't see you, right?"

"They'll spread out in a minute, then we'll have a hell of a time," he said, reloading and glancing up at the rocks behind them. "We have to get higher. When I say go, you move up behind that big rock. See it?"

"Yes, but—"

"Now. Go!"

He began firing, and she ran, turning her ankle and scraping her hands as she raced up and over the sharp rocks. And then he was following, dodging bullets, and at brief intervals swinging to fire a few himself.

He was right. The outlaws had split up and were shooting at them from three different angles. McKaid threw down his empty rifle and drew his pistols. She watched, mortified, as he tried to protect them, knowing if she weren't at his side, he could easily outmaneuver them. She was holding him back. He was staying with her even if it meant that he got killed.

He braced himself against the rock, ignoring the bullet that nearly hit him, took careful aim, and fired. A loud cry came from below. Elizabeth slid herself closer to the cover of the rocks, her cold blood chilling her entire body. She couldn't believe this was really happening. She was sitting in the middle of a real live shoot-out. People were being killed. She was going to be killed. She didn't want to think what it meant, but at that moment, she wanted very much to live, and she wanted McKaid alive as well. Those men out there had no right to take that from her.

Her ears were ringing so that she almost didn't hear the soft burring warning at her side. When it did penetrate all the thundering sound in her head, she thought she was going to faint. She very slowly turned her head, keeping the rest of her body as still as her trembling limbs would allow. Out of the corner of her eye she saw it, big, huge, and coiled not far from her bare arm. She watched, paralyzed, as the ugly head with its slanted, evil eyes rose and moved from side to side, its tongue flicking hungrily.

Her lips felt frozen stiff, her tongue was no more than a wad of dry cotton in her mouth, and the whole world was beginning to spin crazily. She closed her eyes and took a slow breath. She had to get control of herself. If she fainted, she'd fall over. And the snake would ... She opened her eyes, staring at the monster.

"McKaid," she whispered hoarsely. He didn't hear her. How could he. He was shooting. She tried swallowing, but she had no saliva. She was amazed that her mouth could be so dry when her skin was prickling with cold sweat. "McKaid," she croaked again.

He heard her that time and glanced around sharply. "Jee-zus," he swore, and spun away from cover behind the rocks, shooting right toward her.

She watched in a horrified fascination as the demon creature came apart in mid-air and flew in two directions. All her mind could manage to think was that McKaid was a good shot after all.

Another volley of shots rent the air, and she turned her head just as McKaid spun around, groaned, and crumpled to the ground.

"McKaid," she screamed. "Oh, my God, no."

Ignoring any danger to herself, she jumped up and ran to him. He was still alive. Several more shots hit the nearby rocks, and Elizabeth knew she had to get them both out of the open. She hooked her hands under McKaid's arms and pulled with all her strength. She slipped several times on the loose dirt and stones, falling sharply on her behind, but finally managed to get them to safety behind the boulder again. At least temporarily. Someone below was moving around. She could hear his feet dislodging loose rocks as he climbed upward. In a minute he would be behind them, and she and McKaid would be trapped. At the mercy of men who had no mercy.

McKaid still held one gun loosely in his limp hand. The other was out there in the clearing. She took the gun from his hand. It felt strange to her. She expected it to be cold, but it was comfortingly warm. She held it in both hands and looked around. It was up to her now, but she hadn't the slightest notion what to do.

"Throw the gun out, missy," a man yelled at her. She turned

and saw someone standing off to their side by a clump of brush. Without thinking she pointed the gun and squeezed the trigger. The gun jumped in her hands, and she gripped tighter and shot again.

"We know McKaid's dead," came the voice again. "We won't hurt you."

She pulled the trigger again, pointing at the voice. Then again. But nothing happened. Her gun was empty. She dropped it and dodged out into the open for the other gun. The men laughed at her and let her return safely to McKaid's side.

"You ready to come out now?" he taunted. "Hey Corbett," he yelled to his partner. "You see what we got here? We can have us some fun."

A cold chill raced over her arms. She'd rather the snake got her than these two men. The thought of what they would do to her before they killed her made her stomach churn with nausea. At least the snake, for all its ugliness, was clean, a part of the earth, a natural way to die if she had to die. She pressed her back against the solid strength of the rock.

"Hey, Corbett," called the bandit again. The man named Corbett didn't answer.

Elizabeth didn't know where Corbett was either. Had McKaid shot him, too? Or was he sneaking around the other way, trying to get a clear shot at them.

Another bullet glanced off the rocks over their heads. "McKaid," she cried, trying to wake him up. "Get us out of this mess." A movement out of the corner of her eyes brought her head up, and she saw the bandit standing on top of the rocks behind them. She lifted the gun and shot, missing her target completely. She pulled the trigger again and knew a moment of real dismay when the hollow click of another empty chamber met her ears. Her breath whooshed out of her and she slumped back against the rock. It was over then. She had lost. It was going to happen.

The bandit laughed evilly, then raised his own gun. Almost dreamlike, he let go of the gun, grabbed at his back, then pitched over the edge of the rocks, tumbling like a limp rag doll to the hard, unforgiving rocks below.

"Gordo?" someone called from below. "Where are you, Gordo?"

Elizabeth stayed where she was, motionless, holding her breath, completely confused by the turn of events. She should be dead, or at least in the hands of the man called Gordo. But Gordo had been killed, and not by Corbett. Not by any gun.

She heard Corbett curse and begin scrambling down the rocks, and then she heard a horse gallop away. Had he gone then? Why? She was completely defenseless now. She peered up over the edge of the rocks, still holding the empty gun. It was all like a bad dream. She could almost believe it hadn't happened.

The buckboard was still where they left it, and not a creature moved save for the horses, whose ears twitched occasionally and whose tails swished lazily from side to side. The only reality in the entire nightmare was the sight of the two dead men. And the unconscious man at her feet. She placed both arms along the top of the boulder and dropped her head wearily onto their softness. Now what was she to do? How was she going to get McKaid down the hill to the wagon?

Well, she would! She spun around and kicked McKaid's boot. "Wake up, darn you. How dare you do this—" Her words were strangled on a gasp of fear. There before her stood six black-haired, dark-skinned, almost naked Indians. Every horror story she'd ever heard about what Indians did to white women ran through her mind in that second.

"Stay there," she shouted, raising the empty gun threateningly. She kicked McKaid's foot again. "McKaid!" Where had they come from, these savages? They hadn't so much as rattled one stone. "Go away," she shouted courageously, but her wobbly voice betrayed her fear.

The leader, decked out in a few more baubles than the rest, a few more feathers dangling from his long hair, stepped toward her.

"I mean it," she threatened tremulously.

The Indian kept coming until his chest was inches from her gun. He wasn't a great deal taller than she was, not like McKaid, but his broad chest and folded arms were layered with thick corded muscle that gleamed slickly in the bright sunlight. She looked up at his face. His jaw was long and blunt on the end, his prominent cheekbones bracketing his aggressive hawkish nose. His jet black brows rose over almost black eyes that stared into her own.

"You are McKaid's woman?" he asked in a deep, rumbling voice.

Her eyes widened. He spoke English. McKaid's woman? Did

81

he think she and McKaid were . . . She drew herself up indignantly. "Indeed not," she answered, bristling. Then, "Yes! Yes, I am." Oh, lord, she didn't know how to answer him, and she blushed furiously as a broad grin spread his hard lips.

"No, she is not," groaned McKaid from the ground.

"McKaid," Elizabeth cried, dropping to her knees beside him. "Are you all right?"

"No, Lizzie, girl, I'm not. I'm in a great deal of pain. My side . . ."

"Don't talk," she said. "McKaid, what do I do now? About these Indians?"

"You said not to talk."

The Indian leader pulled her to her feet. "McKaid friend of Straight Arrow. Straight Arrow come to help friend."

Her choking fear erupted into anger. "Why in the world didn't you say so earlier, instead of startling me half out of my wits?" she demanded, meeting his puzzled black eyes.

"Straight Arrow does not understand your anger. I shoot man for you," he said pointing proudly to the high rocks behind them.

"You shot him?" Yes, of course he did. And here she was raving at him for scaring her a little. And he obviously hadn't understood a thing she had just said.

She took a deep breath, rubbing her eyes. "I am sorry. I am not angry," she said slowly. "You scared me. I've never seen an Indian before. Thank you for helping us."

The Indian nodded, satisfied, and spoke to his men in a strangely guttural tongue. The other men were quick to gather around McKaid and lift him from the ground. They moved carefully down the hillside and placed McKaid on the ground beside the wagon. The leader released Elizabeth's arm when they, too, were down the treacherous hill.

Very quickly Elizabeth tore McKaid's blood-soaked clothes away from his side and examined the wound. She had seen worse. While the Indians watched silently, she retrieved her previously torn petticoat from her trunk along with a bottle of whiskey from the box of supplies. Whiskey wasn't the best antiseptic, but it would do for now.

She wiped the wound clean with a soaked cloth, then padded the wound and bound McKaid tightly around his lower ribs. He didn't feel a thing. He had passed out again on the way down the hillside. He looked so white and lifeless.

She leaned over him and kissed his cold lips. "Don't you die on me," she said. It was then she noticed the swollen abrasion on the side of his head. She pushed his hair aside. He must have hit his head when he fell. That's why he was unconscious for so long. When she'd cleaned that also, she made a place for him in the wagon and waited worriedly as the Indians lifted him in.

Straight Arrow touched her shoulder. "You are afraid again?" he asked.

She had never stopped being afraid, but she didn't want him to see her weakness. "I don't know how to get to the ranch. Or back to town," she confessed.

"You go to Circle K?" he asked. "I draw picture for you."

"You know where the ranch is?" she asked in relief.

"McKaid and Straight Arrow friends," he said in tones that left her in no doubt that he thought her of limited mental capabilities. "You look," he said, pointing to the simple map he was drawing in the dirt. "Go this road to fork. At fork, go west. This way."

She looked up and nodded her understanding.

"Go over . . ." he hesitated, searching for the word, "bridge. Go over bridge. Around bend in road is Circle K Ranch. Lizzie girl find now?"

She wanted to laugh at his use of McKaid's name for her but she didn't dare. "Yes, I hope so. Thank you, Straight Arrow." She held out her hand to him. "We are friends?"

He laughed, as did the other men. "You are woman," he said, ignoring her outstretched hand and ordering the men to lead the team back onto the road.

She followed, put soundly in her place, which she wasn't about to protest. Still, she felt she owed them something. She thought of the cigars she bought for her uncle and rummaged among the chaos in the wagon until she found them. She took a handful and offered them to Straight Arrow.

"For McKaid's friend," she said simply.

His eyes lit up. "For McKaid's friend, from McKaid's woman. I will take." He slipped a handful of bullets from McKaid's gunbelt and loaded one of McKaid's guns for her. He helped her onto the wagon seat, handed her the reins, and placed the gun in her lap. "If you need shoot, hold very still and pull trigger. Don't shoot Lizzie girl," he warned.

His face was as stern as ever, but his eyes were laughing at her, and she knew he'd watched her pathetic attempts to protect McKaid and herself. She felt heat rise up her neck into her cheeks.

"I'll be careful. Thank you, Straight Arrow," she said, but he was already striding away. They disappeared back up into the rocks from where they had come, and Elizabeth was left alone to get McKaid to the Circle K. Well, surely she could do that much and get it right.

Straight Arrow's directions were simple and easy to follow. She found the fork in the road and followed the rough-hewn sign with the brand, a Circle surrounding a large K, and an arrow pointing the way burned into it. She traveled for another twenty minutes, looking around often to check on McKaid when he groaned. She knew he was in pain, but there wasn't much she could do. She thought of the whiskey then, and stopped the wagon. She found the half-empty bottle and knelt by McKaid's head, lifting him and tipping the whiskey into his mouth.

"Swallow, McKaid. It'll help the pain." She didn't want to make him choke. Coughing would only cause him more misery. He was bleeding again. The bandage she had wrapped around his waist was stained a vivid red.

"Come on, drink some more."

"Lizzie," he moaned.

"It's okay, McKaid. We're almost there." She poured a few more swallows into his mouth until he shook his head. She corked the bottle and set it aside. Impulsively she leaned down and kissed him again. "Hold on. I'll hurry," she whispered as he slipped into painless sleep again.

He needed attention quickly, but there seemed nothing she could do about it, nothing more than she'd already done. She slapped the reins and again headed down the empty road that Straight Arrow said would take her to the Circle K. They should be getting close now. Where was the bridge?

She'd heard tales of the savage Indians who massacred whole wagon trains of people and dragged off the women and children to be their slaves. She'd read blood-curdling accounts of how barbarous and merciless the Indians were to their captives, how cruel and inhuman was their vengeance against the white man's intrusion into their world. She couldn't help the niggling thought that Straight Arrow could easily have directed her into just such an ambush. She pushed those thoughts away again, as she'd done several times already. She couldn't believe that of Straight Arrow. If he and his men had wanted to harm her, they would certainly have done so when they had her at their mercy. Mercy? Hadn't she just now thought of them as merciless? She couldn't picture Straight Arrow torturing a woman. He seemed, somehow, too honorable for that. But what did she know of Indians? What did she know of anyone out here in this lawless land. McKaid killed men without blinking an eye. Did everyone? Was life so unimportant? Suddenly she felt totally alone. What was she doing here? Everything about the West was alien to her. She was a total misfit here, just as she had been back home.

Anxiety began to twist and turn in her stomach. She was lost. She looked around frantically for some sign that would tell her she was on the right road. What if she'd made a mistake, missed the bridge, taken a turn where she shouldn't have? Blinking back tears, she slapped the reins and drove the team onward, faster toward wherever the dirt track would take them. She simply had to trust Straight Arrow. She had to.

Finally, with a great surge of gratitude toward McKaid's Indian friend, she saw the bridge. Then she saw the two horses grazing nearby and the two men who were lounging under a nearby tree. They rose as she approached. Her hand automatically tightened on the gun hidden in the folds of her dress.

"Afternoon, ma'am," one of the men said, lumbering forward, eyeing her curiously. "Can we help you find your way? You're on Circle K land."

She gave a great sigh of relief. "Are you from there?" she asked eagerly.

"This is Clint's buckboard," the other of the two men said, looking at her dubiously.

"How far is the ranch?" she demanded.

"Ma'am, you better explain where you got this . . ."

McKaid groaned again from the back of the wagon, and Elizabeth turned quickly to check on him. When she did, the gun slid out of her lap onto the floorboard at her feet. She grabbed for it, but before she could get a grip on it, a large hand clamped over hers.

"I'd better have that," the larger of the two men said, wresting the gun from her fingers. He was a big man, broad through the shoulders, built like a giant, but the thick reddish hair that curled riotously under his tilted hat softened his looks, as did his easy brown eyes when they met hers.

"I must go on," she pleaded. "Please let me go."

"It's McKaid, Russ. He's been shot," the younger man said from behind them.

The man called Russ looked at the gun in his hand, McKaid's gun, then at Elizabeth.

"I didn't shoot him, you blasted fool idiot," she exploded. "I'm trying to help him."

Russ's brows raised in surprise at her outburst. "Who did, then?" he asked calmly.

"I don't know. Now are you going to shoot me or are you going to help?" she demanded impatiently.

"Joe, you take my horse and go on ahead. Tell Clint what to expect."

"Right, boss," said Joe. He mounted up, and taking Russ's horse by the reins, rode down the road and around the bend.

Russ climbed up beside Elizabeth. "I'll drive," he said, taking the reins from her and slapping them against the horses' backs.

"Who are you?" she asked.

"Russ Packard. Foreman of the Circle K."

"Oh, lord," she groaned, slumping wearily back in her seat. "Look, I'm sorry. I didn't mean to call you an idiot."

"No?" he said, raising a sardonic brow at her.

"No. I'm usually a very controlled person," she explained, her voice almost frantic. "It's just that—well, the whole trip— I mean, first the stage is robbed, then McKaid jumps into my life, shooting people and dumping them out of stagecoaches, then I find out I have to ride all the way here with—*him,* and he's such an insufferable, arrogant man, and we're attacked again by bandits, then that dreadful huge snake, and he got himself shot, McKaid, that is, and those frightful Indians came. So, I guess you were the last straw."

His look, as he turned his head toward her, was incredulous. "Come, now," he said, shaking his head.

"You think I'm making that up?" she asked in a squeal. Then she thought of that darned book again and how she'd scoffed at the author's wild imaginings. She chuckled, and when she looked at Russ's sympathetic frown, she broke out laughing. She laughed so hard that her sides hurt and tears flooded her eyes, and then she was crying just as hysterically.

"Hey, hey," Russ said, wrapping one big arm around her and pulling her to his shoulder where she buried her face and cried like a fool. "It's all right now. You're safe."

"McKaid?" she sobbed.

"McKaid's tough. He's made it this far. He'll be fine now. Look. There's the ranch. We're almost there."

"Oh my," she cried, and sobbed again, "I must look a fright." She reached instinctively to adjust her glasses, but they were gone. Where had she lost them?

"You look fine. Here," he said, handing her a red bandana from his back pocket. "It's clean."

"Thanks," she replied tearfully and mopped at her tear-streaked face. "My hair!" She fumbled with it, trying to find enough pins to hold it in place. They were gone, and in the end, she had to leave it loose.

"Okay, now?" Russ asked, throwing a warm smile her way. He didn't know what had happened out there, but she sure was something. He wondered who she was, but he was certain he'd find out momentarily. At any rate, she was with McKaid. And McKaid wasn't blind.

"I'm really sorry about crying all over you. I don't usually come apart like that. Your shirt . . ."

"Don't give it a thought. There's Clint. He and Emma are waiting for us. They'll take care of everything. Do you know Mr. Colfax, miss?"

"He's my uncle."

"Your uncle? Well, then, you must be the one come to teach those youngsters. I should've figured that out, only I wasn't expecting anyone so young and pretty." He looked down at her and smiled again. "There, now, that's better. You have some color in your cheeks again."

"Thank you, Mr.—"

"Russ. Just Russ."

Clint Colfax did take over when they arrived at the house, issuing crisp orders for the men around him to get McKaid up the stairs to his bedroom, to see to the supplies, and to take care of the horses. Everyone jumped to his bidding, and Elizabeth stepped out of the way as they did.

"Russ," Clint bellowed from inside the house. "See if there's any sign of Mac. We're gonna need him to get this slug out."

"Sorry, miss. That wasn't much of a greeting for you." Russ

87

apologized, uncertain what to do or say. He didn't want to leave her stranded and alone on the porch. She'd been through a tough day if only half of what she said was true.

"You better find Mac. Who is he?"

"He acts as doc around here. He ain't a real doc, but we can't always wait for someone to go all the way to town and fetch Doc Mason."

"You better go, then. I'll be fine," she assured him and watched him nod and hurry off. At least there was one friendly face at the Circle K. That wasn't true, she admitted. McKaid had been friendly, in his way. And the others hadn't had a chance to befriend her yet. She turned and walked tiredly into the unfamiliar house.

She looked around the spacious foyer. A grandfather clock ticked loudly in the corner and a gigantic rack of antlers was mounted on the wall next to it with several hats and coats suspended from the horns. To her left was a comfortable-looking room, darkened against the warming sun by deep green drapes. A stone fireplace took up most of one wall, the others were covered with bookcases full of colorfully bound books. A cluttered desk sat at an angle in one corner and several sturdy chairs were placed around it. Clint's office.

The room to her right was shut off by a sliding door. She could open it and look around her new home, but somehow she couldn't work up the energy. She just wanted to lie down and sleep for days. She stood in the foyer, staring at the long, wide staircase, listening to the buzz of voices from above. She supposed she should go up and see how McKaid was doing.

She'd just started up the stairs when the young ranch hand named Joe burst in the door and rushed past her, taking the stairs two at a time and murmuring a timid, "Excuse me, ma'am."

Ma'am. Was every female a ma'am out here? She hurried her pace and found the door to McKaid's room. Emma stood by the bed, wringing her apron, two children stood solemnly to the side, watching wide-eyed and tearful; and Clint was gaping at Joe.

"He's where?" Clint demanded harshly.

"Up at the north quarter, sir. It'll take us an hour to find him and get him back here."

"Dammit," Clint cursed. "I'm no good at this sort of thing. Emma?"

Emma blanched. "I've birthed many a babe in my life, Mr. C., but I never dug out a bullet. What if I hurt him?"

Elizabeth closed her eyes wearily. Her day wasn't over yet. She couldn't let these well-meaning people get McKaid into worse trouble than she had done herself.

"Russ," Clint cried, relieved. "Good, you're back. You can do it."

Everyone turned to look at him. "Do what?" Russ asked. His brows rose questioningly, then just as quickly they lowered and he shook his head resolutely. "Oh, no, Mr. Colfax. I can't."

"Someone has to," Clint bellowed.

"I'll do it," Elizabeth heard herself say. She looked into Russ's alarmed eyes. "He got shot saving me from a rattlesnake."

"Elizabeth?" Clint said, as if he only just now realized she was there. "Elizabeth."

She turned and looked at his strained face. "I'm sorry. I didn't mean for him to get shot, Uncle Clint." Everyone was staring at her. She moved to the side of the bed and looked at Emma. "I'm Elizabeth," she said unnecessarily. "I'll need some water boiled, and some clean bandages, and any instruments you have for this sort of thing—scissors, tweezers, if you have any, a needle and some silk thread. And perhaps James and Ruthie can help you collect those for me."

"Yes, miss," Emma said, relief giving her renewed strength. "Come on, children. Let's hurry."

"And Emma, some alcohol and any salve you have for infection. And you better bring a bottle of whiskey."

"Right away, miss."

"Uncle Clint, you and Russ get his clothes off him and get him—properly covered. I'll wait outside. Try not to waken him. He'll do better to sleep through this."

She stepped out into the hall and leaned against the wall. It took only moments for everyone to complete their assigned tasks, moments when she wondered if she were out of her mind. It had been years since she'd tended a bullet wound. But at least she'd done it. She was the only one who had, apparently. But she was so tired.

"Tea, Miss Elizabeth," Emma said, pressing a cup into her hand. "Drink it down."

It was hot and strong, and very sweet, and she was grateful

for one person, at least, who saw that she was at her wits' end.

"Elizabeth," Clint said, coming toward her. "We're ready. Are you sure you can do this? I know we haven't given you much of a welcome, but if you can help McKaid . . ." His voice trailed off, and Elizabeth could see that he loved McKaid like a son. They all loved McKaid. Maybe she did, too, if only a little.

"I've done it before, Uncle Clint, during the war. I'll do what I can for him, I promise."

Clint relaxed visibly. "Bless you, child."

Elizabeth cut the bloody bandages away from McKaid and slid the soiled material from under him. The wound was an angry purple, still oozing blood. She scrubbed her hands with strong lye soap, then she cleansed McKaid's torso and the area around the wound. After that she scrubbed her hands again.

Ruthie came in with another pan of hot water, and James followed with clean towels and some torn sheets. Both stood at the foot of the bed and watched in silence.

Elizabeth placed the long tweezers and the threaded needle in the hot water, then turned to McKaid. Very gently she probed the swollen area below his ribs. He groaned and his left arm flew up and caught her on the side of her head.

"I'll get you for that, McKaid," she said, holding her hands away from contact with him. "Restrain him, Uncle Clint."

Clint, looking astonished at Elizabeth's reaction to being slugged, held McKaid's left arm while Russ hurried to do the same with his right. McKaid's eyes fluttered open.

His fever-bright eyes met hers, wandered around the sea of faces, and came back to rest with hers. "Lizzie, love," he slurred.

"Oh, damn," she sighed. "You better give him a good long swallow of whiskey. This is going to hurt."

A strange look passed between Russ and Clint before Clint released McKaid's arm and turned to bring the bottle to McKaid's lips. "Drink up, my boy."

McKaid drank, then pushed the bottle away, reaching out to touch Elizabeth's long hair. "You're gonna save me?" he asked her.

"I'm still thinking it over," Elizabeth retorted. "Some hero you turned out to be! Give him some more, Uncle Clint. Drink it, McKaid. I don't want to be slugged again."

He obeyed. "I was saving you from the evil serpent, Lizzie. She likes to be called Lizzie," he told the assembled group.

90

She ignored them. "Couldn't you have shot the snake from where you were? Did you have to make a target of yourself?"

"I'm good, love, but not that good. I could have shot off your pretty nose. Did you kiss me?" He swallowed more whiskey.

"You're delirious. Go back to sleep." She felt herself blushing, but kept her head down so her hair would shield her face from all the curious eyes.

"You mean you didn't? I'm disappointed." His words were slurring more now.

"You'll get over it," she bantered, giving the liquor time to do its work. She was going to have to cause him pain. A great deal of pain. The thought made her throat close up.

"Kiss me now, then. Just for luck."

"I just washed my hands," she argued.

"I don't want to kiss your hands. Come on, Lizzie. For luck?"

Russ sputtered, and she threw him a quelling look. She looked at her uncle, too, but he was quick to wipe the grin off his face.

"You don't need luck, McKaid. I'm the best there is."

"We'll see," he answered, grinning foolishly.

"Careful," she warned, glaring at him. "You're at my mercy now."

"Be gentle, love. It's my first time."

Russ did laugh at that, as did her uncle and Joe who stood beside the children. Elizabeth looked over at Emma and rolled her eyes heavenward. Shaking her head in exasperation, she turned to her uncle's smirking face. "He's drunk enough," she declared. "Let's get on with it. This is going to hurt, McKaid, but it can't be helped."

"Heartless woman," he answered.

"You better bite down on this, boy," Clint said, placing a folded belt between McKaid's teeth.

Again Elizabeth probed the wound, gently at first, then more firmly. She felt McKaid stiffen and heard him groan, but she kept working, blinking back tears that threatened to cloud her vision.

"His rib is broken. The bullet must have hit that and veered off. I'll have to find it."

She lifted the tweezers from the hot water and dried them and her hand to keep her grip secure. As carefully and as quickly as she could, she probed the ugly hole in McKaid's side. Bright red blood oozed out and covered her hand. McKaid groaned again, turned a sickly gray color, and passed out.

Elizabeth let out her breath in a long sigh. "Thank God for that."

She worked more surely now that he was no longer in pain. It took several long and anxious minutes but at last she felt the hard edge of the piece of lead.

"I have it," she said quietly, clamping the tweezers around the projectile and withdrawing it with skillful fingers. She dropped it on the bed beside him, and let out the breath she had been holding.

"Good girl," Clint praised her, and she looked up into his misty eyes.

His gentle smile encouraged her and gave her strength. Taking another deep breath, she cleaned and sterilized the wound again, then put in several neat stitches to hold the skin together. Lastly, she applied the potent-smelling ointment that Emma had brought and bound his abdomen as firmly as she dared. It was all she could do. The rest was up to McKaid.

She stood up on very shaky legs and washed her hands again. Everyone was praising her, telling her what a fine piece of work she had done, but their voices became very muddy in her ears. She turned to face her uncle, and the room began to spin around her.

He reached out to her, and she touched his fingers with her own before a complete and blessed blackness wrapped around her.

Chapter Six

Elizabeth woke up slowly and reluctantly from her pleasant dreams. She was in a narrow, comfortable bed with linens that smelled of sunshine. After a minute of being deliciously lazy, she opened her eyes to glance out of her warm, snug cocoon. The room was bathed in gentle light that filtered through the pink floral ruffles of the curtains, giving it a patterned rosy glow. The furniture was elegant, a small writing desk, carved chairs covered with needlepoint cushions, a large but delicately carved wardrobe, a dressing table with a shiny bevelled mirror attached. Everything was polished to a deep gloss. She wondered for a confused second what hotel she was in, and how she'd gotten into bed.

She sat up and let the covers fall to her waist. She was dressed in her own thin lawn nightdress, but couldn't for the life of her remember anything past . . . And then the events of the previous day came back in a rushing torrent. She was at the Circle K. And McKaid . . .

She shoved the bed clothes aside and slipped out of bed, searching the immaculate room for her trunk. She must go check on McKaid. She had to know he was all right. A faint knock sounded at her door, and before she could answer, the crystal knob turned, and a little blond head appeared around the portal.

"Hello, Ruthie," Elizabeth said. The little girl looked surprised to see Elizabeth out of bed and almost retreated into the hallway before Elizabeth could stop her. "Could you help me find my clothes, please?"

Wordlessly, but with curious eyes, Ruthie entered the room, went to the wardrobe, and pulled open the double doors.

"We put your things away while you were sleeping," she said timidly. "I didn't think you would ever wake up."

Elizabeth reached for her robe then hesitated. "What time is it?" she asked.

"It's after noon. You almost slept a whole day."

"Goodness. I better get dressed. What will everyone think of me?"

"That you were tired," Ruthie answered logically.

"I probably need a bath," she said absently, considering the pixielike face that had yet to smile.

"Miss Emma gave you a wash when she put you to bed. Are you going to have a baby?"

Elizabeth was pulling a pair of stockings from a drawer she'd been searching, and her hand froze in its upward movement. "A baby? Now wherever did you get that notion?" She tugged the thin stockings out of the drawer and sat on the bed to smooth them over her lap.

"Mama used to faint, like you did, when she was going to have a baby."

"I'm not even married yet, Ruthie. I fainted—well—because I was so tired, I guess. I didn't know you had a younger sister or brother."

"I don't. Our two babies died before they could get borned."

"Oh. That's too bad." She looked in more drawers until she found her underclothes. Ignoring her lack of privacy, she began to dress.

"James said that it was a blessing because him and me couldn't have took care of a babe."

"He and I couldn't have taken care," Elizabeth corrected gently. "And maybe James is right."

"He said God had His ways, and He must have known Mommy and Daddy were going to die."

"What do you think?"

"I think God must be mean," she said pensively.

Elizabeth felt her heart go out to Ruthie. She remembered times when she cried herself to sleep, cursing God for leaving her all alone in that old run-down, drafty orphanage. Time and again she'd watched other children—younger children, prettier children, boy children—find homes. Time after time she'd trudged back to her room to battle the wretched disappointment and loneliness, to hide away until the tears had stopped.

94

"Maybe it was the men who killed them who were mean. Maybe God was just as heartbroken as you were," Elizabeth offered gently, as she hastily pulled on the first dress she came to.

Ruthie was unconvinced, but Elizabeth knew it would take more than a few words to ease the pain and loneliness of a child torn from her parents.

"Could you help me with these buttons?" Elizabeth asked. "They're difficult for me to reach."

Her tactic worked. Ruthie brightened and applied her deft little fingers to the back of Elizabeth's dress.

"How is Mr. McKaid this morning?" Elizabeth asked her small companion.

"He's still sleeping. Emma was trying real hard to keep everybody quiet, but Mr. Colfax kept stomping around anyway. I think he wanted to wake you and Mr. McKaid up. You have pretty hair," she said, reaching out to touch Elizabeth's long tresses, now brushed free of tangles. "Mama's hair was dark brown. James has brown hair, too. Mine isn't any color."

"Nonsense," Elizabeth said, turning on the vanity stool to face Ruthie. "Your hair is beautiful. It's the color of white desert sand, and apple pie right out of the oven, and . . ."

"Ruthie," came a hoarse whisper from the hallway. Ruthie flinched and turned pleading eyes to Elizabeth.

"In here, Emma," Elizabeth said calmly.

Emma pushed open the door with her hip, her hands bearing a tray laden with breakfast.

"Oh, miss, I hope she didn't wake you. I warned them not to bother you none. If she did . . ."

"She didn't. I was awake, and Ruthie's been helping me get dressed. We're getting acquainted, isn't that right, Ruthie?"

"Yes, ma'am."

"I guess that's well and good then," Emma replied. "I brought you some tea and soda biscuits. If you want something more substantial, I'll be happy to fix it for you."

"No. This is fine, and I'm grateful. I assure you I haven't made it a habit to sleep the day away. I'm usually up very early."

She pulled her hair into her usual twist and secured it with several long pins. She found her spare glasses, slipped them on, then sat at the little desk and poured her tea, relishing the sweet brew. She looked up to see two pairs of eyes surveying her curiously.

She smiled self-consciously. "Tell you what. Let's go down to the kitchen. I'm more comfortable eating there. My father never brought me breakfast in bed, so let's not start a precedent now. I don't want to get lazy." She lifted her tray and marched to the door. "Coming?" Bemused, they followed.

James was sitting at the table with Clint, both wolfing down cookies and milk when Elizabeth walked in. They both swallowed hastily and jumped to their feet.

"Good morning," Elizabeth said, putting her tray on the long oak table. "Or rather, good afternoon. May I join you?"

"Elizabeth," Clint said, giving her a warm hug. "Welcome to my home. I see you've met Emma and Ruthie. This lad is James."

"Afternoon, ma'am," James said politely.

"Good afternoon, James. Oh, please, everyone, call me Elizabeth. I've been ma'am to everyone I've met since I left Virginia. I don't think I can bear anymore."

"Elizabeth it is then," Clint said heartily. "Sit down, sit down."

"You look different," James observed.

"She pinned her hair back," Ruthie explained.

"And you have glasses on now."

"Oh, yes," Clint said. "We found a pair in the back of the wagon, of all places. Unfortunately they were under a bag of feed. Broken, I'm sorry to say."

"Never mind, I have these."

"How did your glasses get under the sack of feed?" James asked. "Weren't they on you?"

"Yes," she answered. She spread butter and honey on her biscuit and took a bite, trying to ignore the inquisitive eyes watching her. She knew they had probably all been dying of curiosity about her unusual arrival at the Circle K, and she couldn't really blame them. In a reverse situation, she would be, too.

"All right. I'll tell all, but first I'm going to eat my breakfast. Or lunch, I guess. Do you think I might have some cookies and milk? I have a dreadful sweet tooth."

With her appetite sated, and between sips of fresh, hot tea, she related the events of the last few days of her life, joining in the spirit of adventure by playing up the excitement, and poking fun at herself and at McKaid for everything that had happened. At the same time she minimized the actual danger so she wouldn't frighten the children.

"Were they real Indians?" Ruthie asked, awestruck. "And was it a really big snake?"

"Terribly big. And yes, they were real Indians," she answered, glancing at her uncle.

"They're Jicarilla Apache," Clint explained for her benefit. "They live, for the time being, up north of us, on Circle K land actually. They're an agricultural sect, tend to stay put with their crops and herds of animals, unlike the more nomadic groups of Apache. Straight Arrow has been assured that they're welcome to stay and to hunt the land as long as they don't take to raiding the ranches and killing our stock. Occasionally, when the winters are bad, they come by to trade their goods for a few head of cattle, but for the most part, they keep to themselves. Unfortunately, if the politicians and military men have their way, they'll be rounded up with all the rest of the Indians and sent to a reservation."

"Why, if they're peaceful?" Elizabeth asked, liking the thought of Straight Arrow's people living nearby.

"Just because they're Indians. It doesn't make much difference to some people, including influential men, how peaceful they are. They don't want to be bothered differentiating between the gentle and the aggressive. Indians are Indians."

"I'm pleased you're not one of those men, Uncle Clint. I liked Straight Arrow. I owe my life to him." If he hadn't happened by, she and McKaid would surely be dead now. It was a sobering thought.

"And you said the man who escaped was called Corbett?"

"Yes. The other man was Gordo. He's the one Straight Arrow shot. I don't know who the other man was. Is it important?"

"It will be to McKaid."

"How was his night?" Elizabeth asked.

"Emma and I took turns sitting with him. He was restless and developed a fever, but not by half what he'd have if you hadn't taken out that slug so expertly. You're going to put Mac out of work. I dare say everyone on the ranch has heard about you by now."

"Mac don't know what he's doing anyway," Emma gruffed

from the sink where she was peeling apples. "Sure are a bunch of bruises on these apples."

"That's my fault," Elizabeth admitted. "Let me help you with that." She didn't want to think about the night before. She'd hated hurting McKaid, and she'd been terrified that she'd do him more harm, but she hadn't been willing to trust him to the hands of this Mac or the others who didn't know what they were doing. She prayed she'd done the right thing.

"Goodness no, child. You'll want to look around a bit, no doubt. James, why don't you and Ruthie show Miss Elizabeth the ranch."

"I'd love that, but let me go up and look in on Mr. McKaid first."

Elizabeth slipped into McKaid's room and set a bowl of broth on the table by his bed. She moved closer and laid her cool hand on his forehead. He was still a little warm, but not bad.

He moved once then settled into sleep again. He looked peaceful, he even smiled a little, and she thought again how wonderfully handsome he was. But not as handsome as when his piercing eyes bore into hers and stole her breath away, or when they turned to the color of the warm, clear sky when he was mocking her, laughing at her, challenging her.

She knew she was dangerously close to caring for this big man in a way that her rational mind told her would be unwise, unacceptable, and could only lead to frustration and heartache. Yet, for once in her life, her emotions seemed to be laughing at her, daring common sense to intercede. No matter how she tried to ignore it or put a reasonable name to it, something warm was blossoming inside her that defied repression. No matter how they fought, or insulted each other, or just teased in fun, the anger, resentment, and the humor added fuel to some mysterious, fascinating, and very elemental attraction between them.

Elizabeth, who had never experienced anything of the sort before, found she was inexplicably protective of the feelings burgeoning with a life of their own within her breast, and of the man who caused them. The arrogant scoundrel was right. He was thoroughly irresistible.

She reached out and brushed his dark hair back from his forehead, letting the natural wave caress her fingers. Suddenly he stiffened, and his face contorted into an agonized grimace.

His hand reached out and locked around her wrist in a painful grasp.

"Rosanna," he cried out, his voice strangled and hoarse, his grip fiercely tight. Elizabeth gasped, both from his hold on her and from the surprising pain of some emotion very akin to jealousy.

His eyes flew open, and he tried to sit up, but the searing agony in his head and his side sent him limply back to his pillow and forced his eyes shut against the painful light.

"McKaid," Elizabeth cried. "My arm."

McKaid was battling his way to consciousness. Someone was calling to him, and he wanted to go to that voice. There was peace there, away from his chaotic emotions that were a mixture of pain and remorse, hatred and self-loathing. But those turbulent and unbearable emotions were his private purgatory, his tribulation for what he had let happen to Rosanna, and in a way he welcomed them. He deserved them. She had nothing to do with any of it. All she'd done was love him as he had loved her.

His hand went limp and fell to the bed. Ramirez. Ramirez. The name tumbled over and over in his mind. Ramirez. The man was a devil, cunning, swift, brutal. And elusive. Four years McKaid had searched for him. Four years. Still he had not avenged Rosanna's suffering and death. For four years he had carried the guilt of that within his conscience. For four years he had suffered the nightmares of that day, a day he swore never to forget, as if he had that choice.

Rosanna had been afraid for him, but she had understood his dedication to his work. Since they would be living with her father in San Antonio, and she would have support and comfort while he was away, she had agreed to marry him. It was all so perfect. He'd been happy for the first time since his parents had died.

That was before he had interrupted a particularly nasty robbery in town and had shot two men, both relatives of the gang's leader, Ramirez. It was because of that that McKaid had set out to destroy him. But fool that he was, McKaid wasn't worried. He knew he was good, and Ramirez soon learned the same. Only McKaid had made one mistake. He underestimated Ramirez's hatred, and the lengths to which he would go to get his revenge. Never had it crossed his mind that he would use Rosanna.

"McKaid," Elizabeth said again, taking his tightly clenched fist into her hands.

His eyes fluttered open, and he winced at the stabbing pain the light caused him. Elizabeth left his bedside and drew the drapes across the windows, easing the room into shadows.

"Is that better?" she asked, once more at his side.

"Don't yell," he murmured, relaxing now that his nightmare had finally and mercifully passed. His heartrate settled back to normal and he began to feel peaceful again under the watchful scrutiny of his feisty Lizzie.

"Oh, McKaid, I'm barely talking," she cajoled. "Can you eat a little? Emma sent up a bowl of chicken broth."

"Don't know."

"Can you try? You need to eat something to keep up your strength."

"What I need right now isn't soup. Where's Clint?"

"Downstairs."

"Get him."

"What is it? Can I help?"

"No," he barked, then groaned as pain splintered through his head. His hand went up to cover his eyes. "Just get him, Lizzie."

She finally realized what it was he needed. "Okay, McKaid, but if you think I would be embarrassed, you're wrong. I worked in a hospital, remember? There weren't always men around to assist when someone . . ."

"Lizzie," he groaned impatiently.

"I'm going."

She entered the kitchen, and when Clint looked up at her, she told him that McKaid needed his assistance. Clint chuckled and went to McKaid. "Tell the beast I'll be up in a minute to change his bandages, and he better get that soup in him."

Emma had taken a seat at the table with her pans of apples around her as she worked. She lifted her eyes briefly, and a mischievous grin tilted the corners of her lips. "Beast?"

"The devil's sidekick, at least," Elizabeth said unrepentantly. "Who's Rosanna?" The question popped out before she could stop it.

"Rosanna," Emma answered carefully, "is very much the past. Having another nightmare, was he?"

"Yes, I guess. Where is she now?"

100

"She died."

"Oh." She was sorry, of course, but at the same time she felt relief that the mysterious Rosanna was gone. What an unkind monster she was becoming. "That's too bad," she said, hoping she sounded more sincere than she felt.

"As I said, it's the past," Emma responded, continuing with her apples.

"How long have you been here, Emma?"

"Ten years now."

"Then you knew McKaid's grandfather?"

"To be sure. Now there was a fine figure of a man. My husband, rest his soul, worked for him, and when my Tom was killed, I stayed on. There were very few women out here in those days, just the Spanish ladies in town, a few wives of merchants and military men, and most of them left when the army took over the territory and got the Indians and Mexicans riled up. Old Man McKaid was my protector, and whether he took care of me out of duty or friendship, I was very grateful. He died trying to bring peace back to the area. He never succeeded. By then no one would listen to anything but the sound of a gun.

"I had a few uncomfortable moments, myself, before Clint arrived. A woman alone, you know. I was better-looking in those days. Now I don't fuss much with my looks."

Elizabeth tried to picture Emma ten years younger. She was a pleasant-looking woman still with her gray-blond hair, her slightly plump figure, her soft hazel eyes. She could imagine Emma was once very attractive indeed. Time, the sun, the wind, all had taken their toll, as they did on everyone.

"Oh, I forgot. I brought you a present. I wonder where it is," she said, glancing around the large kitchen for her parcels.

"There's a pile of packages in the library that we didn't open. Are they yours?"

"McKaid made me buy more suitable clothing. He didn't like my city shoes. After meeting up with one of his reptilian friends face to face, I begin to see the wisdom."

Emma clucked her tongue, remembering Elizabeth's story. "Must have scared you to death."

"I know one thing for certain. McKaid is going to teach me how to shoot a gun." With that declaration, she went to the library and returned to place Emma's gift in her lap. "Mrs. Stanhope helped me select it, since she knew you, and I didn't. I hope you like it."

101

"Goodness, child, you didn't have to buy me anything," she said, wiping her hands on a dishtowel. She pulled the string loose and unwrapped the present, her eyes glowing and filling with tears when she saw the fabric.

"I got some lace, too, and the prettiest buttons to match. Do you like it?"

Emma cleared her throat. "Thank, you, Miss Elizabeth. Are you sure you don't want it for yourself? It'd be so pretty on you."

"Heavens, no. I have more dresses than I need now. Mrs. Stanhope said you'd had your eye on it."

"But it was so impractical."

"That's what makes it fun. I'll help you sew it up."

Clint returned, eyeing Emma's lavender gift. "That will look lovely on you, Emma. She wouldn't let me buy it for her," he told Elizabeth.

"Actually," Elizabeth said, grinning crookedly, "you did. Until you permit me to reimburse you, that is. Which I'm sure you will in the name of fairness, won't you?"

"Shoot. What can I say to that, my dear." He laughed softly. "McKaid said you were a determined woman. I can see by your stubborn chin that you are."

"And I'm equally certain McKaid didn't use such fine words in saying it," Elizabeth responded, her soft lips curling into a wry twist.

Clint grinned at Emma who choked on a laugh. "Well, not exactly," he admitted. "He said you were the prickliest, sassiest, most mule-headed female he'd ever run into."

"That's McKaid," she said, rising from the table. "I think I'll change his bandages now. A little pain might make him realize he hasn't reached sainthood quite yet."

McKaid was propped up in bed when she returned to his darkened room. He held out the empty bowl to her. "All gone, Miss Elizabeth," he said. "Just as you ordered."

"Lucky for you it is," she retorted, snatching the bowl from his hand and setting it on the table.

"You're enjoying this, aren't you?"

"I'm sure I don't know what you mean."

"Come on. I'm flat on my back, helpless, harmless, at your tender mercy. You love it."

"Hmmm. I admit the idea has certain appeal, but strangely enough, I prefer you out of bed."

"You don't know that yet, Lizzie. I'm at my best in bed."

She felt a queer heat invade her body at his outrageously suggestive remark. He had no way of knowing the wayward thoughts that had sprung to life in her mind, this impossible man who was her cousin yet not her cousin. And he must never know. Yet he seemed able to hit her at her weakest point every time he started with her. How long could she keep her secret?

"I'm sure you would think so," she retorted sardonically.

"Do you want references?"

Lord, she couldn't believe the gall of him. "It would undoubtedly take me weeks to wade through all the references you could supply, but I'll have to forego such enlightenment. I don't have the time to waste."

"Are you afraid to find out what you've been missing all these years? Are you afraid you might find you like being a woman after all?"

Her eyes snapped to his, and she felt his taunt go through her like a lance. How could he know of the dreams that had been snatched from her because she was a woman. How could he know how many times she mightily regretted that she hadn't been born male.

"Hit a nerve, did I?" he persisted, embarrassing her all the more.

She straightened and went to his bureau to retrieve fresh bandages and the pungent ointment. "I need to check your wound," she said, her voice surprisingly steady for the turmoil she felt inside. Was she so transparent to everyone, or just to McKaid? She returned and let her weight fall heavily as she sat down on the edge of the bed.

She heard his sharp intake of breath and knew she'd hurt him. Well, he'd hurt her, too. Still she managed to feel like an ugly, spiteful child. Her eyes began to burn, and her throat tightened. She shouldn't take it out on McKaid just because he could perceive the unpalatable truth about her.

With utmost care and gentleness she cut away his bindings and removed his bandage. The wound looked a hundred times better. The purple bruise was still there, but the swelling had gone down, and no sign of infection was evident. Satisfied, she nodded, daubed more ointment over the stitched area, and applied a fresh covering. She wanted to apologize, but she couldn't manage to get any words out of her constricted throat. Before she could rewrap his broken rib, a single tear slipped from behind her glasses and fell onto his bare skin.

McKaid had watched her intently. She bit her lower lip as she silently worked, which wasn't uncommon when someone was concentrating on a task, but his sharp gaze also caught the telltale quiver in her chin that she fought to control by biting harder. He'd hurt her with that careless and totally uncalled-for remark, and he felt like a heel. And then he felt that hot tear drop on his abdomen and slide down his side.

He raised his hand to encircle her neck, tilting her head upward with his thumb. With his other hand he removed her glasses and dropped them on the bed by his side. He looked into her misty topaz eyes, and neither moved nor spoke for a long moment. Slowly he pulled her toward him until she was braced over his upper torso.

His eyes burned, fever-bright, into her very soul. Something deep, unspoken, forbidden passed between them, something neither could prevent. She knew it for what it was, though no one had ever looked at her like that before. He wanted her, and, God help her, she wanted him just as much.

Her hand had gone to his naked chest to support her weight, to keep from hurting him, and the feel of his overly warm skin and the crisp dark hair under her fingers sent a great wave of longing through her body. She went hot, then cold, then hot again. Her arms trembled and her breath moved in and out in shallow spasmodic puffs.

"Did I dream it, Lizzie?" One by one he took the pins from her hair and let it fall over her shoulders, and she couldn't stop him. She couldn't pull herself away from the searing touch of his fingers on her face, against her sensitive neck, from her hair. She was being drawn toward him, toward some unknown destination, as inevitably as if she'd stepped into a raging river current.

His eyes roamed over her face, his nostrils flared as he breathed in the subtle wildflower scent of her hair. He shouldn't be doing this, he should put her away from him, but he knew he wasn't going to. She was too sweet, his prickly cactus, blossoming under his very touch. And her own touch on his bare skin was driving him onward, surging through his heated body, sending him into instantaneous and potent arousal. No, he wouldn't stop. Not yet. Maybe in a minute or two. For now he just wanted to savor touching her. He wanted to drown in the rivers of pleasure that were coursing through

104

his body.

His eyes met hers, and he could read the confusion and the surprise in them. Did this strange and compelling desire to explore deeper what he was experiencing also stir within her soul? Did she lie awake at night, remembering that one kiss they'd shared and wondering if it would be like that again? He saw her gaze drop to his mouth. He saw the tip of her enticing pink tongue dart out and moisten the center of her lower lip.

"Oh, God," he whispered and drew her closer. He could feel her arms trembling under her weight, and could envision her whole body trembling beneath him as he made ecstatic and glorious love to her.

He closed his eyes and brushed his lips briefly against hers. She jerked and drew in a sharp breath, her arms stiffening against him. He tightened his hold on her head, letting his fingers and his thumbs caress and tantalize her jaw and the back of her neck. He drew her closer again, and this time she came willingly.

"I know, I know," he said against her lips. His tongue dared to trace the line of her lower lip. "I feel it, too."

"We can't, McKaid."

"I know that, too." He kissed her then, not roughly as he'd done before, but with all the gentle feelings born in him when that single tear had burned into his skin. It was an apology, of sorts, for all the rough times he'd put her through because she'd been willing to leave her life and come out to help him.

At least that's how it started, but something changed in both of them. Their kiss smouldered and flared out of control. His hands pressed into her jaw, his fingers curled into her hair, begging, seeking for more, and as they'd done once before, his thumbs coaxed her jaw downward so he could experience fully the sweet wonder of her mouth.

Elizabeth was spellbound. Her heart was racing out of control. Her body was infused with a wild, wanton heat that clawed at her insides. She couldn't think how she'd let the situation get so out of hand. One minute he was piercing her heart with his careless jibes, the next he was kissing her as if she were the most precious person in the world to him.

She had been surprised when he'd reached out to touch her, but the sensations of his rough fingers against her tingling skin were more than she could refuse. She had told herself she didn't like him, didn't want him to touch her, but none of that

105

was so. She knew the truth of it the instant his fingers brushed against her face. And when his lips touched hers, she lost coherent thought altogether.

McKaid clung to her, buried in the fall of her sweet-scented hair, drifting in a euphoric realm of pleasure as she allowed their kiss to deepen. When his tongue touched hers, she shuddered, and her strength left her limbs. She fell hard across his body.

She knew the second it happened that she'd hurt him. Quickly she got to her feet, staring in mortification at McKaid's pinched and drawn face.

"I'm so sorry. Are you all right, McKaid?"

"It was—worth it," he ground out, going a bit pale around his tightened lips.

"No, it wasn't. It was foolish, and it shouldn't have happened in the first place. Why, anyone, Emma, Clint, the children, could have walked in here and . . . Oh, it doesn't bear thinking about. And my hair!" Where were her pins? She gathered them off the bed and from the floor, grabbed up her glasses, and swung around to leave.

"Lizzie," McKaid called softly.

She turned to face him, her chin raised, her eyes bright. "We have to live in the same house, McKaid. This can't happen again. I won't be able to stay here if I have to keep watching you every minute, wondering when you're going to grab me and . . ." *And knowing I won't be able to resist.* Her hand fluttered to her forehead. "Can't you see that?"

"It won't happen again," he said wearily.

Wordlessly she nodded. She hurried to the sanctuary of her rose room where she could repair the damages to her face and hair. The damage to her shaken emotions would take longer to repair. Much longer.

He made her feel totally out of control, a complete stranger to herself, and she wasn't at all comfortable with that. With all her uncertainties and fears of what he could do to her, how he could destroy her, she wasn't sure she ever wanted to lay eyes on him again. She realized she'd have to, though. She'd forgotten to wrap his broken rib.

For the next three days McKaid was on his best behavior. He couldn't help teasing Lizzie occasionally, especially since she was being so starchy toward him, but he didn't touch her.

She didn't come into his room very often, and when she did,

she usually contrived to bring one or both of the children with her, letting them show off their schoolwork for the day. The children boasted to him about what they'd taught her of the ranch, and exhibited what she'd taught them of the world.

"We made maps. See? This is where Elizabeth used to live," Ruthie exclaimed. "She said there are big cities there with thousands and thousands of people. Could we go there someday, Mr. McKaid?"

Before McKaid could answer, James piped up. "She took the train all the way to Abilene, Kansas. That's here. Then she rode in the stage down the Santa Fe Trail. Where did you rescue her from the bandits?"

"Well, let me see?" McKaid said, his warm glance resting on Elizabeth who was smiling fondly at the three of them. "Here, I'd say."

"I'm gonna mark that on my map," James declared.

"Definitely an historic site, James," McKaid answered, tongue in cheek.

It was the same each day. The children were eager to visit him, and their chatter was non-stop and heart-warming. They were getting back to normal again. It was clear they adored Elizabeth, and were enthusiastic about their lessons. She was exactly what they needed, and he became determined not to make her uncomfortable or, God forbid, drive her away.

She never let the children stay while she checked his wound, and it was during these times alone that she was her most reserved. He could understand it, and found he was just as reserved. He still wanted her, but what she had said had brought him to his senses. He'd been playing light with her feelings, having fun at her expense, not really considering what she might be experiencing. And obviously for the first time.

Even if she hadn't been related to him, she was a properly raised young woman who prided herself on her high standards. He had no right to demean her for that or toy with her unawakened passions. That was for some other man much luckier than himself. All he could hope to offer her was his protection, the security of his home, and his affection as her cousin.

If only he hadn't kissed her before he'd known who she was. He wouldn't now be struggling with memories of her responsive kisses, he wouldn't have this burning desire for

107

more of the same to disturb his peace of mind. What a perverse twist of fate. But what had happened happened. He'd have to live with it. She was his cousin, and neither of them could condone anything other than a purely familial relationship. He'd have to force the memory of her lips from his mind and try to find some way to ease the tension between them.

"You're a good nurse, and a good teacher. I haven't seen those kids so animated since they came here. Not since their parents died."

"They're very apt pupils. They keep me on my toes," she answered. "And as for you, it's time for some fresh air and sunshine. You've lain in bed long enough."

"I've been up and around," he protested.

"So I've heard," she scolded. "But now you don't have to sneak around behind my back. You're released from bed rest. That doesn't mean you can get on a horse yet, or fix the barn roof, mind you."

"Yes, Miss Elizabeth," he said far too docilely.

"I mean it, McKaid. If you tear out those stitches, I'll put them back with fencing wire."

He looked properly horrified. "I'll see I don't, in that case."

Her mouth tightened in exasperation. "Oh, aren't you ever serious?"

"When I have to be," he answered seriously.

Her eyes roamed his shoulders and chest. He was so perfect. Her gaze rose to his lips, then his eyes. He grinned and winked at her. She jumped and backed toward the door. "Yes, well, I have some work to do, so—eh—I'll leave you to finish your book."

He watched her until she closed the door behind her, then he picked up the book he'd set aside. It wasn't the story he was interested in though, but the latest letter he'd received from the sheriff in Santa Fe. He slid it from between the pages and reread it.

The sheriff had been notified about the ambush and had sent his men to track Corbett, but so far, they hadn't been successful. McKaid knew they probably wouldn't be. If Corbettt had any smarts at all, he'd be riding with Ramirez now. Corbett was another problem he'd have to face sooner or later. Corbett, young, headstrong, and hating, would seek revenge for his brothers. He was rash and careless, and McKaid knew he would probably end up dead. The older Corbetts had set an example for him that Wes Corbett would try with his life to emulate. It was a great pity the older men hadn't considered what might befall their younger sibling.

The sheriff also said that Ramirez had been boasting that he was going to kill Ranger McKaid. That was undoubtedly true. And Ramirez would come to the ranch to attempt it if he thought it necessary. McKaid had to prevent that from happening. When Ramirez was out for blood, he was ruthless and relentless in his pursuit. McKaid would welcome a confrontation with Ramirez, for he, too, had reason to seek revenge, but not at the expense of any of the workers or his family at the Circle K.

McKaid had already alerted Clint to the possibility of trouble, and Clint had ordered a rotation of guards to keep an eye open for anything unusual, but McKaid knew that the dozen or so men left on the ranch since round-up weren't going to be enough against Ramirez and his gunslingers. Inwardly he thanked the sheriff for his foresight in wiring the Rangers in Fort Worth and requesting help to stop Ramirez. Texas also wanted Ramirez, and the Rangers would be quick to respond. And he knew without a doubt which Rangers would come. He only hoped his friends would arrive in time.

Chapter Seven

The next morning McKaid and Clint walked together around the ranch. McKaid was still weak, but mostly plagued by headaches and discomfort from the injured rib. Elizabeth had wanted to go with them just to make sure that he didn't overextend himself, but the men very politely but firmly vetoed that idea. When they returned, they were both so solemn that she became concerned.

"I'm a little tired, that's all," McKaid evaded when she expressed her concern.

She had to accept that as far as McKaid was concerned, but it didn't account for Clint's preoccupation for the rest of the afternoon. Restlessly he stalked around the house, then went out for a long discussion with the workers that left him even more agitated. Something was afoot, she could feel it in the strained atmosphere. The entire ranch felt different.

She fully intended to question one or both of them before supper, but she never had the opportunity. An unexpected visitor arrived late in the afternoon.

The woman who stepped down from the sleek, black and gold carriage was beautiful, with a creamy complexion, raven black hair and eyes, and a lovely and lush figure that would make any woman envious. Elizabeth stared at her mutely, as she climbed the porch steps and met Clint's welcoming hands. She had no idea who she might be, but a heavy weight settled on her heart at the sight of her, and a sick foreboding twisted in her midriff.

If Clint knew this woman, it stood to reason that McKaid did, too. How could he be any less impressed with her beauty than she, herself, was. And knowing McKaid as she did, how could she expect that McKaid had not charmed Lenore as well. Was that why she was here, to see her lover? How many more were there going to be?

"Clint, how good to see you. I hope I'm not arriving at a bad time, but I only this morning learned of McKaid's misfortune. You should have sent for me. I'd have been happy to come and help."

Even her voice was beautiful, Elizabeth thought grudgingly, then reprimanded herself soundly for her jealous thoughts. And they were jealous. She didn't want this woman here, upsetting the way things were, interfering with McKaid. Even as she thought it, she realized the absurdity of her possessiveness. If anyone was intruding on the status quo, it was she. Nevertheless, the feelings persisted, and she fought hard to be pleasant when Clint introduced her to Lenore Beaumont, the widowed daughter-in-law of Pierre Beaumont, their neighbor five miles to the south.

"So you see, there was no need to disrupt your life," Clint explained, relating the circumstances of McKaid's injuries. "Elizabeth handled everything nicely."

"I'm happy to meet you," Lenore said, "and relieved that you were skilled enough to help McKaid. We'd be lost without him, wouldn't we," she said sweetly, sharing a special smile with Clint. "He's an exceptional man. And quite handsome, don't you think?" she said to Elizabeth.

Elizabeth's heart turned over in her breast and seemed to plummet into the pit of her stomach. Never had she felt such a hopeless dread of losing a man's attentions. With Paul there had been no need. With all the rest she hadn't cared enough for such feelings to be formed. Could two kisses from a man who'd treated her so insolently reduce her to such a deplorable state? She was terribly afraid the answer was yes.

"Handsome is as handsome does," she answered noncommittally.

"You've come to teach the children, I understand," she continued before giving Elizabeth a chance to reply further. "McKaid told me he was sending for someone to help him with those two rascals. Have you been a teacher long?"

"Eh—no. Actually, I've never taught," Elizabeth answered, feeling her long-battled sense of inadequacy reasserting itself.

"But you've some experience with children?" Lenore persisted.

112

"No."

"Oh. I see. Well, I'm sure you'll do fine."

Elizabeth seemed to have lost all her sixth sense. Usually she could discern a person's true feelings beneath their spoken words. With Lenore, however, she couldn't. She wasn't certain whether Lenore was trying to be friendly and make conversation, or attempting to make her feel inferior, as she was succeeding in doing.

"I'm sure I will," she answered pleasantly enough, even managing a small smile. Her father had always advocated extending the benefit of doubt. She'd give Lenore that benefit and see how their relationship developed from there.

"Mrs. Beaumont," Emma said, coming from the kitchen, wiping her hands on her apron. "Lenore, what a nice surprise. You'll stay for supper, won't you?"

"Thank you. I'd love one of your wonderful meals. Why, there you are, you two ragamuffins."

James and Ruthie ran to her and received a warm hug apiece. "Hi, Mrs. Beaumont," James said. "How is your new foal?"

"You wouldn't recognize her. She's as tall as I am. And how's my Ruthie?"

"Just fine, ma'am. You haven't been here in such a long time. We missed you."

"You two haven't been running away anymore, have you?" she rebuked teasingly.

"Just once," James admitted. "But we promised Mr. McKaid we wouldn't do it again, and now that Miss Elizabeth has come . . ."

"She keeps you busy, does she?" Lenore asked, throwing Elizabeth a knowing grin.

"And out of trouble," Clint added. "She's a real treasure, our Elizabeth. The ranch hands are completely taken with her. Quite a feat for the short time she's been here. You should see them stumbling over each other to answer all her questions or to be the one lucky enough to act as escort on her brief outings with the children." He chuckled and shook his head.

Lenore's eyes flew to Elizabeth's then. "Oh?" was all she uttered, but her black eyes were no longer unreadable. Lenore hadn't liked what she'd heard.

Elizabeth felt in a small way as if she'd won a victory. She was grateful to her uncle for the praise, such as it was. Her eyes were warm as they met his. He winked at her. He must have sensed how uncomfortable Lenore's confident manner and her pointed questions had made her feel.

"Thank you, Uncle Clint," she said softly, "but you really are exaggerating. Besides, Russ keeps the men well in hand. It's not as if the ranch were falling into chaos because of me."

"Perhaps not, but it is a fact. They hold you in greatest respect, if for no other reason, because you saved McKaid's tough hide."

Elizabeth glanced at the beautiful Lenore and was surprised to see her momentarily disconcerted. A frown creased her elegant Spanish forehead, drawing the finely shaped black arches of her brows together. And her rouged lips were tightened at the corners, drawn almost into a pout.

"Mrs. Beaumont," Emma startled her by saying, "you weren't planning to return home tonight surely?"

"Oh, I had planned to say and help out until McKaid was back on his feet, but I didn't know Miss Hepplewhite was here. I think it best if I go home."

"Oh, no," Ruthie wailed. "Please stay, Mrs. Beaumont. Tell us another bedtime story."

Lenore looked fondly at the big eyes of the little girl and ran her hand down the smooth fall of platinum hair. Elizabeth felt as if a rusty knife was twisting in her heart. Lenore was beautiful, sensitive, warm, and she was obviously quite fond of the children. And of McKaid. Why hadn't McKaid asked Lenore to teach the children? Or why hadn't he simply married her and given the children a proper home with a mother to care for them? McKaid couldn't be immune to such loveliness as Lenore's. Surely he could have come to that decision on his own? Why then had he sent for her, brought her all this way to this strange and alien land, when a more suitable answer lay right next door?

"I don't see how I can, Ruthie, dear," Lenore said gently. "You have a full house now."

"Never mind that," Emma said. "We'll figure out sleeping arrangements later."

"If you're sure you don't mind."

"Emma's right. You must stay," Clint decided.

"May I see McKaid?" Lenore asked, glancing at the stairs. "Is he in bed?"

"He's sleeping," Elizabeth said. The brusque snap of her voice shocked even her. She bit her lip and looked away.

114

"He won't mind if Lenore wakes him," Emma said, her startled eyes looking at Elizabeth questioningly.

"No, of course not," Elizabeth agreed quickly. "He was so tired earlier that I overreacted. I'm sure he'd welcome you." And now she was sounding proprietary. Oh, why had her much-prided self-control taken this moment of all times to desert her?

"I'll go up then," Lenore said, excusing herself.

"Actually, I'm a bit tired myself. I think I'll go to my room and lie down before supper." Glad to get away after making a fool of herself, she followed Lenore up the stairs.

Clint exchanged a long and puzzled look with Emma.

"She's only thinking of McKaid's health," Emma offered by way of explaining Elizabeth's strange behavior.

"I wonder. You don't suppose she's getting sweet on McKaid? Now wouldn't that be a match?"

Emma's brows rose a notch. "Indeed it would, but they're cousins."

"Technically," Clint said. "Elizabeth was adopted."

"Well, now." Her tanned and creased face broke into a broad grin.

"What's adopted mean?" Ruthie asked, tugging on Emma's apron.

Emma and Clint both turned to look at the two children whose quiet presence they had forgotten. Clint cleared his throat, but it was Emma who spoke.

"It's nothing. You two run along and play now. Go on."

"Shouldn't you have explained?" Clint asked as the children scampered out the door.

"That's for Elizabeth to do if she sees fit. I'm not sure she'd appreciate the two of us telling tales behind her back."

"Maybe we should tell them not to say anything about what they heard."

"Then they would for sure. Best left alone, I'd say."

Elizabeth lay on her bed, staring at the ceiling, her stomach churning with emotions she'd never dealt with before, emotions that ran rampant and uncontrolled. Uncontrollable. She was jealous, pure and simple. It made her sick to think of how she'd reacted just now, what unkind and ungenerous thoughts she'd entertained. Lenore was obviously a respected and very welcome guest in her uncle's home. And just as obviously, she and McKaid were good friends. Maybe more

115

than good friends.

She could hear the quiet timbre of their voices through her closed door, McKaid's deep and resonant, Lenore's low and throaty. They laughed occasionally, and then they would begin their private conversing all over again. She couldn't help but wonder what they were discussing, or what they were doing when their voices stopped.

Finally she could stand it no more. No way in the world was she going to be able to sleep. She got up and went down to the kitchen, determined to put McKaid and his lady friend out of her thoughts.

She kept herself busy over the next couple hours. She set out the good china and flatware on the snowy cloth covering the dining room table, a table at which she'd yet to dine. She filled the lamps and cleaned the delicate chimneys. She got the children fed early, bathed, and tucked into their room for the night after reading their favorite story. Finally she decided to have her own bath and change into a more suitable dress for entertaining company.

She banished thoughts of McKaid from her mind and promised herself that she'd be in the most gracious of moods during the meal ahead. She'd made enough of a clown of herself already because of her silly schoolgirl crush on the man, and vowed that in the future she'd return to her normally placid, sensible self. Anyway what did she want with a man who had a woman in every town.

She'd selected one of her favorite dresses to wear, a pale yellow gown, trimmed in a rich dark honey brown, the same color as her eyes. The patterned trim down the side panels, the glossy ribbon at her waist, and the wide, flat bow at the back of her hips all accentuated her slender figure and made the best of the gently rounded curves of her body. She took extra care with her hair, brushing it until it was shiny and smooth before pulling it up at the sides of her face and securing it with her mother's combs into soft, loose waves. The rest was braided and wound into a chignon high on the back of her head, a style not nearly so severe or plain.

Her only adornment was a little gold locket that found its resting place just where the hint of her rounded bosom showed above the demure neckline of her gown. She fingered the small heart, a gentle wistful smile curving her lips. Her parents had given it to her on her fifteenth birthday.

116

Her thoughts drifted to her father, and she wondered how he and Caroline were doing. Did they miss her as much as she missed them? He would have received her telegram, notifying him of her safe arrival in Santa Fe, so at least he wouldn't be worrying about her. She pictured the little brick house with the unruly ivy clinging to its sides. Her home. Yet it no longer felt like her home. It was her father's and Caroline's. She couldn't go back there, now that he'd finally found someone to build a new life with. The Circle K was her home. In time it would be better, in time she would feel less like a visitor.

She wiped her glasses until they sparkled, took one last appraising look at her appearance, and went downstairs. Clint, McKaid, and Lenore were already in the parlor when she entered, and they paused in their lively conversation long enough to greet her.

Her uncle took her hands in his and planted a kiss on her forehead. "You look lovely, my dear," he said.

"Thank you, Uncle Clint," she answered softly, glancing at McKaid to see if he thought the same.

McKaid was also standing, only he had his hand on the back of Lenore's chair. They looked the picture of a perfect couple. Her stomach felt as if she'd swallowed a chunk of lead. She was determined, though, to get through this evening, and to do so with her usual social grace. And if she forced herself to consider Leonore and McKaid as a couple, she would come to accept the fact that much sooner. Not unlike having the mumps or the measles, she thought. Once the initial discomfort passed, it never returned. The body became immune to further attacks. So it would be with her silly, adolescent heart.

"Good evening, Mrs. Beaumont, Mr. McKaid."

McKaid raised a mocking brow at her formality then nodded. "Miss Hepplewhite," he answered similarly. His lips twisted crookedly as he took in her appearance from head to foot. His gaze came to rest on the locket. She held her fingers firmly interlocked at her waist to prevent them from covering the creamy skin exposed to his lecherous view.

"What a lovely dress," she complimented Lenore, ignoring those taunting eyes that rested on her heart. Could he see it pounding?

"My father-in-law chose it for me in Albuquerque last month. He goes there to see a German doctor for his eyes."

117

"Lenore's father-in-law is nearly blind," Clint explained.

"I'm sorry to hear that," Elizabeth offered.

"It's been happening over many years now, so he's grown used to the idea. Still he hopes."

"Yes." She could feel McKaid staring at her, so she turned her attention to him. "You look better, McKaid. Your rest seems to have restored your energy. Or perhaps it was the company."

"Both, I'd say," he answered, actually daring to grin at her.

This whole night was going to be next to impossible, she could see that. He couldn't know how difficult this was for her, yet he seemed to have guessed. And to make matters worse, he was intent on goading her. Well, he was in for a surprise if he thought he'd make her lose her temper again, humiliate herself, embarrass Clint or Emma. He'd see the devil first.

She shrugged carelessly. "It took a woman to lay you low, it only stands to reason that it would take another to get you on your feet again. You should have come days ago, Mrs. Beaumont. He'd be riding the range now." She saw the light of battle in his eyes and decided to rob him of his chance to retaliate. "If you'll excuse me," she said, her words encompassing the three of them. "I'll see if Emma needs any help. I'm starving."

Ignoring Clint's chortles, Lenore's sultry laughter, and McKaid's silence, she swept from the parlor and went down the hallway to the kitchen.

Emma was busy mashing potatoes, all the time watching the gravy that bubbled on the stove. She seemed nervous, which was unlike Emma. Elizabeth wondered why.

"Here, let me do that. I'm good with potatoes," she said, taking the masher from Emma.

"Oh dear. I'm so behind. But you should be in there with the young folks."

"Nonsense. There'll be plenty of time to socialize over dinner. What's left to do?"

"Just that and the gravy. Oh, and these darned peas won't get cooked."

Elizabeth tried them. "They're perfect as they are. Relax, Emma. You look done in."

"Lenore is used to good meals. They have cooks, and servants, and . . . What if she doesn't like roast beef? I had such short notice."

118

"She'll love it. The gravy's done. I'll take care of the rest. You go splash your face and comb your hair. And put on your new dress."

"I'm not eating with you," she announced.

"Okay. Then I'll eat in here with you. McKaid's being his usual irritating self anyway. It would suit me fine to stay in the kitchen."

"Oh, no. You mustn't."

"Whyever not?"

"Because you—you can't, that's all."

"You are not a servant, Emma. We will both eat with them, or neither of us will. Take your pick."

Grumbling, Emma ripped off her apron and tossed it on the table. "Don't know why you call *him* irritating. You can be just as stubborn."

Elizabeth grinned. Dear Emma didn't know the half of it. By the time Emma returned, refreshed and dressed in her lilac gingham dress, Elizabeth had their meal ready to serve. Together they carried the bowls and plates into the dining room and summoned the others to dinner.

The meal was excellent, and Elizabeth managed to eat her share, though she couldn't remember a meal that threatened to choke her more. McKaid's eyes rarely left her, except to glance briefly at Clint or Emma or to smile down into his companion's lovely face. He watched every move Elizabeth made, calculated every response, sized her up this way and that. Her nerves were strung taut by the time coffee was served. The muscles in her cheeks were screaming from all the smiling she'd done. If her father had thought her a good woman for not flying into Arnold with both fists for his patronizing remarks, he'd think her a saint after this meal. She didn't know how many more barbs she could brush aside or how many more quick retorts she could deliver. The top of her head was about to erupt with suppressed anger.

"You don't have to wash dishes," Emma said when Elizabeth cleared the table and poured hot water into the basin. "You've done enough to help today."

"Emma, you're asleep on your feet. You've canned apples, baked bread, cooked meals all day."

"And you cleaned the house, plus lookin' after those kids. And how you've held your tongue all evening, I'll never know. If that McKaid weren't so tall, I'd box his ears good."

"Catch him while he's sitting down."

Emma managed a snorting laugh. "I've heard you talk back to him. Why didn't you do so tonight? Because of Lenore?"

"No. Because of McKaid. He wanted me to lose my composure in front of his guest. Didn't you see how annoyed he became when I didn't? It's a game with him."

"So you changed the rules?"

"I changed the game."

"Maybe he wanted to see if you were jealous," Emma suggested, slanting Elizabeth a sly look.

"I'm sure he likes having women falling at his feet. He's arrogant that way. He thinks they all love him."

"But not you?"

She turned on her sugary smile again. "I wouldn't presume to think of myself as one of his women when he has the likes of Lenore at his elbow. What a lovely couple they make. Don't you agree?"

"Oh, pooh. Don't try that with me."

"Emma," Elizabeth said, voicing a question that had crossed her mind several times since her arrival. "Did you and Clint ever consider getting married? I mean, you get along so well."

"Yes, dear, there was a time when the subject came up, but only because he was concerned about proprieties, me living under his roof and all. We always liked each other, and my husband was a friend of his, but there was never anything more than that. He needed a housekeeper and a cook for his two sons, and I needed a place to call home. Our arrangement suited us, and out here that's all that matters. Life boils down to the basics when you only have the basics to live with."

That was true, Elizabeth thought. Civilization and its inherent mores and rules hadn't reached this far yet. People lived as best they could with what they had. "Whatever the reasons, I'm glad you're here. Now off to bed with you. I'll get the dishes."

"I think I will then. Tomorrow's laundry day. Goodnight, child."

Elizabeth was starting on the pots and pans when McKaid came into the kitchen, frowning at her as usual.

"So here's where you're hiding?"

"I'm not hiding, McKaid. I'm cleaning the kitchen."

"Where's Emma?"

"You can't expect her to do everything. I sent her to bed."

She grabbed the roasting pan and dunked it into the hot soapy water.

"That's what I want to talk to you about. Lenore would like to retire now, but there doesn't seem to be a bed for her now that you're in her room."

Elizabeth's hands stilled. "Her room?"

"What I mean is that she always sleeps in the rose room. She even decorated it with extra furniture and curtains she had at her house. We did invite her to stay, Lizzie."

Who did? Well, what was a bed here or there. She wasn't going to give him the satisfaction of seeing her lose her temper over where she laid her head.

"I see. I didn't know, of course." She snatched up a towel and dried her hands, a little too quickly and a little too vigorously, to hide her feelings. "I'll be out of Mrs. Beaumont's boudoir in two seconds." She turned and strode to the doorway, but McKaid was there before her. He took hold of her shoulders and turned her to face him.

"Lizzie, she's a very special friend."

"I can see that, McKaid." She shrugged free and hurried with as much dignity as she could muster up the stairs and into Lenore's room. With swift, sure movements she stripped the bed and remade it with clean linen from the top shelf of her wardrobe. She was tucking the last corner under the mattress when she turned and saw McKaid standing in the doorway.

"You're upset," he said observantly.

She whipped the pink coverlet over the bed and methodically smoothed it over the bedding. "Don't be silly. I was under no impression when I came out here that there would actually be a place that I could call my own."

"Lizzie—"

"Forget it, McKaid. I'll sleep with the children."

"There's hardly room for them in that bed."

"Then I'll sleep in the library." She marched to the wardrobe and swept the hangers off the rod, folding her meagre supply of clothes over her arm. Then she opened the top two drawers of the bureau and scooped out her belongings, piling them on top of her already full arms and holding them in place with her chin. At the last moment she fumbled to collect her hair brush and comb from the little vanity table and stalked past McKaid out of the room.

"I didn't mean for you to move out . . . Lizzie," he called to her, dismayed.

"No?" She opened the children's door and slipped inside. The room was small, and the children were indeed sprawled onto every corner of the one bed. She took a weary breath and dumped her belongings in the corner.

McKaid leaned against the wall in the dimly lit hallway and rubbed his aching head. He felt awful. She had every right to be angry. She should have a room of her own. But Lenore . . . He couldn't very well ask her to sleep on the sofa when she'd outfitted herself a room at the Circle K. And he couldn't very well refuse her his hospitality. She had a valid reason for wanting to visit the ranch at frequent intervals.

Elizabeth gathered up the pile of linen from the floor and turned toward the stairway. She didn't want to look at McKaid. Her anger bubbled over that he was still there. Why didn't he just go down to his special visitor and leave her alone. She'd had about as much as she could take from him for one day.

"We need a bigger house, don't we?" McKaid murmured, hoping that she'd hear in his voice his regret at asking her to give up her cozy room. She was tired. That much was obvious. She'd been working all day long, and it was terribly unfair to put her out.

"Look, why don't you sleep in my bed," he suggested, hitting on a solution he thought would satisfy everyone.

Her nostrils flared as she rounded on him. If she had not had her arms full, she'd have slapped him. "How very generous of you. Did you offer your bed to Lenore? I'm sure she'll end up there before the night's over anyway. All this is just for show, isn't it?"

He shook her then, causing the sheets to cascade out of her hands. "You little viper," he ground out, temper rising to replace his soft-hearted regret. "Lenore is a lady. A fine lady. And take those stupid spectacles off your face. It's like talking to a mirror." He jerked them from her nose, twisting the wires and hurting her ears in the process. He flung them disgustedly down the hall. "For your information, the Beaumonts offered all the financial asistance they could afford when we were struggling to get back on our feet after we were nearly ruined by a blizzard. If not for them, we'd be out of business. They are valued friends, more so because that same blizzard took the life of Lenore's husband. Now do you get the picture? And Lenore is not someone you slander in such a way."

Elizabeth gathered up the linens. Her eyes shot icy daggers when she looked at him again. "But I am?"

He sighed and turned away, rubbing his head again. "You misunderstood. I—"

"You better stop talking, McKaid. Why don't you go to bed and leave me alone. You look as if you're about to fall over." She turned and walked away.

McKaid listened to her soft footfalls on the stairs. Slowly he leaned against the wall and slid to the floor, his elbows propped on his raised knees, his head in his hands. He hadn't meant that at all. He'd intended to give up his bed and go down to the bunkhouse to sleep. But he hadn't said that, had he? He hadn't said anything right. He'd blundered in and made Lizzie feel like an intruder, unimportant, the one who was extraneous and dispensable. And she was everything but that. The Circle K felt like a home for the first time because of her presence. He'd lain in his bed for three days, and healing sleep had come easily because he could hear her moving about in his room, could hear her voice as she talked to the children, could hear the sweet sound of laughter filtering through his window. Peaceful sounds. Comforting sounds.

Why was he so hateful to her then? Why did he persist in goading her until she stormed off and left him? Why couldn't he be nice to her?

Because misery loves company.

You want her and you can't have her, and it's driving you crazy.

In a couple more days when he was a little stronger, he'd get back on his horse and ride out, pain be damned. It was the only answer, unless he meant to drive her away permanently. Maybe apart from her he could get himself straightened out again. Maybe then he could treat her as she deserved to be treated.

He got to his feet and walked to the end of the hall. He stooped and picked up her glasses. One of the lenses had cracked. He put them to his eyes, lowered them, then lifted them again. Plain glass. He smiled sadly. Her shield against the world. What was Lizzie hiding from? The pain of loss, disapppointment, disillusionment? He closed his eyes and put her glasses to his lips. In that second he fell in love with her all over again.

Chapter Eight

Early the next morning, after a restless night of tossing and turning on the hard sofa in the library, Elizabeth gave up on sleep, tidied the room, and dressed for the first time in her new riding clothes. A good long walk would clear the muddle of her mind.

The golden dawn was just beginning to find paths through the purple clouds of night when she let herself out of the house. She gazed appreciatively at the shapes silhouetted against the waking sky, the stark line of the hills, the silver-highlighted forms of the long rows of fences, the peaked roofs of the barn, stable, bunkhouse, and cottages, the tall windmills that turned aimlessly in the morning breeze but would soon pump fresh water from aquifers below the ground. The Circle K was a beautiful ranch in a beautiful valley. It was all that was fresh and clean and natural. Except for her aching heart and the empty, unsettled loneliness that lodged inside, she could stay here and be content forever.

She was drawn down the stone path toward the stables where an orange glow lit the doorway. Somebody was awake. Somebody to chase away her feelings of estrangement. She hadn't felt this way since she was a child, all alone in a harsh world. Since that time she'd had one or both of her parents to cling to. The Hepplewhites had given her everything: love, acceptance, security, opportunities not afforded to most young ladies. They had filled her world to overflowing. Yet underneath, buried deep in the back of her mind, was a basic sense of insecurity and unworthiness. Her mature and rational mind knew that those feelings were only residual dross from the long ago daily warnings, issued so sternly by the fierce and frightening headmistress of the orphanage, that children needed to be well mannered, hard-working, and spiritually and morally upright to be welcomed into someone else's life, yet she still couldn't completely eradicate them. Her father was far away now, but she had Clint, Emma, and the children. They accepted her warmly and were even coming to love her as she was them. So why did she feel so empty? Because of McKaid? He had never been more than a thorn in her side, but she had come to crave that constant pricking. She had somehow come to love the irksome man.

She'd told him to leave her alone, and he'd done it. She couldn't blame him after the horrible way she'd acted. Was it such a big favor to ask that she give up her bed? She'd have done it willingly and gladly for Caroline if Caroline had asked to spend the night in her father's home.

And it wasn't even Lenore she objected to. She liked Lenore in a way. She was a gentle woman who'd taken her side more than once during dinner the night before. She couldn't blame McKaid in the least for wanting Lenore. It was McKaid's attitude that made her feel shut out and alienated. Since Lenore's arrival he had done nothing but snipe at her, all the while sharing something very different with his neighbor.

When he talked with Lenore, his eyes turned a warm blue. They spoke very eloquently of respect, admiration, approval. That's how Paul had looked at her, with gentle caring, and it had made her feel so good inside. She wanted just once to see McKaid look at her that way. She wanted just once to bask in that warm radiance, to let it wrap around her cold heart and chase away the chill of being alone.

"Well now, good morning to you. You're up early."

She jumped, startled from her troubled thoughts. "Oh, you scared me. Good morning, Russ."

"Still dreaming, were you. That's one of the hazards of living on the range."

"Why do you say that?"

"Oh, in the city there are too many distractions. Out here, once your thoughts get started down a path, there's nothing to stop them. You can lose yourself, forget what you're doing, end up someplace you never intended to go."

"Yes. It's very hypnotic. Are you going somewhere?"

"A morning ride. Some buzzards were circling in the northeast sky last evening. Thought I'd check and see if there's

126

a problem."

"Buzzards?"

"Scavengers. They can smell death before it happens. They've been known to stand fifty feet off for hours until an animal gives up the fight. Or a man."

She shivered. "How gruesome."

"That's life out here."

"May I come with you? I'm not an expert with a horse, but I'll try to keep up."

"You do ride though?" Russ questioned cautiously. "It's a long way."

"I used to ride often, but only as a properly trained Eastern lady rides. McKaid did make me get a riding skirt and boots, so I'm ready to try it your way." She grinned imploringly. "Please."

"How can I refuse?" he asked, shaking his head. "I'm utterly defeated by long, flowing hair, a pretty smile, and big, soulful eyes. Even if those eyes have dark circles under them. Here, hold these reins while I get you a horse."

She touched her fingers to the bridge of her nose. "I didn't sleep very well. I had to give up my room to our company." She watched him begin to saddle a second horse.

"Ah, yes. Lenore's here," he nodded. "Where did you bunk?" He lifted the heavy saddle as if it weighed nothing at all.

"On the sofa in the library."

"There's an extra room in my cottage," he said with a twinkle in his brown eyes. "I guarantee I'll be a gentleman," he added, forestalling the quick temper he knew she possessed. "Actually, I don't see why McKaid didn't think of that."

"You mean me moving in with you?" she teased.

"No, silly. Him."

She thought about what McKaid had said about her sleeping in his bed. She chuckled and shook her head at her stupidity. "Maybe he did. Only I was so irritated with him . . ." He had said she misunderstood. What a foolish idiot she was.

"Here we go. This is Belle. Belle, meet Miss Elizabeth." Russ led the horses out into the sprinkling light of dawn. "Fine morning," he said, glancing around. "Need a hand up?"

"Let me try." When she was comfortably seated, both toes in the shortened stirrups, she led Belle through a few turns. "Not bad. It's much easier astride. I have more balance."

"Far more practical," he agreed. "At least you've a fightin' chance to stay in the saddle that way."

They rode side by side, they talked, they laughed, and when she found her courage, they raced. She found that this big, warm-hearted man, who kept a sharp eye on her as well as their surroundings, laughed heartily at her jokes, showed his own quirky sense of humor, had lightened her heart. She was glad she had come. She was beginning to get her perspective back again and put her self-pity aside. Her life was too good, and the day too glorious to be down.

They rode over the crest of a grassy knoll, and four of the biggest birds she'd ever seen took flight, climbing to soar in wide circles overhead, rising then dropping, then rising again.

"My word, is that a buzzard?"

"Come on," Russ said. "Let' see what they were feasting on. Have you the stomach for it?"

They rode down the hill and dismounted, slowly walking to the mutilated carcass lying in the tall grasses. "A steer," Russ said unnecessarily. "Butchered, by the looks of it."

"By Indians?"

"No. Indians have more respect for life than this. They use all of the animals, the hide, the bones, the sinew, the organs. This was the work of . . ."

"Who?"

He looked up from his squatting position, then stood. "Someone else. Rustlers, maybe. Let's get back. McKaid needs to know about this."

McKaid? Not Clint? Russ knew who had slaughtered the animal, or had a pretty good guess, but he was keeping it to himself to avoid alarming her. If McKaid needed to know, it had something to do with outlaws. Maybe even the Corbett character who'd escaped Straight Arrow's retaliation. But why would he be here? Wouldn't he long since have left the area?

When they returned to the ranch, Elizabeth entered the kitchen by the back door and walked straight into McKaid's temper.

"Where the hell have you been?"

Clint, Emma, and Lenore were all seated around the table drinking coffee, the dirty dishes from their breakfast stacked beside the wash basin. All three of their mouths dropped open when McKaid addressed her in such a discourteous way. What she could tell them!

She was feeling much better now, back to her fighting form after her invigorating morning ride. She threw McKaid a saccharine smile and fluttered her lashes, something she could do, now he'd destroyed her only other pair of glasses. "Riding."

"Riding? Who the hell told you that you could go riding?" he thundered.

She tapped her chin thoughtfully with her kid gloves and pretended to search her mind for an answer. "Let's see. Who the hell did tell me I could go riding? Why, speak of the devil, wasn't it you, McKaid, who insisted I buy new clothes and boots because I would be required to learn to ride?"

"I didn't mean you were to go by yourself. And in the dark, no less."

"Ah, well then you can calm your ruffled feathers, big fella," she said coyly. "It wasn't completely dark, and I wasn't completely alone. By the way, Emma, I've asked Russ to join me for breakfast."

"Russ?" they all chorused together.

She looked around the room at their shocked faces. Emma was all adither, Clint was looking strangely at Lenore, Lenore was staring bleakly at McKaid, and McKaid was scowling down at her.

"What did I do now?" she demanded defensively.

"Russ can eat with the men," McKaid said heatedly.

"I asked him to eat with us. Besides, he want—"

"It isn't done, Elizabeth," he barked, grabbing her shoulders and shaking her again. "And in the future I'll thank you to check with me before enticing men home with you."

She wanted to brain him, she wanted to punch him in the stomach, but because of his injuries, she could do neither. So she resorted to her pointed-toed boots and kicked his unbooted shin.

"Ouch. You damned she-cat. I ought to turn you over my knee for this."

"You think you're big enough, you overblown hothead?"

"Children, children," Clint interceded, grinning from ear to ear.

"For your own sake, you better go to your room," McKaid growled between his teeth, still balancing on one leg and rubbing the other. "And stay there!"

"If I had one, I would," she shot back, unthinking. "As it is,

I'm going to have breakfast." Go to your room? Who did he think he was talking to? She took down two plates and set the table for herself and Russ, aware that during the silent interval, except for the rattle of glass and flatware, McKaid stood over her, glaring, his temper boiling hotter and hotter. She hoped he burst a seam.

She glanced at her uncle as she helped herself to two pancakes and poured thick gravy over them. His face was nearly hidden behind the two hands that held his coffee mug to his lips, but she could see the sides of his cheeks twitching. The whole scene, from where he sat, must have looked ridiculous. She couldn't help the snicker that escaped. Ruthie and James were better behaved than she and McKaid. She jammed a wedge of pancake into her mouth to stop her laughter.

"You think this is funny?" McKaid demanded. He grabbed her wrist and jerked her up off her chair, nearly gouging his chin with the fork she still held.

She choked on her food and swallowed it in one gulp. "McKaid! Good lord."

"Before you get too comfortable, you're going to march right back to the stables and tell Russ Packard that he can forget any notion he has about . . .

The back door opened and banged shut again as Russ stepped into the kitchen. "Did I hear my name taken in vain?" he asked jovially. "Ah, flapjacks and gravy. My favorite." His eyes stopped on Lenore. "Hello, Lenore."

"Hello, Russ."

Russ looked at McKaid and cocked a brow at his grip on Elizabeth's wrist and the fork dangling from her fingers.

"I suppose you've learned the hard way that she can't handle a horse yet," McKaid said derisively to Russ. He turned to glower at his shackled prisoner.

"Can't handle . . . I'll have you know the little darlin' almost beat me in a race."

McKaid's head shot up, and he stared, dumbfounded, at Russ. "A race?"

"It was her idea," he defended himself.

McKaid's fingers tightened on her wrist, and when he turned back to her, she had the nerve to flutter those blasted long lashes at him again. Did she have to be so damned alluring? Did she have to come waltzing in with her hair loose and windswept, her eyes alight, her cheeks and lips flushed

130

with color. Weren't things bad enough?

"You said you couldn't ride," he accused.

"Nooo. I said I won first place at the Academy. *You* said I couldn't ride."

"That was sidesaddle," he argued.

She waved her fork dismissively. "Minor adjustment."

He let out the breath he had been holding and released her hand. "Okay, okay," he relented, running his fingers through his hair.

"He was concerned about you, Elizabeth," Lenore said softly. "Why don't you finish your breakfast."

Lenore's face was serious, but her eyes were unusually bright when she looked at Elizabeth. Was she amused, too, or just pleased that McKaid didn't get along with his wards' new teacher. There wasn't anything she could do about it, whichever the case, so she shrugged and sat back down. "I was safer on the horse," she said dryly to the other woman as she stabbed at her food, which made Lenore laugh.

"Pull out a chair and dig in, Russ," Clint invited.

"Don't mind if I do," Russ accepted, helping himself to the last five flapjacks and the rest of the gravy.

"Can I make you eggs?" Emma asked, needing to do something. What an awful situation. "Scrambled all right?"

"Mmm, that'd be great," Russ mumbled.

"I'll get you some coffee," Lenore said, jumping up to do just that. She returned with a steaming mug for Elizabeth as well.

"I'm sorry about your room. I didn't know. I'll move my things out," Lenore said quietly to Elizabeth.

"No. Don't do that, please. It's all right. Really."

"But you were upset."

"Only with McKaid. He's such a bully."

"So, McKaid," Russ said after a long drink of coffee, "what did you want Miss Elizabeth to march down there and tell me just now?"

"Hmm?" McKaid said distractedly. "Oh, that. Never mind." He sat down heavily on his chair and wrapped his hands around his cooling coffee.

"I haven't told them yet, Russ," Elizabeth said, winking intimately at the foreman. "It would be better coming from you, I think. Man to man, you know. McKaid would say it was all my fault somehow, just because I enticed you into taking me

131

with you. Try not to upset him when you break the news."

McKaid went very still, eyeing them both with that frozen look he could summon so well. His mind conjured up the image of the two of them locked in a lovers' embrace, murmuring words of love, promises of forever after. "Let's hear it then," he said, barely moving his rigid lips.

"We found a dead steer. Slaughtered for meat. Half the carcass was still intact." Russ's face was poker straight.

McKaid said nothing. He couldn't. His mind wouldn't function yet. A dead steer? Elizabeth was smirking. Damn her hide. Damn them both. Russ threw back his head and laughed.

"Where was it?" Clint asked.

"Northeast corner by the ravine."

"I'd better go take a look around," Clint said thoughtfully, his eyes darting to McKaid.

"I'll come with you," McKaid answered too quickly.

"You can't go out there. You're not fit to be on a horse yet," Elizabeth protested.

"I'm fine. And don't think just because you took that bullet out of my side that you can order my life around, lady."

Lenore wisely interceded. "You'll set your recovery back days if you aggravate your injuries."

He sighed and leaned back in his chair. "I suppose you have a point." He knew she did. He didn't want to be flat on his back again either when Ramirez decided to show his face. On the other hand, Clint didn't know what to look for. He hadn't been trained to read signs or track.

"I'll have a good look, McKaid," Clint said, seeming to read his mind. "I'll give you a full report."

"You think it might have been Corbett?" Elizabeth asked.

McKaid shot a questioning look at Russ who subtly shook his head. He turned to Elizabeth. "It's unlikely. Don't worry about it."

She rolled her eyes heavenward. It was said so patronizingly that she was both hurt and angered. He either thought her stupid, or he plainly wanted her out of his affairs.

"If you'll excuse me then, I'll get the children up and fed," she said, and cleared her dishes from the table.

"Stay close to the house today," McKaid ordered imperiously. She didn't answer as she left.

Later that morning Clint and McKaid closeted themselves in the library.

"What did you find?" McKaid asked.

"As far as I could tell, it was the work of one man. That's not to say he didn't join up with others after he got what he came for."

"But you tracked him?"

"Only as far as the rocks. I lost him there. Do you think it was Corbett?"

"If he suspects I'm still alive, he'll stick around."

"But it could be one of Ramirez's men?"

"He wouldn't have butchered that steer there. He'd have led it back to camp. Ramirez rides with maybe twenty men and who knows how many women who all need to eat. He wouldn't waste the meat."

"So you've two men gunning for you? Do you think Corbett was letting you know he's around?"

"Corbett is just a kid. He may be mad as hell right now, but he's probably just as scared. He's not thinking beyond survival at the moment. My guess is he didn't expect us to find that carcass."

"What are you planning to do?" Clint asked, concerned for his nephew.

"Get well first. But I would like to get word to the sheriff about this. If Corbett is in the area, he might try something in town."

"I'll send a couple of men."

The sun was working its way down that afternoon when Elizabeth walked hand in hand with the children to the corral where a group of men were boisterously watching one of their friends saddle-break a horse. The men sat on top of the rough board fence, shouting encouragements and occasional jeers at the sweating, dusty man who was frequently pitched from the horse's back.

The children, entranced, climbed the fence and hung over the top rail as they watched. Elizabeth, too, looked on curiously. She'd never seen the procedure before. By turns the young man calmed the animal with low, soothing words, stroking its long neck muscles, then lifted himself into the saddle for another rough and tumble ride.

"*Buenas dias*, señorita," a man said at her side. "You like to watch the taming of a horse?"

"Hello, Julio," she answered, proud that she was beginning to know some of the ranch hands by name. "The children

133

wanted to watch, so I agreed. But I admit it's fascinating."

"It is sport for the men. They make the bets on who will succeed first."

She chuckled. "And did you bet, Julio?"

"Sí. I, too, placed a bet." But win or lose, Julio stood to gain from his temporary work at the Circle K. He was very pleased to have been taken on to help with the branding and cutting while the regular men were droving the herd to market. "Mr. McKaid, he is getting well?"

"Oh, yes. He gets stronger each day. He even wanted to go riding today, but Mrs. Beaumont talked him out of it." A fact which still rankled, but she didn't let it show.

"Mrs. Beaumont, she comes to visit often? I think she is a little sweet on McKaid, no?"

"Perhaps," Elizabeth said indifferently. "Who's to say?"

"This does not upset you?"

She wanted to snap at Julio for even asking such a painful and personal question, but she held her tongue. It would be unbearable if the men of the ranch knew how she really felt about McKaid. Doubly so when they could see for themselves that McKaid spent most of his waking hours on the porch swing with Lenore.

She raised her brows and shrugged. "Why should it?" She spotted Russ walking toward them and called out to him, waving her arm. Anything to discourage Julio's curious prying.

"Miss Elizabeth," Russ greeted her affably, removing his hat and ruffling his head of curls. "How was your day? Are you stiff yet from our morning ride?"

"Some," she answered honestly, grinning impishly. "But more in my wrist than anywhere else. One of the hazards of life on the range, I guess."

Russ tossed his head back and laughed. "I heard all about it from Clint," he admitted.

"Humph," she grunted. "I can stand a few bruises. May I come tomorrow, too? I did enjoy starting the morning with you. I also want to take the children on a picnic at noon. You will come won't you? Emma's sending an apple pie."

Russ noticed Julio's avid interest and gave him a dark look. Julio grinned and walked away, his gait a little too slow not to be deemed insolent. Russ scowled and turned to Elizabeth.

"Maybe it would be better if we don't."

"Because of Julio?" Elizabeth asked. "Or because of

McKaid. Russ, I may be just one of his paid employees, but I will not be dictated to by McKaid or anyone else. If you don't want me with you, I'll ride by myself." She turned and lifted the children from the fence. "Time to get cleaned up."

"Another bath?" James grumbled.

"No, not a bath if you don't want one today. But a good wash, and clean clothes, young man."

"Elizabeth," Russ stalled her.

"Go on, children. I'll be there in a minute." She turned to face Russ. "Yes?"

"It's not that I didn't enjoy our ride, because I did," he said uncomfortably. "But you have to understand. There's a sort of pecking order at the ranch, not unlike the army. Some men are privates, some lieutenants, others captains and majors."

"And the general and his family are off-limits?" she finished, beginning to see. That was what McKaid must have meant this morning when she'd invited Russ to breakfast and he'd said that it wasn't done. "But you're the foreman, Russ. You must be at least a colonel," she returned, not at all amused by such an hierarchical system.

"It's something Old Man McKaid started years ago when his men got to wrangling about their duties. Clint kept it on, since it seemed to work. And of course there was Emma to protect."

"But I'm in no danger with you, am I?"

"Certainly not. And it is fitting that you go with me, since McKaid's laid up, but . . ."

"Then let me go. Please, Russ. I'd really appreciate it."

He gave in. He was sure to hear about it from McKaid, and the other men would give him the business about it, but if it would make Elizabeth happy . . . "All right. Same time though. I won't wait around for you."

"Thank you, Russ." Impulsively, she took his shoulders and stretched up to plant a quick kiss on his bristly cheek.

That evening was as difficult as the previous one, not because McKaid badgered her, but because he went out of his way to avoid talking to her at all. Even the children, who dined with the grown-ups that night, noticed it.

"Mr. McKaid, are you mad at Miss Elizabeth?" Ruthie asked. "You're not going to send her away, are you?"

"Send her away?" McKaid repeated, his brow creasing into a deep frown. "Why would I do that?"

"When you look at her, you frown. Like now," Ruthie said

with innocent frankness.

"Ruthie, hush!' James warned.

"Did I say something wrong?" Ruthie asked her older brother.

"No, darling," Elizabeth answered, smoothing the little girl's fair hair. "Mr. McKaid still gets tired, and sometimes a little cranky. Isn't that so, Mr. McKaid?"

"Yes. Quite," he said, returning his attention to his meal.

"It's late, children. If you've finished, you'd best prepare for bed. I've an outing planned for tomorrow. We'll take a picnic lunch to the caves, shall we?"

"Who has won the distinction of escorting you?" Clint asked. "Which of my eager men drew the long straw?"

"We, that is Russ and I, thought it best if he accompany us. It wasn't hard to convince him in the face of Emma's apple pie, and it seemed best since . . ." Her voice trailed off when she noticed all four pairs of eyes turned disapprovingly on her. "Excuse me, please. I'll have my coffee after I've tucked the children in. I'll do the washing up, Emma." She received no response, and very curiously felt like a naughty scullery maid who'd displeased the lords and ladies of the house, though she couldn't guess why. She had a wild impulse to bob a curtsy as she backed out of the room, but pride and better sense came to her rescue. As soon as she'd left the room, she expelled her breath and sagged against the wall.

She took the stairs quickly and rushed in to help the children in case McKaid came after her again. He looked positively murderous. Did he hold some grudge against Russ? If so, why didn't he simply let the man go? She couldn't give that fleeting thought credence. Russ was too good a foreman, too fine a man, and his loyalty lay entirely with Clint and McKaid.

Clint had said she was to take someone with her if she left the ranch. Since learning about that foolish ranking system, she'd asked Russ to go with her for the express purpose of avoiding trouble with the rest of the men. He was the obvious choice, and she liked his company. So if that wasn't it, and she didn't see how it could be, then what was it? The picnic? Did they have some other unwritten rule about eating out in the open?

Maybe they thought she was loafing. Maybe they felt she wasn't holding up her end of the bargain. She'd tried diligently to help where she could around the house, as well as taking

136

over the total care of the children. She'd helped with cooking, cleaning, the laundry. What more did they want of her?

When morning came she met Russ as planned, and their ride again lifted her spirits. Russ seemed able to restore her good humor with a few well-chosen words, and put her emotions in balance anew by simply laughing at her exaggerated verbal abuse of McKaid's foul temperament.

"You don't think he's regretting that I came, do you?" She voiced the thought that had been hounding her all night in the dark library. She'd lain awake for hours, turning events, words, expressions over in her mind. Finally she'd resorted to counting the books that lined the walls, but that didn't help either when she saw how disordered they were. They needed sorting.

"Regretting? Not at all. He has nothing but good to say about you, miss."

That surprised her. "You're just saying that to make me feel better." She couldn't contain her laughter at his faked indignation. "Come on, Russ. You haven't seen him in days except for yesterday morning. He spends all his time with Lenore now. You couldn't have talked to him about me. Besides, you saw for yourself how fondly he treats me. He had the affrontery to order me to go to my room."

"Which you don't have. You must resent Lenore—Mrs. Beaumont," he said, staring off at the pink-crested mountains.

"No. I like her very much, actually. She's very sweet. Did you know her husband?"

"Yes. I was with the men who found his body. I helped bring him back."

"That must have been devastating for her."

"It took her a long time to get over his death, but she finally has, it seems, and she deserves to be happy again. I hope McKaid appreciates that fact."

Elizabeth said nothing as her worst suspicions were inadvertently confirmed. They rode on in silence for a while. After a time Russ broke into her thoughts, he too still thinking about McKaid and Lenore.

"Have they ever mentioned getting hitched?"

"Not in my presence. Are they planning to be married soon?" McKaid's marriage to another woman was not something she wanted to think about, but she supposed she'd have to get used to it sooner or later.

"I imagine it's inevitable, both of them being ranchers, both alone. At least McKaid isn't beneath her station, and he is a good man."

"What do you mean he isn't beneath her station?" she asked, picking up the hint of bitterness in his tone. "Was her husband? But I thought they were very wealthy." He said nothing, and Elizabeth finally understood. "Are you referring to this foolishness about ranch rank again? That's positively archaic. And where does that put me? I'm just the hired help, too, you know."

"You're family, Elizabeth."

"I suppose you could say that."

"You sound doubtful."

"I'm not blood kin at all. I'm not sure I can legally claim to be family to anyone but my adoptive father."

"Ahh. You're feeling unsure of yourself and your rightful place here, is that it? And McKaid adds to it by kicking you out of your room. Poor little Lizzie," he commiserated facetiously, using McKaid's pet name for her.

"I see you're all sympathy."

"Clint thinks you're marvelous, and I did hear that directly from the man's lips. And I also see you stand up to McKaid's sharp tongue. I was even a party to some bedevilment on your part, young lady. You don't need my sympathy."

She laughed, both at herself and at Russ's forthright honesty. "Nor do I want it. I need your plain-speaking far more."

Elizabeth held her breath as she entered the kitchen later, braced for another confrontation with McKaid, totally unprepared for what she met. The four adults were chatting and laughing easily with each other, and all four turned and bid her a cheery and bright good morning.

"Did you have a good ride, Lizzie?" McKaid asked, filling her coffee cup for her. He held out her chair. "Sit down. We're having oatmeal this morning. You like oatmeal, don't you?"

"I love oatmeal," she replied, thoroughly bemused. Emma served her, pouring creamy milk and a large dollop of honey over her hot cereal. Elizabeth took a spoonful and glanced around the table as the easy chatter began again. One of her finely shaped brows rose curiously, but she wasn't about to question her good fortune.

She finished her cereal and helped herself to a small bowl of

138

stewed cinnamon apples from the pot on the stove. They continued discussing ranch matters and local gossip, directing remarks and explanations at her and questioning her about her opinions as often as they could, including her in their conversation. Something was going on. They were just too unusually casual.

"Where did you ride this morning, Elizabeth?" Lenore asked.

"We went south to the bridge, then west to check on the lower well. One of the vanes had come loose on the windmill, but we fixed it."

"You didn't climb up that contraption, did you?" McKaid asked.

"Someone had to steady the arm while Russ tightened the fitting."

"You could have been hurt," Emma admonished.

"That's what Russ said. He wanted to come back for one of the men, but that seemed a waste of time when I was right there."

"Nevertheless," McKaid said sharply, but stopped when Lenore laid a hand on his arm. He looked from Lenore to Elizabeth, then glanced at Clint. He shrugged. "You're right. It would have been a waste of time, and you were obviously capable of handling the task."

"Thank you, McKaid." For whatever reason—probably Lenore—he had decided not to yell at her. He'd even admitted she'd been of help, however slight she knew that help to be. She still couldn't figure out his change of attitude toward her, but neither could she curb the well of warm satisfaction that bubbled up in her breast to finally be in McKaid's good graces.

"What are your plans for today?" he asked her.

Surprise flickered in her gold-flecked eyes, and McKaid frowned again. Had he been that bad that his interest in her day-to-day activities came as such a shock to her? He'd been fully aware of where she was and what she was doing every minute of the time since she'd arrived, but no one else had seen it that way.

Lenore had scolded him soundly the night before about how callously he treated her. Emma and Clint had each had a go at him, too. They even asked him, as Ruthie had, if he wanted her to leave, if he was trying to force her into going home.

He didn't know how to answer them. How could he explain

to them what was going round and round in his mind, what logical thoughts and illogical emotions were battling each other. He wanted her here, needed her here, but if Ramirez ever learned why, he'd use Lizzie to get to him. He didn't want history to repeat itself through Elizabeth, so he wanted her gone. Safe. Away from danger.

But the thought of never seeing her again was too much to bear. What was getting even worse, though, was watching her lithe body in graceful motion all day long, hearing her laugh with other people, seeing her discover her new world and trying patiently to ignore his peevish tantrums so she could enjoy it, when all the time he was longing to grab her, hold her tight against his body, and kiss her until they were both utterly mad and writhing in the heated, pulsing, passionate act of love.

"McKaid," Elizabeth said for the second time, finally getting his attention.

"What—" His head snapped up. Everyone was grinning at him.

"When you ask a question, the least you could do is listen to the answer."

"Lizzie, I want you to tell Russ he's not to go with you today."

"You want what?" Elizabeth said very quietly. "Listen, McKaid—"

"Wait. I didn't say that right. Would you please ask Russ if he'd mind if I took his place today? That is, if you don't object."

"You actually want to come?"

"If you'd rather Russ go, then . . ."

"No. I just . . . Are you serious?"

"I'm tired sitting around here. I need to get out. Besides we need to have a talk. We could take the buckboard and go down to the creek. The children could splash around in the water."

"That's a terrific idea," Lenore said to Elizabeth. "He needs some sunshine. Russ won't mind, I'm certain."

"Then you'll be coming? I mean, shall I make lunch for five?"

"Goodness, no. I've promised Emma to help her with her baking. Isn't that so?"

"I—a—yes," Emma sputtered.

"I better fire up the bakehouse then," Clint said, smiling

140

broadly and winking at Emma. "Are you up to a chocolate cake as well?"

"Chocolate cake?" exclaimed two sleepy urchins from the doorway.

"Lizzie?" McKaid asked again.

"Yes, McKaid. That sounds lovely." Her voice was calm. She hoped her eyes didn't betray the fact that her heart had done an erratic leap and then settled again to a less than mild gallop. He wanted her company. Hers. Was this an olive branch? Did he, too, want an end to the exhausting tension that stretched between them?

Her heart thudded to a breathless stop. Or did he want to tell her of his marriage plans? Had he discerned her feelings, was he hoping to let her down easily? Did he want to apologize for dragging her away from her once well-ordered life only to realize he didn't need her after all, and now politely offer to see her safely returned to Virginia?

Suddenly she wasn't sure she wanted to go on this picnic. Not knowing was better. Hoping was better. The tension, the bickering, his glowering at her was better than never seeing him again.

Chapter Nine

McKaid and Elizabeth reclined on a blanket in the shade of a giant cottonwood, watching the children cavort in the cool waters of a stream. Some miles away the town of Las Vegas lay resting, quiet and unsuspecting, complacently enjoying the noontime siesta hours.

Las Vegas, a hard day's ride from Santa Fe over the Sangre de Christo Mountains, was a trading center along the Santa Fe Trail as well as a service point for surrounding ranches and small villages. The town and its occupants also saw a steady stream of the lonely men stationed at nearby Fort Union.

As with most of the Spanish towns of the Southwest, Las Vegas was rapidly being inundated by merchants, bankers, tradesmen, and new settlers from farther east who were determined to find a place for themselves in a newly opened territory away from whatever it was they wished to leave behind. In most cases it was the devastations of war, creditors, memories, and in some cases a misdeed or two.

Heedless of approaching danger, the town took its usual mid-day nap. The shopkeepers lazed or snoozed on rough benches and chairs outside their shops, the banks, postal office, and business establishments closed their doors, the town sheriff even gave up and stretched out on a cot in one of the cells. In the next cell lay an unkempt and odorous man still sleeping off a drunk. The sheriff had locked him up the night before after the man had stumbled and fallen through one of the expensive painted glass windows of the saloon.

Some parts of the town had no time for siesta. The blacksmith was overloaded with work, the lumber mill and brick kilns worked two shifts a day to keep up with the steady

143

demand for building supplies, the restaurants and the new telegraph office remained operational, and the priest at the chapel of the old decaying mission welcomed worshippers day and night.

Two men rode slowly into town, tethering their horses at the hitching rail in front of one of the saloons. Their alert black eyes took in the somnolent town from one side to the other. One of them nodded toward the swinging doors of the saloon, and they moved in that direction. After a few minutes two more men rode in, stopping at the livery. Two more entered the hotel. In a slow, unnoticeable trickle fifteen men invaded Las Vegas that afternoon with a well-planned strategy.

Ramirez, himself, stopped for a brief visit at the home of the banker. He let himself through the unlocked door, startling the Spanish woman who was the cook and housekeeper for the wealthy *gringo* bank manager. The cook saw the long, deadly pistol he held and backed away in silence.

Ramirez grinned insolently at her fear, flashing his gold front tooth at her, and strode through the door into the dining room where the family was seated around a large black-lacquered table. A child of five was seated in a chair nearest him, and while surprise was still on his side, he grabbed up her wriggling body and held his gun to her head.

Terrified of the squat ugly man, the child screamed and flailed her arms and legs to get away. The wife cried out in terror, clamping her pudgy hands against her mouth. The banker rose and began to shout, but thought better of it and sat back down.

"You will instruct the *niña* to stop kicking," Ramirez ordered, and waited until the banker had done so and the child lay quiet in his grip.

"What is it you want?" the banker asked, afraid he already knew the answer.

"We will trade. Your child for the gold in the bank," Ramirez answered calmly.

"That money is not mine," the banker began. "I'll be ruined."

"*George*, please," the wife implored.

"*Sí.* It would be wise to heed your wife. Or perhaps the child is of no importance to you."

"Don't hurt her," the banker said, scowling. "All right, just

144

don't hurt her."

"Very well. We go to the bank now. You will keep the others of the house quiet until we are finished," he warned the woman, who could only nod mutely in response.

The sheriff met a much worse fate. On the verge of sleep he heard the two men enter the jail. He sat up slowly and shook his head to clear away his drowsiness. When he looked up he saw who his visitors were. He came instantly awake, and the hair on the back of his head bristled. He knew the two men. A poster hung in his office, offering a reward for the Dawson brothers. They rode now with Ramirez. He reached for his gun, but found his holster empty. His eyes flew to the cot where he'd laid his weapon, but he never had the chance to reach it. The hot, searing pain that exploded into his chest robbed him of his breath, his strength, his life.

The gunsmith's son was taken, the wife at the general store was abducted. Five hostages in all followed the men to the old mission where the bandits met after ransacking the town. With their mocking laughter filling the air, they loaded the stolen horses with their loot and mounted up.

Ramirez alone remained on foot, his gun held on the five hostages and the young priest. The priest, recruited from Europe by the Archbishop Lamy to help bring order and a more traditional form to the churches of New Mexico, stood his ground, unflinching under the hard onyx eyes of Ramirez.

"Your souls will suffer the damnation of hell for this," the Padre intoned.

"*Silencio,*" Ramirez shouted, swinging his gun toward the priest. "You will take back your curse."

"I cannot, for it is God, Himself, who curses those who steal and kill for their own greed."

"Let's go, Ramirez," one of the men coaxed. "Leave him."

But Ramirez could not. The priest had unknowingly hit upon his worst fear, his only fear, that of dying outside the forgiving grace of the Holy Church.

"I will have your blessing, Padre," Ramirez demanded. "You will remove the curse."

The priest stood in silence for a moment. "If you wish to make a confession, you will have to come into the church with me."

The Dawsons rode over, pulling their horses up beside the

145

huddled group of hostages. The older brother knew Ramirez was obsessed with the hereafter. The Mexican had deep respect for the church, a fearful respect. Dawson had seen him shoot a man between the eyes because the man had robbed a church. Ramirez had ugly scars on his arms and his back from a fire he'd escaped as a child, a fire he believed was caused by a *bruja's* curse. He feared the unknown, he feared fire even more, and he never sat too near one even on the coldest of nights. The priest couldn't have selected a worse prediction for Ramirez, one sure to drive him over the edge of sanity, than the threat of slowly roasting in Hell.

Ramirez was insane, dangerously so, but coupled with that insanity and separated only by a hazy thin line was a brilliance that Dawson had to admire. Ramirez lived like a king in Mexico in a palatial hacienda with beautiful women, wealth, and prosperity, and an army of minions at his service until his restless greed for more violence sent him on another unholy rampage. The ghosts from his past that rose up from time to time to haunt him would not let him rest for long.

Dawson wanted to get moving, but he knew Ramirez wouldn't budge with damnation hanging over his head. There was one thing to do, and it was a good idea at that.

"Ramirez," he advised, "the whole friggin' town will be down our necks in a minute. Let's get the hell out of here."

When Ramirez hesitated, uncertain what to do, Dawson spoke again. "We take the priest with us. He can spend his time in prayer for your immortal soul. Get the Padre on a horse," he said to his brother. "You," he directed his order to the gunsmith's son, "go back to town and tell them if they follow, we'll shoot your priest. The rest of you get inside the church."

"*Si,*" Ramirez said. "You are wise, *amigo.* Me, I lose my head for a moment. We go."

Satisfied, they rode out of Las Vegas with their booty, leaving the hostages to return to their families, certain no one would risk any danger to their priest.

The town stood in the wake of the Ramirez gang, stunned and devastated, their sheriff dead, the bartender at one of the saloons dead, the telegraph operator shot, two women brutally violated, the bank emptied, the cash boxes all over town looted, the horses and weapons gone, the priest kidnapped. Never again would they take for granted the peace that had been

146

theirs lately. Never again would they rest easy in the shadow of Fort Union, forgetting that they lived in a hostile and lawless land.

McKaid leaned back against the rough bark of the tree, replete after their bountiful picnic. Elizabeth was gathering their dishes and utensils and the remains of their food and packing them back into the wicker basket. He watched the graceful movements of her body as she worked.

She'd put on a few pounds in the last week, though she was still on the slender side of womanly. Her cheeks and arms had taken on a peachy hue from her hours in the sun, and her hair, hanging freely to the middle of her back except for the front and sides which she'd tied back with a ribbon, was sun-kissed with golden highlights. She was more relaxed today than he'd ever seen her, and she laughed and joked openly with the children and him. He found her very attractive and very bewitching. The thought that he could have a family like this flitted on the edges of his mind and his emotions, like a butterfly trying to decide whether or not to light on a delectable flower, but he was quick to wisk it away. A man in his line of work couldn't afford thoughts like that, no matter how beautiful or how sweet the nectar.

"You said you wanted to talk to me, McKaid," Elizabeth reminded him a few minutes later when she'd finished her chores and had checked on the children.

He looked at her and nodded. "Yes, I did. Clint and I both think you should be fully aware of what living here could mean."

"I like living here," she said quickly, hoping he wasn't going to ask her to give it up.

"I know you do. I was concerned when I first learned who you were. You seemed too rigid to fit in out here, but I've been proved wrong. That's not the issue," he said, seeing confusion cloud her amber eyes. "Hear me out. Then you can argue if you like. You see, Lizzie, my life isn't my own. I've made commitments and promises to people that I have to see through."

"To Lenore?"

His brow rose at that, but he shrugged and nodded. "Among

147

others, yes. I promised her husband that I'd see her married to someone who would love her and care for the ranch and his father."

"You've made a lot of promises to dying men," Elizabeth said.

"I have, and I take them seriously. But—"

"I understand, McKaid," she interrupted, staring at her clenched fingers.

"I'm not sure you do," he replied, watching her closely. "Those children are mine now, my responsibility, just as Lenore and her father are. But I'm digressing. Lizzie, I'm a lawman. I'm a Texas Ranger, and now I'm a deputy marshal of this territory."

"Deputy marshal?"

He nodded. "Since before you arrived. Things have changed here in a way I hadn't anticipated when I sent for you. I'm not sure I have the right to ask you to stay."

She bit down on her lower lip. Well, hadn't she expected it? Now that he'd decided to marry Lenore, there was no place for her here. "You want me to go. Is that what you're saying?"

He didn't answer, and she glanced up and caught him staring into the distance with an almost haunted look on his face.

"McKaid," she said, touching his arm.

He looked back at her and caught her hand in his. He pulled her closer until she was kneeling at his side, face to face with him. He dropped her hand and took her shoulders in his strong grip.

"It's not a matter of what I want. I can't have what I want," he said almost savagely.

"McKaid . . ."

"No. I don't want you to leave, but neither will I allow anyone to harm a single hair on your head."

"Why would they want to?"

"Because of me, Lizzie. Because of who I am, what my life's been all about."

"I don't understand." She didn't. She was more confused than ever. This wasn't what she'd expected to hear.

"You're a very practical woman, sweetheart, but underneath that tough exterior you're also romantically idealistic. You once called me your hero."

"I believe I said you were a little disappointing in that area,"

148

she corrected him teasingly.

His grin mirrored her own, and for a brief minute he couldn't draw his gaze from her soft tempting lips. Those lips. A sweet langorous heat swelled within his body as it did whenever he got too close to her. Hell, he didn't even have to be close to her anymore. He only had to watch her cool indifference from across the room to fantasize himself kissing her, caressing her until she turned hot and wild in his arms and begged him to take her. He only had to see her smiling at the children or Emma or Clint to imagine that same smile of pleasure on her face after he'd fulfilled the hungers of her woman's body. For a week now, an interminable week, he hadn't been able to keep his erotic imaginings at bay. She filled his mind, night and day, and his thoughts kept his body in a constant state of stress. He didn't know how to put an end to it aside from actually taking her, which he couldn't do, yet he didn't think he could tolerate much more of it without losing his sanity completely.

"McKaid," Elizabeth said, bringing him back to the moment.

"Yes." He set her firmly apart from him and sat up, draping his arms over his drawn-up knees. "What I'm trying to say is that I'm no hero. I'm a killer. I shoot people for a living."

"Don't talk nonsense. You're no more a killer than—"

"Elizabeth!" he barked. "Don't whitewash it."

"You're a lawman. You said it yourself," she persisted.

"I kill people, and occasionally people get killed because of me. Innocent people."

She'd heard it all before, from both Union and Confederate officers. Some men, hardened men, played with their soldiers' lives as if they were mere chess pieces in a game of wits, as if they were no more important than those little colored pins stabbed into the desktop maps in combat headquarters. Somehow they had learned to shut out the screams of agony, to erase the color of blood from their eyes. It was a means of survival for them. Others had a more traumatic time dealing with the nightmares of war and all the rivers of crimson they saw dripping from their own hands.

"Why do you continue with it then?" she asked.

"I can't stop. Not yet, anyway. Not until I stop Ramirez."

"Who is Ramirez?"

149

"He's the leader of an army of *bandoleros*. He's the reason I wanted to talk to you. For years I've hunted him, and when I'm not stalking him, he's stalking me."

"Why?"

"I killed his brother—in the line of duty." Duty. What a little word to absolve so much death.

"And?" There had to be more.

"And he killed my fiancée."

"Rosanna?" She nodded sadly at his stunned expression. "You called out to her once when you were asleep."

His face cleared of all expression, became inscrutable. "Yes. Rosanna."

"He killed her because you killed his brother?"

"It was more than that by then, not nearly as simple as revenge, if revenge is ever simple. Ramirez is obsessed with me now. He's obsessed with some sick game of cat and mouse. He stalks me until I almost have him, then he kills someone I care for and retreats back across the border to his mountain hideout in Mexico, leaving me to gnash my teeth in frustrated fury."

This was a side of McKaid's life she knew nothing about, and one she wasn't at all sure she liked. At one level she recognized that lawmen were important, crucial to an area as new and undeveloped as New Mexico, especially when lawlessness was rampant, but at another level the chasing, tracking, gunplay, and killing didn't seem real. Even after what she'd experienced with the Corbett gang, had seen McKaid in action, she couldn't associate herself or him with it. Maybe she just didn't want to. But she couldn't hide from it just because she didn't want to see it. It was part of McKaid. That's what he was trying to make her see. If she wanted to be a part of his life, she'd have to accept what his life was. Good and bad.

"Who besides Rosanna has he killed?" she asked. "Tell me about it."

He drew a breath and let it out slowly. He hated talking about the past, but this once he had to, and she was ready to listen. She was making it easier for him.

"One man was my partner. I won't describe how I found him except to say that both his ears were missing."

"Oh," she gasped. "Why?"

"Ramirez was just a boy in '41, when Governor Manuel Armijo took on the Texans who were seeking to annex the

150

territory east of the Rio Grande. Armies of men marched into New Mexico. It was a disastrous trek even though they came prepared with huge wagons of supplies and arms. What was left after the Indians attacked, Armijo finished. He was unconcerned that the first Texans to arrive were on a diplomatic mission to discuss terms and the benefits of annexation. Armijo ordered them locked up and starved, and those who weren't shot at the wall were then led with the rest—who were easily captured because they were practically dead already—back to Texas on foot with no food or supplies at all. Any who fell behind or tried to escape were shot and their ears returned to Armijo as proof that no Texan remained in his province.

"Ramirez learned at Armijo's feet how to be cruel. He learned to despise the Texans and all North Americans, and fought with Armijo to keep them out. In the end Armijo, smarter than most, saw the futility of the battle and sold out. Ramirez never forgave his idol for letting New Mexico fall to the enemy. Ever since then he has looted towns, rustled horses and cattle, killed indiscriminately in both Texas and New Mexico, always escaping across the border where he cannot be touched, where he lives as a legend."

"And now he's become your crusade?"

"Maybe he has now, but it wasn't always that way. All of the Rangers wanted him. I just happened to be the one in town when they attacked, I was the one who killed his brother and his nephew. You have no idea how many times I've wished I'd turned my back and let them go."

"You could never do that, McKaid."

"No," he admitted wearily. "But so many lives . . ."

"Who else?"

"Another was an old trail hand I'd found buried to the neck by the Comanches. After I nursed him back to health, Seth rode with me, cooked, kept my life in order. A good man." He shrugged off the memory. "Once it was a mangy dog I'd picked up along my journeys. That old mutt was as crafty as the devil. I actually believe he could read minds. Got so he could spot a crook before I could. I found him hanging by his neck in my own hotel room. Like Seth and my partner, he was minus his ears. After that I rode alone, kept to myself, stayed away from the ranch. I didn't want anyone to be in any way connected to me."

Elizabeth wondered if Rosanna had been mutilated as well, but decided she didn't really want to know that answer. "What about Jack and Sophie?"

"The only reason I can look those kids in the eyes is that I know Ramirez didn't have their parents murdered. That was a freak attack, though one not so uncommon out here. I didn't see them often, and when I did, I made sure Ramirez was back in Mexico."

"Why are you telling me this, McKaid?" she asked, then answered her own question. "Ramirez is back."

"He's let it be known that he's here and gunning for me."

"He'd come to the ranch?" she asked, incredulous.

"It's a possibility none of us dares to ignore."

"You're afraid for us."

"Yes, I'm afraid. I'm terrified. It won't be hard to select a victim this time."

"Why doesn't he just come out in the open and face you? Why hit at you through others?"

"He's demented. He loves to cause pain. And I can assure you this is more painful to me than a showdown would be. I'd love nothing better, but Ramirez won't end it so easily. Besides, when you blow all his bravado away, he's a coward."

Elizabeth sighed and studied the branches of the tree above them. "This is all so—unbelievable."

"You'd be well advised to believe it. It's the way things are out here."

"Why does it have to be this way?"

"What better place to go to escape prison or a rope around the neck than to a land where lawmen are so few and far between. This territory is full of society's rejects and refugees from the law back East. Some even take up a respectable trade and start fresh. Others just go on . . ."

"What are you going to do, McKaid?" she asked quietly.

"I was going to ask you the same thing. Do you want to go home? None of us will blame you if you do. This is not something you should be expected to deal with."

"I thought I *was* home."

"Ah, Lizzie," he said, his heart melting. "For as long as you want, this is your home. But think very carefully about what we discussed before giving me a decision."

"All right. I'll think about it."

"You could be killed."

"Yes. So could you."

"Yes."

Their eyes met, and the world slipped away. The sound of children's laughter faded, the birds and insects hushed, the leaves stilled. Elizabeth felt her entire soul reaching out to McKaid, and knew without doubt that she loved him and always would. She could never bear it if this man died. She'd rather lose her own life.

He reached for her, and she went to him, burying her face in his neck. She held on to him with all the strength she had, wishing he could somehow take her strength into himself so that he'd have that little bit more when he needed it. "Don't get killed. Please promise you'll be careful."

Fear glittered in her eyes and pulled at the muscles of her face, and he reached out to comfort and assure her. Her soft pleas against his neck, as much as they aroused him, stunned him more. She wasn't afraid for herself, but for him. She was worried about him. She cared. How his heart soared.

He smiled sadly and pressed his lips to her temple, remembering who she was. "Hey, what's this? I'm your hero, remember?" Then he tickled her.

"No, no, McKaid. Don't," she squealed and struggled frantically to get away. He wouldn't let her go. Instead he rolled her to the ground and held her down while he tortured her by drumming on her ribs.

Peals of laughter rang out, and he joined in with laughter of his own, ten fingers tickling her mercilessly.

"Blast it all, McKaid," she laughed. "Stop this. Let me up."

"I like to hear you laugh. And I like you lying under me like this. Do you realize what you do to me?"

Her laughter died as the hand that teased at her midriff stilled, then began a very erotic tour of her rounded breast. She closed her eyes and fought to catch her breath. Desire rose in her like the unstoppable wash of the tides, turning over and swamping her reservations like so much flotsam that had dared to get in the way. Helplessly she sank under its wake.

Never had she lain with a man, never felt the strength of masculine legs restraining her, muscle against muscle, a man's hard need pressed against her lower abdomen, teasing at her very womanhood, firm hands exploring her so intimately and

153

sending showers of wondrous bliss through her body. It felt wonderful, exciting, compelling, free.

The tingling, the heavy fullness of her breasts, the hollow ache that grew between her thighs were not new to her. They had been part of her long restless nights ever since McKaid had kissed her the first time. But this one moment of reality was better, more powerful, more urgent than any of her dreams had ever been.

She looked into his eyes, dark with desire but for the thin rim of silver-blue, and she slid her hands up over his broad shoulders until her fingers framed his face. Slowly she pulled his head downward toward her waiting lips, seeking to deepen the erotic feelings, prolong them, take them even further.

She felt his whole body stiffen against her and draw away. Bewildered, she let him go, feeling at once bereft and rejected. She didn't hear the children until they were on them.

"What are you doing to Miss Elizabeth, Mr. McKaid?" James asked. "You're not kissing her, are you? Yuck."

"No, you rascal," McKaid said, grabbing him and tossing him carefully to the blanket. "I was tickling her, just like this."

"And you too, young lady," Elizabeth said, doing the same with Ruthie until all of them were laughing.

The children squealed and giggled, their bodies thrashing to escape expert fingers. Above them McKaid's eyes met Elizabeth's. She looked away, back at her laughing young charges. What was there to say? He had Lenore, she had her responsibility to the children. It had been wrong, a mistake. It shouldn't have happened. Why had it? Why, when they weren't arguing and tearing into each other, did they end up flirting with danger, albeit a very seductive kind of danger.

He hadn't actually kissed her. At least that hadn't occurred again. But that thought didn't bring her the relief it should have, because what he had done to her was going to be far more difficult to forget.

Elizabeth didn't see much of McKaid over the next two days. He delivered Lenore back to her ranch and began to resume his normal activities, including short rides on Lucky Lady, his chestnut mare. She was concerned about him, but Clint assured her that he was taking it slowly. His absence from the

154

house was both depressing and relieving. She hadn't been able to put their picnic out of her mind, and neither had he, it seemed, for when he was around her, he was withdrawn and evasive. Yet the tension was still there and straining tighter with each day.

Clint sensed it, too. On the afternoon of the third day he asked Elizabeth to join him in his office.

"You've been very quiet lately, Liz—Elizabeth," he said, coming directly to the point. "I wanted you to be happy here, but I get the feeling you're not."

"Oh, no, Uncle Clint. I love it here."

"McKaid said he talked to you and explained what we're up against."

"Yes. He did, but . . ."

"Would you rather remain out of it? Is that what's been bothering you?"

"No. I'd rather stay, unless you want me to go."

"I can't make that decision for you."

"Then I'll stay. Besides, everyone here is in danger. I want to help."

"Is it McKaid then?" he asked pointedly. "Has he offended you in some way? I'll have a talk with him if—"

"No," she said quickly. Oh, Lord, what was she to say? "No. Don't do that. You know McKaid. McKaid is—just McKaid." She looked away quickly, damning the heat rising in her cheeks.

"He's a good man, you know. You couldn't do any better."

Her eyes snapped around to meet his. In what way couldn't she do better? "I'm not sure I know what you mean," she said hesitantly.

"You're a clever woman, Elizabeth," he said, inwardly grinning at her flustered state.

"Are you suggesting that . . . But . . ." She jumped up and began inspecting books.

"I'm not suggesting anything," he said.

She wasn't fooled by his insouciant manner. "The heck you aren't," she retorted, her amber eyes stabbing at him from across the room.

So much fire buried under that cool exterior. He shrugged. "Maybe I am."

"Why? And aren't you forgetting Lenore?"

"Lenore?" he asked stupidly.

"Oh, really, Uncle Clint. You can't be that blind. He's smitten with her. They were practically inseparable the whole time she was here. And you saw the way he treated me when she was around." That may be true, but it was those other times that had her worried. How could he kiss her, touch her, look at her as he had, if he loved Lenore? How could he be so unfaithful to his betrothed, unless he was the sort of rake who wanted a wife and any other woman he could seduce as well. She couldn't accept that McKaid was like that, which left her more confused.

"Men have always proclaimed women to be odd and bewildering creatures, but I've seen more than my share of strange behavior in men as well."

"In McKaid? Do be serious," she said facetiously. "Besides we're already family. How can you even think . . ."

He didn't answer that, but he stopped her with a lifted eyebrow, the same look she used on the children when they tried to get away with mischief.

"Oh, this is ridiculous. I'm not listening to anymore." She stalked to the door, but couldn't make herself open it. Slowly she turned to face her uncle. "Why?" she asked again.

"Why not? You said you love the ranch and those two kids. I just thought I'd let you know that if you want to take on McKaid as well, you have my blessing."

She gave a soft snort. "I'm not sure I want your blessing, and I'm not at all sure I want anything to do with your strange and temperamental nephew." With that parting shot she did open the door and walk out, but only to hear his low chuckle following her all the way to the kitchen like the mocking laughter in her own head.

Emma was kneading another batch of bread, and Elizabeth washed her hands and took over. "Let me do that. I need something to drive—my—fist into right—now."

Emma backed a safe distance away. "Who put the burr under *your* saddle blanket?"

"I don't want to discuss it."

She'd just begun to regain her composure when McKaid and the children came in. The door slammed after them.

"Are we having lessons this afternoon?" James asked, snitching a cookie from the cookie crock.

156

"No. Go play. You have a day off."

"Oh, boy." James beamed. "Come on, Ruthie. Let's play in the tree house."

Ruthie, always sensitive to people's feelings, looked at Elizabeth uncertainly, then swung her apprehensive eyes to McKaid.

"It's all right, muffin," McKaid said. "Go on." When Ruthie had followed her brother out of the house, Elizabeth let out her pent-up breath and pressed the back of her hand to her forehead. She had to get a grip on herself. She felt as if she were flying off in a dozen different directions—hither, thither, to and fro, near and yon.

"Headache?" McKaid asked.

"No." She started forming the kneaded bread dough into loaves, rather forcefully for the good of the loaves.

"You sure?"

"I'm all right," she snapped irritably.

"You don't look all right, and you've been on edge ever since—"

"Leave me alone, McKaid," she gritted through her teeth.

"Ho, ho. Don't tell me our sedate spinster schoolmarm is having a temper tantrum." He clucked his tongue. "You don't suppose there's a real live woman under all that starch, do you, Emma, me darlin'. Who would have thought. And taking it out on the bread, no less."

Without pausing to consider what she was doing, she hurled the ball of dough at him. She watched, horrified, as he deftly dodged to the left, and the dough splatted on the wall and thumped to the floor inches from Clint's foot.

"Uncle Clint," she cried, mortified.

"Was that intended for me, my dear?" Clint asked drolly. He stooped to pick up the squashed dough and strolled on into the kitchen.

"Let me have that," Emma said. "I'll see if I can salvage it. Flour is expensive these days, but I'd gladly give up bread for a week to have seen this hit its mark."

McKaid, grinning widely, stuffed his thumbs in his back pockets and rocked back on his heels. "Ah, shucks, Emma. You don't mean that."

"Don't I? You've been giving this poor lamb the dickens ever since she came here. If I had my way . . ."

157

"Stop it," Elizabeth cried. "Just—stop it." She turned and slammed out the back door, racing for the stables.

She met a few of the men coming off the range and leading their animals toward the corral. She appropriated one of their horses, and unmindful of the amount of leg she showed as she mounted with her voluminous skirts hitched above her knees, she kicked the horse into a gallop and headed south, anywhere away from that house and those two infuriating men.

"Hey, wait," one of the cowboys called to her. "You can't go riding off alone like that. It ain't safe."

"That danged horse ain't half tamed yet, either," another yelled.

"Jee-zus H. We better tell McKaid."

"What's the problem?" Russ called to them from the stables where he was reshoeing his own mount. "Why all the yellin'?"

"It's Miss Elizabeth, boss. She took my horse and rode out of here."

"I'll go after her," Russ said. "Let me have your horse, Cal, and you better tell McKaid that I'll be with her, in the off chance he's even interested."

Russ rode hard, following the cloud of dust kicked up as Elizabeth raced across the valley floor. This was probably McKaid's doing again, he thought. He'd caused Miss Elizabeth no end of grief, and then he was always sidling up real cozylike to Lenore. For two bits, he'd punch the bastard in the jaw.

"Ho. Wait up there, gal," he yelled as he closed the gap between them.

Elizabeth looked around. If it had been anyone but Russ following her, she would not have stopped. As it was, she wouldn't mind Russ's company. Right now she needed his calming influence. He made her laugh, he made her feel good about herself again.

"Hey, you okay?" he asked, taking hold of her horse's bridle.

"Yes, Russ. I just needed to get away before I threw something deadlier than a ball of bread dough."

"Beg your pardon?" he said, laughing.

"It doesn't matter. I didn't hit him," she said disgustedly.

"Let me guess. McKaid?"

"Honestly, sometimes he gets me so angry I think I'm going to explode."

Russ chuckled lowly. "Maybe you should. It's not always good to hold your feelings in such a tight fist. You gotta let 'em out."

"What do you suggest—that I scream my head off?"

"That sounds as good a way as any. Why not?" he said challengingly.

She did it. She opened her mouth and let out a grinding scream that released all the pent-up anger and frustration that she'd been tamping down for days.

She didn't hear the eerie echo that returned from the high bluffs on their west, for when her piercing cry emerged so spontaneously from her throat, her horse reared up and came down hard on all fours. She felt the reins slide from her fingers, and at the same instant felt herself falling. She made one last grab for the saddle, but it was too late.

Russ dismounted, steadied the horses, then squatted down to Elizabeth. "Are you hurt?"

"Only my pride, and my backside." She grinned ironically. "So much for screaming my head off." She looked up at Russ, and they both sputtered then broke into laughter.

"You did it beautifully," he praised her. "They probably heard you clean back at the ranch."

"Oh, no."

He pulled her to her feet and dusted her off. "I'd bet my horse McKaid's on his way now."

"Hah. If so, it's only to yell at me again. I don't care. It was worth it."

"You feel better?"

"Infinitely. Except . . ." She cleared her throat. "I think I ruined my voice. You're fun to be with, Russ Packard."

He laid his hands on top of her shoulders and looked down at her with his laughing brown eyes. "So are you. If I weren't already in love, I'd be tempted to . . ."

"You're in love? That's wonderful. Who's the lucky lady?"

"Never mind that." He blushed faintly and turned away. "It can't work anyway. Let's start back."

They rode side by side in silence. Elizabeth's mind raced with questions. Who was the woman and why couldn't it work? Was she already married or promised? Had she left the area? Did she not return his love? But he had said no more, and she was too well mannered to pry for an answer. It was disheartening that they were both doomed to suffer through loving the wrong people.

"Brace yourself, Miss Elizabeth. Here comes Ranger McKaid, and he doesn't look happy."

She harumphed. "Does he ever?"

"But you still love him." It was more a statement than a question.

She shrugged and grinned crookedly. She wasn't surprised that Russ had guessed. He knew her very well. "I thought I was in love once before, but it was so easy then. Not at all like this."

"Love is a violent emotion and very often painful. It's rarely easy to love someone wholeheartedly."

"Are you a romantic, Russ?" she teased.

"No more than you. Neither of us wants the world to know, do we?"

He had surprising insight. Innately she was a romantic. She did dream of a forever kind of love, a passionate love, a home, and a family. It took loving McKaid to make her admit it though, to dig down deep inside to where she'd buried her dreams and bring them to the surface again. Now they were dusted and polished from all the times she toyed with them. Yes, she had her dreams. Much good as they'd do her.

"What a hopelessly pitiful pair we are," she said dramatically.

"Pathetic," he agreed, and they both laughed.

McKaid had stopped some distance from the two riders and watched furiously as they approached. Why couldn't she be as relaxed with him as she was with Russ? Why couldn't she laugh freely with him the way she was doing now? Why did she hold herself so apart and so aloof, ignoring him most of the time, as if he were some spectre she could see right through? He didn't want her to ignore him.

"I see I wasted a trip coming after you," he said shortly when Russ and Elizabeth reached his side. He swung his horse around to keep pace with theirs.

"Didn't Cal tell you I came with her?" Russ asked.

"Yes, but we heard her scream. What happened?"

"Nothing," Elizabeth answered quickly.

"Then why scream?" he demanded, irritated.

"Why not?"

McKaid's brow cocked curiously when he heard Russ's deep chuckle, but he let the subject drop. He wasn't sure he could control his temper if he pursued it. She'd taken a year off his life when she'd screamed. His stomach had twisted into a cold hard knot, and he felt a chilling sweat break out on his skin, head to toe. And for what? A "why not?" And how could she look so carefree when his insides were still churning and curdling?

Chapter Ten

McKaid lay wide awake for hours that night, listening to the lonely sounds in the valley. Sounds that mirrored his own state of mind, like the solitary owl that hooted and the coyote that called in the distance, then called again, beckoning for an answer from another of its kind. The night was warm and unusually still, a sure sign of a coming storm. What was one more storm, more or less. His whole life had been a tempest since Elizabeth rode into it.

What was he to do about her? He couldn't be without her, he couldn't be around her. There was no answer that he could see. He'd been furious when he'd found her laughing together with Russ. He'd lashed out again, upsetting her all the more. And Russ was disgusted.

She'd been very quiet that evening. She ate in her room, she refused to come out even to put the children to bed.

"Something has to give," he said into the night. He was terribly afraid it would be him.

He threw off the light blanket and got out of bed, deciding to go outside for a smoke. He pulled on his trousers and slid his feet into a pair of leather moccasins. As he reached for his smoking material, he heard a whimpering cry come from the next room where the children slept. It would be Ruthie.

Emma's room was off the kitchen, so she wouldn't hear the child, and Clint could sleep through a cyclone. The only one who would possibly hear the muffled crying was Elizabeth. He didn't want her awake. He had enough trouble knowing she was asleep across the hall. Quietly he left his room and went to the children's room. He knelt beside the bed and smoothed his hand over Ruthie's tousled hair. She had so many disturbed nights.

"Ruthie. Wake up, honey."

She quieted for a moment, then opened her eyes. When she saw McKaid, she leaned up and threw her arms around his neck.

"Was it another bad dream, sweetheart?"

She nodded and burrowed into his warm arms. He lifted her small body and settled into the rockingchair with her as he'd done countless times in the last months.

"It's all right now. Go back to sleep."

"She won't go away, will she?" Ruthie asked, her little girl's voice trembling against his neck.

He looked down at her. "Who, muffin?"

"Miss Elizabeth."

"Is that what you were dreaming about?"

Again she nodded. "Is she angry with us? Doesn't she like us anymore? I promise to work harder on my sums."

"She's not going anywhere. She told me she wanted to stay here with us. And I'm sure she loves you just as much as I do."

"I heard her crying. I thought . . ."

"When was she crying?"

"When you took Mrs. Beaumont home and didn't come back till the next day."

"I see." His emotions took a wild leap, then settled into a weary despair. He cautioned himself that it made no difference how she felt, how either of them felt. The situation and his ticklish conscience wouldn't permit him to go beyond their present impasse.

"Mr. McKaid, what does adopted mean?"

"Adopted? Well, it's like with you and me. Your mommy and daddy died, so I adopted you. I made you my children. There's nothing wrong with that."

"No. I'm glad you took us. You're nice."

"Why did you ask?"

"I thought it was what made Miss Elizabeth so sad. Uncle Clint said she was adopted. He didn't mean for us to hear, and he wouldn't tell us what it meant, and I thought it was a bad thing. But it isn't, is it, so it couldn't be why she's not happy anymore."

"Wait a minute." He sat her up on his lap so he could look at her. His mind was reeling. "Say that again."

"What?"

"About Elizabeth being adopted. Clint said that? When?"

"Emma said she thought Miss Elizabeth was sweet on you, and I don't remember what else. Then Uncle Clint said Miss Elizabeth was adopted. We asked what that was, but they made us go outside to play. Why didn't he tell us it's not a bad thing?"

McKaid was having trouble drawing a straight breath. He felt as if he'd been punched in the stomach. Why hadn't Clint told him? Why hadn't Lizzie said anything? Relief and outrage struggled to see which would prevail. At least he didn't feel so damn guilty anymore for all those crazy fantasies, but what kind of dirty game were they playing?

"Mr. McKaid, does that mean Miss Elizabeth's mother and father died, too? She's just like us?"

He looked down at her and smiled gently. "Yes. That's what it means." And that's why she'd come out to New Mexico to take care of James and Ruthie. Hadn't she said on the way to the ranch that it was the least she could do to repay a kindness. It hadn't made any sense to him at the time, but it did now.

"Can you sleep now, kitten?"

He tucked her back into bed, kissed her forehead, and left the room. He stood in the dark hallway, listening to the hall clock tick away the minutes, his emotions raging in his breast. His overwhelming relief gave way to resentment. Did everyone know except him? What a fool he'd been. Resentment turned to anger, to the memory of days and nights when he dared not touch her as he wanted, when he could only dream and imagine and curse the damned irony of a Fate who'd let him again love a woman he wasn't going to be permitted to have.

Why hadn't she told him?

Finally his anger and frustration won out, and he took the long steps that led to her door. Careless of the noise that might disturb others of the household, he threw open her door and strode to the side of her bed.

His breath whispered from his lungs, leaving a vast empty space that was filled with the heavy swelling of his thudding heart. She was more beautiful, more tempting and desirable than he'd ever imagined.

Her arms were thrown wantonly over her head across the spill of her long hair. Her sheer, white ruffled nightdress was opened at the neck as if she'd clawed it away from her body, freeing her from the heat of the night. The gentle curve of one

165

glorious breast was exposed almost to the darker rosy circle of her nipple. A little tug and his eyes could drink in the sight of her that he'd so thirsted for.

The hem of her gown had bunched up around her hips, covering those woman's secrets, but leaving the length of long, subtly molded legs exposed to the cooling air. One leg lay fully extended, the other bent outward at the knee in an unconscious invitation.

His masculine parts began to throb unbearably at the sight of her. She was covered, kept hidden from view, but a more provocative sight he'd never seen.

His hand went out to touch her, but with a grunt of actual physical pain, he pulled it back. He had not come into her room for that, he had come for straight answers. He had come to make certain she knew how detestable he found her little games. He'd come because, in a strange way, he felt she had betrayed him, and he wanted revenge for that. She made him love her, all the while making a fool of him.

Some small sound, some disturbing presence in her room, some movement at her side roused Elizabeth from her sleep. She opened her eyes to see the shadowy form of a man, a man she'd know anywhere.

"McKaid?" she said. She knifed to a sitting position and jerked her flimsy gown over her legs. "What's wrong? What are you . . ."

As her eyes adjusted, her voice wavered and died. He was naked to the waist. He was standing beside her bed—her bed—with almost nothing on. And he was beautiful. His skin glistened with a fine sheen of moisture. The moonlight brought the masculine lines of his body into sharp relief. His tanned skin was a deeper shade of bronze, stretched over a rippling musculature. His dark hair blacker. She remembered the feel of that hair. Coarse, springy silk. He made her head spin.

She'd seen his broad bare shoulders, his muscle-layered arms. She'd even touched him. But he'd been hurt, bandaged, safe. He stood now, all dominating man, his legs slightly spread, his hands on his hips where his low-riding pants clung, defying the forces of gravity.

He was well. No bandages, no stitches, no headache.

The tension stretched between them, as strained as a tightwire, and Elizabeth felt herself poised on that tightrope,

166

trying to keep her faltering balance, trying to keep from reaching out to steady herself against that rock hard chest. But to touch him would be to lose her balance completely.

A slow heat began to invade her feminine body, unfurling, billowing, swelling, until she was flushed from head to toe. She searched his face, shrouded in shadows, trying to read the sharp angles and planes. Why had he come? Why was he simply standing there staring at her?

When he spoke, his voice was pure ice. "Get up."

"McKaid?" she said questioningly, her ardor dying an instant death. Her previously overheated body shivered.

He reached out and his hand clamped like a manacle around her arm. Effortlessly he drew her off the bed and toward the door.

"What are you doing, McKaid," she whispered hoarsely. "Wait a minute. My shoes."

He said nothing, only stopped long enough to let her slip her feet into her impractical city slippers, then hauled her with him out the door, down the stairs, and out into the night.

"What's going on? For the love of heaven, McKaid—"

"Quiet," he silenced her. "I don't want the whole ranch in on this."

"On what?" she demanded as she was pulled with him past the well house, the bake oven, the smoke house, the root cellar. He didn't answer, and she knew he wouldn't. Not until he was good and ready.

At the back of the barn he opened a narrow door and led her inside, locking the door behind them. The room was pitch black and smelled of linseed oil and leather. He dropped her arm and left her. She shivered again, though not from cold.

She heard him fumbling with something, then a match flared and a lamp was lit. She glanced around at the workbench of tools, the bridles, saddle parts, halters, broken harnesses hanging on the walls. In the corner was a low bunk, and beside it a small table with an old leather-bound book lying beside the lamp.

"Whose room is this?" she heard herself ask.

McKaid turned to face her. His eyes, she saw by the orange glow of the dirty lamp, were coldy angry, turning his angled face into a macabre mask. "You lied to me," he said through stiff lips.

167

She gasped. Her mouth opened to protest, but no words would come out. Lied? Mutely, she shook her head, and took a tentative step backward from the menace of his glaring eyes and intimidating stance. Lied? She shook her head again.

He closed the distance between them in two long strides and clamped his hands around her shoulders, dragging her close to his smouldering glower.

"Why?" he ground out, strong, hard fingers digging painfully into her soft flesh. "Have you any idea of the torment, the agony you've put me through? All for a sick joke. Or was it to get even for the way I kissed you in front of Bert and Amos?"

"McKaid," she said, caught helplessly in his grasp. "I don't know what you're talking about. Please, I really don't."

"I had you up on a pedestal. You were my brave, compassionate angel, my prickly little virgin. Or did you lie about that, too?"

"No. I never lied."

"Never? Then I'll have to confess to you that I'm a hopeless degenerate, because I've thought of nothing these last weeks but making long, passionate love to my own cousin. Do you know what that's done to my sanity, my self-respect, my peace of mind?"

"Oh, no," she breathed in an outward groan. Her eyes dropped, and she pulled against his restraining hands.

"Look at you. You look as guilty as sin. As guilty as I felt."

"No," she said sharply, finding some of her spirit. "I'm not guilty. I didn't know how you felt. How could I? All you ever do is yell."

"Because you're so damned indifferent. I ache for you, but you look at me and see right through me. Yes, I yell. The only time you react to me is when I can make you fight back."

Her mind tried desperately to sort out what she was hearing. She knew she was awake, but it was like a confusing dream. All this time, so much effort to hide her own feelings, when all along he . . .

"Why?" he demanded again.

She looked up into his eyes. They weren't quite so fierce now, rather they seemed to be begging her for an explanation.

"I didn't know what Clint had told you. First you acted as if you didn't know, then you kissed me again, and I thought you

168

surely must. Then I wasn't sure again."

"Why didn't you just tell me you weren't really my cousin?"

"Because Lenore came, and I thought it didn't make any difference anyway. I thought you and she . . ." Her own anger surfaced at how much she'd suffered in her own way. "How can you say you want me, if you're going to marry her? And don't accuse me of not seeing you. I didn't even exist when she was in the room."

His eyes widened incredulously, then frowned. "That's not true, and you know it. None of it. I know where you are every minute of the day. And don't think there haven't been a few times I wanted to strangle you. When I saw you kiss Russ, when he could touch you and I didn't dare, when you laughed with him then scowled at me. I've half a mind to boot him off the ranch."

"You're jealous," she crowed.

"Dammit, yes. I'm obsessed with you." He released her and ran his hands through his hair. His stomach was tied in knots. He was obsessed. Bewitched. He didn't know if he could believe her or not, yet he still wanted her so badly he hurt with it. Never had he felt like this about another woman.

"You could have told me," he persisted doggedly.

"Yes. But how? The subject never came up," she answered reasonably, studying the assorted paraphernalia hanging on the wall. "I couldn't just come up to you and say it. How would that sound? 'By the way, McKaid, in case you're interested in a little dalliance before you get married, I'm not really your cousin.'"

He crooked his finger under her chin and tilted her face up to his. His lips twitched into his crooked grin, making her heart tumble over in her breast. "That does sound a bit forward, Lizzie, love," he teased. His mockery was back, but with it came a look so intensely male that she was left speechless. "Did you really think about making love with me?"

She wanted to look away, to hide from his probing eyes, but he wouldn't permit it. He was after the truth, he demanded it with his every essence, and she couldn't lie.

"All the time. I didn't want you to know." She felt very vulnerable, very exposed, and it frightened her. But it also felt good to finally admit it, to be open and candid with her feelings, instead of struggling to keep up an impassive front.

He brushed the back of his knuckles across her cheek, down her slender neck, and over the pert tip of one of her breasts, and watched in fascination as her whole body responded to his touch. She gave a little gasp of surprise, then relaxed. Her body of its own accord leaned into his hand.

"And now? Do you want to make love now?"

"I'm scared," she admitted breathlessly.

He smiled gently. "You won't be for long." Slowly he drew her into his warm embrace. Just as slowly his lips covered her own.

For all his gentleness, his kisses were an assault on her senses more powerful than if he'd ravaged her. He held her tenderly, he cupped the back of her head caressingly, and laid kisses as soft as rose petals on her eyes, her nose, her cheeks. Her whole body melted and flowed into his masterful hands.

His lips brushed hers tantalizingly, tempting but not satisfying. He nibbled at her lips, he teased with the flicking tip of his tongue. His warm breath mixed with her own.

She felt her head begin to spin. She wanted him to kiss her as he had the first time, wildly and forcefully. She wanted him to crush her in his strong arms. She dug her nails into his shoulders and coaxed him closer, but still he resisted.

"Are you afraid now?" he asked, lips against lips.

"No." She was, only she feared now that he would stop. "Kiss me, McKaid. A real kiss."

"If I kiss you the way I want to, I won't be able to stop. Do you understand?"

A wild, wanton flame of desire leaped to life at his seductive words. She didn't want him to stop, she knew that. For the first time in her life she didn't want to consider what was proper, reasonable, right or wrong. She wanted what she wanted. She wanted this moment. She wanted McKaid.

"Don't stop," she answered. "I don't want you to stop."

"Why?"

More soft kisses rained over her face, down her neck. "I want to belong to you."

"Why?"

"McKaid . . ."

"Why?"

He wanted all of her, she realized. He wanted the words that

170

would remove the last of her protection. He wanted absolute possession, total commitment, complete surrender. Did she trust him enough to give him so much of herself? Foolish thought. He had it already.

"I love you," she confessed honestly.

She had what she longed for and more. His arms tightened convulsively, pressing her fully into his hard body, and his mouth claimed hers in kiss after kiss that demanded all she had and left her weak and shaking in his arms.

With fingers not quite steady he stood her away from him and untied the bows at the front of her gown. Very slowly, letting his fingers trail over her sensitive shoulders, he pushed the loose garment aside until it slid from her body.

Instinctively she wanted to cover herself again, but McKaid's eyes prevented her. She could feel them on her flesh. They had warm, velvet fingers of their own, touching and caressing.

Gradually she began to relax, and as she did, her breathing slowed and deepened, and her blood began to roll like hot honey through her veins. Her breasts seemed to fill and grow weighty, and her body to swell with a deep heavy ache. He was here with her. His hands were on her shoulders, his eyes on her body. This was no dream. She closed her eyes and let her head fall backward. He was going to make love to her. Her whole body opened to him in urgent invitation. It was shamelessly erotic, this power of the flesh. Erotic, and beautiful, and with McKaid it was so right.

"God," McKaid groaned and scooped her into his arms. His mouth came down on hers again and didn't release her until they were both lying together on the narrow bunk.

"You are unbelievably beautiful," he murmured against her lips and kissed her again, taking possession of the sweet warm cavern she offered so freely. His hands, hot and callused, traveled from her shoulder to her thigh, exploring, cupping, loving. He wasn't gentle, neither was he rough. He knew just where to touch her and how. He knew without being told what words she needed to hear. He was all experience to her innocence, and she gave herself into his expert care.

His lips and tongue trailed hot kisses down her neck, to the edge of her ivory shoulder and back. Slowly, maddeningly, he moved to her waiting breasts.

171

Don't rush her, he warned himself repeatedly. Take it slow. Very slow. She was eager and responsive, and he wanted to please her. He wanted her first time to be unforgettable. He wanted her to like it, because he knew for a certainty he'd never get enough of her. But he didn't know how much more he could take. He was on the verge of losing any control he ever had. He felt like a young kid again with his first woman.

He flicked his tongue over the hard swollen center of her rounded breast. Once, twice. Then he moved to plant tender kisses on the warm velvety mound around it.

Elizabeth buried her fingers in his thick, dark hair, urging him back to her expectant breast. Her body pressed upward against his, wanting more, needing more, reaching for she knew not what. She was burning up inside, and that empty ache was growing larger, more demanding. Why didn't he hurry. Why was he tormenting her so.

She pulled his head down to her breast. "Please, McKaid," she groaned.

He chuckled deep in his throat. "In a hurry, are we?" he teased, but turned his ardent attention back to the swollen, hard nipple standing so erect for him. He saw no need to keep her waiting when he was just as impatient as she. His heart and his body soared with anticipation at the knowledge that she wanted him.

Elizabeth was whirling on a plane of pure sensation. Her body, flesh she had known so well and controlled so effortlessly, was foreign to her. Her mother had taught her the facts about a woman's body, her father had explained what happened with a man. Both had said there would come a time when passion would be natural and right. Neither had prepared her for the awesome and overpowering changes taking place inside her, or the ravenous hunger that was consuming her.

Every secret place McKaid touched cried out for more of him. His lips, torturing her breasts, drew soft whimpers of need from her throat and arched her body into his roaming hands. When he finally took one hard nipple into his mouth, she thought she surely must die of the pleasure. Ecstatic curents of shock rocked through her body as he drew on her, nibbled, laved his tongue over her sensitive flesh. From one taut peak to the other he moved, and back and forth again, covering the warm satin valley between with hot open kisses. She cried out

172

his name and held on tightly as he devastated her senses.

He felt so wonderful in her arms. For an eternity of days and nights she'd longed to hold him, touch him, kiss him. Now her hands were full of him, sliding possessively over his broad back, down his taut-muscled arms, back into his thick hair.

And that voice, that wonderfully male voice that had often teased, mocked, yelled at her, was filling her head with dark, velvety words of praise and adoration, of need and desire. She loved him so much, and she was drowning in his passion. It was glorious, but it was not enough. She wanted more. She wanted it all.

"McKaid," she said his name softly, lifting his face to hers. "Could you—uh—I want to feel all of you against me."

His nostrils flared and he drew a harsh breath. "I won't be able to control myself," he warned. She only smiled.

He rolled to his side and removed his trousers, the only barrier between them. She gave him only enough time to kick the offending garment aside before she urged him back to her, pressing her body into his.

Her soft cries and sighs and her sinuous movements against his aroused maleness nearly drove him crazy. McKaid was stunned by the depths of her reactions. He'd thought her responsive when he'd kissed her before, he'd seen a glimmer of her sensuous nature, but he never expected such a generous wealth of passion. She was giving everything she had to him. Him. He didn't deserve it, but how could he resist what his lonely heart had longed for, for so many years.

Love, warmth, passion, caring. A woman of courage and strength and spirit. She was everything he'd ever wanted, and more. He knew he was being selfish. He should be thinking of her safety, her future and happiness. Could he guarantee her any of that?

Brutally he shoved the questions away. He was a lawman, yes, but he was a man, too. Didn't he have the right to love, a home, a family. Didn't he have just as much right as any other man to reach out for what was good and bright and shiny in life. Well, he was reaching now. He intended to have this woman, and to cherish her, and to keep her for as long as was humanly possible. And he'd fight anyone or anything that threatened to take her away.

He kissed her then, and it was a kiss that demanded her soul.

She knew his patience was gone. He'd been so careful with her, so considerate of her innocence, but she'd driven him beyond that with her own seductions. He was all man now, staking his claim, taking his woman, and he was all the more thrilling for it.

His tongue filled her mouth, mating with hers in a rhythmic movement older than the ages. It was all excitingly new to her, but she wasn't frightened. What he wanted she gave freely, and gloried in the wondrous pleasure he gave in return.

His mouth took hers almost savagely, demanding more and more of her, and his hands ran feverishly over her body, stopping to knead and mold her breasts, to roll the hardened tips between fingers and thumb. Elizabeth felt herself spiraling downward and downward into a deep dark vortex of desire. Her body felt heavy and insatiable with a raging hunger to be touched, to touch, to join, to mate with her lover. The throbbing ache between her thighs became an unbearable pain. Restlessly she twisted and arched against him, searching for, begging for relief.

McKaid placed his hand under her hips and drew her hard against that tumescent length of his arousal. She was wild in his arms. No passive lover this. He'd never wanted a woman more in his life. His whole body was pulsing with his need of her.

His lips left hers and trailed again to those pert breasts that she was pressing against his chest. His lips closed over one tip and he drew it firmly into his mouth. At the same time his hand slid around her hip and cupped her womanhood. She writhed against him and cried his name with such longing that he could wait no longer.

She was hot. So very hot. And ready for him. Parting her legs, he settled his weight against her. "I love you, Lizzie," he said and kissed her wildly. With one sure stroke he entered her, quickly, without hesitation, releasing her from her innocence and her virginity. She was a woman now. His woman. He groaned in sheer ecstasy.

He held her tightly in his arms as he buried his body in the hot, tight sheath of her femininity. Her head thrashed backward, exposing the long column of her delicate neck. He lowered his head and buried his face there, kissing, nibbling, fighting to regain his control. It was a difficult task when her

174

silken legs were tightening around his flanks, when her fingers were clutching at his shoulders, when her tiny cries of pleasure were echoing in his ears.

Elizabeth had for so long been in such a state of frenzy that the pain of his entrance was sweet bliss. He was in her, the full swollen length of him filling the innermost part of her. The deep ache she'd felt was abating, and something far more rapturous was taking hold of her senses. A bud of tingling warmth was blossoming deep inside and spreading outward to all her limbs. She was floating free of the world, yet she wanted to stay, to be with McKaid.

"Are you all right?" his deep voice asked, washing over her like a sweet warm breeze.

She tightened her legs and moved beneath him, moved to get closer, to take more of him into her being. "I don't know. I feel so . . . so strange."

"I know. I know. Let it happen, Lizzie. I'll be with you. I'll be right here."

He lowered his lips to hers and kissed her with so much love she thought her heart would burst. Then very slowly he began to move, and she stopped thinking altogether. Slowly at first, and then more forcefully, he taught her the exquisite art of loving, and with each filling stroke took her higher and higher into a realm of carnal pleasure where the only reality was the two of them joined together as one.

Elizabeth could do no more than hold on to McKaid and go where he was taking her. Her body was no longer her own. He controlled her, leading her further and further from this narrow and mundane world. The more he gave, the more she wanted. The more he demanded, the more she gave. Onward and onward he drove her until in one shimmering moment all her senses, all her energy, and all her nerves seemed to focus in one rapturous spot deep within her womb.

McKaid's head was spinning. His mind and body were full of her, the feel of her flesh fused with his, the heady scent of her, the taste of her, the uninhibited responses of her untutored body. He wanted to possess her totally and for all time. And in a very human and masculine way, he wanted to plant an indestructible part of himself deep inside her, to mark her so all the world would know she belonged to him.

His skin prickled from head to toe and a film of perspiration covered his body. He could feel the tingling heat gathering in his loins. It was at that same moment he heard Elizabeth cry out and felt her body still, then begin to contract in powerful pulses around him.

"Yes," he cried, for he too was lost to any restraint. They held tightly to each other as their individual worlds came apart in shattering splendor. Free of the world, they soared together, their bodies glorying in the act of love, in the final climactic transcendance. Slowly, as their worlds righted again, as reality once more intruded on their rhapsody, their eyes locked.

"He's part of me, now and forever," she thought in wonder.

"I'll never give her up," he vowed in his love.

Chapter Eleven

For long silent moments they lay still, closely entwined, hearts beating as one. Finally a tear, two tears, a flood of tears rushed down Elizabeth's cheeks and onto McKaid's shoulder.

Alarmed, he propped himself up and looked down into her face. "Tears. Did I hurt you?"

"I'm sorry, McKaid. It's silly of me to cry when I'm so happy. It was so beautiful."

His frown disappeared, and his cocky grin peeped out. "I told you I was at my best in bed." Gently he wiped her face, kissing the damp trail of her tears.

"McKaid," she chided, "you're a rake." Then she pulled him back so she could snuggle in the peaceful aftermath of their loving. He complied, wrapping his arms securely around her, fondling her hair, brushing her forehead with little kisses.

She ran her fingers through the crisp hair on his chest. "Your heart is still hammering," she said, letting her fingers rest against his breast.

"I don't wonder. I've never experienced anything quite like that. You take my breath away."

"I was concerned, you know. I don't know what I'm supposed to do. Will you teach me, McKaid? I want to know everything I should know to make you happy."

"Right now? Have some mercy."

"Hmmm. Perhaps I should have a look at those references you offered me once. I'm fresh and new at this. Maybe you're old and worn out already."

"I'll show you worn out, you wretch," he growled, pinning her to the bed and tickling her.

"No, don't. Anything but that. Please, McKaid."

"Take it back?"

"Take what back?" she asked innocently, laughing and squirming against his marauding fingers.

He tickled her more. "Have it your way then."

"Wait. Stop. Truce, okay?"

"Truce? You don't just call truce when you please. Take it back."

"Okay. I take it back. Satisfied?"

He rolled to his side, grinning devilishly. "Only temporarily," he answered.

She scowled at him. "What do you mean by . . . Oooh. Maybe you're not so worn out."

"I'm not old either. Not much older than you."

"That's just in years. In experience, I feel like a mere child next to you."

"Lord, woman," he groaned. "I just got over being your cousin. Don't have me seducing schoolgirls now."

She laughed. "Poor McKaid. If I'd known what you thought, I could have turned the tables on you but good."

"Was I that hard on you?"

"Yes."

Both listened to the cry of the owl high overhead somewhere in the rafters of the barn, both lost to thoughts of their own. Elizabeth remembered Lenore and felt sorry for her, though she couldn't begin to think of giving McKaid up. She wondered how he was going to handle that situation. She decided to ask. It was better than worrying.

"What will you tell Lenore?"

"Why should I tell her anything?"

"Don't you think she has a right to know?"

McKaid came up on one elbow again. "What are you getting at? What's Lenore got to do with you and me?"

Elizabeth frowned. "I thought you . . . Well, isn't she in love with you?"

"She's in love, all right, but not with me. Wait a minute. You don't mean to say you really thought Lenore and I . . ." His lips twitched humorously.

"What's so funny, and don't you dare laugh. I was insanely jealous."

"Don't worry about Lenore. She wouldn't have me. She thinks I'm not quite civilized."

"Why? Because you live by your guns and your wits, with a

178

good horse thrown in for luck?" It was a line out of *Desert Sunset*, but it seemed to fit.

He laughed. "Among other things. I kissed her once. I scared the wits out of her."

"Did you plant one of your Ranger Dash Darling McKaid specials on her by any chance?"

His smirk was unrepentent. "It didn't scare you."

"But then I knew you were an uncivilized brute before you took all those liberties with my body."

"I only kissed you," he protested defensively.

"It was more than a kiss and you know it. It was a deliberate challenge."

"You were altogether too—unruffled. I was more shook up than you were, and it wasn't right. Accusing me with your nose in the air. You needed to be set down a peg or two."

She grinned, remembering. "Did Lenore?"

"No. She was just so jumpy around me that I thought if I simply kissed her and got it over with, she'd relax."

"Did she?"

"Hell, no. She went home and I didn't see her again for months. By then we'd both decided we'd make better friends than lovers."

Elizabeth clucked her tongue. "Such charm. Who is she in love with, then?"

"This might surprise you. Russ Packard." He rolled to his back and placed one arm under his head, watching her reaction out of the corner of his eyes.

It was Elizabeth's turn to leap up. "Russ? Oh, no. But he said he was in love with some . . . Who is he in love with? Lenore?" Of course. He'd asked enough questions about her at any rate. How had she missed it?

McKaid slanted a dark look her way. "You had us all pretty worried for a while. Especially Lenore."

"All?" she asked. Then she remembered the scowls, the shocked silences, the glances that passed between them all. And McKaid's temper. "I see. You, too?"

"I was ready to wring your neck."

"I remember that," she said, nodding. "Wouldn't it have been easier to tell me?"

"I couldn't. You were still my cousin then, and despite what I felt personally, you deserved a chance to find someone to love. And who better than Russ. But between my loyalty to

Lenore, my duty to you, and my own desire, I was coming apart at the seams."

"I remember that, too," she said, and they both fell quiet again.

"Lizzie, we need to talk about what's happened between us."

"Okay," she said absently. "McKaid, if they love each other, why haven't they . . . why are they . . ."

Turning his gaze toward the ceiling, he searched for that answer. "I don't know. Neither does Lenore. That's why she was so worried about you. Russ never took her riding. He never went for long walks with her."

"He was only standing in for you. He's the next man in the status order around here. He felt it was his duty in the circumstances."

"Status order? Ah, yes. My grandfather's idea, that."

"Russ said, when we both thought you and Lenore were going to be married, that at least she'd be getting someone worthy of her. I think he feels he's not in that category."

"Russ? He'd be perfect for her. He's fond of old Beaumont, and he could run that ranch with his hands tied behind his back."

"Then why don't you talk to him?"

"Some things a man has to decide for himself, Lizzie. He's the type of man who would want to take care of a woman. He'll have to come to grips with Lenore's wealth before he can make a commitment to her. Talking to him now would embarrass him. Best to stay out of it."

Elizabeth thought about that. Russ appeared to be level-headed and reasonable, sure of himself and his work. Could something so seemingly insignificant really be standing in his way? Men were strange creatures indeed. Uncle Clint was right about that.

Poor Lenore. Elizabeth knew the agony of wanting a man who she thought didn't want her. How much longer Lenore had suffered that painful knowledge, false though it was.

Lenore was a beautiful, charming, and sensitive woman. She was also clever and persistent if her frequent surreptitious visits to the Circle K were any indication.

But Russ was obviously a proud man under his gentle manner, and far too noble and self-sacrificing for his own good. He must love Lenore a great deal to be willing to step aside for another man he thought more suitable. What he didn't realize was that he was denying Lenore, too.

Surely, between herself and Lenore they could figure out some way to get Russ off his behind. McKaid said to stay out of it, but Elizabeth liked happy endings. She resolved to find a way to talk with Lenore.

"Lizzie?" McKaid broke the peaceful silence between them.

"Hmmm?"

He turned to face her, propping up his head. "I want you to listen to me. This is very important."

"All right."

"It's about you and me. I shouldn't have let this happen. Now don't misunderstand. I couldn't help myself, and I'm not sorry, but it does present a problem. We can't let anyone know about us. It's imperative to your safety that we keep this between the two of us."

"Because of Ramirez?"

"Exactly. He has eyes and ears everywhere to feed him the information he wants. He'll find out about you, maybe even from someone from the ranch, if we aren't very careful."

"You mean a spy?"

"Possibly, but more likely from loose talk or a careless comment from one of the men when they all go into town."

"I see. And Emma and Clint?"

"That's another problem. If they know, they'll insist on a wedding. They won't want you compromised."

"But there can't be a wedding," Elizabeth finished, understanding his train of thought.

"No. Not yet." He lay back down. "Not until that snake is dead," he said bitterly.

"So much killing. Doesn't it bother you to kill a man?"

"Not men like Ramirez. They don't deserve to live."

He sounded cold-blooded, and it was the one side of him that bothered her. She couldn't understand why men had to solve their differences only through death. Duels, shoot-outs, hangings, wars. Whatever became of common sense, compromise, compassion?

"Couldn't you just send him to prison?"

"No." They retreated again to silence. She could feel McKaid withdrawing from her, separating himself emotionally. To compensate, she snuggled closer physically.

"Listen, sweetheart. You have to understand how a mind like his works," he said. He wanted her to understand. He

181

didn't like the feeling that came when he thought she disapproved of what he did. "Men like Ramirez and the Corbetts don't care about anything except getting what they want. They know nothing of fairness. There was no reason to kill Jack and Sophie Warren. When Jack refused them his hospitality, they could have ridden on. Jack had that right. He had a family to protect, and he knew those men meant danger. The Corbetts attacked them out of pure spite because they were denied what they wanted. Men like that think of nothing but themselves. And Ramirez is ten times as bad as the Corbetts.

"Decent people live in fear of them. Most people, by nature, are reluctant to kill. They go that last little distance to avoid it. Outlaws know that, they depend on it. It gives them the edge.

"Do you know what would have happened to a regular family if the Corbetts had come by? The husband would have been beaten, if not killed, probably tied up and forced to watch as the men took turns with his wife and daughters. Their home would have been ransacked and everything of value taken. After all that, after the scum had taken what they wanted, they would have killed them all anyway.

"Jack was a Ranger once. He knew what was coming. He wouldn't have hesitated. Still it made no difference. One man against five? What I do, what my conscience demands I do, evens the score a little, and maybe prevents another family of good people from suffering a like fate."

"But you're only one man against all of them. How can you hope to win?" The picture he painted with his words was a gruesome one, and the thought of McKaid fighting such men chilled her to the core.

"I'm good at what I do, and I won't be alone. There are men everywhere who have learned from experience that the only way to deal with these outlaws is on their own level. The sheriff in Santa Fe already sent for a few of my friends in Texas."

"More Rangers?"

"We'll have our own army."

"It's very frightening."

"I want you to realize the full extent of the danger, Lizzie. I want you to understand why it's imperative that no one, not even Clint or Emma, knows of our feelings for each other."

"I won't say anything. I promise. Do you really think Ramirez would come after me? Even with all the men around?"

"Ramirez is insane. The real world doesn't exist for him. He lives only for the sense of power he gets from subduing others.

Even his own men are terrified of him."

"Why do they stay with him then?"

"Because no one defects and lives to tell about it, and death at the hands of Ramirez is a long and merciless ordeal."

She sighed audibly. "Must you go?"

"Do you want me to stay? Do you really want me to do nothing?"

She wanted to scream yes. She wanted him safe at the Circle K. She wanted him never to strap on those guns again. But did she have the right to ask that? Did she have the right to be so weak and selfish when so many others depended on his strength? Could he live with that? Could she?

How strange, she thought, that not once in *Desert Sunset* had Penelope feared for Colt Starling or doubted the outcome of any of his battles. Was the woman simply shallow, or was she superhuman? Was she confident or blindly dense?

That was fiction, she reminded herself. The fantasies of some imaginative mind. A male mind. It was still strange that he had spent so many words describing the rough male society and the continued jousting with words, fists, or weapons to see who was the better man, and so little time considering what the women experienced and endured. Was it the heroine's lot to suffer in silence?

Heroine. Was she cut out of the same cloth as such a woman? Was she equal to McKaid's strength? Could she dig deep down into herself and find the courage to stand and fight beside her man? She would do anything for McKaid. Anything. Couldn't she then do this for him?

"You could never live in peace with yourself if you did nothing," she answered. "I know that much about you. I won't say I'll not worry, but I do understand. Just take care of yourself."

He rolled her into his arms and held her tight against him. His heart swelled with love and with relief. He'd not been wrong about her. She was his soul mate, she understood him. It wouldn't be easy for her, but that didn't matter to her as much as his peace of mind. She was giving him what he needed most right now: acceptance, her blessing, her unconditional love. And one day soon, Lord willing, he would return that gift tenfold.

"You are one woman in a million, Lizzie. I won't let you down."

"You better not," she threatened teasingly, "or I'll go after

Ramirez myself."

"A little tigress showing her claws here, eh?" he bantered.

"Haven't you heard? There's nothing so dangerous as a female protecting her own."

"And nothing so savage as a woman's revenge. Maybe I should turn you loose on Ramirez."

"Now you're being foolish. I can't even hold a gun right. Your Indian friend actually laughed at me. He was sure I'd shoot myself."

"We'll take care of that."

She shuddered at the thought. She hated guns. "Do you think we should be getting back in the house?"

He rolled over, pinning her securely to the cot. "I don't know. I'm in no hurry. Actually, I'm feeling very young and strong right now. For one so old and worn out, that is."

"Yeah?" she asked, chuckling. "I'm still not convinced. Words are easy."

"Words, my love, are unnecessary."

He kissed her, igniting a brand new flame of desire in her body, and she had to admit that he could speak very well without saying a thing.

Into the early hours of morning the revellers continued to celebrate. Empty bottles of whiskey, tequila, and mescal lay strewn around the dying campfire along with the discarded food containers, dirty tin plates and utensils. In the shadows, but visible nonetheless, one of the men was making use of one of the women. Another man stood nearby, smoking a cigarette, watching, waiting impatiently for his turn with her.

Wes Corbett slumped back down behind the rocks. This was it, Ramirez's hideout. He'd been lucky to get this close. He would have been killed on sight if the guard closest to him hadn't been as drunk as the rest of the gang. As it was, he'd been able to slip by the man unnoticed.

Wes Corbett had been in the saloon when the Ramirez gang took Las Vegas. He'd never seen anything like it. His brothers would have stormed the place, shot up the town and the people, and left with only a fraction of what Ramirez and his men got away with. Ramirez was a genius. Corbett's friends, both dead now, had known that. Hadn't they both said their only hope was to join the Mexicans. They'd be alive now except for his own unreasonable desire to kill McKaid.

Corbett still wanted McKaid. He felt duty bound to avenge his brothers. He also wanted that Indian who'd shot his friend. But he was smarter now. The red veil of rage had lifted, leaving him with a cold, calculating determination, and far more patience. He'd set things right, only he'd do it with Ramirez: And while he was at it, he'd learn all he could at the hands of a master. The tricky part would come next. He had to get to Ramirez.

He waited and watched as, one by one, the *bandoleros* sank into a drink-induced stupor. Hours passed before the camp fell into a deep enough sleep for him to move in. From rock to bush to tree he moved in painstaking slowness down the hillside and into camp. He saw the priest tied to a tree. A nice touch, kidnapping a man of the Church. He saw half-naked women sprawled beneath equally exposed men, he saw one man stir, roll over and empty his stomach, then fall unconscious again.

Stealthily he crept through camp, searching. At last, in a secluded niche away from the main camp area, he found the man he'd come looking for. He, too, was locked in the sleeping embrace of a naked woman, both fully exposed to the chill of the damp night air, neither feeling it.

He sat down, his guns drawn and pointing at the man's head. Ramirez. In sleep he looked harmless enough. He was a small man, smaller than he'd thought he'd be from all the stories he'd heard. But his face, even relaxed as it was, held all the menace of a natural born killer.

His right hand was curved around one of the woman's breasts. She was a good-looking woman, full figure, decent face, lots of long black hair. She must be Carmen, the woman his older brother had tried to steal from Ramirez. If so, she was worthless trash, a whore. He couldn't understand how his brother could have let her come between him and a man like Ramirez. No woman was worth that.

He waited patiently, wide awake and alert, until just before dawn. As Ramirez began to stir, so did he. He moved very close, wrapped an arm around Ramirez's neck, and pulled the man up against his chest. With his other hand he brought his gun to Ramirez's head, very close to his ear, and cocked the hammer.

The ominous click brought Ramirez instantly awake, and he reached for his gun, dismayed to find himself naked and defenseless. He swore viciously.

185

"No need to be alarmed, *señor*," Corbett said smoothly, pressing the gun into his captive's temple. "I only want to talk."

"Who are you? You are a dead son of a bitch, whatever is your name."

Carmen woke up, took one look at the situation, and cried out for help. Corbett smiled. The more men to witness his victory, the better for his standing in the group. He wanted all of them to know who he was.

Within seconds a crowd of half-dressed, armed men stood around them, waiting for instructions from their leader.

"My back is against a rock, Ramirez. On both sides I am protected also. To shoot me your men must first shoot you, and even if they manage to miss you and get me, I will have time to take you to hell with me."

"Damn you. What is it you want? Money? I have money, but you won't live to spend it."

"I don't want your money, Ramirez. What I want will cost you nothing. I want to ride with you. I want to learn from you. You and your *bandoleros* are the best there is. And I want McKaid."

"McKaid! No. He is mine. Mine alone. Get me a blanket," he shouted to the woman.

"You can kill him in the end, my friend, but I want to be there to look into his eyes when you do. I want to prove that he's not indestructible. I want to see him cower in fear and beg for his life. I want him to know it was me who helped to bring him down. That will be my revenge for my brothers." He had no intention of stopping there. He was going to kill McKaid himself if he had to kill Ramirez first, or if he had to die doing so. But for now the Mexican didn't need to know that.

"Your brothers?" Ramirez asked, buying time.

"Dink and Lefty Corbett."

"Dink is dead?" Carmen shrieked, unthinking, then covered her mouth with her hand.

"Go, *puta*," Ramirez ordered her hatefully. "Go and cover your nakedness, and weep for your lost lover. Get me a blanket," he shouted again just as one was tossed in his lap.

"No. He was not my lover," Carmen cried. "I am *your* woman. Only yours, I swear. I'm glad he's dead. I bless the man who killed him."

Corbett stiffened, and his tightened muscles brought the

186

gun sinking into Ramirez's head even further. Corbett's eyes narrowed on the whore. So she was glad, was she? She blessed McKaid, did she? She'd pay for those words before he was through with her.

Ramirez, too, stiffened. Would he die because of his woman's careless words? "Get her from my sight," he said to his men. "It no longer matters to me how many men you lift your skirts for. I want no more of you. My men can have you."

"No, please, Ramirez. Don't do this to me."

"Now! Get her away from me."

The men obeyed. Only after she'd gone did he speak again. "So you are Dink Corbett's brother. And what are we to do about the gun you hold to my head?"

"My name is Wes. Wes Corbett. Nothing will happen to you if you'll be reasonable."

"What's to stop me from agreeing to your wishes then shooting you in the back? You play a very dangerous game, *amigo.*"

Wes was scared clear through. Ramirez was right. He had no guarantee. But he wanted to belong so badly that the risks weren't worth considering. If he could work with Ramirez, he could be the best. Better than Dink or Lefty. Anything less would never do. Not now. Not while McKaid still lived.

"I got past your guards, I walked through your camp, I spent the night sitting beside your head. If I'd wanted to, I could have slit every throat here last night, yours included. You should be more careful."

"What guard?"

"On the south rocks. He was drunk. As drunk as the rest of you."

"Get him," Ramirez ordered his men. "Bring him to me."

"I want to ride with you, Ramirez. Unlike my brother, I have no interest in your woman. You can't hold that against me. I was fifteen at the time. And I've proved that I mean you no harm, or any of your men. I came here last night to show you that I can be of use to you. I can handle myself."

"I do not like being held at gunpoint."

"Neither do I. But we both know you'd have put a bullet in me if I'd rode in here any other way. Your men are fast with the gun."

Ramirez chuckled evilly. "I think you are right. They would have killed you. What is it you wish to learn from me?"

"I want to shoot like you, I want to think like you, I want to be your right-hand man. I want to be as famous as you are."

"A *gringo?*" scorned Ramirez, and his men laughed with him.

"A *gringo*, one who is not so well known as the Dawsons here, could go where your men could not. I could walk freely down the streets of any town, scout out the lawmen, learn which stages carry money. I could help you get McKaid."

"We've done well enough without you," Ramirez replied. "We do not need you."

"I told you, I need you. Shall I shoot you then?"

"Don't be hasty. We will think a moment."

The guard was brought forward, shoved from behind by the two men who were sent to find him.

"The kid was right," one of the men said. "Juan was out cold." He threw the empty tequila bottle at Ramirez's feet.

The guard, hung over and very ill, trembled before Ramirez. "It won't happen again, I swear on all that is holy. I meant only to have one little drink."

"You left us unguarded by your craving of the bottle."

"Please, another chance," the man pleaded, falling to his knees. "I won't take another drop."

"Because of you, I sit here, naked, with a pistol at my head. Am I to forgive that?"

The man was speechless. His head dropped. What he'd done was unforgivable, and he knew the punishment. He damned the fates that had let him draw guard duty while the others were left to drink and enjoy the charms of the women. It wasn't fair. He'd needed a woman in the worst way, and he only drank to dull the ache in his body.

"Corbett," Ramirez said, "you will show me how loyal you are to me. This man loves his liquor more than he loves me. What do you think his punishment should be?"

"Only a fool would trust him again. He is useless to you now."

"You will shoot him for me?"

So this was his test. He had only to pull the trigger to be one of Ramirez's men? A deep sense of power and satisfaction swept over him. He would kill for Ramirez, but he would show him the full extent of his loyalty at the same time.

"I'll kill him, but in my own way. Stand, you weakling. Stand and die like a man, if you can," Corbett spat at the guard.

188

The guard, still begging for his life and sobbing out his abject apologies, was pulled to his feet. All the other men, guns still trained on Corbett, stepped aside in silence.

"I'm going to release you now, Ramirez, while I shoot your guard for you. You don't have to worry that I'll shoot you, no matter what you decide to do with me. All I ever wanted was a moment of your time. You gave me that."

Wes stood and pulled Ramirez to his feet. With the respect afforded only to one held in high esteem he guided his mentor to the side and lifted his gun. His first shot caught the condemned man in the right arm, the second in the left hand. Two more shots followed, both directed at the man's knees.

The guard screamed out and crumpled to the ground, writhing in an agony of searing pain.

"We must be able to trust the people we depend on, eh, my friends?" he said to Ramirez.

Ramirez didn't answer. He stood to the side, arms folded, watching the young man. A little foolhardy yet, but he had courage. He'd actually had the nerve to hold a gun to his head. And now he was standing alone, knowing that with one softly spoken command, he would be as dead as Juan.

Another shot rang out, then one more. The guard was dead. Wes Corbett holstered his gun and turned to face Ramirez.

Seven men raised their guns, hammers cocked back, waiting for one word from their boss. Corbett waited too, staring directly into the deadly black eyes of Ramirez.

"Let him live," Ramirez said at last, and motioned with a slight nod of his head for his men to leave them. His eyes never once left Corbett, even when he stooped to pick up his pants and slide his legs into them.

"You are a puzzling man," Ramirez said. "You were not afraid?"

"Only a fool would not fear you."

Ramirez laughed unpleasantly. "You want McKaid badly enough to risk your life to get him?"

"Yes."

"Then we must have an understanding. You may bring him as much pain as you like, but it is my knife that will cut his heart out. I will not be cheated of his death. I have waited too many years."

"I want to be there," was all Wes said.

"You will. But a warning." His gold-toothed grin was

189

chilling, diabolically evil. "If you cross me, I will hunt you down, and you will wish you never heard the name of Ramirez."

"A rider." The voice came from one of the lookout points up on the ridge.

Wes was spared answering as the men, Ramirez included, grabbed up their guns and turned their attention to the intruder.

"It's okay. He knows the signal," the voice called again.

The men waited while the rider crested the hill and rode down into camp. When they saw who the man was, they relaxed again and went about their business. Corbett held his ground and watched.

"*Amigo*," Ramirez greeted the rider and held the horse's bridle as the man stood down. "You bring the information I seek?"

"*Sí*. I know who you want."

"The new one? The woman from the stage? The one he met in Sante Fe?"

"No. Beaumont's widow."

"And the other? Are you certain?"

"*Sí*. They do not like each other. A very cold one, she is, except with the foreman. No, it is the Beaumont woman you want. She will bring McKaid to your feet."

"Good. She will be easy to take. Go now before you are missed." He withdrew a pouch from his pocket and spilled out a gold coin, passing it to his friend. "You have earned your money well. I will not forget this."

"It is my honor, *señor*."

"Any other information you can bring to me will be equally rewarded."

The man mounted his horse and looked down at Ramirez. "Then know that McKaid is well again and has been in touch with the sheriff at Sante Fe. Know also that he will come for you."

Ramirez watched the man ride away, waving his men off as they prepared to shoot the informer. "Not yet. He may still be of use to us."

Slowly, Ramirez turned and walked to Wes. "That is your first lesson, my young friend. Know your enemy. Find his weakest spot. With McKaid it is his soft heart. He allows himself to care for others. That will be his death."

"You're going to kill his woman?"

"Eventually. After we use her as bait to bring McKaid to us."

"You think he'll ride into a trap?"

"I have seen McKaid in one of his rages. When his heart is involved, he does not follow the rules. Because he cares, he becomes careless." Ramirez laughed. "It is funny, no?"

"But a woman?"

"You have not the stomach," Ramirez bit out scornfully.

Wes stared into implacable eyes and saw for the first time the evil that lay there. Weak spot? He didn't want Ramirez to find one in him, not even his distaste for killing women. He knew then that he must never show it. He shrugged indifferently. "It matters not to me who I kill, so long as McKaid dies in the end."

"I thought you would see it that way."

"So we go after the woman?"

"I think not. We will play with McKaid first, just to get his temper roused. The more anger that burns in his soul, the less clearly he will think."

"One other thing, Ramirez. There was a band of Indians."

"Apache. They killed your friend, no? I hear about this. They are a small tribe that would not be held at Bosque Redondo with the other Apache and Navahos. Even your famed Kit Carson could not keep them there."

"I want them."

Ramirez shrugged. "That is your fight. It does not concern me."

"Some of your men—could I ask them to help?"

"It is their decision. My men love a fight, but I will not order it. Do not be too hasty to take on the Apache. I think you do not know them. You forget already your first lesson."

"I can handle myself," Corbett countered.

"As you wish. Go from me now." Corbett did so, and Ramirez let his gaze follow the young man. His eyes narrowed speculatively. A man with a vengeance who did not fear for his life was a dangerous man. "We will see," he said softly. "We will see."

Chapter Twelve

McKaid had already gone out when Elizabeth rose the next morning. She sat down to breakfast, feeling decidedly apprehensive. Did anyone know what had happened between her and McKaid? Could they see it on her face? What would they think of her if they knew? She ate little, hurrying to begin washing up, hoping to avoid Emma's too astute eyes.

But Emma was busy, as usual, and only spared a brief comment, saying she hoped Elizabeth was feeling better today.

"Oh, yes, I am. Actually," she said, wanting to put Emma's mind at ease and to explain what would be an obvious difference in McKaid's attitude toward her in the future, "I had a talk with McKaid last night. We—ah—understand each other better now."

"That's good, dear. It pained me to see him treat you the way he did, and him being such a nice man. I don't know what got into him."

Elizabeth wanted to say more. She longed to talk to Emma about her love for McKaid and explain his misunderstanding and why he had been so hard to get along with, but she remembered what McKaid had said and how strongly he felt about keeping their relationship to themselves. So she held her tongue.

McKaid and Clint came in a few minutes later, both helping themselves to coffee and sitting at the table. Elizabeth busied herself scrubbing at the oatmeal in the iron kettle to keep from looking at McKaid. It was too soon after their long night of passion for her to hide the love in her eyes. Or was it too late to prevent it from forever being there?

"Had breakfast yet, Lizzie?" McKaid asked casually.

193

"Yes, of course," she answered over her shoulder.

"Emma, can you watch the children this morning? Lizzie's decided to stay on with us, and Clint and I think it's time for her to learn to handle a gun. I'm taking her up to the north range for a lesson."

Surprised, Elizabeth turned, soapy water dripping from her hands onto the linoleum floor. "Gun," she croaked in dismay.

"It's a good idea," Emma concurred. "Oh, I'm so glad you're staying. I was afraid that you'd . . . Well, that's not important now. McKaid's right, Elizabeth. You have to be able to defend yourself. Everyone else out here knows how to shoot."

Elizabeth looked from Emma to McKaid. He couldn't have picked a better subject to take the light of passion from her eyes. Guns, shooting, blood, death. She shuddered.

"Do I have to?"

"It's best," Clint said. "You may never need to use a gun, but if you do, you better use it well."

McKaid drew her eyes to his. Neither spoke, but they understood each other. McKaid had taken her virginity last night, and now he was going to take the rest of her innocence. She was his woman, and as such, she would have to learn his way of life. She had spirit enough, but he doubted if it had ever been tested to the extent it would be if she stayed with him. She had to be prepared for whatever came her way because of him. He didn't intend to protect her from life's crueler side as he had done with Rosanna. He wanted Elizabeth to be able to protect herself if it became necessary. She had to be prepared for anything, even his death.

Elizabeth knew. She'd made a commitment to him last night, an unconditional commitment. Even though she hated guns, recoiled at the thought of actually shooting another human being, she never again wanted to be a hindrance to McKaid as she had been when the Corbett gang attacked them. Never again did she want to endanger McKaid's life because she couldn't support him in a fight for their right to live and do so in peace. She knew she had no other choice but to do as he said.

"I'll go change. I'll only be a minute."

They watched her leave. "I hope we're doing the right thing," Clint said.

"We are. She's stronger than she looks," McKaid answered.

"As her uncle, I could insist that she return to Virginia."

194

"She stays," McKaid said adamantly and stood to refill his cup at the stove.

Clint and Emma looked at each other and grinned.

They rode together up the valley floor on the west side of the Rio Grande. Elizabeth was stunned anew by the vastness of the country. "It's beautiful here," she said, meeting his shining eyes with her own sparkling gaze.

"I was afraid to see you this morning. And when we came in, and you kept right on washing those damned dishes, I thought for sure you regretted last night."

She smiled at the question in his eyes. "I don't regret a minute of it. I was afraid to look at you. I was certain my face would give us away."

He laughed. "It didn't."

"That's because you announced I was to learn to shoot."

"You do understand, though?" he asked seriously.

"I understand."

They rode in silence for a while, and all the time she could feel his eyes on her, warming her blood, stirring her senses, making her remember.

"I like your hair loose like that," he said, breaking the silence. "You have a lot of hair. It shines like spun gold in the sunlight."

She brushed a few blowing tendrils away from her face. "It's also bleaching. And I'm getting freckles."

"I know. I counted them. You have eleven on your nose and cheeks."

"You're keeping count of my freckles?" she laughed.

"I notice everything about you. When you're agitated, you stand on one foot and tap the other, when you're really angry, you stand squarely on both feet and your chin goes up. One eye, your left, squints more than the other when you glare, and a little line appears right between your brows."

"Well, for goodness' sake," she sputtered.

"You walk with a lilt when you're happy, and your eyes turn gold when you laugh. When you're about to cry, your chin dimples and quivers, and you always bite your lower lip to stop it. Your teeth are perfect except for two on the bottom that are slightly crooked, but that's endearing. You broke a fingernail yesterday, on your left hand."

"I don't believe this," she said, looking at her broken nail.

"It didn't work, you know. Last night didn't work."

Her eyes flew to his. "What didn't work?"

"I was sure that once I'd had you, I'd be able to get you off my mind, for a few hours, at least. It hasn't worked out that way. I woke up this morning wanting you again, and it hasn't gotten any better."

"You wish you didn't want me?" she asked.

"I wish," he growled in return, "I could take you up into these hills right now and ravish you for days on end."

She grinned impishly. "Let's go." She was teasing, and he knew it, but she would have gone. She had been living with the same frustrations as he had, and she was feeling the same desires now that he was describing. She, too, had been able to think of little else than making love with him again.

"You're not trying to get out of your lesson, are you, teacher?"

"I thought you were offering another lesson."

"Oh, there are a few things left for you to learn. Shall I tell you about them?"

She blushed. "I'm not sure, McKaid. Enough. Tell me about this area. What's that?" she asked, motioning to a large mesa that jutted up out of the flat valley.

He laughed, but let her change the subject. "That's Black Mesa. It sits out here in the valley like a lone sentinel from the mountains. It's covered, like most of the hills, with piñon pine and juniper. Clint has found a lot of Indian artifacts around it."

"What sort of artifacts?"

"Old pottery, tools, that sort of thing."

"From the Apache?"

"No. From an extinct sect of Indians. There are cave dwellings all over this area. I'll take you to see them sometime."

"I'd like that. Does no one live there now?"

"No. There are pueblos around where large societies of Pueblo Indians do exist though. They're peaceful Indians who don't categorize themselves as part of what we consider today's Indian cultures. As far as they're concerned, this was their land, even before the Spanish arrived. The Navaho, Zuni, the Apache, and Comanche, all of them, are as much interlopers as the Spanish, Mexicans, and Americans. Which,

196

of course, is all true."

"But they didn't fight?"

"They weren't happy about being invaded, but they've been able to compromise and find a way to coexist."

"Where do you market your cattle?"

"We ran eight hundred head up the Sante Fe Trail for the first time this year. Most of the cattle go to Sante Fe or Albuquerque or other towns in the river valley. A large number go to the forts. We sell horses to the army, as well."

"Do you have sheep?"

"No, but it's a good market. Cattle and horses are easier. Sheep are the orneriest critters alive, except for women."

"Oh, really?" she retorted sarcastically. "And how is that?"

"Cattle, like men, are predictable. You try to get a bunch of sheep together, and they're apt to go off in a hundred directions at once. And none of 'em know what they're doin'. Like women, they need a firm hand and constant watching over."

"Yeah? Well, let's see how good you are at it, shall we?" She dug her heels in and sent her horse galloping away from his smug, smirking grin.

She heard him calling to her to stop, but she threw back her head and laughed. The speed and power of the sleek-muscled animal beneath her was exhilarating, and she urged the mare on, faster and faster, laughing freely as they flew together across the valley floor. She could hear McKaid behind her, gaining on her, but she dared not turn to look. And then he was beside her, pulling her horse to a stop. She didn't look at him, she knew he'd be scowling. She slid off the horse almost before the mare had stopped, and she started running in the opposite direction.

"Lizzie," McKaid yelled again. "Don't you dare make me chase you."

"Ba-a-a-a," she bleated back to him.

She heard him swear, then heard his horse following her. She should have expected him to play dirty, but she didn't, not until she felt the rope breeze over her head and shoulders and jerk her to a quick halt. She landed again on her bottom, her already bruised bottom.

She tried to loosen the rope, but he tugged it tighter, dismounting and walking slowly toward her, his cocky grin in place as he wound in the coils of the rope.

"Not fair, McKaid," she grumbled laughingly, getting to her feet. He pulled her closer, each reluctant step drawing her nearer and nearer to the retribution she knew was coming.

"Are you going to run again?" he asked.

"I'm tied up. How can I?" She tugged again at the rope binding her arms to her sides.

He pulled her against him and held her there, chuckling at her struggles. She couldn't decide whether to laugh or spit fire at him.

"I never roped me such a fine-looking heifer before," he goaded.

"I thought I was a sheep."

"Ewe."

"Me what?"

"No. I mean ewe, E-W-E."

"Oh." Reluctant laughter bubbled up from her chest like a fountain of sparkling joy.

"I used to hate Russ because you laughed for him like that."

"I used to hate Lenore because you'd bend your head down to hers and tell her some secret that made her laugh. I thought you were laughing at me."

"No. Never that. You know how I felt about you, and Lenore thought you were delightful because you dared to sass me."

"But you didn't."

"Yes, I did. Everything about you drove me crazy. You're driving me crazy right now." To add proof to that, his right hand glided down the long curve of her back and pressed her hips to the hard shape of his arousal.

"McKaid," she murmured, turning her face up to meet his descending lips.

"God, it feels so good to be able to do this without guilt tearing at my conscience."

He kissed her, gently at first then more insistently, moving his mouth persuasively against the soft pads of her lips. Sweet shafts of pleasure spiraled through her body.

"I want to kiss you again and again," he whispered, his mouth moving against hers as he spoke, his warm breath melding with hers. "Every time I look at you and watch your lips as you talk or eat, as your slow smile curves your mouth, I want to kiss you. I'm becoming obsessed with you until I can't think of anything else."

"It's that way for me, too," she said softly. "Oh, McKaid,

how can I want you this much when only a few hours ago . . ."

He didn't let her finish, but took her mouth in a kiss that robbed her of her breath, her will, her very soul. She wriggled loose of the lariat and slid her hands up the firm wall of his chest to encircle his neck.

She loved losing herself in his kisses. She loved the deep rhythmic thrust of his tongue, she loved when he drew her tongue into his mouth. It was a new world of sensations for her, being kissed by McKaid, a world she didn't want to leave. She ran her fingers into his thick lively hair and drew him hard against her mouth.

Her pulse was racing, hammering against her chest, her blood was beating thick and hot through her veins. Her breasts, where they pressed against McKaid's chest, were heavy and straining to feel McKaid's touch and kisses. And lower in her body a place was opening to him, aching, preparing itself to receive him as it had done only one other night in her life. How strange the power of the flesh that, once tutored, would not meekly accept being denied its desires.

Her fingers went to his waist and freed his shirt from his trousers. Hastily she worked at the buttons until she could run her hands over his firm heated flesh, could feel the texture of the mat of dark hair sprinkled in a triangle down his chest.

She tore her lips away from his and pressed hot kisses across his shoulders and collarbone. She let her lips explore until she felt the hard pebble of his flat nipple. She slicked it with her tongue and nipped at it with her teeth.

McKaid's hold on her hips tightened, and his breath hissed inward through his teeth. Elizabeth felt a wild exultant surge of feminine power that she could also give him pleasure as he did with her. She moved to his other nipple to caress and tease and heighten his enjoyment. At the same time she dared to let her hands slide to his taut buttocks and, with fingers that molded to his contours, press him more firmly against her abdomen.

"Lizzie," he groaned, pulling her away from him. "We better stop right now, before we can't stop."

"No," she objected, placing kisses against his chest again. "I don't want to stop. Don't talk, McKaid. Just let me make love to you."

He groaned again, fighting his own insistent desire. "Look where we are, love. Any one of the men could come by. We're out in the open."

"Right now I can't seem to care about that. All I know is that I want you." Boldly she ran her fingers up and down the evidence of his own need.

"Don't do that," he said roughly and pulled away from her reach entirely.

She looked at him with stricken eyes that suddenly dropped as a deep flush crept into her cheeks. She clenched her hands at her waist and turned away in embarrassment. "I'm sorry. I didn't think you'd mind. I only wanted . . ."

"Wait. Stop," he said and turned her to face him. "It is all right. Look at me, Lizzie. I want you to touch me more than I can say. I want to make love to you, I can't hide that. But not here. Not now. Remember what we talked about last night. It was risky enough coming out here together. If the men don't soon hear some target practice, they'll begin to wonder. And Lizzie, I meant it about being out here in the open. We can't take the chance someone will see us. We could be shot."

"I'm sorry. I know you're right. It just happened so quickly." Her eyes dropped again. "I couldn't think."

He cupped her chin and tilted her face up, smoothing the hair back from her face. "I knew when I first kissed you that you had a passionate soul, and I'm very glad you do. Hell, if I could, Lizzie, I'd marry you this minute."

She gave him a tremulous smile. "Me, too."

He draped his arm over her shoulders and steered her toward their horses. "Come on. Let's go shoot something. And starting now, we'll be very careful where we kiss each other. Stopping is too hard to take at my advanced age."

When they finally got down to business, McKaid made her work. Time and time again she loaded the little gun he'd decided was to be hers. Over and over she emptied it, learning to steady her arm in several positions, and even managing to hit the target a good percentage of the time.

When he was satisfied with her progress with that weapon, he began with his rifle. By the time they headed back to the ranch for the noon meal, her arms were sore and her right shoulder much the worse for wear. She had to admit, though, that she no longer dreaded the weapons, she felt confident and comfortable with them. What a little knowledge could do. Hitting tin cans, bottles, and stumps was a challenge, it was fun. Yet, as McKaid had said, target practice wasn't the final end. She'd have to prepare herself mentally to use the weapons

200

on a human being. She couldn't practice that.

"Most people die because they hesitate," he told her as they approached the ranch. "And the killers out there don't. They no longer have a conscience where right and wrong are different. They don't care if they kill. When the time comes to defend yourself or those you protect, you'll have to face the fact that it's their lives or yours. It's very difficult to pull the trigger. You'll have to be strong, and you'll have to be quick."

"What if I can't do it?"

He didn't answer.

"Won't it make me just as bad as they are?"

"I've asked myself that question a hundred times. All I can say is that it depends on motivation. I've never killed out of spite or malice. Whenever possible, I've turned the criminals over to the judges who decide their fates. I kill when my life is threatened, or the lives of good folks who cannot defend themselves. It's very much like war. It is war."

"I'll remember."

He was filled with pride for her. She was a strong woman, equal to this land. "That's my girl. Let's get something to eat. I'm starved, though I could make a meal of you."

"Is that E-W-E?"

"No, that's you, Y-O-you."

Dessert that evening was bread pudding, and they had just started on it when the messenger arrived from Santa Fe. Both Clint and McKaid went with him into the study. Russ, who had brought the man to the house, stood in the doorway of the dining room, unsure whether he should wait or go.

"We're having pudding for dessert, Russ," Emma offered. "Will you have some?"

"Don't mind if I do, thanks. Actually, I missed chow line altogether, so if no one's going to eat that last piece of chicken . . ."

Emma clucked her tongue. "You sit yourself down. I'll get a plate and feed you proper. I always said you should take your meals with us. There's too much gets discussing over food and a good cup of coffee around here for you to miss."

"Thanks, ma'am. I just don't know if that'd be right."

"Course it would. You're the foreman. Now make yourself at home. I'll be back directly."

201

"She's right, Russ. You know you're more than welcome here."

Russ sat down and looked at Elizabeth. His voice was for her alone. "I heard McKaid that morning I came to breakfast. He didn't want me here."

She grinned at the memory. "He thought you and I were sweet on each other. He was afraid we'd hurt Lenore."

"Lenore? Why would we ever hurt Lenore?"

"Because she's in love with you."

"Nah. She couldn't be, not a woman like her."

She'd shocked him with that news. Could he really not have guessed? "I realize it's farfetched, you being such a rotter, and all," she teased. "And anyway, you're already in love with some mysterious woman, whose name remains a secret to me. I assure you it's true. McKaid explained it to me. That's why she comes to visit so often."

His eyes narrowed on her questioningly, then he shook his head and chuckled. "Because of me?" he asked, grinning like a schoolboy. "Well, now, what do you know?"

"Here you are, Mr. Packard," Emma said, placing a heaping plate of warmed-up food in front of him.

"This looks wonderful."

"Course it does," Emma returned. "Now, get yourself on the outside of it while it's hot. I'll be in the kitchen if you want seconds."

"May we be excused, Miss Elizabeth?" James asked. "We want to play checkers."

"Finish your milk, then yes," she answered fondly, watching as they drained their glasses and scampered from the dining room.

"They're fine kids," Russ said as footsteps raced up the stairs.

"Yes, they are," Elizabeth agreed.

"How are they doing?"

"James is fine, I think. He's adjusting well, and is very bright. Ruthie still clings. She tries so hard to please everyone. I'm afraid she's still very unsure of her world."

"It was an awful thing they went through. It'll probably take time."

"I hope we have that time," Elizabeth said, glancing toward the closed library doors. "What does that man want?"

"He's delivering a message to McKaid from the sheriff in

Santa Fe."

"Is it starting then?" she asked.

"It started for McKaid a long time ago. He can't seem to get away from it anymore. Trouble has a way of trailing him."

"Do you think he wants to quit?"

"He's wanted out for years, but there's always one more gunslinger who wants to prove he's better than Ranger McKaid, and there's always Ramirez."

"If he wanted to, couldn't he simply walk away from it?"

"Maybe there's been no real reason for him to do that until now."

"He's afraid for all of us. He thinks Ramirez will try to kill one of us."

"Is that why he gave you a shooting lesson?"

"Yes."

"I'm glad he did."

"Then you think we're in danger, too?"

"Yes. I do indeed. I've seen what was left behind after Ramirez swept through a town. It was not a pretty sight."

Russ was on his second cup of coffee when the men emerged from the library. Clint called to him, and the four of them walked out the door. The house seemed vaguely tomblike with the men gone. She busied herself with chores, and soon the kitchen was clean, the children were put to bed, and Emma had gone to her room to read. Emma read when she was nervous. Elizabeth paced.

She walked from room to room, tidying this, straightening that. The house creaked in places she'd never heard it stir before, as if it, too, knew something ominous was about to happen and was as restless as she.

When she heard the first footsteps on the front porch, she jumped, the sound going through her like a shot. With her heartbeat leaping in her throat she raced to the door and flung it open.

Clint stopped, his hand still reaching for the door latch, and looked at her for a long silent moment. He raised his hand to cup her cheek, running his thumb over the tight little line of worry between her brow.

"I wish . . ." he said hesitantly, then let his hand drop. "Goodnight, Elizabeth." He walked past her and up the stairs, his feet moving as if they were weighted with the cares of the whole world.

She turned to call to him, to somehow ease his mind, but McKaid's soft words halted her.

"Can we talk, Lizzie? Out here?"

She looked into his serious face and his troubled eyes and found herself speechless. She nodded and followed him to the porch swing. They didn't touch, and for a while the only sound they heard was the rhythmic creak of the swing, ticking away the seconds.

"I have to go," he said finally.

"I know," she sighed.

"Ramirez and his gang raided Las Vegas and took their priest with them."

"A priest? Why a priest?"

"Apparently he damned Ramirez for what he had done in town, and Ramirez took him along so the padre could pray for his soul. Incredible, isn't it?"

"Unusual, to say the least. I thought men like that didn't have consciences."

"It's not what he's done in this life that Ramirez is worried about. He wants everything his way now and he wants to be assured of heaven as well. The Church is his one weakness."

"Why must you go? Why can't the sheriff handle it?"

"The sheriff in Las Vegas was killed. The sheriff in Santa Fe won't leave town in case Ramirez comes there next. He has an army of men deputized to protect his people. He has to stay. It's up to me as marshal to go after the priest."

"What if Ramirez comes here while you're gone?"

"We've talked with the men. They'll be ready if he does."

"I don't like this, McKaid. He's following the same pattern you told me about. He gets you to chase after him, then he comes around behind your back and kills someone you care about."

McKaid ran his hand agitatedly through his hair. "I know that, but what am I supposed to do? He kidnapped a priest. I'm duty bound to try to get him safely away from that outlaw camp, wherever it is."

"Is Uncle Clint going? Or Russ?"

"No."

"You can't go alone."

"The sheriff said that my two friends from Texas are due in

204

Sante Fe tomorrow. I'll have all the help I need."

"Are they Rangers?"

"Good ones."

The tight coil of apprehension in her stomach relaxed at that news. "I'm glad to hear that, anyway."

"Lizzie, you and Emma and the children are going to have to stay very close to the house until this is over. No more outings, no more playing in the creek or swimming in the river, or climbing around that tree house. The men will see you have plenty of food and water. Promise me, Lizzie. Your lives may depend on it."

"Okay, I'll see to it. I promise."

"Good."

"When will you leave?"

"First light."

Into the silence that followed they both spoke at once. "Lizzie . . ."

"McKaid—"

"Go ahead," he said, touching her long hair where it lay across her shoulder.

"Could we go somewhere tonight?"

"I was afraid that's what you were thinking."

"You don't want to?"

"Oh, I want to, but I don't think it's a good idea. What if I don't come back? It may be too late already, but I'd hate to die knowing I'd left you with my child to raise alone."

Her throat tightened, and her eyes began to sting with tears that scratched to be set free. "If I can't have you, if fate decides to take you away from me so soon, I'd want your child more than anything else in the world."

"People can be very cruel to a woman in that situation."

"I don't care. The rules of most societies hold little appeal for me right now."

"And what of the child?"

"He'll be a McKaid."

"Or she will. A little girl with sun-touched hair and tawny eyes."

She stood and held her hand out to him, tempting with eyes that promised and a smile that lured. He was only a man, a man deeply in love. He took her hand.

They rode bareback on Lucky Lady away from the ranch, becoming just another dark shadow among the juniper and piñon while the moon played elusive games behind the low-riding clouds.

McKaid wanted more for her than a few minutes in a room that smelled of leather, oil, old wood, and old wool. He wanted the memories of their loving to come to her with the clean smells of the earth, the sounds of moving water, and the fresh air and the scent of nature. He wanted their joining to be a natural and wholly beautiful part of life, as it was meant to be, not a sneaking rendezvous that felt tainted by the very act of hiding. Apart from the marriage bed, the nearest place he knew of was his secret refuge, a secluded cave of overhanging pine boughs at the curve of the river, where stately cottonwoods and aspens stood watch around them. He'd spent many hours there, searching his soul for some meaning and validity in his life, and he'd never felt the desire to share his special place with anyone else until Elizabeth.

"This is beautiful," she whispered reverently when he pushed aside a curtaining bough and ushered her into his private chamber. The moon decided to show its face at that moment and sent a long slender finger of silvery light through the openings between trees and branches, adding a cathedral-like atmosphere to their sanctuary.

"I'll start a small fire," he said, smiling indulgently at her awe. He'd felt the same way the first night he'd camped out here.

She watched as he gathered kindling and wood from his private cache and put a match to it. The fire pit, ringed with rocks, was perfect, resembling what she'd always imagined the altars of bygone days had looked like.

She was deeply touched by the sensitive side of McKaid, that he could recognize beauty in a simple setting and seek not to mar it by a blackened mass of scattered ashes, but to erect a monument to enhance its specialness. Her heart swelled with love for him, a magnificent man in body and soul.

"There," he said, satisfied with his efforts. He stood and retrieved the thick bedroll from beside his horse, spreading it on the soft mat of last year's leaves and needles. He looked up and smiled. "Will this do?"

"Oh, McKaid, I love you. There don't seem to be any adequate words in my head to tell you how very much you mean to me."

He held open his arms, and she was propelled into them as if

206

she'd been held apart from him by an invisible restraining hand that had suddenly been lifted. Bodies melding and lips meeting, they came together with a force of such overpowering love and need that neither could deny it.

"My darling, sweet woman, I love you, too."

Slowly, yet impatiently, they discarded the raiments of cloth and leather that separated flesh from flesh, and together sank to the soft bed, covered only the flickering golden warmth of the fire.

In her giving arms McKaid found the answers to the mysteries of life that had brought him so often to this place. This then, this loving, caring, sharing with one special mate, was what life was about. This was living, this was being, this was continuity. This gave his bare existence its meaning, this gave credence to his work. This was what had unknowingly drawn him to Jack and Sophie. How could he accept happiness and not do what was possible and often necessary to insure all other men and women the same freedom? How could he take his unbounded joy and close his eyes to the rest of mankind?

With Lizzie to love he was no longer torn asunder by questions and recriminations. With Lizzie his soul found peace, wonderful, complete peace.

"I'm nervous, McKaid," Elizabeth whispered. "I feel as if this is the first time all over again."

"Perhaps, in a way, it is. Perhaps in the space of a day we've both uncovered some truths and made some commitments we weren't aware of before. I have. I know my life has no meaning without you. I want you beside me as my wife more than anything I've ever wanted before. I wish to God we were married now. And I promise as soon as we can, we will be."

Tears, hot and unstoppable, pooled in her eyes and overflowed to cascade down the sides of her face. "I couldn't be more married to you than I am at this moment. No declaration by some man we barely know, or signature on a parchment, could make me any more a part of you than I am right now."

"I know that, but it's the possessive part of me that wants the whole world to know it."

"That day will come, my love."

His lips met hers and they made their eternal vows of love in their tabernacle of land and trees and sky with the fire and the water to bear witness. They lay entwined, creamy skin and bronze, gilded by the gold and orange flickers of the firelight. Silver eyes met gold, each drinking thirstily of the promise of love, each giving in abundance to fulfill that promise to the other.

Hands and bodies, eyes and lips worshipped and adored, and passion blossomed forth with a fervor so intense it defied the mystical and whimsical powers of Destiny to keep them apart.

Cares and worries of the coming days were temporarily forgotten, but the unconscious sense of impending danger lingered and lent an urgency to their lovemaking.

McKaid's hands moved relentlessly over her newly awakened body, seeking out the most sensitive flesh, drawing her into his sensuous web of desire. Elizabeth, herself, found a new and surprising need to explore the rippling muscles of his back and buttocks and the sinewy length of muscled limbs, and the boldness to let herself touch and caress the most masculine part of him, an intimacy she had been too shy and uncertain before to dare. Now, more than her own pleasure, she wanted to please McKaid, to be his woman and meet his needs.

"Ah, sweet Lizzie," he groaned, delightful sensations stirred by the very touch of her fingers. "If you don't stop, I won't be able to control myself. Your hands are . . ."

"Why should you be in control when I'm not? I want you so much I ache for you."

"Sweetheart," he murmured and pulled her closer, rolling her beneath him. He kissed her deeply, possessing all the sweet nectar of her warm, inviting mouth. He wanted her, too. He wanted to make love to her until he absorbed her very being into his own, until they were totally and irrevocably inseparable.

With a groan of utter delight he entered her, easing himself into the deepest part of her, allowing her body time to become reaccustomed to the full, hard length of him.

Elizabeth needed no time, she needed McKaid. She needed his kisses, his touch, she needed to be filled again with the strength of his passion. Her hands slid down the taut curve of his back until she could mold them to the tight muscles of his buttocks. She urged him closer, taking him deep within that part of her that cried out to be joined with and fulfilled.

Together they climbed to the heights of passion, together they traveled to that other bright world where the vivid pleasures of love are found. Together they found their fulfillment, and together they lay spent, bodies still inter-twined in the aftermath of their union, sharing the small spasmodic pulses that throbbed like fluttering heartbeats within their bodies.

McKaid felt her shiver as the night air touched their damp skin. Reluctantly he withdrew, but only so he could cover them with a blanket and keep them warm.

"I thought you were leaving me," she said, burrowing into his embrace, trying to ignore a chill of a different kind that her own words brought.

"I'm not going anywhere," he replied, knowing that eventually, in the real world, he must.

"Will you be back soon?" she asked quietly.

"As soon as I can. It depends on Ramirez."

"Hold me then. Hold me very close so that I can remember this night until you return."

"As I'll remember you."

"No. You must forget about everything except what you're doing. No distractions."

"That's a tall order. I couldn't get you out of my mind before we made love. How am I to do it now?"

"You have to, that's all."

He leaned up and looked down at her, smiling tenderly. Such a rush of love filled him for this woman that he was almost bursting with it. Right along with it came a surge of desire, desire to possess her all over again.

"It's still tonight, my love," he said, leering comically.

She laughed. "So it is," she said and wound her arms around his neck, bringing his lips to hers.

Chapter Thirteen

The clouds grew thick and solid, a heavy blanket rolling over the mountains to cover the valley. The moon slid behind them and retired for the night. Over an hour passed before the lovers emerged from their trysting place to find that complete darkness had closed around them like a black shroud. McKaid mounted Lucky and pulled Elizabeth up in front of him, kissing her one last time before turning his mare homeward.

"What's that, McKaid? Look."

"I see it."

An orange glow arched into the sky in the near distance like an isolated piece of sunset that had dropped from the sky. The arm around Elizabeth's midriff tightened, and the mare, picking up McKaid's tension, began to dance under them.

"What is it?" Elizabeth asked.

"Fire. Hold tight, Lizzie. It's at the ranch."

They raced across the valley, McKaid's eyes alert for obstacles in their path, the horse surefooted under his guidance. So it was to begin like this again, he thought. Striking out at him in unexpected ways, baiting him, testing him, frustrating him. He was very tired of the games Ramirez played. He had to put a stop to them. For Lizzie's sake, this must be the end of it.

They crested the last rise nearest the ranch compound, and McKaid pulled Lucky to a stop. Men were shouting orders to each other, running around seemingly without direction in the eerie orange light of the blaze.

"The children?" Elizabeth asked in alarm.

"It's not the house. It's the barn." It's where they would have been if he hadn't taken her to the river, but he didn't tell

211

her that. She would ask the same questions he was asking himself. Was it an accident or was it deliberately set? Had the fire been meant for them? Did someone already know? Was someone now waiting with gun in hand for him to return to the ranch? He dismounted and helped Elizabeth down.

"Why are we stopping? We have to help," she argued.

"We're going on foot from here." He slapped his horse on the rump and sent her off into the night. She'd return in her own time.

"Take this," he said, handing her one of his two six-shooters."

"No, I—"

"Lizzie," he interrupted sternly. "Take it. Now, work your way below the house and come in from behind the pumphouse and bake oven. If anything moves, shoot it."

"What if I shoot you," she asked, shaking her head in denial.

"I'm going the other way. If anyone's out here, he's not one of the Circle K men."

"You think Ramirez . . ." She couldn't finish for the knot of fear in her throat.

"I have to think that, and I don't want you anywhere near me. Do as I say now, and be as quiet as you can."

Elizabeth's hands shook on the gun. All of her muscles were frozen. How could this be happening? Only with conscious deliberate effort could she make her legs move. One step, two, right foot, left. What was she doing? She couldn't do this on her own. She stopped and turned around to tell McKaid, but he was already gone.

With wide eyes she stared into the darkness at the ghoulish shadows formed by the dancing, licking tongues of the fire. Did that shadow move? Was someone there? Or there? Back and forth, all around, her eyes darted.

Go, her mind screamed. *Get hold of yourself and move!*

Tamping down her fear, she took one more step, then another. Her blood started to run again, and the paralyzing fear that held her immobile slid away. Soon she was moving rapidly down the incline, staying as much as she could in the shadows of the scrubby piñon. She slipped and fell only once, and for a few terrifying seconds scrambled on hands and knees to find the gun she'd dropped, but she was back on her feet and pushing on as soon as her hand closed around the weapon.

The last stretch, an open clearing from the brushy perimeter of the hillside to the bake oven, lay before her. She surveyed the area and took the distance in a quick sprint, pressing herself against the hard brick wall as soon as she reached her destination.

She stopped for a minute to catch her breath and let her racing heart slow to a more normal rate. An hysterical giggle welled up inside her, but she choked it back. What she must look like, her hair a mess, her clothes askew, dirt and mud all over her from slipping and sliding into an invisible wash, braced against a wall with a gun in her hand. It was not a scene in which she could picture the lovely Penelope.

Gathering her wits, she eyed the distance to the well house. From there it was only shouting distance to the house. She stepped out of the shadows and ran.

McKaid didn't like leaving Lizzie, but he didn't want her near the barn. Whoever started the fire would be vain enough to stick around and watch the effects of his handiwork. McKaid wanted that man.

Though the activity around the burning barn was chaotic, he knew Clint and Russ would have it well enough in hand. He stayed back and circled the area, looking for anything or anyone out of place.

When nothing turned up, he holstered his gun and made his way to Russ. Acrid smoke filled the air and stung his eyes, and the heat from the burning timbers was daunting.

"How's it look?" he asked the foreman.

"Not good. Cal was quick with the alarm, but the flames moved so fast we couldn't do much. The brick walls'll hold all right, but we'll lose the loft and the roof. How's Clint?"

"Clint? What happened? Where is he?"

"At the house. I thought that's where you were."

"No . . . I . . ." he faltered, guilt riding heavy on his shoulders. He swore. "Never mind that. What happened to him?"

"He went in to get the animals out. As far as we can tell, he must have hit his head. Part of the loft fell in on him before we realized he was still in there. We found him trapped under one of the beams. He's not good, McKaid, he's hurt bad."

McKaid moved to go to his uncle, but Russ stopped him.

"McKaid, we found this in Clint's hand. I thought you ought to see it."

McKaid looked at the gold coin Russ dropped in his palm, turning it over with his thumb and fingers. His hand clenched around it. Stamped in Mexico. Mexican gold. Ramirez.

"Thanks, Russ," he managed and turned away. He was almost to the house when the first blinding flash of lightning rent the sky. A second followed in the next instant, accompanied by a crack of thunder that set the earth to trembling. Rain began to fall in big, cold drops. Too late.

When Elizabeth entered the house and bolted the door behind her, she was too relieved to notice how quiet and still it was. She looked around the empty kitchen, silent except for the pots of bath water that gurgled on the stove top. The hall clock chimed three times. Her eyes went to the water again. Three o'clock in the morning? The barn was burning outside. This wasn't bath water. Something was wrong.

"Emma," she shouted, racing through the house. "Emma."

No one answered, but she found them, Emma and the children, huddled around her uncle's bed. Emma looked up as Elizabeth burst into the room.

"Thank God you're here," she said, coming to stand between Elizabeth and the bed. "I'm going to take the children back to their room. See what you can do for him. I've already given him as much laudanum as I dare."

Elizabeth stood motionless as the three left. Her heart started to thud sickeningly. *Not Clint,* she prayed silently, squeezing her eyes shut. *Not Clint.*

"Liz-beth, that you," came a throaty whisper from the bed.

She went to him. "Yes, Uncle Clint. I'm here. Oh, God, what happened?" she cried. "I should have been here."

His faded eyes looked up at her from hollow sockets in a paper white face. "You and McKaid?" he managed.

"Yes, Uncle Clint. Don't talk now. Save your strength."

"Good. Good." His face seemed to relax a bit, and she was glad she could give him that little bit of comfort at least.

"How bad are you hurt. Let me see."

"No use," he croaked, seized by a stab of pain.

Gently she lifted the bloodstained sheet from his torso. Emma had packed the torn flesh with thick pads of bandaging,

214

but they weren't enough to curtail or contain the amount of blood he was losing. The bed beneath him was soaked a vivid red. His abdomen above the deep puncture was swollen and discolored from his internal injuries. From the look of the soiled towels and sheets on the floor she could see that he'd been hemorrhaging for a long time. Too long. Even if she knew what to do for him, it was too late.

"Are you in pain?" she asked, lowering his blankets again, wiping the tears from her face with her shoulder.

"Cold."

She threw another blanket over him. "I can give you more laudanum if you're still in pain." What would it hurt? He had so little time left. She took his hand and held it between her own.

"You'll stay with McKaid?" he asked again, seeming to want that reassurance. She saw no need to deny him such a simple wish. She told him of their love for each other and about the misunderstanding that had prompted so many of their arguments. "I think McKaid is the most wonderful man in the world," she finished at last. "I'll stay with him always, Uncle Clint. I promise."

"And children?"

"As many as he wants."

He took a feeble breath and let it out. "Good. He's been alone," he said, struggling for breath, "for so long."

"I know. Hold on, Uncle Clint. McKaid is coming now," she said, hearing the heavy, leaping footsteps on the stairs.

McKaid stepped into the room, followed by Emma, whose eyes and nose were blotched and red from weeping. McKaid's face was drained of all its color. He looked inquiringly to Elizabeth. Her chin trembled, and she gave a slight shake of her head.

"Clint," McKaid said, his voice cracking. Falteringly he made his way to his uncle and took his other hand, noticing with a grimace of pain the charred and blistered patches of skin on his exposed arm.

"McKaid, my boy," Clint said, his lips twitching into a semblance of a smile.

"Dammit, not again," McKaid cried helplessly. "Not again."

"I've had a good life, son. Don't fret for me." He took several shallow breaths and began to speak again.

215

"Don't talk, Clint."

"Have to. Hear me out. Deed to land is yours. My will—in my desk. Carlson has copy in Santa Fe. It's legal."

"No. The ranch is unimportant next to you. You have to get well."

Clint's head rolled slowly from side to side. "The ranch can work, my boy. You can make it work?"

"Oh, God."

"Someone set the fire. Hit me from behind."

"I'll find him," McKaid said through clenched teeth.

"One more thing," Clint said, exhausted. "Gold. Old Man McKaid—told me—he found gold."

"Gold?" McKaid repeated numbly.

"On Circle K. Don't know where."

"It doesn't matter, Clint."

"McKaid, you—find it. Money to—buy breeding stock." He was gasping for air.

"Rest, Clint. He knows now," Elizabeth said.

Clint turned his head to look at her. "Glad you came," he croaked. "Emma," he called, a frantic quality to his voice.

"I'm here."

"My true friend," he said. "Should have married you."

"Why spoil a good thing?" Emma bantered bravely through her tears.

Clint grinned weakly. His eyes moved to each of them one last time before they closed, never in this world to see again.

As dawn broke, McKaid stood on the front porch, turning the gold piece over and over in his fingers. At his feet were his hat, his range coat, his bedroll, his packed saddlebags, and his rifle. His guns were already strapped to his lean hips. A gold star, proclaiming his authority as a lawman in the territory of New Mexico, was pinned to his leather vest.

"Are you sure you don't want to wait until after the funeral?" Elizabeth asked, daring to break into his stony silence. "It's only one more day."

"I'm sure," he answered brusquely, not taking his eyes from the brightening horizon.

Oh, McKaid, her heart cried, *where are you? Where are we?* He hadn't said a dozen words to anyone since Clint had died. He just stood, rigid and still, and stared out the door at something in his mind that no one else could see. He was in pain, as they all were, but more than that, he blamed himself. And her.

"I should have been here," was all he had said in those long endless moments following Clint's passing. He had looked at her with such disdain that she inwardly cringed from her own guilt. She had been the one who'd lured him away, and even though he didn't voice it, she could see the accusation in his eyes. Since then he'd refused to speak to her or even look at her.

"I know you hurt, and you blame yourself and me, but you said you loved me and wanted to marry me. That has to mean something, McKaid. Must you go without talking about this?"

"I was wrong about all of that. It can never be that way for me. If I forgot it for a while, I've been brutally reminded." He stooped to pick up his hat and put it on with abrupt force, as one would slash an exclamation point behind an especially heartfelt declaration.

She looked away as if tearing him from her sight could erase his words from her mind. How could he mean that after what they'd shared? How could she accept it? What did he want from her—tears, begging, an argument? She raised her chin and faced his stiff back. He may have ripped the bottom from her world, but he'd not get a scene like that.

"Very well. Take care of yourself, McKaid." She walked toward the kitchen, then stopped and turned for one last try. "Good-bye," she said quietly, hopefully. He didn't answer, just picked up his gear and walked out the door.

Two men, both dear and precious to her, both bringing love and happiness to her life, were gone within the space of hours. She stared for a long time at the empty doorway, her ears filled with the hollow echoes of empty promises, those made to her in the heat of passion, those she had made to her uncle. What a fool she'd been to think dreams had any substance. She was far better off in a world of cold reality, where she wasn't left to hope for things beyond her grasp.

She finally knew why McKaid had cut himself off from close relationships over the past years. Life was safer that way. It was unfortunate that she hadn't learned it before yesterday. She was sorry she had made a promise to Clint that depended on someone else. At least when McKaid gave his word to the dying, he made sure he could fulfill it. Maybe she'd have to be

217

dying before McKaid's promises to her meant anything.

The screaming painful lump in her throat turned cold and hard and brittle. Bitter gall rose in her throat, strangling off the breath of life from her softer, more vulnerable emotions. Her tears dried up, and with them went the sparkle from her eyes. If McKaid could so cruelly deny what had sprung to life between them, then he wasn't the man she thought she knew. She'd made a mistake. And she'd learned a lesson. Happiness, and if not happiness, at least contentment, came only from within. To trust it to another was a fool's folly.

McKaid did not spare his horse as he rode away from the Circle K. He covered the miles as though he thought he could outrun the demons of pain and guilt that followed, but no matter how fast he went, the shadow of Ramirez still hovered overhead, laughing, jeering, stabbing with its sardonic accusations. Fool. Idiot. Have I taught you nothing. Ranger? Marshal? Pompous titles. Where were your shiny badge and fast guns this time? Where were all those lessons I gave you while your barn burned. Where was your mind while your uncle lay dying? What incurable fools you *gringo* lawmen are with your minds full of the idealistic principles and the glory of justice. How many times must I show you?

"Damn you," McKaid shouted to the wind. He pulled his horse to a stop and slid from the saddle, falling to his knees in the muddy wagon track. Tears rolled unchecked down his face. "Damn you," he repeated brokenly.

While his tears gave release to his pain, the calm of hopeless acceptance settled over him. Clint was dead. Another man's life now lay on his conscience, a life he could have saved, if he'd been tending to business instead of playing out a fantasy. Fantasies were for children.

He thought of the street urchins, hungry, deprived, sometimes homeless children who roamed the streets of Philadelphia, begging for any small handout they could get. He remembered one Christmas, in particular. He and his mother had been in a little toy shop. It was a child's delight, that store. He looked up from the brightly painted firewagon, complete with a team of four carved horses, to see one of those tattered children with his nose pressed to the window. There was such pathetic longing in his eyes at the sight of the toys that after all

218

these years McKaid could still remember it. And he could feel the boy's hopelessness as if it were his, for it was. What dazzled his mind and body, what he wanted above all else, was kept from him by an invisible barrier much like that pane of glass that said clearly, "Look all you want, dream, covet, but do not touch unless you can pay the price." For him, like the boy, the price was too high.

He'd hurt Lizzie, he'd hurt her dreadfully. But better that than the realization of the ghostly premonition he'd seen beside his uncle's bed when Clint's white and sunken face had fleetingly become hers.

Oh, God, he prayed silently. *Please don't let that happen. Not that. I'll do anything. I'll give her up, I'll send her back to safety. I'll give up my own life, only let her be safe.*

He remounted and rode on. McKaid was a strong man, a self-reliant and capable man, but he never felt more helpless in his life, or more scared. He was truly, desperately scared this time.

Julio Ortega was already in Santa Fe when McKaid arrived. He was seated at a table in the corner of the cantina, playing poker with a couple vaqueros and two old men who were drifting through town. After a long losing streak his luck was changing. He wished impatiently that the man he was to meet here would show soon. He needed his money.

"That's all for me," one of the old-timers said, gathering his winnings and dropping the coins into his shirt pocket. "You comin', pardner? It's time we found us a bath and a shave. You, especially."

"Yeah. I can only eye these cards for so long, then they all take to lookin' alike."

"Wait," Julio barked. "You have all my *dinero*. You stay. You play more."

"Sorry, pal, but you're the one who roped us into this here game. It ain't our fault you ain't no good at it."

"Come on, Tex. Time's a wastin'. Let's hightail it."

"No," Julio spat, jumping up and drawing his gun. "I will take my gold."

"Hey, *amigo*," one of the vaqueros interceded. "It was a fair game. You did not think of our losses when you raised the stakes on us."

Biff and Tex eyed each other. They were both armed, as most

219

men in the Southwest were, but they didn't care to draw on a man who already had his finger on the trigger, especially if there was any alternate solution. That solution walked through the door in the forms of Sheriff Wade and Ranger McKaid.

McKaid saw at a glance the predicament his two friends had gotten themselves into. And he saw the man who was holding the gun on them.

"Julio," he said, making his way to their table. The room hushed as all eyes turned to the tall Texan. McKaid was a friendly sort, and well liked, but no one took odds against him when it came to a fight. And a fight looked a sure thing.

"What's going on, Julio? These two men cheat you?" He glanced inquiringly at his friends. It wasn't out of the question that they had. They'd cheated him enough times. But, on the whole, they were just damn good players, especially when they decided to use their "crazy old drifters just passin' through" ruse. Biff had learned all the tricks on the Mississippi River.

"It was a fair game, McKaid," the bartender piped up. "Rafe, there, said so hisself."

"That right, Rafe?" McKaid asked.

"Yes, sir. Me, I got no quarrel with it."

"Put your gun down, Julio."

Julio was weakening. "They were leaving. I only want a chance to win my money back."

"Put the gun on the table or use it, Julio."

"Hey, it ain't you he's pointin' it at," Tex protested.

"No. But I'll be the one who kills him."

The blood drained from Julio's dark skin, leaving it sallow against his black hair. He lowered the gun and laid it on the table, slumping back down on his chair. The whole cantina gave a collective sigh, though from relief or disappointment, McKaid couldn't tell.

"What are you doing in town, Julio?" McKaid questioned. "The rest of the ranch is in mourning because of my uncle's death, and you're here playing cards?"

A buzz of comments filled the room at the news of Clint's death. Old Man McKaid and Colfax had been very respected men in Santa Fe, as was the young McKaid.

Sheriff Wade thought it strange also. "He rode in here early this morning. I didn't think nothin' of it at the time, your men gettin' regular leave time and all. But it is a mite strange, under the circumstances."

220

"Flashin' a lot of gold, too," Biff said. "Show him the pot you won, pard." Tex spilled the gold coins onto the table.

Julio stared hungrily at them. "It means nothing. I quit the ranch. I come to town."

McKaid picked up one of the coins and held it to the light. "That's funny. You quit, yet you didn't draw your pay. But then maybe you had no need of it since you carry Mexican gold. Where did you get it? Not from me, that's for sure."

"I earn it."

"Doing what? You were in my employ."

"I—eh—I do not stay to listen to this. I—"

"Sit down," McKaid spat, advancing on his former ranch hand. "When Packard found my uncle lying unconscious in the burning barn, he found this coin in his hand." McKaid drew out a coin that matched the one Julio had gambled away. He tossed them both on the table. "Clint didn't die right away. He told us what happened."

"No. It is not so," Julio cried defensively, sinking back further into the chair.

"McKaid," Tex said thoughtfully, "he was spoutin' off about meetin' some friend who was going to pay him more money."

McKaid's brows rose. "Very interesting."

Julio Ortega was visibly trembling, but McKaid showed no pity. As swift as lightning he grabbed the man's shirt front and hauled him to his feet.

"I'll tell you what I think. I think Clint Colfax offered you work, gave you a comfortable place to live, kept you well fed, and paid you a better than fair wage, and you betrayed him for a few stinkin' coins which you've already lost. I think you started that fire for money. I think you dropped your precious gold, and when you went back for it, Clint had already found it. I think you hit him over the head and left him there to die. And he did die, Ortega. You murdered him."

"You have no proof," Julio cried, defending himself against a sure hanging.

McKaid jerked him even closer. "But I'm right, and you know it. And before I'm finished with you, you'll beg to tell me so. And you'll tell me who hired you to kill him."

"I was not hired to kill anyone."

"And when you've spilled your guts to me, I'll turn you loose and tell the world that you confessed that you work for

221

Ramirez. I'll let them know you told us everything, where his hideout is, how many men he has, who they are, what he plans to do. When Ramirez hears that—and he will—he won't be happy with you. And when Ramirez is unhappy, he gets downright mean. I couldn't think of a better punishment for you than to let Ramirez have you."

"No. Sheriff, you have to protect me. Put me in jail."

"Sorry. You're Marshal McKaid's prisoner, not mine."

"Marshal . . ." Ortega repeated, feeling the sure and deadly jaws of death snapping at his heels. If McKaid didn't kill him first, Ramirez would. Sweat ran down his face. "I meant only to start a little fire, to provoke you. No one was to be hurt, I swear to you."

"Except Clint was hurt, and you left him there to die."

"I was afraid. I ran to get help."

"You just ran, Ortega. You took your gold and you ran. And you don't know what fear is yet. Wait until you're standing on the gallows with a noose around your neck and counting the seconds until the floor drops out from under you. You'll hear the latch give, and then you'll be falling. Your neck will snap, but you won't die right away. Did you know that a man's legs twitch for several minutes after he's been hung?"

"You cannot do this," he said with false bravado. "I have rights. I know the law."

"You have nothing, Ortega. When you deprived my uncle of his right to live, you forfeited yours. You are dead. The judge will hear your pitiful case tomorrow, and if he doesn't hang you, I'll be somewhere around, waiting. And when I'm not there, there will still be Ramirez."

"Please, *por favor*, I beg of you, have some mercy," Julio cried, his countenance crumbling in fear and dread.

"Mercy? Was it mercy when you couldn't even drag an unconscious man out of a flaming barn, when you left him where the roof could collapse on top of him? Is that the mercy you seek?"

"Enough, McKaid," the sheriff interceded. "I'll lock him up for you. Have a beer and cool off."

McKaid eyed the sheriff and his two friends, then nodded and released Ortega. He went to the bar and accepted the mug of draft the bartender handed him.

"Sorry about your uncle."

Without looking up he nodded, then lifted the mug and

drained half the contents. A loud cracking report sounded from somewhere across the town square. Very slowly McKaid lowered his beer and turned toward the door. His feet carried him to the commotion outside.

Halfway down the block the sheriff stood and turned to McKaid. "He's dead."

McKaid looked at Ortega's lifeless body, then let his eyes search the rooftops for any sign of movement. He didn't expect to find any, nor did he.

"I'll get my men together and go after him," the sheriff said. "This *is* my jurisdiction."

McKaid said nothing, he felt nothing. He went back to finish his beer.

Chapter Fourteen

"For everything there is a season, and a time for every matter under heaven: a time to be born, and a time to die, a time . . ."

The reverend's voice resounded melodiously in her ears, as it did with all those gathered around the simple pine box embracing the body of her uncle now at rest. Clint's wishes had been observed: a plain burial, no guests, no lengthy mourning, a plot beside Old Man McKaid.

She stared not at the coffin with its one bouquet of wildflowers, but at the hole. Deep, dark, empty. Abysmal. An intriguing door to the earth and to time without end that waited to welcome one of its own back home.

"Ashes to ashes, dust to dust. May the Lord . . ."

She lifted her eyes and numbly looked at the others standing around that portal. Emma was weeping, sobbing into Russ's dark coat. Russ sniffed back his own grief. The children were crying, though quietly, and Lenore, her eyes red and wet, held them in the shelter of her arms. Beside them Mr. Beaumont wiped his clouded and nearly sightless eyes. The ranch hands stood, hats in hand, shifting uncomfortably. Several cleared restricted throats, one ducked his head and blew his nose.

Dry-eyed, Elizabeth watched it all, even when the coffin was lowered and when the first shovel laid a scattering of dirt over it. She felt like an observer, removed emotionally, as if she'd never been part of their lives at all, as if she could walk away and no one would know she'd gone or remember that she'd been there. Emma, Beaumont, Russ, Lenore, and the children. A nice family unit. Where did she fit, now that her only connection with the ranch had been severed?

A time to kill, a time to heal, a time to weep, a time to laugh, a time to mourn, a time to dance. The words repeated themselves in her mind. She couldn't weep, she couldn't mourn. Not yet. Not until she was stronger. If she let the pain in now, it would be too devastating to bear. She had lost her uncle and she had lost McKaid, and both because of her irresponsible, wanton behavior. And she had caused so much heartache and sorrow.

She deserved the pain. It would be just punishment for her transgressions, but some part of her mind, a part intent on protecting her from herself even if against her will, had turned off her feelings. Now she only felt cold, cold and as empty as that hole had been moments before. In a way, it was better, in a way, worse. Maybe her terrible aloneness was to be her penance.

"I'm worried about her, Russ," Lenore said late the next night. "Maybe you should have a talk with her. She's close to you."

"What can I do? She's grieving in her own way. Give her some time."

"It's more than that. She doesn't cry, she doesn't talk, she won't eat, she just sits up there in her uncle's room and stares at the walls. It's not natural. She's dealt with death before. Emma told me she lost her parents when she was young, then her adoptive mother. You said she even lost a fiancé. No, Russ, something else is bothering her."

"She's probably worried sick over McKaid."

"And that's another thing. How could he go riding off without even giving his uncle's funeral a care. As far as I'm concerned, they're both acting strange. Talk to her, Russ. I've seen the way you draw her out. She responds to you."

"Listen, Lenore, it's not the way you think it is with Elizabeth and me."

"That doesn't matter. What does matter right now is that poor woman. She's going to make herself ill."

Russ gave in and climbed the stairs to Clint's room. What he found gave him pause to wonder. Elizabeth was indeed a wretched sight, her eyes lifeless glass in her ashen face, her cheeks hollow, her lips bloodless, her hair dull and uncombed. But she wasn't sitting in any chair or staring at any wall. She was hanging different curtains at the window, plain yellow curtains to match the faded yellow and white quilt on the bed.

A trunk sat by the door, and in it were all of Clint's belongings, except for a tintype of Clint and McKaid that rested on the bedside table and Clint's gun-belt and gun that hung over the bedpost.

"Elizabeth?" he said, questioningly.

Her hands stilled, and she turned her head his way. "Hello, Russ."

"Elizabeth, what are you doing?"

"I'm moving into this room. I'd be grateful if you'd take Uncle Clint's things to the bunkhouse. If there's anything there that the men want . . ."

"What's wrong with your own room?"

Elizabeth finished hanging the curtains, then fluffed them out to her satisfaction. Not until then did she get down from the chair and face him.

"I've been doing a great deal of thinking. As a matter of fact, I'm glad you've come. Close the door, please."

"But, Elizabeth . . ."

"I don't care about proprieties. I care about privacy. There are some facts you must know now, even though I promised McKaid my silence."

"If you promised . . ."

"Promises are just words, easily forgotten when situations change. Believe me, I know. Sit down."

He frowned, but did as she said. He was afraid not to. She was different. She wasn't the happy spirited sprite he had once known. Lenore was right. Something was definitely on her mind, and weighing heavily by her looks and actions. He was almost afraid to know what. Almost, but not quite.

"All right. Let's have it," he said.

"First of all, I want you to tell Lenore how you feel about her."

"What?"

"Don't deny it. I thought at one time that I could employ a more devious method to make you both realize what you're doing to each other, but there isn't time for that. You've lost years already, and you may not have much longer, especially if you remain around me. Lenore wants to marry you."

Russ couldn't find any words. Marry him? Remain around her? She wasn't making much sense.

"Are you listening to me, Russ Packard?"

"Yes. Yes, of course, but . . ."

227

"This idea you have that you are somehow beneath her is just plain balderdash. You're making her as miserable as you've been. You're throwing away precious time together."

"What about McKaid?"

"Forget about him. They've never been more than friends and neighbors. He told me that the night . . ." She gave a shuddering sigh, then lifted her chin and pressed on. "The night we first . . . ah . . . made love."

"Sweet God, Elizabeth, you don't have to tell me this." He stood up and walked to the window.

"Yes, I do. It's important. I want you to know that Lenore only came here because of her need to see you. We gave them a good scare, Russ. They both thought you and I were falling in love." A bittersweet curl turned her lips.

"Then McKaid returns your love? Well, that's wonderful. That makes it . . ."

"No," she said bluntly, stopping him when he would have come to her. "It seems he was mistaken about that. His very words, I might add."

"Well, that's just too bad, isn't it," Russ ground out, fury sparking in his eyes. No wonder she was upset. That bastard? "I'll break his neck for hurting you like this."

She shook her head. "It doesn't matter."

"Like hell! Clint would have his hide if he weren't . . ."

"Dead," Elizabeth said expressionlessly. "But he is dead. Because of me, my uncle is dead."

"That's not true. Why are you doing this to yourself?" he demanded, pounding his fist against the bedpost.

Impassive eyes met his. "When McKaid told me he was leaving to go after the priest who was kidnapped, I begged him to take me away where we could be alone for a while. If I hadn't, McKaid would have been here, and none of this would have happened."

"You don't know that."

"No? Ask McKaid."

"Did he say that? That you were to blame?" he asked, incredulous.

"In words? No. But it was in his eyes, and on his face. It couldn't have been plainer if he'd shouted it for the world to hear. When Clint died, McKaid just stood there. For a long time he was quiet. Then he looked at me with those icy eyes. Have you ever seen his eyes when they turn to the color of cold

228

steel? They're no color at all. They simply glitter. Anyway, his eyes narrowed, his nostrils flared, and his lips curled as if he'd just looked at something disgusting. 'I should have been here,' he said, and that was all he said to me, even though my own heart was breaking, until he told me it was over between us, that all the talk of love and marriage was a mistake."

"Elizabeth, honey, he was in pain. He'd just lost his uncle."

Her back stiffened and she turned away. "Are you implying I didn't love the uncle I just lost?"

"One would have to wonder," Russ said provokingly. He couldn't stand her stoicism a moment longer. He wanted tears, screaming, a single word uttered in anger, anything but this blank face and monotonous voice. "You haven't shed one tear. All you care about is that McKaid scorned you. All you can think about is hating McKaid. Have you given a thought to Emma or the children? Emma's worried sick about you. When did you turn so selfish?"

For one brief tick of the clock, he thought she would break. Her eyes clouded over and her chin started to pucker. But she was tough. Before he was even certain of what he saw, it was gone. Her slender shoulders stiffened and her chest muscles clenched as if forming a shield around a very battered and broken heart.

She drew in a deep breath and relaxed, the tension flowing out of her, and the emotion that was fleetingly revealed on her face rolled away with it. She turned lifeless eyes to his face, absolute control in place again. He sighed.

"You're very wrong, Mr. Packard. For the first time in my life, I'm not thinking of myself. I don't deny my life has been centered on self and self-pity. I pitied myself when my parents died, when my mother died. I felt sorry for myself when I lost my fiancé. I was indignant and resentful of being unfairly treated by my employers and prospective employers. And I felt sorry for myself when I loved McKaid and thought he loved Lenore. Oh, yes, I have been selfish. But not now. I accept my responsibility for Clint's death, and now I have to do whatever I can to make it up to everyone, especially McKaid. That's why I have to break my promise to him."

"I don't understand this." He sat down hard on the edge of the bed.

"It's Ramirez, Russ."

"Ramirez? What does he have to do with your promise?"

"Everything. You know as well as I that he was responsible for the fire.'

"Maybe, but . . ."

"Listen to me carefully. Ramirez always goes after someone McKaid loves. It's become a pattern with him."

"But he couldn't have known Clint would go into the barn, or that he'd be struck by falling timbers."

"No. I don't think he intended that anyone be hurt. Not yet. He was playing with McKaid. But he will come for someone. And I believe it will be Lenore."

"Lenore," he gasped, jumping up again. "Why should he . . ." His words fell off as he began to see.

"We, you and I, thought they were lovers. They acted like lovers. All the men think they're three steps from a wedding. My promise to McKaid was to keep silent about the two of us in order to protect me from Ramirez. He wanted no one to know we'd resolved our differences. He didn't want word to get to Ramirez that McKaid had a sweetheart. I don't think he gave Lenore a thought, not because he didn't care, but because the idea of them as lovers, or even giving the appearance of lovers, never crossed his mind."

"Oh, my God," Russ breathed, stunned. "You could be right."

"Is Lenore still here?"

"She and her father are preparing to leave now. Her father has to go to Albuquerque tomorrow morning."

"Is Lenore going with him? Could he keep her there until this is over?"

"No. He's taking the stage so his men can stay at the ranch. Besides, she'd be no safer in Albuquerque if Ramirez really wanted her."

"Can you persuade her to stay here? Maybe you could get some of their men to come here, as well. If all the possible victims, the people McKaid loves, are living in one place and heavily guarded, Ramirez might think twice."

"She'll stay. I'll tell her you need her. I don't want to alarm her."

"Alarm? Isn't it better for her to be on her guard? She's a strong woman. Don't underestimate her."

It was the first softening he'd seen in her since he'd come to talk to her. "You like her, don't you?"

"It's hard not to like Lenore."

"Does she really love me?"

"Yes, I think she does. Why don't you ask her? She's been waiting a long time for you to come to your senses."

"What if you're wrong?"

"Then you'll be exactly where you are now. What if I'm right? You don't look like a coward."

"Ouch. Easy on my pride there."

She grinned, and it was an easy smile that reached her eyes. He felt himself breathe easier. "What about you? Will you be all right for now?"

She gave a short dismissive huff and turned away. "I'm fine. Russ, I think you should move into the house. I'll put clean linens on McKaid's bed for you."

"Do you really think that's necessary?"

"Yes. And I want four men on guard around the house at all times. I don't intend to see McKaid lose anyone else. See to it, please."

With Clint dead and McKaid gone, Russ knew she was mistress of the ranch. If McKaid was killed, she could possibly even inherit it. If he had doubted her ability to assume that role in the past, he did no longer. Something had changed inside her. She didn't need him anymore to tease her out of a sulk or give her someone to lean on. She'd found her strength.

McKaid had put him in charge, but he hadn't seen fit to explain the situation as Elizabeth had. Maybe he was trying to protect Elizabeth, and maybe he hadn't seen Lenore as being in danger, but that didn't excuse the way he'd left things. How did McKaid expect him to keep the women from harm when he didn't know which of them to protect, or why? Hang McKaid. From now on he would work with Elizabeth.

"Consider it done."

"No arguments?"

He grinned cheekily. "Not yet. No guarantees though. If I ever think you're wrong, I'll speak my mind."

"Fair enough."

"This is gettin' us nowhere," Biff grumbled to his longtime partner. "He gettin' addle-brained on us, or what?"

"I dunno. I ain't never seen him in such a state as this." Tex pushed back his hat and rubbed his stubbly jaw. "It's like the devil hisself is ridin' his arse."

231

"And pokin' at him with that red-hot pitch fork," Biff added.

"It ain't like him to be so close-minded. He ain't listened to one piece of advice we give him. Why'd he bring us out here if he ain't gonna let us help him?"

"Well," Biff drawled, "let's cut him some slack for a time longer. He just lost his uncle."

"The hell of it is," Tex went on, "we ain't got a while longer. The more time we waste on a cold trail, the more time Ramirez has to do his worst. Why, right this minute he could be stalkin' that ranch."

Biff chewed on his inner lip, his eyes squinting thoughtfully. "Grievin' or no, it's time we took a hand in this. It's time he listened to sense."

They caught up with McKaid in a matter of seconds and physically blocked his way, drawing their mounts to a stop in front of Lucky Lady.

"We got a piece to say, McKaid, and you're gonna hear us."

"Get out of my way."

"You're a Ranger," Tex argued. "It's long, damn past time you started thinkin' like one."

"Hell, man," Biff added his voice to his partner's, "you ain't doin' no good out here. Use your head. This is a fool's mission."

"You won't find Ramirez this way, not if he has a mind to stay hid. You ought'a know that by now. Shee-it, ain't he done this enough times already?"

"What's that supposed to mean?" McKaid snarled.

"Don't waste your breath," Biff said sarcastically. "Can't you see he loves this. Ramirez strikes, McKaid chases, Ramirez strikes again, McKaid changes directions. He ain't savvy enough to outwit the pissant, so he don't even wanna try. He just wants to go round and round in goddamn circles."

McKaid's jaw clenched and he glared menacingly at his friends. "If you're so damn smart, what would you do?"

"Are you askin' finally?" Tex taunted. "The young know-it-all wants some advice from us older and wiser experts."

"Dammit, Tex, if you aren't going to help, quit hindering. Get out of my way."

"Now simmer down," Biff placated. "Let's take a hard look at this. Here we are, chasing phantoms, and Ramirez is off, who knows where, havin' a good laugh."

"And?"

"You ain't never caught him, and he knows it. Time you learnt it, boy, this ain't the way."

"He's not getting away with it this time," McKaid swore.

Tex laughed jeeringly. "No-siree, bub. Looks like you got him hog-tied good, don't it."

"You looking for a fight, Donner?" McKaid snapped, shards of fury spitting from his frozen glower.

"Could be," Tex drawled. "A good kick in the arse might just get your brains to workin' again, seein' as that's where they are."

"All right. I've had enough, you jackass. Get off that horse."

"That's a good idea," Biff agreed. "Let's have a nice long brawl. Right here. We got nothin' better to do. Let's kill a little time while Ramirez kills one of them young 'uns of yours."

McKaid took off his hat and raked his fingers through his hair. He took several deep breaths to get himself under control. "Sorry, boys. I guess I am over the edge."

"I say we get back to the ranch," Tex said. "If we're ever gonna get that jackel, we'll have to get him by bein' as crafty as him. We have to make him come for us on *our* terms, not his."

"I don't want him anywhere near that ranch."

"So that means he's gonna stay away? What you don't want don't matter beans to Ramirez. If he wants something at the Circle K, by crakey, he'll go after it. Now, I suggest we make tracks. We got some miles to cover."

"Well?" Lenore asked, coming to his side as Russ walked into the kitchen. Emma was refilling Mr. Beaumont's coffee cup and stopped to look up, wanting to hear the answer.

"She's some woman," Russ answered enigmatically.

"So I've heard," Mr. Beaumont said, sipping his coffee. "Is she as pretty as the men say she is?"

"Miss Elizabeth is beautiful," Ruthie answered staunchly.

"She is that, child," Emma replied. "More cornbread, James?"

"No, ma'am, I'll finish Ruthie's."

"Russ Packard, are you going to tell us or not?" Lenore demanded, her fists resting on the curve of her hips.

Russ studied her, grinning boyishly. Did she really love him? Could he be so lucky? "I'm not a rich man, Mrs. Beaumont. I have some money saved up, but not much as

233

you'd see it. And I haven't gone to fine schools or anything like that. But I am a passably intelligent man, and I work hard."

Lenore frowned quizzically. "Mr. Packard . . ."

"And if you stay on with us, I give you warning I'll use the time to my advantage."

"Are you trying to say something, young man?" Mr. Beaumont asked.

"Yes, sir, I'm asking your permission to court Lenore."

"You have it. And about time, I'd say."

Lenore was blushing when Russ turned to look at her. "And you, Lenore, do I have your consent?"

"I—" She dropped a spoon on the floor and glanced around at the curious eyes watching her fumbling response. Russ wanted to court her. Relief and excitement bubbled to life, and for a second she wanted to throw herself into his arms and hug him for sheer joy. Instead, she squared her shoulders and scolded him.

"I sent you up there to see about Elizabeth, not come back with notions of courting."

Russ was mesmerized by her expressive face, the way her dark eyes lit, the way her creamy pale skin flushed, the way she struggled not to grin. Her full bosom rose and fell with every quick short breath she drew. He'd never really had much chance to sit and look at her the way he wanted. She was a truly exquisite woman, and he could hardly wait to unwrap all her mysterious secrets, layer by layer.

"Well, ma'am, the notion's in my head. What's your answer?"

"I say I'm surprised. I thought you had an eye for Elizabeth."

"No, ma'am. I mean, she is a woman to turn a man's head, but it's you I have an eye for."

"And I'm not a woman to turn a man's head?"

"No. I mean yes. I mean that's not what I meant. You're the most beautiful woman I ever saw."

Her finely arched brow rose thoughtfully. "I haven't turned your head in three years."

"Yes, ma'am, you have, but I thought you were sweet on McKaid, so I held my tongue."

"You were afraid of the competition?" she baited him.

"Of McKaid? Definitely not. I just figured he could offer you more. As I said, I'm not a rich man."

234

"And you think I'm only interested in men who have large bank accounts. That doesn't say much for my character."

"I meant no harm or insult, Lenore," Russ said passionately. "A woman as fine and lovely as you should have the best, that's all."

"I see. Very well, you may come to call, but I make no promises, Russ Packard."

"Gee," sang Ruthie in wonder, her wide eyes darting from one to the other.

"Ugh," James answered. "Sweet talk. Let's go upstairs and draw on the slate boards."

Emma, grinning smugly, cleared the table as the children left. "You said something about Miss Lenore staying on here, Russ. Are you invitin' her?"

"No. Not that I wouldn't, mind you. It's Elizabeth. She says Lenore is to stay here while Mr. Beaumont goes to visit the doctor."

"Oh, I can't impose at a time like this," Lenore demurred.

"I agree with Elizabeth," Russ said. "You really must, for your own protection."

"Elizabeth talked to you, then?" Emma asked.

"She didn't so much talk as give me my orders."

"Orders?" Elizabeth never ordered anyone around, not even James or Ruthie.

"Yes, ma'am. I think you have a new mistress at the ranch. And a smart one." Omitting the personal parts of their discussion, Russ explained why Elizabeth thought Lenore could be in danger and why she should stay at the Circle K.

"I have to agree with her," Beaumont said. "You'll be safer here with Russ. I'll send as many men as I can spare to help you out."

"I could go with you, Father."

"You'd be on the road for hours in a wagon that's no protection at all, and I'm no good to you. No. I'll take the stage this time, and you will do as Russ tells you."

She bristled. "Father, I'm not a child to be—"

"She's a headstrong woman, Packard. Use a firm hand with her."

"Yes, sir," Russ answered, unable to hide his grin as he helped the older man to his waiting carriage.

"Now look here, you two." Lenore marched after them indignantly.

235

Emma laid a restraining hand on her arm. "It's nothing but talk, dear. They like to think they have the upper hand." She winked conspiratorially. "Just mind you, it's the women who pull the rugs out from under their feet."

Russ heard them. He looked back toward the kitchen and rolled his eyes heavenward. So it was starting already, the battle of wit and wile. He would have laughed if what Emma said weren't so pathetically true. He hadn't had his feet firmly on the ground once while Lenore was around. He doubted that he ever would again, because he intended to have her around permanently.

Emma patted Lenore's hand. "He's a fine man. You've loved him a long time, haven't you?"

"He's so different from my late husband," Lenore said in place of a direct answer. "Jacques was so formal and correct, not given to showing his feelings. And Jacques didn't often laugh. Everything was serious to him. I think I fell in love with Russ the first time I heard his laughter. I felt myself smile from inside out with him." She looked at Emma and sobered. "You think me unfaithful for feeling that way while my husband still lived?"

Emma shrugged. "You were never anything but a good wife to Jacques. How did you meet him?"

"Ours was an arranged marriage. I was young and thought him terribly sophisticated, but we were very different. Oh, I had great respect and admiration for him, and I truly cared for him . . ."

"But he didn't make your heart smile."

"No. We had much together, but not that."

"It's a rare thing to find. Now, let's see if Elizabeth needs any help. I dreaded clearing out his room. I used to nag him something fierce about keeping his belongings picked up." Tears sprang to her eyes. "If I had him back, I'd let him throw his shirts anywhere he wanted."

"Don't, Emma. You have your memories. Keep them and let the rest go."

Emma sniffed and wiped her eyes with her apron, putting on a brave front. "Yes, I know you're right. He meant a lot to me, that man. I'm glad Elizabeth will be in his room. He'd like that. He took one look at her and decided she was the one for McKaid. You should have heard them when she was taking that bullet out of him. She was exhausted and going on nerves

236

alone, he was in pain and drunk out of his mind, and still they were arguing, just like they do now. And poor Clint. There was his nephew, bleeding all over the place, and a niece he knew nothing about except that she'd almost been killed. She was doing what no one else could do, she was saving McKaid's life, and there Clint was trying to keep from laughing at them both. He felt awful when she fainted. That was it, as far as he was concerned. Elizabeth was pure gold, tough, strong, courageous, and not intimidated by calamities. Right up there with McKaid. He wanted to see them get together. It's too bad he never did, it would have made me happy."

Two days later their guarded peace was shattered. One of the ranch hands rushed into the house interrupting their late evening meal, and announced that a large band of Indians was riding their way.

"How many?" Russ asked, getting up abruptly from the table and grabbing the rifle that was never far from his side.

"Twenty—thirty. It's hard to say. They're east of the river, coming from the north. What do you want us to do, boss? We're scattered all over the ranch."

"I thought the Indians were confined to reservations," Lenore said. "We haven't been bothered in a long time."

"The *Daily New Mexican* reported two Apache raids on small farms and ranches just this week," the young man answered. "Brutal massacres, the paper said."

Elizabeth could see he was disconcerted, and quite possibly overreacting. She knew there were still Indians in the area, she'd met some of them firsthand. It would be foolish to assume these Indians were as friendly as Straight Arrow's men, but it would be disastrous if the men at the ranch acted hastily and provoked a real attack when none was intended.

"Russ, could I speak with you, please?"

She went into the study and closed the doors after Russ had followed. She paced the room once, then turned to see Russ waiting nervously for her to speak.

"What do you think?" she asked.

"I was hoping you'd have the answer."

"Oh. I don't, so let's think like McKaid. They could be Ramirez and his men, disguised as Indians, so keep that uppermost in your mind. Then they could be real Indians ant on mayhem. Or they could be Indians who mean no harm, in which case, we dare not show hostility. I'd hate to think we shot Straight Arrow after he saved our lives."

Russ understood. He nodded his head, his mind outlining what needed to be done. "I'll sound the alarm and get the men back here to the house. If you don't mind a few windows shot out, we'll turn this place into a fortress. We'll be ready for whichever way it goes."

Russ barged back into the hall, rapping out his instructions as he sent the young man to the emergency bell mounted by the side of the burned barn, and went himself to organize the men. Outside the clang, clang, clang of the bell sounded in its prearranged signal, and hurried footsteps and shouted commands permeated the air. Ammunition had already been collected at sentry points around the house. It was hauled onto the porches, both front and back, where rough planks were being laid in place to act as protection for the men.

Elizabeth gave out her own orders to the two women and the two frightened children, explaining, as she did, what they were planning. Medical supplies were collected as well as all the guns and ammunition in the house. Furniture was moved hastily to free the windows, and the children were given strict instructions to follow in case of an attack.

All this, Elizabeth realized belatedly, should have been organized before. McKaid would have thought of it, but McKaid, blast his hide, was conspicuously absent.

"No, no!" wailed Ruthie. She broke away from her brother and threw her small body against Elizabeth's legs, clutching at her with desperate little fingers. "Don't leave us. Stay with us. You can hide with us. You'll get shot like my mommy if you don't hide. She made us get in the cellar, and she never came back. She should have stayed with us. She should have."

Elizabeth dropped to her knees. "Oh, sweetheart," she crooned, holding Ruthie close. How terrible that these two children couldn't seem to escape violence, that they couldn't find peace and security again. It wasn't fair. Life was never fair.

She looked up at James, and he bravely squared his shoulders and came to pull Ruthie away.

"Ruthie," Elizabeth said gently. "Your mother cared first about your safety, just as we do. But she also cared about your daddy, and she knew he needed her help. She had to help him, you know that, don't you? And now I have to help Russ, and

238

you have to help me. You can do that best by going with James."

"Will you come back?" she asked tearfully.

"She'll come back," James said. "The men won't let her get hurt. Daddy was alone. He couldn't fight all the outlaws who came. But Elizabeth has dozens of men to help her."

"James is right," Emma said sternly. "You're not to worry, just do as Elizabeth says now."

Elizabeth stood and took a bracing breath. With a last look at Ruthie and a nod of thanks to Emma and James she turned and left the room. Shouting outside the front door drew her attention back to their predicament.

Elizabeth raced upstairs and strapped her uncle's gun around her hips, an incongruous sight against the gathered material of her blue calico dress. She withdrew the weapon and weighed it in her hand. Two months ago, if someone would have told her she'd be standing in a bedroom in New Mexico sighting down the barrel of a gun at her own reflection in a mirror, she would have had a very good laugh. She thought of dear Arnold and what he'd say if he saw her, and she did laugh.

A low rumble, like distant thunder, sobered her. They were coming, and they were many. She dashed out the door and down the steps, heading for the front door.

"Elizabeth!" Emma shouted. "What are you doing? You can't go out there."

"I have to. I have to be sure it's not Straight Arrow's people out there." Without waiting for the argument she knew would follow, she slipped out the door and closed it firmly behind her.

Russ's reaction was much the same as in Emma's, and got the same reaction. Shaking his head in exasperation, he checked her gun to see that it was loaded.

"You're sure you can shoot this now?"

"Taught by a master," she quipped. "Russ, did you tell the men to hold their fire until you give the signal?"

"They'll wait," Russ said, lowering the spyglass.

"Where are they?"

"Just over the hill."

Painted in grotesque patterns, heavily feathered and beaded, lances and guns at their sides, the large Apache war party crested the hill and rode toward the house.

*   *   *

239

Biff, Tex, and McKaid rode toward the Circle K from the south. They were silent, each occupied with his own thoughts. Biff, his rheumatism acting up in his hip joints, wanted his hot bath and his bottle. Tex was looking forward to a good meal, anything but jerky and beans and dried bread. McKaid thought of Clint and how unlike home the ranch would be without him.

Clint and the Circle K had always been there for him when he wanted someone to talk to and a place of refuge for a while, when his harsh life began to press in on him. He was returning, but with a certain reluctance this time. He didn't want to think about how he'd failed his uncle, he didn't want to face the pain in Emma's eyes, he didn't want to see Clint's stallion and know he'd never see his uncle ride him again. And he didn't want to see Elizabeth. Not yet. He was too confused. Anger, fear, love, hate, guilt, remorse. Every demoralizing emotion he possessed was at play inside him. Rather than sort them out, he ignored them.

It took a few minutes for the three weary Rangers to recognize the faint distant sound that rode on the evening breeze.

"Are we near to bein' there, McKaid?"

"Sounds like church bells."

McKaid reined in his horse and listened, a chill running through him. "It's the alarm bell at the ranch. There's trouble. Let's ride."

Chapter Fifteen

Even through the paint Elizabeth recognized the Indian who broke away from the war party and rode alone up to the house. She rushed down the steps. "Don't shoot!" she called over her shoulder as she heard Russ call her name and heard the men on the porch come to their feet. A few of them cocked the hammers on their guns. She spun around.

"Don't shoot. Russ—" she implored urgently.

Russ signaled the men, and they lowered their guns, though none of them was ready to trust the Apache chieftain just yet. Neither was Russ. He'd heard of the Indians who made their home to the north and sometimes traded with Clint, but he'd never met the man Clint considered his friend, the man Elizabeth claimed saved her life. He didn't know Straight Arrow.

Elizabeth stopped a few feet from Straight Arrow's horse and looked up into his impassive dark eyes. She remembered those eyes.

"Welcome, Straight Arrow," she said.

Straight Arrow lifted his eyes to all the armed men surrounding the house. "Welcome?" he asked, looking again at the woman. McKaid's woman. "I will speak to McKaid," he said, looking dismissively at the door of the house.

And yes, she remembered that, too. To him she was a *woman*. "I'm sorry, but McKaid is not here."

"The old man?" Straight Arrow asked, still addressing the air between himself and the house. "I will speak to him."

"Clint Colfax is dead," Elizabeth said stiffly.

Almost imperceptibly his chin rose, but it was enough to let Elizabeth see that he was affected by the news.

"He had a sickness?" the deep voice asked of someone. Certainly not her, though she answered.

"No. The barn was set on fire. Uncle Clint was badly hurt trying to save the livestock. He died that same evening. One of the men on the ranch was gone the next morning, and we think he started the fire."

"McKaid looks for this man?"

"No. He doesn't know the man left. He looks for Ramirez." The Indian looked at her then, and his eyes spoke of understanding. "The guns."

"We didn't know who you were. Ramirez could have tried to trick us."

"There is a man who is boss?"

"Yes, of course." It certainly would not do to talk of such matters with a woman. She motioned to Russ. "This is Russ Packard, the foreman in charge. Russ, this is Straight Arrow."

Straight Arrow dismounted and shook hands with Russ in the white man's way. He then turned to his men and signaled that all was well.

"Can we offer your men anything—food, water?" Elizabeth asked.

"My men need nothing. We will talk," he said, turning to Russ. Elizabeth felt dismissed.

She glared at his broad, bare back, then turned and strode to the porch. "Relax," she said to the men. "He's McKaid's friend. His men won't attack us. And Ramirez won't come while the Apache are here. Take turns on watch, and get some rest."

"Riders coming," one of the guards shouted. "Three of 'em."

"Let me have the glass, please," Elizabeth said, making her way to the lookout man. She raised the glass to her eye and scanned the area where the guard had spotted the riders. Wide shadows fell across the land from the western mountains that rose upward into the orange and purple sky. It was impossible to see other than dark shapes, but one shape, in particular, caught her eye.

"Be on your guard, but hold your fire. It might be McKaid. If it is, send him to Russ and Straight Arrow."

She went into the house. She alerted Emma and Lenore that McKaid was home, then walked directly to the stairs. She wanted no part of McKaid's homecoming.

"Wait a minute," Emma called. "What happened out there?"

"Some friends came to call. No need to worry. Russ will tell you all about it."

"When?" Emma demanded. "Elizabeth . . ."

She didn't answer, but went to her room and locked the door behind her. She unbuckled the gun belt and looped it over the bedpost, pausing to finger the tooled leather of the holster. Sitting heavily on the edge of the bed, she pressed the tips of her fingers against the bridge of her nose to ward off the tears that were threatening. She felt bruised and battered on the inside, and so very tired. She lay back on the bed and closed her eyes to rest for a minute. Outside she heard McKaid's voice rapping out staccato questions and orders. The burden of responsibility slid from her shoulders. McKaid. Weariness from the past tension-filled weeks overcame her and she slept.

Elizabeth was up before the sun rose the next morning, and the appetizing aromas of bacon, biscuits, and fresh coffee filled the kitchen by the time the others appeared.

"Morning, dear," Emma said, hurrying out from her small bedroom. "What's left to do here?"

"Thought I'd fry some pork chops and scramble a platter of eggs. Who were the men with McKaid?"

"Friends of his. Rangers Biff Story and Tex Donner."

She nodded and began dipping the chops in light batter for frying. "Did you learn what Straight Arrow wanted?"

"Didn't you? You talked to him long enough out there last night."

"Straight Arrow doesn't talk to women unless it's absolutely necessary."

"I see. Well, it seems some of Ramirez's band attacked their camp while the hunting party was away. They killed three of their men, including Straight Arrow's father, and took two of their women. One of the women is Straight Arrow's first wife."

"First?"

"He has two."

She shook her head. "From all I've heard, that sounds like Ramirez's style, all right, but I can't see him getting involved with the Indians."

"According to Straight Arrow, it was the same man who

attacked you and McKaid, along with four Mexicans. Ramirez wasn't with them though."

"Corbett." She clucked her tongue in exasperation. "Corbett's riding with Ramirez then."

"That's right. Corbett released one of the women after the men had beaten and raped her. She was sent back to camp to tell Straight Arrow that Corbett wanted McKaid. Corbett blames the Indians for cheating him of McKaid that time they attacked you. He says that Straight Arrow is to make it right, or he'll never see his wife again."

"Corbett wants Straight Arrow to bring McKaid to him? An exchange?"

"That's about it."

"That's crazy. I hope McKaid told him so. Straight Arrow's wife is probably already dead. Or as good as. Can you imagine what they'll do to her?"

"Which is exactly why McKaid is going."

Elizabeth slumped onto a chair. "Yes. That's precisely how he'll see it. My God, that man is diabolical."

"McKaid?"

"Ramirez. Don't you understand? He's setting up a war. Straight Arrow needs McKaid to get his wife back, our men aren't going to let the Indians deliver McKaid to Ramirez. So we fight, we become enemies, we kill each other to protect and possess what we love. It's very astute really. And the *coup* is that McKaid has to watch his friends die, both red and white, because of him. It will drive him mad. It's very neat."

Emma had stopped in the middle of cracking eggs, motionless as she listened to Elizabeth analyze the situation. How did she know this? She'd been asleep during the long discussion that had taken place around the kitchen table last night. She'd repeated almost word for word what McKaid and the two Rangers had said to Straight Arrow. Emma opened her mouth to speak, but no words would come.

"But naturally, McKaid won't let that happen. He'll go willingly before he'll be the cause of that, even if only to foil Ramirez's plans. And if he does, if Straight Arrow trades McKaid's life for his wife's, we'll still become bitter enemies in the end."

"Clint," Emma choked out through her restricted throat muscles, "worked so hard to be good friends and neighbors to those Indians. This would break his heart. Isn't there anything

244

we can do?"

"When are they leaving?"

"McKaid sent Straight Arrow and his men down to the river to camp. He's going to meet them at mid-morning. Straight Arrow is to deliver McKaid at sunset tomorrow at some place in the mountains. Even that was well planned. Indians don't like to fight after dark. Ramirez will be long gone with McKaid by daylight."

"The men at the ranch don't know, do they?"

"No. McKaid didn't want to take the chance that they'd do something rash."

"And the Rangers?"

"They're going along, disguised as Indians. Don't worry, they're all aware that this could be a trap."

"Yes, but for whom? Where's McKaid now?"

"He and Biff and Tex bunked in Russ's cottage. He insisteed that Russ stay in the house. He was impressed with how you managed the ranch, and the Indians, and Russ."

"I don't manage Russ. Russ is a strong man in his own right. I'm going to talk to McKaid. I'll send the other two up for breakfast."

There was nothing Emma could say. This new Elizabeth was not to be argued with. She was just like McKaid when her mind was set.

Elizabeth pounded on the door and waited impatiently for someone to answer. She paced the stone stoop, then knocked again.

"Dad-blast, I'm comin'," came the gruff answer. Biff jerked open the door with one hand, rubbing his sore hip with the other.

"Good morning," Elizabeth offered, eyeing the old man standing in worn brown trousers and gray long johns, his suspenders dangling to his knees. "Emma has breakfast waiting for you at the house. I'll give you a minute to get dressed, then I'm coming in to talk to McKaid."

"You must be Miss Elizabeth. We heard all about—"

"One minute," she repeated and pulled the door closed. His voice carried through the heavy wood as he yelled for Tex and McKaid to shake a leg, that there was a fine-lookin' woman waitin' outside to bend McKaid's ear, and she wanted to talk to him privatelike.

In less than a minute the door opened, and Elizabeth looked

245

up into McKaid's wary blue eyes. "Mr. McKaid," she said, gathering her scattering wits. He seemed bigger, broader, more intimidating than she remembered. After days of convincing herself that she could be just as indifferent as he, she was shaken at what the mere sight of him was doing to her senses. He didn't answer, and she had the urge to babble to fill the silence.

A momentary reprieve came in the form of the two old men. These were the Rangers who were going to help McKaid defeat Ramirez? Inwardly she cringed.

"Lizzie, meet Tex Donner and Biff Story," McKaid said perfunctorily. "Miss Elizabeth Hepplewhite."

"Gentlemen," Elizabeth said politely as they scuffled past her, darting glances at both her and McKaid.

"Ma'am," they chorused.

"Mr. Story," Elizabeth called after them, "Emma has some strong lineament for your hip."

"Oh, this," he patted the back of one thin buttock. "It ain't nothin'. Just stove up after all the ridin' we done."

"Nevertheless, you had better take it."

Biff looked at her and then at McKaid and could sense the tension between them. He wasn't about to argue. "Yes, ma'am. I believe I will, thank ya kindly."

"You wanted to talk," McKaid said coolly.

"Yes." She went into Russ's quarters and waited until McKaid closed the door and sat down.

"I could do with some coffee," he said.

"Were you planning to see me before you go?"

"What makes you think I'm going anywhere?"

"I see. So I was not to know, either, hmm? Did you tell Russ to keep it from me?"

"For your own good."

"What gives you the right to decide that? You weren't here when those men rode in last night. You wouldn't have been here if they had scalped us all. We were here, and we used our own good sense to decide what was best for us."

He stood. "I didn't want you to worry. Dammit, I'm trying to protect you."

"Well, in your misguided attempts to protect, you could be putting us in grave danger. If I hadn't met your Indian friend, if I hadn't stopped the men from firing, we'd have ended up killing each other. No one on the ranch knew Straight Arrow

246

except you and Clint. And who among us has ever seen Ramirez? You're the only one who knows what he looks like. If you're going to keep your damned secrets, you better stay around. If you're going to go riding off on some crazy mission, then we all have to know what we're up against. That means all of us, the men, the women, those two children. What if you don't come back?"

"If I'm dead, Ramirez won't have any reason to bother you."

"So, you're sacrificing yourself?"

"No," McKaid shouted. "I'm going to do everything within my power to survive and to get Ramirez before he can hurt anyone else I love."

"Just like always." Her tone was derisive.

"Meaning?" he demanded.

"You're a puppet on a string, always dancing to whatever tune Ramirez plays. Don't you think he knows you'll go?"

"Of course he knows it. He planned it. But whatever the risks, I have to try to save Mary Runningwater. I have no choice."

"Mary?"

"She's a halfbreed. Her father was a trapper. He named her after his mother. She has hair as black as midnight, skin as dark as copper, and eyes as green as spring leaves. Straight Arrow has loved her since they were both children."

"Then why did he take a second wife?"

"He could afford it."

She took a deep breath and let it out. Knowing Mary's name and what she looked like made everything more complicated. "Is there any other way?" she asked.

"Not and keep peace with the Apache. Corbett threatened to kill Mary if Straight Arrow didn't deliver me."

"Think about this, McKaid. Corbett would be that stupid, but I can't see Ramirez waiting to be surrounded by angry Indians. And I can't see him giving you to Corbett, not after all these years of trying to get you himself. It just doesn't sound right to me."

"All I know is that I have to try. If a trade is made, I'll be closer to Ramirez than I've ever been able to get. I'll have a chance. Maybe only one, but I'll have a chance."

"Will you explain to the men?" she asked.

"No, Elizabeth. I don't want them to know. As far as they're

247

concerned, I'm going with Straight Arrow to talk peace with the other Apaches who have been raiding the farms before a full-scale war breaks out."

"I don't know, McKaid. It feels wrong."

"Let it go, Lizzie. It has to be this way. And as territorial marshal, I'm asking you to abide by my decision."

"Just as marshal?" Is that all she was to him, one of the citizens he'd sworn to protect?

He came to her and took her shoulders in his large, gentle hands. For a moment she thought she saw his eyes soften, or maybe she just wanted to see that, but it was gone as quickly as it came.

"I'll have your promise, Elizabeth."

She sighed and stepped away. "*Promise?* Sure. Why not?" She turned and walked to the door.

"Lizzie . . ." McKaid called, reaching out to her.

"Your coffee will be ready when you come in for breakfast."

McKaid stood later that morning at his uncle's grave, paying his last respects. He wished now that he'd stayed for the funeral, but at the time, he simply had to do something, anything, to ease his guilt and pain. And he did find out the truth of that night.

"Thought I'd find you here," Russ said, coming up behind McKaid and laying a consoling hand on his shoulder.

"Julio Ortega killed him. He set that fire. Clint found him looking for the gold he'd dropped, and Ortega hit him over the head and left him to die. Ramirez paid him to spy on us and to cause trouble."

"Where's Ortega now? In jail, I hope."

"Dead. One of Ramirez's men shot him to keep him quiet."

"Typical."

"Sheriff Wade has the man who shot him in custody. He'll swing."

Silence fell between them. Russ had so many questions, so much to discuss, but he didn't know where to begin.

McKaid sensed it. "Something on your mind, Russ?"

"A great deal. Have you talked to Elizabeth?"

"Early this moring. She promised to keep quiet about this business with Straight Arrow."

"You asked her to make a promise to you, when you don't

keep your own to her?" Russ asked, feeling again an urge to punch his boss in his unreasonable jaw.

"I never made her any promises."

"That's low, McKaid, and unworthy of you."

"What did she tell you—that she promised not to?"

"Only what I needed to hear, that you weren't Lenore's lover because you were hers. Until you decided it was a mistake, that is."

"Dammit. Who else knows?"

"No one, McKaid."

"Why the need to confess to you?"

"Because you took off and left her to face the threat of Ramirez hurting McKaid's woman. Who, to all appearances, is Lenore."

"Lenore? Oh, my God. I never thought, Russ." He shook his head incredulously. "I didn't see that. It was so far from the truth that it never crossed my mind. I swear it. Is that why you brought her here?"

"That's why Elizabeth brought her here, along with eight of Beaumont's men."

"Elizabeth did all that?"

"She's determined not to cause you another moment of grief—like she did with getting you shot and getting Clint killed."

"None of that was her fault. That's absurd."

"She's convinced you blame her since leaving the ranch that night was her idea."

"I don't blame her," he denied.

"Hmm. Did you put your arms around her and share her grief, did you tell her you were sorry she didn't have longer to get to know her only uncle? Did you do any of that, McKaid, after she'd just shared the most wondrous gift she could have given you? Or did you look at her with those frozen eyes and tell her you should never have gone with her? Do you have any idea how much you've hurt her? She hasn't shed one tear, she's as frozen inside as you are. Maybe you should go. Maybe everything you touch gets frostbite."

"Is that all, Packard?" McKaid asked warningly.

Russ knew he was risking life and limb by pushing McKaid, but he wasn't nearly done. "Where's your last will and testament kept?"

"I don't have a will."

"This ranch is yours, McKaid. Those kids are your legal wards. There's Emma to consider, and possibly a son or daughter since you've seen fit to treat Elizabeth so irresponsibly."

"Is there?"

"How should I know? Don't tell me that's another thing you didn't think of."

"Yes, I thought of it. Okay?" McKaid bellowed.

"Don't yell at me, McKaid. I'm just trying to open your eyes. You'll be leaving an unbearable amount of responsibility on Elizabeth's shoulders if you get yourself killed. She'll try her damnedest to keep your family together. How will she manage that?"

"All right, all right," McKaid sighed. "I'll make a will."

"Will you tell her how you really feel, or will you leave her to always believe she was used?"

"Let it alone, Packard. It's best this way. She'll forget me faster."

"You're a fool if you think that. The memory of you will always be an open sore on her heart. And if she does carry your child, that child, instead of bringing her peace and joy, will remind her of how you deceived her. Well, now I've said my piece. I used to admire you." He shook his head sadly. "Good luck, McKaid."

McKaid stayed there for a long time after Russ left, staring at his uncle's grave, thinking about Elizabeth. God, he didn't want to go through the pain he'd experienced with Rosanna again. And somehow, he knew it would be worse with Elizabeth. Much worse. But how much worse her pain would be, thinking he hadn't loved her after all. It was a risk to let anyone know about them, but maybe it was a risk worth taking. He looked at his pocket watch and wound it automatically. He'd have to hurry if he was to get everything done and still leave on time.

His saddle bags were packed, his heavy coat rolled in his bedroll, and his guns were loaded when his partners rode up later that morning in war paint and borrowed Indian attire.

"You ready, McKaid?" Tex asked.

"Almost. I have a couple important matters to take care of in case I don't come back, so you two go on down to the camp and explain to Straight Arrow."

Biff and Tex glanced at each other. "We'll do our best to

cover your backside," Tex said. They rode off, and McKaid went into the house to find Russ.

Russ was waiting in the library, staring out the window, his feet propped up on Clint's desk. When he saw McKaid, he stood.

"Here it is," McKaid said, withdrawing a paper from his shirt pocket. "Put your name on it as witness. Emma's already signed it. It covers all—contingencies. I'm afraid I had to let Emma read it. She wasn't very happy with me."

"Are you?"

"Just sign it, okay? And lock it up somewhere. I have to get going." He stopped at the door and turned. "Russ, I'm sorry about Lenore. Hell, I'm sorry about this whole mess. Look, take care of everything?"

"I'll do my best, you know that."

"Thanks. I better find Lizzie."

"She's out back with the kids." Russ's face relaxed as McKaid left. He sat down and propped up his feet again. McKaid would do right by her, he was sure.

"Mr. McKaid," the children yelled together when he stepped out of the house.

"We thought you'd be gone by now," James said.

"I'm leaving in a minute. How about one more hug from my two favorite kids. Then I'd like to have a few minutes alone with Lizzie."

"Good," Ruthie said, smiling her relief. She gave his neck a squeeze, then danced into the kitchen where Emma stood at the window with tears in her eyes.

James was more sedate. "This isn't dangerous, is it?" he asked.

"There's always danger out there, James, but I'll be very caerful. Now you take care of Emma while I'm gone. That's my boy."

McKaid rose and turned toward Elizabeth. "Walk with me to my horse?" He held out his hand to her, but she folded her arms and walked quietly beside him.

"Elizabeth—Lizzie, I owe you an apology. I've been way out of bounds with you."

"If you're going to apologize for making love to me, then don't. Please. Leave me that memory, McKaid."

"No, that's not it at all." He stopped her and turned her to face him. "I'm sorry for trying to deny to myself and to you

251

that I love you. I thought that if I denied there was anything between us, that I'd be protecting us both. I was afraid for you, and afraid that I'd be hurt again."

"Rosanna's death must have been awful for you."

"But at least I knew she loved me. That was a comfort to me, as well as knowing she was secure in my love for her. Telling you and telling myself that I don't love you won't make the pain any less if something should happen to you. That was a crazy idea.

"I've been so caught up in my fears and my hatred and desire for revenge that I haven't been able to think straight. You and Russ have both shaken some sense into me. I might even be able to do some good this time. But if I can't, if I don't come back, I want you to know that I love you and have from the first. I'm more sorry than I can say that I hurt you."

Tears, all the tears she'd refused to release before, rolled down her face. McKaid, with a few precious words, had torn down her protective wall and let all the grief and pain and fear be felt.

"Don't, ah don't," McKaid soothed, pulling her into his arms as she sobbed out her misery. "What have I done? Sweetheart, I'm so sorry. I've let you down so often. I should have been there for you when Clint died, I could have spared both of us so much pain. Forgive me, please, forgive me." He held her close while she cried, burying his lips in her soft hair as he calmed her. He didn't care any longer that they were standing between the house and the rest of the ranch where any or all of the men could see them. He didn't care if the whole world knew he loved Lizzie, just as long as she knew it. How could he have been so thoughtless and cruel?

"I've missed you so much, McKaid," she said raggedly as she tried to wipe away her tears.

He tilted her wet face up to his and cupped her head with his hands. Her amber eyes were drenched, but at peace. His own vision blurred.

"I've been cold for so long, Lizzie. When you came, you brought the sunshine back into my life. I woke up in the mornings just to be near you, even when you were prickly. If I never see you after today, take comfort in knowing you've given me warmth and joy, and the freedom to love again."

"Please don't talk that way, I can't bear it. You sound like you're giving up."

"Giving up? I think I've just started to fight. I have something worthwhile to fight for. I have a future. I'll be careful."

She nodded, her throat working convulsively. Her chin started to quiver, and McKaid couldn't resist her a second longer. He enclosed her in his strong arms and lowered his lips to hers. It was a kiss they'd both hungered for and needed for a long desperate week. Her lips, already parted, welcomed the gentle probing of his tongue, and she brazenly drew him into the greedy warmth of her mouth. He needed no more encouragement to kiss her the way his heart and body longed to, completely and thoroughly possessing her.

He tore his mouth from hers and buried his face in the hollow of her neck, kissing his way upward to her small, perfectly shaped ear.

"I have no time. God, do you know what I'd like to do right now, Lizzie. I'd like to take you to our place and very slowly remove your clothing so that you're standing before me as you were the first time we made love. You were so very beautiful that night that I was trembling inside. I wanted to touch you, but I was afraid if I did, you'd vanish like a dream when you try to hold on to it. And I would be left devastated.

"I want to run my lips over your silken skin and taste you, I want to take your breasts into my mouth and draw those sweet cries from your lips. How the sound of your pleasure thrills me.

"I want to hold you tight to my heart and fill your body with my own until we are one, you and I, together, no longer separate and isolated and alone.

"I want to rock with you until the fires of passion build and burn so hot within us that we lose ourselves completely in the beauty of loving each other. And I do love you, Lizzie. You are my heart and my soul."

"McKaid," she whispered brokenly and turned his head with a gentle hand to meet her lips. Her kiss tasted of renewed tears, but not tears of sadness.

"I wish I could, sweetheart, I wish I could."

"You just have, my love. I couldn't feel more joy than at this moment."

The soft thud of hoofbeats broke them apart, and they looked up to see Straight Arrow observing them.

"We must go far, friend," the Indian said.

McKaid looked down at Lizzie. "Be strong," he said and gave her a swift, hard kiss.

As McKaid turned reluctantly to walk to his horse, Elizabeth looked up at McKaid's friend sitting so straight and tall and somber on his well-trained horse.

"I hope you find Mary Runningwater. If you hadn't stopped to help us, Corbett wouldn't have taken her." Her wayward chin trembled again.

He looked directly into her eyes, and she could read his sincere regret. "And you would be dead, and my friend McKaid," he said. "I will find Mary. Ramirez and Corbett will know Apache justice." He tilted his head to the side. "You are strong and brave, Lizzie girl. You are much like Mary Runningwater."

He turned his head, his bronze body straightening. He'd said all he was going to, which, to Elizabeth, was enough. He joined McKaid, and they rode away.

"*Estupido!*" Ramirez bellowed, raging back and forth in front of Corbett. "*Estupido. Bastardo.*"

"No, wait. It's brilliant. Think about it. We can't lose."

"With Apache you cannot win."

"I did win. I did just like you. I waited till the men were gone, then rode in and took Straight Arrow's woman. Slick as can be."

"Straight Arrow, he is chief. Idiot."

"He's also McKaid's friend. What do you figger'll happen when Straight Arrow goes after McKaid so he can trade him for the squaw?"

Ramirez began to think about that, his beady eyes squinting. "*Nada.* McKaid will come."

"Then we have him," crowed Corbett gleefully. "At last we have him."

"And fifty Apache with him. What will you do with the Apache?"

"No. I told that other squaw to tell Straight Arrow to come alone or I'd kill his wife."

"They will be there. When they have the woman, they will come for you from every side. You will not hear them. You will hear only the breath of arrows before you die. Have you defiled the squaw?"

"Sure. We all had her. So what? She's just an Injun."

"Better for you to kill her."

"Nah. You'll see. When I bring McKaid to you, you'll see."

"When is this meeting with the Apache?"

"Tomorrow night. Just think, by tomorrow night McKaid will be dead."

"You do this thing on your own, Corbett. My men do not go."

"But I'll need them."

"I need them. They are nothing to me dead. If you wish to be stuck full of slivers of wood like a porcupine and hung by your toes over a fire to roast alive, or have your skin removed in strips, or have your manhood cut from you as you watch, then you go. Face the Apache whose woman you raped. They will want revenge."

Corbett turned a sickly shade of green. Ramirez spat in the dirt and walked away, taking with him Corbett's dreams, his victory, his glory, and McKaid.

The Apache and the three Rangers approached the gorge north and west of the Circle K. The mountains had turned rugged, with sheer bluffs rising from rock-covered floors where streams made their twisted way to the Rio Grande. The evening sun illuminated the flat piñon-covered mesas, but down in the gorge the shadows deepened.

They rode in silence, keeping to the cover of the pines, cottonwood, aspen, and cedar that grew in profusion along the waterways. One by one the Apache broke off from the main body as Straight Arrow gave only the slightest of silent commands.

McKaid didn't need to be told that somewhere out there, unseen and unheard, his Indian friends were surrounding them, waiting, watching.

Tex and Biff were the only two who remained behind McKaid and Straight Arrow as they neared Maiden Rocks. They stopped fifty paces back and waited, guns at the ready.

"It is here we stop, McKaid."

McKaid looked up at the three spires of sandstone, formed and pitted by time, weather, and water to vaguely resemble three women. How many centuries had they stood sentinel over the wild and virgin gorge.

McKaid took in every rock, every tree. He didn't like their position. They were situated at a point where Ramirez could easily enter, attack, and leave the canyon from several directions, all well protected, while they had only the long, narrow canyon and the natural cover of nature for protection. It was a perfect place for an ambush. But if Ramirez had seen them approach, if he knew Straight Arrow had brought the braves along, he wouldn't go through with it. He would kill Mary. Elizabeth was right. It wasn't at all like Ramirez to suggest a meeting with an Apache chief. Where did that leave Mary?

The more McKaid thought, the less he liked what he was thinking. If Ramirez knew Straight Arrow, and he would if he were going to fight him, he would know that the chief would not make the trade and ride away. He would fight as valiantly for his friend as for his woman. His honor would demand it. Ramirez never intended to come. They would be dealing solely with Corbett or no one at all. Which left him to wonder where Ramirez was.

Time passed slowly, although darkness fell with the speed of a great hand snuffing out a candle. The four men at the Rocks tethered their horses in a thicket where they could fill their hunger grazing on the thick grasses and made camp. No fires were lit as they sat together waiting for morning. No one spoke, but they all knew Mary Runningwater was not coming. Corbett had realized the folly of his plan. Biff and Tex unrolled their bedding and put on their own clothes.

Chapter Sixteen

After their scare Russ and Elizabeth tightened the security at the ranch. At noon on the day McKaid and the Apache left, they held a practice drill. That time each man knew exactly where to go and what to do.

"From this moment on, the sound of the bell will mean serious trouble. There will be no more drills," Russ explained to his men. "We will sleep in shifts, eat in shifts, and never for a single second leave our posts unguarded. The women have agreed to take over the cooking as a special reward for your efforts. You will also find extra in your pay packets this month as our way of saying thanks."

A chorus of cheers went up. Russ wasn't sure whether it was because of the food or the money. The men dispersed and went to their various duties, none of which took them out of the immediate area.

Elizabeth came out onto the porch to join Russ. "How are they taking this? It's not exactly ranch work."

"They're fine. I gave them a raise in pay. Hope you don't mind."

She laughed. "Not at all. It's not my ranch."

He didn't tell her that it might soon be. "You look better today. Did McKaid come to his senses at last?"

She smiled shyly and nodded. She sobered as the silence stretched between them. "Do you think he'll be all right?"

"Well, he's stopped thinking with his guts, at least. Whenever Ramirez was involved in the past, McKaid seemed to go into some sort of black trance where all he could think of was getting his hands around the man's throat. He'd do stupid things—like riding off in a fury, as if he could find Ramirez in these mountains all on his own. This time it will be different. Ramirez will have the real McKaid to deal with, the underhanded, conniving, deceitful, ruthless McKaid. That man of yours is a good lawman, Elizabeth. Not many get past him."

"Just Ramirez."

"In a way, I always felt there were two powers at work in McKaid where Ramirez was concerned. One wanted to see the man dead, the other . . ."

"To let Ramirez go on punishing him for getting Rosanna killed?"

He looked at her in surprise, then chuckled in amazement. "You are one wise woman."

She shook her head. "It wasn't hard to see. Do you think he's over it then?"

"I think loving you has set him free." He threw his arm over her shoulder and walked her into the house.

Russ sent the women and children off to bed early that night. The children were cranky, Elizabeth was plainly exhausted, and Emma, trooper that she was, was dead on her feet.

"You ladies did a fine bit of cooking today," Russ complimented Lenore, refilling her cup with the hot chocolate she'd made for them. "You need to get to bed, too."

Lenore closed her eyes and leaned back in her chair. "I don't know what we'll do tomorrow. There's not a scrap of food left from today. You'll have to refill the larder before breakfast."

"We'll manage. I'll have the men set up a grill beside the back porch. It'll be easier to cook all that meat at once. I'll have Cookie come in and help."

"Emma will love that," she answered sarcastically.

Their eyes met, and a force, charged with a life of its own, held them bound together. Russ let out his breath and drew another lungful.

"Lenore . . ." He pushed back his chair and stood.

She stood as well, their eyes never parting. "It's late, Russ." She tore her eyes from his and turned, her heart pounding rapidly in her ears.

"Dammit," he muttered and swung her around. "No more," he said fiercely. "I've tiptoed around you for years, hiding every little desire and urge I've felt in case it might offend you, but not this time. I'm a man, Lenore. A flesh and

258

blood . . . Oh, hell."

He pulled her into his arms, against the rock-hard, massive strength of his body, and he kissed her. There was nothing tentative in him when his mouth met hers. His lips moved with surety across and against hers, his tongue probed until it found access and plunged onward to total possession.

When her husband had shed his fastidiousness and kissed her in such a way, she had greeted it with passive acceptance. When McKaid had kissed her, she'd been surprised and frightened. But with Russ, with the big man whose body had intrigued her, whose laugh and easy smile delighted her, whose warm brown eyes warmed her, none of those feelings came. Instead, a wild surge of excitement and physical desire rose within her.

Her legs lost their strength to support her, and she wrapped her arms around his neck and held on, letting the wondrous new feelings sweep her away.

Russ, encouraged by her pliant surrender, deepened his kiss. She was so sweet, so soft in his arms, so responsive.

When he at last drew his lips from hers, they were both breathing hard. He could feel her full breasts burning into his chest, he could feel the softness of her abdomen pressing against his aroused manhood. A hot throbbing began there, and he drew back, sure she'd be able to feel it.

"I . . . I . . ." he faltered, looking down at her raised face, her slumberous eyes, her parted lips, swollen from his kiss. He groaned deep in his throat and kissed her again.

"You are so beautiful, my sweetheart," he said a moment later. He kissed her finely shaped brows, her darkly fringed lids, her aristocratic Spanish nose. "I've loved you for so long, and God help me, I think my knees are about to buckle."

It struck her funny, since hers had long since ceased to work. Her black eyes lit with humor, and a sultry chuckle broke free.

"You dare to laugh, woman?" he scowled playfully. Before she knew what he was about, she found herself swung off her feet, cradled in Russ's arms.

"What are you doing, Mr. Packard?"

"Putting you to bed. I'm half afraid you don't know what you're doing. In the morning you may club me with the skillet for taking advantage of you. Do you think I could convince you this was a dream?"

"Not at all. Russ, the lamp."

"You get it." He dipped her head toward the glass chimney.

"Don't drop me."

"You're light as a feather. There's not much to you, except in all the right places."

She blew out the lamp then settled her arms around his shoulders, daring to kiss his neck and touch her tongue to his ear. "If I'm so light," she asked huskily, "why are your arms trembling?"

"It's nothing to do with your weight, I can assure you," he groused.

This was all new to her and terribly exciting, this light bantering with intimate innuendos. She'd always loved his sense of humor, but she'd never imagined how freely it would show itself between the two of them, or how much fun it would be to tease him in return.

"Are you going to carry me all the way up the stairs?"

"Now that I've got you, I may never put you down."

"Well, if you think I'm going to shoe all your horses for you just because you have your arms full, you'd better think again."

"Maybe they can go barefooted."

"Oh, Russ, horses don't go barefooted. They go—shoeless."

"That's barefooted."

She laughed and buried her face against his shoulder to muffle the sound. She felt so happy. When he stopped moving, she looked up.

"We're here."

"Yes. I guess you had better put me down."

"That's the hard part." He lowered her legs and let her body slide slowly down his. He shut his eyes hard and gritted his teeth when, for a split second, their bodies met. He took her shoulders and squeezed, then stepped away.

"I'll say goodnight, Lenore. Sleep well." He was gone so fast she wondered for a minute if he'd really been there. She looked up and down the hallway and took the few steps necessary to turn down the wick in the wall lamp. She went back to her door, but she couldn't make herself open it. She felt deflated and alone, when only seconds ago in Russ's arms she felt warm and secure. She wanted him back. Why had he gone? Because he thought she'd be afraid of his passion? She thrilled at his desire for her. She welcomed it. She felt her body stir to life for the first time in years because of him, and she wanted him with a longing of a lifetime.

A slow devilish smile spread across her face. He may as well know what she wanted and expected right from the start. She had no intention of getting herself into another marriage where she had to curb her desires because she made her husband uncomfortable when she exhibited them. She wanted a real man, and she wanted to be a real woman. And after her husband's immaculate ways, she hoped Russ threw his clothes on the floor.

She knocked softly on his door, and when he opened it, she slipped around it and pressed it closed behind her. "I have a problem, Russ."

"What is it, Lenore?" He grabbed his shirt off the chair and slid his arms through the sleeves, but not before he'd seen her black eyes travel over his upper torso. He had to get her out of his room before . . .

"Well," she drawled, "Eve, my maid, isn't here, and you sent Emma and Elizabeth to bed, and I can't reach the buttons on my dress. Could you help me?"

He ran a shaky hand through his thick curly hair. "I don't know if I can."

"I'll have to sleep all trussed up then. You can do it. They're only buttons." She turned her back and waited

Finally he gave in. One by one he slid the buttons through the eyes, his fingers clumsy appendages he couldn't seem to control. And more than his fingers was going beyond his control.

Her bodice fell to her waist, and he drew a sharp, painful breath. Dear God, he thought. She tugged at the fastenings at her waist, then stepped out of petticoats and dress in one motion.

She turned and smiled sweetly. "Now if I can get out of this thing, I'll be able to breathe again."

Right before his eyes she unlaced her corset and tossed it on the heap at her feet. He stood, mesmerized. His blood had reached the boiling point and was hammering in his ears and throat and his lower parts. He swallowed, but didn't know why. His mouth was dry.

She took a deep breath and stretched. "Ahh, that feels better." Her full, lush breasts threatened to burst the seams of her lacy chemise. He couldn't take his eyes from their creamy

261

curves or their erect nipples outlined clearly against the soft material.

His eyes jerked to hers. "What are you doing, Lenore?"

She tossed one hairpin then another and another on the floor. "I'm taking my hair down." Another pin.

He grabbed her upper arms and shook her slightly, as if to wake her up. Her long raven hair came loose and tumbled down her back. She shook her head and the heavy weight of her black mane swirled over her shoulders, over his hands.

He shook her again. "I don't mean your hair. Why are you here? What are you trying to do?"

She shrugged. "I wanted to see if I could take advantage of you. You had your chance and threw it away. I, on the other hand, am more persistent. Shall I help you with your boots? Your knees look weak again."

Like a dazed puppet, he sat on the bed while Lenore turned her backside to him and tugged off his boots. Suddenly he shook his head and came to his senses.

"That's enough, young lady. You've had your fun."

"Don't scowl. And don't be a curmudgeon."

"Now you listen to me, you little tease. I mean to court you proper." He got up, and she sat down.

"So?" One stocking, two.

"How can I do that when you undress in front of me?"

"I don't know. You think of something."

"Lenore, I'm warning you . . . Leave that on!"

She dropped her hands from the tie at the neck of her low cut chemise. "Oh, piffle. I like to sleep with nothing on."

"Lenore," he growled, hot, red color seeping into his neck. She stood and reached for him. "Let me have your shirt."

"Leave my shirt alone."

"I'll unbuckle your belt for you."

"This is no game. When I asked for your permission to call on you, you said you were giving no guarantees. To me this is a guarantee. A commitment."

The crisp sandy hair on his broad chest tickled her fingers. She pushed him back until his legs hit the bed. A little more pressure and he toppled completely.

"Make love to me, Russ," she whispered in his ear, nibbling the lobe between her teeth. "I know you want me."

"Damn right I do," he said fiercely and rolled her beneath him. "But it has to mean we get married."

She grinned, triumphant. "Are you asking?"

"Yes!"

"Yes."

"Yes?"

"Yes."

"You'll really marry me?"

"It took you long enough, Russ Packard. Heaven only knows how much longer I'd have had to wait if I hadn't helped a little."

"But your father—" He sat up.

"Has been waiting, too."

"I think I'm having palpitations."

"Let me see." She pressed her hand against his heart then slid it up and over his shoulder, removing his shirt. "I think your clothes are too tight. Let's get this off. And those rough old trousers. How can you stand them?"

"I can't. I can't stand any of this. Come here."

She wanted to know what kind of lover he would be, and she was finding out. He kissed her, pressing her to the bed with the weight of one leg and his chest, holding her a prisoner to lips, teeth, and tongue that tasted, touched, drank deeply from the enticing sweetness of her mouth.

Hands that until now had been wary to touch such delicate beauty slid over her body, lifting and caressing the weight of her breasts, testing the curve of her hips, the softness of her belly. She was beautiful and she wanted him. He couldn't believe his good fortune. He may have nothing else in the world, but if he had her, he'd be a rich man.

The remainder of their clothes, thin barriers between them, were discarded, and they came together, flesh to flesh.

"I've never felt such excitement, such need and desire before," she cried out softly. "I want you so much."

She didn't ask permission to touch him, her hand found its way from the hard, tense muscles of his back to his stomach and lower, all on its own, out of a need to give him the same pleasure he was giving her. The freedom to do, even that was new to her. Russ didn't hold himself aloof and apart from her as if he were afraid she'd find some flaw. She was enchanted to know so much more existed between a man and woman than she'd been allowed to experience before, and she was delighted that she would learn of it with Russ.

Russ was so in love at that moment that he could only think

of holding her, caressing her, and filling her with as much joy as he was feeling. He'd found in her a surprising impishness and playfulness that he knew would match his own sense of fun and adventure. She was strong, she was brave, she was everything, and she'd agreed to marry him. He couldn't have been happier. He felt like shouting.

"I love you. I love you," he avowed.

"I love you, too. I've been in love with you since I first met you."

"You, too? It was so hard for me to watch you go home with another man, even one I respected. I wanted you to be mine, even if I didn't deserve you. It's hell to covet another man's wife."

"You were very discreet. I never guessed. And all the times we visited, I'd listen for your voice and watch to catch a glimpse of you. I knew I'd never hurt Jacques, but I still wanted to be near you, if only once in a while."

"I'm glad we were honorable people. I wouldn't want any guilt to mar this moment. I want to make love to you with a heart free to give, I want to love you knowing you're mine to cherish for as long as we live."

"I want that, too, Russ."

Their lips met tenderly at first, and passion, long suppressed in them both, burst to life like buried coals receiving the vitalizing breath of life.

He covered her face and throat with warm kisses, found the sensitive cords of her neck, traced the delicate ridge of her collarbone. He felt her arch toward him, he felt the tight, hard centers of her full breasts pressing into his chest. He heard her strangled cry as he cupped one breast and raised the nipple to his lips, drawing it into his hungry mouth.

She clung to him, holding him to her, unaware that her nails bit into his shoulders, leaving small curved marks. She had never felt any urgency to complete the act of love before, but now her own impatience and Russ's leisurely pace were driving her mad. She had waited for so long for this moment, testing it in her fevered dreams and imaginings, that the incredible reality of it actually happening, and her newfound and surprising capacity for enjoyment, left her mindless and racing headlong for fulfillment.

Russ was overwhelmed by her passionate response. She'd always been so reserved and proper, that he could only hope she'd welcome his lovemaking. But maybe she'd learned that reserve from her first husband, her first lover. Maybe she'd been denied for as long as he had. She'd said she had never felt such desire before. Could it really be that he was to be blessed with showing his lovely Lenore her body's capacity for love? The thought filled him with wonder and a powerful sense of possessiveness. His dark eyes, when he looked into hers, burned with it.

A matching desire to give herself to that possession rose in her, and, making a place for him in between her slender thighs, she urged him to her. His first thrust, tentative and careful, was not enough for her. She gripped his hips and pulled him fully inside her, locking him with her legs in that most intimate of embraces.

In the next few minutes he taught her what true intimacy was, not just a calculated and dutiful joining of bodies in the hope of begetting an heir, but a true uniting of body, mind, and spirit. She no longer merely surrendered her body, she demanded his. She no longer waited for the end to come, she craved his body and yearned to remain in her euphoric ecstasy forever.

Their passion mounted swiftly, driving them to give and take of each other wildly and with not the slightest self-consciousness. Together they moved until they exploded in a wondrous climactic burst of pleasure, holding tightly to each other in the glorious realization that what they'd found in each other would be theirs to enjoy for all the years of nights to come.

"Russ, oh my darling Russ, this must be what heaven is like. I feel so wonderful. I hope we can get married very soon, because I'm not going to be able to do without you now."

He chuckled, his chest vibrating against her sensitized breasts. She felt a new stirring of desire, and when he would have withdrawn from her, she held him locked to her.

"Don't go yet," she implored. "Let me enjoy the feel of you."

"I have a suspicion you're going to turn out to be one handful of woman." His eyes gleamed with masculine pleasure.

"You have capable hands," she quipped. "Would you mind?"

"No man alive would mind."

That wasn't true, but she didn't say so. She put the past behind her and embraced only the now and the future. A future with Russ.

"What if I start chasing you around the house to seduce you?" she asked.

"That will never happen," he answered.

"Why not?" she challenged.

"Because I ain't runnin'," he drawled.

"You mean whenever I want you, you'll be there for me?"

He grinned wolfishly in response. "Will you seduce me the same way you did tonight?"

"Perhaps. I felt very wicked, and I think I enjoyed it."

"So did I, believe me. I may dress you so you can do it again while I'm not so dumbstruck, although I don't think there's ever going to be a time that I can watch you undress and not swallow my tongue."

"What a pity that would be," she said provocatively. She laughed delightedly when she felt his stirring response within her own body. How good it felt to be carefree and totally open with this big, adorable man. And to laugh.

"Who would ever believe that the refined, aristocratic young woman who'd visited the Circle K with her distinguished father-in-law would be lying now in bed with her black hair spread out on my pillow, her face and body flushed from my lovemaking, and be begging for more like the wanton seductress of every man's midnight fantasies?"

"I've had dreams like that, too, where I would sneak off into the night and come to you while you slept."

"Have you now? I can't wait."

She ran her fingers along the contours of his brows, his cheekbones, his jaw. Her touch feathered over his lips, all the while her body moved tantalizingly beneath him.

"Surely it must be near midnight." She urged him to his back and rolled herself on top of him, looking darkly into his eyes, letting her hair hang in a bewitching curtain around them, brushing her voluptuous breasts against the crisp hairs matting his chest. "Close your eyes, my unsuspecting victim, and let me show you my dream."

Chapter Seventeen

As the light of morning reached the windows of the room down the hall, Elizabeth stirred and frowned in her sleep. A church bell was ringing, summoning friends and neighbors to the marriage of Elizabeth Hepplewhite to Ranger Dash McKaid. She was snuggled cozily in McKaid's arms when Emma, anxious and excited, burst into the room and disrupted them.

"Hurry, hurry! They're coming. You must get dressed now," Emma demanded.

But Elizabeth was in no hurry to break away from McKaid's embrace or the velvet words he was murmuring in her ear, making her body ache and burn for his lovemaking.

The bell chimed more insistently, spitefully, as if it were jealous of the musical quality of McKaid's voice and strived to drown it out.

She wanted to scream for the sound to stop, for Emma to go away and leave them alone. But the bell rang, and Emma's voice droned in her ears.

"Wake up. Oh, please wake up!"

She blinked awake and sat up with a jolt. Bell? It was no church bell, it was the alarm.

"I thought you'd never wake up."

"Did you wake Russ?" she asked, not yet able to think clearly.

"I reckon he's already outside by now."

Elizabeth flung her robe on and dashed out of the room. Just to be sure, she knocked on Russ's door and swung it open. Stunned and thoroughly embarrassed, she turned away. Russ and Lenore were both grabbing up garments from the floor and

267

holding them in front of their scantily clad bodies.

"I—ah—the bell—" she stammered, glancing from one to the other. She ducked out of the room and closed the door.

"Embarrass yourself, did you, my dear?" Emma laughed.

"Yes. Let's go down and see what's going on." She took Emma's arm and steered her toward the steps. If Lenore decided to dodge across to her own room . . .

"You'd better dress first," Emma said, slanting the younger woman a reproving look.

"Oh. You go on down. I'll only be a minute."

Emma tilted her head back and gave Elizabeth a curious look. Then her eyes turned to Russ's room.

"I'll wake up Lenore first," Emma said.

"No. I'll do it," Elizabeth almost shouted.

Emma's brows rose, making gathered folds on her forehead.

"Fine. No need to shout." Without another word she turned and went down the stairs. Elizabeth sighed with relief. Emma laughed. Did they all think her addle-pated?

Russ bounded out of his room, still fumbling with his gun belt, and almost collided with Elizabeth.

"Sorry," he said, stepping aside.

"I'm sorry, Russ. For barging . . ."

"Never mind. I'm going to marry her." He winked and bolted down the stairs.

Elizabeth tapped on Russ's door. "You can come out now."

Lenore, blushing, opened the door a crack. "Is Emma gone?" she whispered.

"You'll never fool Emma. Forget about it, she'll be pleased."

The bell pealed again, James poked his head out of the doorway. "Is this a drill?" he asked sleepily.

"No, it is not. You and Ruthie get dressed and go to your posts."

"Yes, ma'am," he answered. "Ruthie!" His door slammed shut behind him.

"Let's get moving, Lenore."

Russ was standing on the porch when the women joined the men a few minutes later. He raised the spyglass to his eye again.

"What is it?" Elizabeth asked.

"I don't know. Five wagons, a dozen or so riders. And . . . women."

"Women?" Emma cried, her eyes lighting. "It's a barn-raising. That's what it is. I reckon the preacher told everyone

268

what happened, and they've come to help."

"What's that mean?" Elizabeth asked. "What happens with a barnraising?"

"Oh, it's wonderful. The women bring food, the men work on the barn, there's music and dancing. It's like a church social, only they build a barn."

Elizabeth glanced at Russ. By the look on his face he wasn't any more pleased than she was to have dozens of people around who hadn't the slightest idea what was really going on at the Circle K.

"Can we ask them to come back in a week or so?" she asked quietly.

"No. We can't do that, Russ," Emma pleaded, grabbing his arm. "They've come out of neighborly concern. To turn them away would be the worst kind of offense. It's not done. McKaid would tell you. It's just not done."

Russ turned his concerned gaze back to Elizabeth. "She's right, Elizabeth. It would be an affront not soon forgiven. They've gone to great lengths to help, taking time from their own businesses, preparing food, hauling supplies." He looked again at the long caravan. "They must have left Santa Fe before dawn."

James and Ruthie came out the door at a run. "Is it him?" James asked.

"It's a barnraising," Emma said, excitement building.

"A barnraising," James squealed. "It's a party, Ruthie."

"Is it really?" Ruthie asked, turning big blue eyes to Elizabeth. "With other children and everything?"

"I—guess it is. All right. But I don't like it, and for as long as they're here, we all remain on our guard."

"But these people are friends," Lenore reasoned. "I agree with Emma. We have to show them every hospitality. They'll expect it. We can't have guards standing around with guns trained on the women and children. What will they think? What will our own men think? Ramirez wouldn't dare show his face with half the town here."

"This is a godsend," Emma added. "We've all had a difficult two weeks. A party is exactly what we need. The men as well. You can understand, can't you, Elizabeth? They'll be gone by late afternoon. Everything will get back to normal then, and we'll all be the better for it. Clint used to say there was nothing like a party to lift the cares of the world."

Elizabeth, against her better judgment, gave in. How could she not when everyone was looking at her so expectantly. Even Russ. Suddenly she felt every inch the schoolmarm with the entire population of the Circle K as her class. Somehow, at some time, for some reason, they'd all begun to look to her for the decision-making. The very fact that she had the final say put a great weight on her shoulders.

She gave one last sigh of resignation and turned to Russ. He patted her shoulder.

"It'll be fine, Elizabeth. You'll enjoy it."

He left the women and turned his attention to the waiting men. "Let's get this place back to the way it was. And hurry. We're having a party. We're gonna build a barn." Cheers and whoops of delight rose from the men. "Cal, you take some of the men and start cleaning out the debris in the barn. Joe, you round up a crew and get out the ladders and all the tools you can find. The rest of you . . ."

He went on, but Elizabeth didn't care to hear more. She went back into the house and started straightening furniture. She had only one other thing to say, and she said it as soon as Lenore came in to help her.

"I want a promise from you, Lenore. At no time are you to be alone. I don't know these people, and because of that, I'm worried. But you know whom you can trust. Stay with someone you know."

"Oh, I will. I promise."

Lenore fairly floated around the room as she helped put the furniture to rights. Elizabeth knew that more than a party had her dancing on a cloud. She smiled indulgently as she lifted a lamp table to return it to its usual place. A small porcelain figurine slid the length of the surface and toppled off, shattering into pieces. She tried to stop it, but she couldn't without upsetting the lamp and music box as well. Just like this day, she thought. Everything was happening too fast, slipping out of her control, and she couldn't stop it without causing more havoc. All she could do was hold her breath and hope the result wasn't as disastrous for them as it was for the little figurine.

More than five wagons came. It seemed that all of Clinton Colfax's friends showed up, as if to do one last good deed for a man they had respected and would miss.

Fascinated, Elizabeth watched as dozens of men unloaded

270

lumber and adobe bricks from the wagons, kegs of nails, cedar roofing shingles, long hand-hewn beams.

"This'd be a sight easier, ma'am, if McKaid's grandpappy hadn't insisted on putting up buildings that look like they belong in Georgia," Mr. Murphy groused good-naturedly. Murphy was the man who had agreed to oversee the repairs. He owned the lumberyard.

She grinned crookedly. "I understand he was as eccentric as the young McKaid. Once a McKaid gets hold of an idea . . ." She shrugged prettily and threw up her hands helplessly.

She turned from Murphy to meet three ladies who introduced themselves and pulled her with them into the general confusion around the long plank tables being set out with an assortment of food for every taste. She was asked countless questions about her family, her past, Virginia, her misadventures on her way to the Circle K. It seemed that everyone had heard one story or another about her unusual arrival, most bearing only a vague resemblance to the truth. They enjoyed their own versions so much she was loathe to disillusion them.

The day went on and on for Elizabeth, and her head began to throb with every rap of the hammers. She stood on the porch and watched Emma help herself to a plate of food, which she had nothing to do with cooking, and laugh at something Mrs. Morales had said. Or was it Mrs. Mendoza? She pressed her fingers to her temples and turned around to come face to face with Mrs. Murphy. At least that name she was sure of.

"Have you a headache, dear?"

"I think it's from trying to remember all their names, Mrs. Murphy."

"Agatha, please."

"Agatha," she repeated. Another name to remember. Last names weren't enough?

"Have you some powders?"

"No need. I'll fix a cup of tea. Won't you come in?"

"Yes, dear. I'd like that. Oh, this is lovely."

"It's very masculine in taste, but it's comfortable."

"Still, you have some lovely pieces of furniture. I'll wager the late Mr. McKaid had them transported when he built this house."

"Do you remember him?"

"Oh, yes. Had more bluster than sense most of the time."

"Sounds familiar."

"You've heard that before? I'm not surprised."

Elizabeth smiled, but didn't explain herself. "Do you know all the people here?"

"Oh, no. Certainly none of the ranch hands. New people are always moving into the area, and they welcome a chance like this to get acquainted with their neighbors. It's fun, isn't it? Have you eaten? That may help your headache. I'll get you a plate of food. Take your tea out to the porch. You can't hide away in here."

Dazed, Elizabeth did as told. Faster and faster her grip on the situation was slipping through her fingers. Once when she was little, she made a Christmas tree ornament out of a snowball and bright red holly berries. She took it inside to show her parents. She was so proud of that little ball. At first she didn't feel the water running through her fingers because her hands were cold, but when she realized her polka dot ball was melting, she held it even more tightly, as if she could keep the snow together that way. It took two stories on Micah's knee to dry her tears.

Maybe that's just how life went.

She looked out over the sea of faces. James and Ruthie were playing with a group of children, mostly black-haired, dark-skinned children. Ruthie's white gold head stood out like the moon in the black sky. But they were all the same in one way, their eyes were lit by excitement, their faces split by broad laughing smiles.

Elizabeth greeted Mrs. Murphy with a smile, hoping it wasn't as strained as she felt. She accepted the food for which she had no appetite and even managed a bite or two until she choked on a pickle that set her mouth on fire.

"Oh, my God," she gasped, draining her cup of tepid tea. "What was that?"

"Eat some bread, dear. I'm so sorry. That must have been one of Mrs. Cerillo's pickles. I guess I wasn't paying attention to what . . . Well, never mind that. She pickles them in hot peppers. They're always too hot, but she won't listen if you tell her so."

Elizabeth set her plate aside. "Mrs. Murphy—Agatha—do you know that young man with Lenore? The one with the limp? He seems to be smitten with her."

"I think I heard someone say he works at Pedro's leather

272

shop. I think they're new in town."

"He has a family then? Are any of them here today?"

"Oh, I don't know that, dear. This is the first I've seen him. He's a handsome young man, bad leg aside."

"I wonder what Russ would say if he knew Lenore had an admirer."

"Now that was a surprise to everyone, Russ announcing their betrothal. Can't say it surprised me though. I saw it coming."

Elizabeth wondered how she could have, when no one else had, but tact held her tongue. The musicians struck up a lively tune, and Elizabeth made her excuses to the talkative Mrs. Murphy and went in search of the children.

One by one she took James and Ruthie with her on a whirling spin around the dance area, laughing, making up silly steps, having fun. Other children wanted to join their gaiety, and she found herself scooping up a young boy of three or four and taking him for a spinning ride in her arms. A very shy little girl held back from the rest, and Elizabeth spotted her and coaxed her into the fun, taking her by the hands and sashaying around the musicians. It was something she needed to do, and not just for the children.

The barn walls were declared sound after a minimum of repairs. The roof rose quickly over it, many hands making the work light and fun. New beams were laid, the framework set up, and the long shingles laid in place. Laughter, jokes, and teasing banter rose from the boisterous collection of busy men. Murphy was enjoying his moment in the limelight to the fullest, taking in his stride the good-natured grumblings and complaints as he drove the men to keep them working instead of lazing around the food tables and barrels of cider and ale.

"We're gonna lose out on the apple pies," one man protested.

"You make damn sure they save us that chocolate cake," another shouted down from the peak of the roof. "We gotta get some reward for puttin' up with a slave-drivin' ramrod like you."

Russ came up to Elizabeth and squeezed her shoulder briefly. "Having a good time?"

He was, obviously. Aside from the fact that his shirt was soaked and covered with soot from handling the dirtiest part of the work, that of clearing out the charred wood and beams, he was exhilarated. They found an empty bench away from the crowd and sat down together.

"I can't wait to see McKaid's face when he sees this new roof. It's better than the old one, and while we were at it, we put in a double loft, front and back. We'll have twice the storage space."

"Who paid for all the materials? I don't know how these affairs are usually handled, but we can't let these folks . . ."

"Whoa, there. It's all been charged to McKaid. Murphy knows he's good for it. All the people do is lend a hand and have a good time."

"Are they having a good time?"

"Sure. Look at Emma. You have to admit she doesn't get to town very often. Look at her face. These people loved Clint and they share Emma's grief as well as her memories. She'll begin to heal much faster now."

Elizabeth felt choked up and a little guilty. "It's really very nice of them, isn't it?"

"Yes, it is. If the barn hadn't burned, they'd have thought of another reason to come out."

"I feel ridiculous now for being so suspicious."

"It takes time to learn a place. You haven't been here that long. Don't be so hard on yourself."

She nodded and changed the subject. "Mrs. Murphy said she wasn't at all surprised that you and Lenore are going to be married."

"Mrs. Murphy likes to think she has a finger in every pie in town. A true busybody she is, but in a mother hen sort of way, I suppose. She was instrumental in getting a new school built."

"Oh. She didn't mention that."

"She didn't? That's unusual."

"Have you seen Lenore?"

He glanced around. "A little while ago. She was surrounded by the Potter sisters and the reverend."

"She has an admirer. A good-looking young man with a bad leg."

"I noticed. He looks harmless enough, but if he tries to rustle my woman, I'll break his other leg."

"My, my. You're sounding ferocious today. Maybe I better warn him off. You never know about the fickle heart of a woman. Just because she loved you and waited for you for years on end doesn't mean that you can trust her, does it?"

He laughed and shook his head self-deprecatingly, his ruddy cheeks tinged with color. "I'm a fool, I know it."

"You're in love. Love makes fools of us all. Can't you see Cupid sitting up there on his cloud, whittling out his arrows, taking aim at his next victim, and laughing his head off at our mortal follies?"

He turned serious. "I've put you in danger, you realize that. I swear I didn't do it purposely."

"When you announced your wedding plans?"

"I was so happy, I blurted it out without considering what it would mean to you."

"Russ, I don't want Lenore in danger because of me. I never did. I'm relieved that the truth is known."

"I know. You've been wonderful, Elizabeth, taking precautions on her behalf the way you have. Still, I can't help feeling guilty."

"Don't. There is absolutely no reason. Knowing I don't have to watch her every move as well as my own has given me some peace of mind about this gathering."

He stood and pulled her to her feet. "I think I'll see if there's any peach cobbler left, then I have to get back to work."

"Stay away from the pickles."

He threw his head back and laughed. "You actually tried one? Those pickles are legend in New Mexico. The men make wagers on who can finish one."

"I don't believe you. No sane man would inflict such pain on himself."

Impulsively he pulled her into his arms and off her feet. He planted a kiss on her cheek, very close to her lips. "You are a delight. I'm very glad we're going to be neighbors."

"Russ," she scolded and extricated herself from his bearlike embrace. "Good heavens. What will people think?"

The people around them didn't notice, or if they did, they didn't think anything of it. The young man at Lenore's side did, however.

"Isn't that your fiancé?" he asked.

Lenore looked at Russ and Elizabeth and smiled fondly. "Yes, it is."

"And it doesn't upset you to see him kiss another woman?"

"Not Elizabeth."

The man beside her looked at her thoughtfully, then turned his gaze to the foreman and the teacher. How could Mrs.

Beaumont not care that they were looking at each other with love in their eyes and laughing together as if they shared an intimate secret. He looked back at Mrs. Beaumont and felt his insides churn with jealousy and white hot desire. She was more beautiful than any woman he'd ever seen. He singled her out the minute he laid eyes on her, and she'd welcomed his presence. He thought she'd be one of those uppity bitches who looked down their noses at men like him, but she wasn't. She'd talked to him as if he was someone who interested her, asked him questions, made him feel important. She was polite and kind, and a real lady. She deserved better than Russ Packard. If she were his, he'd never touch another woman.

"Mr. Kent," Lenore reprimanded him, recognizing the look in his eyes for what it was. "I must remind you that I am spoken for. If you'll excuse me, I think I'll check on Emma."

"Wait, Lenore," he demanded, taking her by the arm and steering her roughly to the side of the house where they couldn't be seen.

"Mr. Kent . . ."

"You have to know I'm in love with you, and I know you like me or else you wouldn't have spent so much time with me. Don't you see now, you can't marry that two-timer. He ain't— he isn't right for you. He'll hurt you."

"You're the one who's hurting me, Mr. Kent. Please let go of me."

"I can't let you go. I love you. All my life I've never had anything or anyone my own. My brothers always took everything from me. But not you. They can't take you. Don't you see? I love you, and I can have you. I'm strong and smart, I can protect you. I can give you anything you want. I never saw a lady as beautiful and nice as you. You're everything I ever dreamed of."

"I'm sorry about that, but I am going to marry Mr. Packard."

"Mr. Packard, Mr. Packard," he sneered mockingly, his lips drawing into a tight line. "That don't sound very loverlike to me, Lenore."

"Let go of me." She struggled, horror and panic filling her at the wild, frantic glint in the young man's eyes. "Please, I'm sorry if you misunderstood. I didn't mean to give you any false impressions. I love Russ."

"No. It's me you'll love. Me! You have to love me."

"Don't be ridiculous." She was getting angry now. He wouldn't listen to reason or apologies. He was mad. Mad, if he thought she could care for him over Russ. "You're just a foolish boy with a crush. Let me go, and we'll forget all about this. I'll never mention it."

"You'll never forget me, I promise you that." He forced her arms behind her back and drew her hard against his slender body, taking her mouth in a hard and clumsy kiss.

He knew how he was supposed to kiss, how women liked to be kissed. He knew what women wanted. He'd learned from experts. He forced her chin down and showed her what a good lover he'd make.

Lenore thought she'd be sick. She gagged and turned her heard from side to side to escape him, but he held her throat so tightly she couldn't move. Couldn't breathe. She began to struggle harder, kicking, twisting, fighting for her breath, her life.

He tightened his grip on her arms, raising them painfully higher behind her back, and pressed her full breasts into his chest. His hard arousal felt wonderful to him. He couldn't wait to take her. He tightened his hand at her throat, plunged his tongue into her mouth, and ground his pelvis against her hips.

Russ, oh, Russ, where are you? was her last thought before she slid away into unconsciousness.

Elizabeth went in search of Emma to see how she was holding up under the excitement of the day. Emma was more than fine. She was collecting all the gossip of the last six months from the original source of it, Mrs. Murphy.

"Hello, dear. Isn't this wonderful? You see, I told you it would be. Elizabeth has never been to one of our get-togethers before," she explained to Agatha.

"We ought to do it more often," Agatha said. "But then we will when Mr. Packard and Mrs. Beaumont get wed."

"Oh, I imagine Mr. Beaumont will have a grand celebration, with a big church wedding, and a party in the town square."

"With the governor and all those distinguished politician friends of his. We'll have to have new gowns, of course. It'll be the event of the year. When is the wedding? We must know that if we're to be ready."

"I don't know," Emma answered. "Elizabeth?"

"I don't know either."

"We simply must find out."

"Elizabeth, dear, why don't you go ask Lenore," Emma suggested.

"You must remember that her father-in-law is away right now. I'm sure they'd want to speak with him first before making definite plans."

"Yes. That must be it. We'll have to wait, Agatha."

"Not too long, I hope."

"Excuse me, ladies," Elizabeth said, wanting to find Lenore for her own reasons. She'd bet her front teeth that Russ and Lenore hadn't ever considered any such affair as was being planned for them behind their backs. Lenore needed to be forewarned.

She walked through the milling throng, thicker now that the men were almost finished with the barn and were joining the general merriment of the day. She couldn't see Lenore or her deep pink dress, which was what she looked for amid all the other black-haired partiers.

These people, at least most of them, were Lenore's people, she realized. The blood of Spain ran deep in Mexico, Mexican blood ran deep in New Mexico. A chilling thought struck her. Ramirez was Mexican. For all she knew, he could be here. She would never know. Russ would never know.

Her feet moved faster. The need to see for herself that Lenore was still safe urged her on until she was practically running. Russ. She had to find Russ. Maybe they were together. She looked back at the crowd she'd pushed through. She spotted him across the milieu, a head above the rest of the men, but Lenore wasn't with him. Her pink dress was nowhere in sight.

She raced into the house and called to her. She took the stairs two at a time, hitching her skirts to her knees All the rooms were thrown open, all stood empty of Lenore's presence. Real panic seized her then. She'd known it. She'd felt it all along. She raced outside and collided with Mr. Murphy.

"Easy, girl," he said, righting her as she lost her balance. "We're finished. I come to fetch you so we can christen the barn."

"Mr. Murphy, who organized this barnraising?" Please say you did, her mind pleaded silently.

"Don't rightly know. They came to me to manage the

278

buildin', but the stone was already rollin' by then. Why?"

"I wondered whom to thank," she lied. "I'll thank you instead. You've been wonderful, all of you. Please convey our sincere appreciation, and Mr. McKaid's. He'll be deeply touched."

"Sorry he couldn't be here, but I reckon he has duties he can't ignore. I heard he's on a peace mission with the Apache."

"Yes," she lied again. "Please excuse me. I must go find someone. Go on without me, Mr. Murphy."

"But . . ." He raised a hand to stop her, but let it fall again as she raced off. "Women!"

Frantic now, Elizabeth leaped off the porch and ran around the far side of the house. The wide skirt of her dress caught on the sharp edge of the porch and threw her off balance. In her headlong flight she took several more unsteady steps, tearing her skirt free, before she tumbled to her hands and knees.

"Damn," she cursed. She pushed herself upright and stopped, her heart lodged in her throat. A few feet in front of her lay the ornate ivory comb that had adorned Lenore's hair that morning. A rage unlike anything she had ever felt before boiled to life inside her. Blindly she raced on, to the deserted back of the house, to the well house, the root cellar, the privy, the bake oven.

She nearly ran into his back, but like a predatory cat, he jumped away and spun around, drawing a gun from a holster that hadn't been there before.

Lenore lay on the ground, her feet tied, her hands bound behind her back, a dirty gag stuffed and tied into her mouth. She was conscious, but dazed.

"Lenore," Elizabeth cried and made a move to go to her.

Mr. Kent grabbed for her and they both tripped and fell to the ground. He rolled on top of her, clamped a hand over her mouth, and pushed his gun into her belly. "Keep away from her, you filthy bitch. You whoring slut! I ought to teach you a lesson right here and now. Lenore's a lady. You're not fit for her company."

Elizabeth was dumbfounded and more frightened than ever before in her life, but she was angry too, and her anger leapt from her eyes. She bit down on the fleshy part of his hand that found its way between her teeth. She bit and kept biting until she could taste the metallic tang of his blood.

He dropped his gun and prized her jaw open, swearing

279

volubly at her. He drew his hand away and struck her across the face with the back of his knuckles.

While her hand was still ringing from the blow, he holstered his gun and drew a long knife. "I can't shoot you here, but I sure as hell can slit your throat if you so much as make one more sound. You thought you could fool me, didn't you, but I'm no fool. I got eyes. It's you what's lifting your skirts for Packard, not her. That stuff about a weddin' was a trick to keep me from my woman."

His woman? What was going on? Who was he? Elizabeth glanced over at Lenore, who was able only to shake her head and utter agitated, muffled grunts.

"You can't stop me, so you may as well quit thinkin' it. She's mine now. All mine. Even Ramirez won't take her from me."

Elizabeth had no need to ask who he was then. She had no need to question who had set up the whole barnraising. They had done it again, just as McKaid had described.

"You're making a mistake, Corbett," she said.

He was surprised for a second, then he laughed. "So you recognize me, do you? I bet you didn't think I'd be smart enough to see through your little tricks though."

"Ramirez won't think you're so smart when you come back with the wrong woman. You've already made one bad mistake in getting the Apache involved. Ramirez didn't think you were so clever then, did he?" That was a safe guess. Corbett wasn't where he'd arranged to trade Mary Runningwater for McKaid, and she knew Ramirez wouldn't be there, so Ramirez must have decided to use Corbett's ill-conceived plans to his own advantage.

"How do you know so much?" he demanded sarcastically.

"Because Ramirez is too smart to antagonize the Apache."

"Ramirez decided he didn't want McKaid, not till he got his woman."

"*I'm* his woman," Elizabeth said, ignoring Lenore's protesting struggles.

He laughed again, a wild uncertain laugh. "I don't believe you. Why should I? I seen Packard kissing you. I got the right one, the one Ramirez sent me to get. And she ain't McKaid's no longer, she's mine."

Where was Russ? Surely he would know something was wrong when neither she nor Lenore came for the dedication ceremony. She had to stall Corbett. Even if she risked her neck by screaming, she doubted anyone would hear over the increasing cacophony of music and noise coming from the front of the house, but somehow she had to give Russ time.

"Yours?" She gave an incredulous snort. "If she were McKaid's woman, do you think she could feel anything for you except pure loathing? There's no way another man could hope to match McKaid, in bed or out of it. Every time you touch her, she'll compare you to McKaid and find you woefully lacking."

Her words took him aback for a second, then he shook his head. "McKaid'll be dead."

"Is that going to erase her memory?"

"Shut up!" He slapped her again.

She squeezed her eyelids shut and drew a sharp breath, holding it in against the stinging pain. Slowly she opened her eyes, glaring directly into Corbett's confused ones. He was straddling her, and enjoying it even while he was trying to decide which of them to take. She felt him harden against her, and she goaded him further.

"Do I excite, you, Corbett? Here's the man who claims you are his lady, Lenore, aroused in your presence by another woman." She laughed victoriously. "It's me you want, Corbett. It's me you must take with you."

"Don't believe her. I love you," he said, turning pleading eyes to Lenore. "I don't want her."

"Your body proves you a liar. You can't love her and still feel desire for me. And you do feel it, don't you? I excite you. I make your blood run hot. I'm the one you really want. I'm the one who controls your passion. Not her. Never her. She won't do for you."

"No! She's a witch. She's trying to bewitch me," he cried to Lenore. "I love you."

Elizabeth laughed wickedly, picking up on his suggestion. "Witch, am I?" she said. If she couldn't save Lenore from this madman, and it didn't look as if she could, at least she might be able to buy her some time, help her in another way, if only for a while.

"How clever of you to guess. I've fooled everyone so far, even McKaid. He was a difficult man to possess, his will is very powerful, but I have him now. He belongs to me, just as you will. Just as she will."

He jerked, and the tip of his knife broke her skin. A trickle of warm blood ran around her neck. His hand was not steady as he listened to her vitriolic words.

"She belongs to me," he cried with a wild, desperate forcefulness, as if by saying so he could make it so. "You can't have her."

"I'll let her alone if you give me your soul instead. Prove to her how much you love her. Leave her and take me. I'm the one who holds the power over McKaid."

"No. I don't want you. I want her."

"Then I curse you, Corbett," she spewed in her most wretched voice. "I call on the old ones, the powers of the occult, on the great Octogenarius to curse your very manhood."

He got up and yanked her to her feet before she could finish. "What does that mean?" A curse? Ramirez was certainly wary enough of curses and evil powers. They must exist. Could she really be a witch?

She laughed again. "It means, you mortal fool, that if I can't have you, no woman will. Everytime you try to take this woman you choose over me, me, Ellspeth of Micah, your manhood will shrivel up and die on you."

She caught a brief flash of movement from the corner of her eye before his fist slammed into her jaw. There was an explosion of light, terrible pain, then blessed darkness.

Chapter Eighteen

She could hear her name being called. The voice was far away, but it made her feel good, and she wanted to go to it. It called again, beckoning her closer and closer. She opened her eyes to the most beautiful sight she'd ever seen, McKaid with misty tears in his eyes, tears for her.

"Lizzie."

"McKaid," she spoke at the same time he did, and the effort sent a sharp pain through her jaw. Her fingers went to the side of her face. It was as swollen as when she'd had the mumps. And her lips hurt. She remembered then and bolted upright in bed.

"Lenore," she cried, turning anxious eyes around the room in search of her. She wasn't there, but everybody else was, Emma, the children, Biff, Tex, McKaid, Straight Arrow, and Russ, sitting dejectedly in the corner.

"Easy, honey," McKaid said, lowering himself to the edge of the bed and trying to get her to lie back.

"Lenore?" she demanded again, looking over at Russ.

"She's gone, Lizzie. We've been waiting for you to tell us what happened. Russ got worried and sent some of the men to find the two of you when you were gone for so long. They found you behind the bakehouse, but they couldn't find Lenore. Was she with you? Do you know where she is?"

"He took her. Corbett. Russ, I'm so sorry. I tried to stop him."

Russ lifted his face from his hands and shook his head in abject denial. "It's my fault, Elizabeth. I should have listened to you. You warned us to be on our guard. You've been right all along. It's my fault. What he did to you, what he'll do to

Lenore, it's all my fault."

"Russ," she said and winced in pain.

"Lie down, Lizzie," McKaid coaxed. "You're hurt."

Elizabeth turned her gaze to the man standing tall and watchful behind McKaid. "Mary Runningwater? Did you find her?"

"Nobody showed," McKaid answered. "It was a ruse to get to you. Or Lenore, as it happens."

"I tried to convince him that Lenore was the wrong woman. He even heard Russ announce their engagement, but he just wouldn't believe it. He said it was a trick, and that he was taking Lenore because she was the one he was sent to get. I tried everything I could. I stalled for time, I argued, I insulted him . . ."

"Okay, okay. Don't get yourself upset. Emma, where's that cloth? Her lip's bleeding again."

"Never mind my lip! What are we doing here? We have to find her." She pushed McKaid away and got off the other side of the bed, grabbing the night table until her head quit spinning.

"She's right. We've waited long enough," Russ agreed, getting up. "We've seen she's all right, now let's go after Lenore."

"It's dark, Russ. Even Straight Arrow can't track what he can't see. Get back in bed, Lizzie."

"I'll be fine." He started to argue the point, but she waved his protests aside. "A punch on the jaw never stopped you, McKaid. It won't stop me either." After such fine words, the room began to tilt crazily.

"Sit down, for pity's sake," Emma scolded. "Here, take a whiff of this."

She did and recoiled away from the ampule. "What is that?"

"Smelling salts, child. Surely in your vast experience, you must have come across it once or twice."

"Not at that close range. Good Lord, that'd wake the dead." But her head was clear again.

"I'll bring you some tea."

Ruthie came to the bed and laid her fingers gently on Elizabeth's swollen face. "Does it hurt bad?" she asked softly.

Elizabeth hugged her. "Not much, sweetheart. You two must be exhausted. Why don't you go off to bed now. I'm fine, I promise."

284

"That's a good idea," McKaid said to both the children. "You'll need your sleep if you're to take care of Elizabeth tomorrow."

After they'd gone, she turned to McKaid. "Tomorrow? I'm going with you, McKaid."

"Now, Lizzie . . ."

"Don't 'now, Lizzie' me. I'm going and that's final."

"You're staying right here, and *that*'s final."

"And who's going?"

"We are. Us men."

"And what happens when 'us men' are gone, and Ramirez comes for me? He will, you know. Sooner or later."

None of the men had an answer to that.

"McKaid, have you ever played chess?"

"Chess? Lizzie, lie down. You're delirious."

"Even with my head spinning, I can outthink you, McKaid. You're probably the poker type."

"He ain't no good at that either, ma'am," Tex drawled from across the room.

"At least I don't cheat," McKaid rejoined.

"Chess is a game of strategy," she said.

"I know what chess is," he barked, irritated.

"If you move your men directly across the board," she continued as if he hadn't spoken, "straight toward the king, your opponent will slaughter you man by man. On the other hand, if you set up your own moves at the same time you second guess your opponent's . . ."

"What are you getting at?" McKaid said, his eyes widening incredulously. "That we turn this into a game?"

"It is a game to Ramirez, and a dangerous game for all of us."

"Hold on, boy," Tex said, coming to her side. "Let's hear what she has to say."

"She's been right so far," Russ interjected. "Right about Lenore, right about Straight Arrow, right about Mary Runningwater, right about the barnraising. She's had a bad feeling about that all day long. And look what happened. It's my woman involved now, and I want to hear what Elizabeth has to say."

McKaid looked at her, hurting inside at the ugly bruise on her face. Had he done that? Could he have prevented it simply by listening to her? She was waiting for him to accept or reject her help. So far, in his arrogant blundering, all he'd done was

285

push her aside, and it had gained him nothing. It had nearly gained her a broken jaw. It could have gotten her killed.

"Are we partners, McKaid, or are you setting limits?" she challenged.

Her question hit him squarely between the eyes, right where she'd aimed it. He'd asked her to marry him, and marriage wasn't a unity in body only.

"We're partners, Lizzie," he answered. "I'll listen to you." He turned to his Indian friend, wondering what his reaction would be. "Straight Arrow?"

"Mary Runningwater much like your woman. She sees with eyes that look beyond my sight. I will hear Lizzie girl."

Elizabeth sighed with relief. "Good. We all have to plan this together. All of us. Let's go to the kitchen and talk. I'm hungry. Will you help me down, McKaid. I do need your support."

"You have it," he said and lifted her gently into his arms. "Lead on, Tex. It looks as if we have a new Ranger."

He paused only long enough after the others left to brush his lips tenderly across hers. His arms tightened as he held her, and he buried his face in her neck.

"When I knew we'd gone all that way for nothing, I was so scared for you."

"I knew you would be. I tried to prevent—"

"No, it wasn't your responsibility. If there's blame to be had . . ."

"No talk of blame or guilt. Never again. Let's start fresh from now."

"I hate for you to be involved."

"I am involved. Everyone who wants Ramirez stopped has to be involved."

"Let's go have that conference then. You know, you're a pretty smart lady. I'm beginning to think you're some kind of gypsy soothsayer."

"It's only my woman's intuition, although Corbett thinks I'm a witch," she quipped.

His left brow shot up. "You'll have to explain that later."

"Just as soon as I feed my stomach. I didn't have much to eat all day."

The bell rang again late that night, only this time to gather all the men together and set their collective plans into motion.

*   *   *

By dawn the Indians were gone, except for the six who remained with Straight Arrow. And by dawn every wagon at the Circle K and the Beaumont ranch was loaded with all the items of value from the house and headed for safekeeping in Beaumont's spacious stable.

Most of the books had to stay, of course, to Elizabeth's regret. She loved books, and Clint had a truly fine collection. She withdrew one and looked at the title, running her finger over the faded gold letters. It was rough and worn around the edges as if it had been read often. It must have meant a lot to someone so she tucked it in the trunk with the rest she had pulled out to save.

"We're ready, Lizzie. We'll have to take the trunk now."

She took the family Bible from the table by the window, a table they were leaving, and put it on the top of the books already in the trunk, closing the lid.

"Is that it then?" she asked.

"I hope you're wrong about this."

"Me, too. But if I were Ramirez and I had the chance, I'd burn the place just for spite."

"We'll be pulling out as soon as the last wagon leaves. Are you ready?"

She looked down at her boots, her dark shirt and split skirt, and the gun belt slung around her hips. "I'm ready."

"You can still change your mind."

"No. I'll be safer with you than anywhere else."

He led her outside and sent two men after the books. Their gruff grumblings reminded her of another time when two men had carried her trunk for her. She smiled fondly at the memory. So long ago. A far different woman she'd been then.

Emma and the children stood beside the last wagon, their faces red from crying. Even James didn't seem to mind being seen with tears in his eyes.

"Come with us, Elizabeth," Ruthie cried and threw herself into Elizabeth's arms. "I'm afraid."

Elizabeth looked up at Emma and saw the same entreaty in her eyes. All three of them depended on McKaid for their security, and when McKaid was gone they'd come to depend on her. It had to be difficult for them when all they could do was worry and pray that neither she nor McKaid would be hurt.

"I can't this time. It's important that I go. And it's important that you stay with Emma and do what she says. Do you understand, honey?"

"Why?" she wailed. "I don't want you to be stolen like Mrs. Beaumont."

"We're going to go and get Mrs. Beaumont."

"That man who hurt you, he'll be there. Don't go."

She glanced at McKaid for help and felt his hand fall reassuringly to her shoulder.

"I'll take care of her, sweetheart. The man who hurt Lizzie won't hurt anyone ever again."

Emma gave each of the children time for hugs and kisses then embraced both McKaid and Elizabeth herself before climbing into the wagon. McKaid lifted the children into the back and tucked a blanket around them.

"You know what to do, Emma?"

"I know what to do," she answered. "God speed you both."

"Nervous?" McKaid asked as the last wagon pulled out, taking with it her last chance to change her mind. "You could really be on that stage tomorrow."

"I'm staying. And yes, I'm nervous. Lenore's life is at stake. I hope this works. I don't want anyone killed."

He took a deep breath and blew it out. "Well, we've set up your chess board. Let's make the first move."

By mid-morning Biff and a posse of six caught up with them, following their clearly marked trail.

"How'd it go?" McKaid asked. "Any trouble?"

"Not a bit. The sheriff wasn't pleased to be woke up, but when I told him what you wanted, he had it arranged before dawn. He wanted to come with us mighty bad."

"I need him there."

"I told him so. He handpicked the posse. Three are his top deputies, and the rest are the best shots in town. 'Course, the whole town would have come if they could. Seems they're outraged at what went on out at the ranch, and how they was used."

"What about the telegram?"

"Beaumont will stay put. He says to do what needs to be done."

"Dynamite?"

"Got it."

"The stage?"

"Amos is holding today's stage till tomorrow. He knows

what to do. He'll be waitin' for his passenger. The hanging is scheduled for midnight, but the word is already out that Jemez escaped, and you and the posse are on his trail. Sure wish I could see their faces when they stop that stage."

"If they do. What about the chemist?"

"He raised an eyebrow at the amount, but in the face of Wade's badge, he nice and quietlike put everything in the saddlebags."

McKaid grinned to himself. If this worked, they had a chance. He looked at Biff, and they both laughed. "You're a conniving old bastard, Biff Story."

"This is beginning to be fun," the old man said.

"Let's make it work. That's all I care about. It's a crazy fool idea, if you ask me."

"At least he won't be expectin' nothin' like this."

McKaid rode ahead to where Tex and Elizabeth rode. He looked at her closely to see how she was doing.

"Jaw hurt?"

She nodded. "With every bump."

"Let your mouth hang open. Don't clench it."

"What if a bug flies in?" she asked, scowling at his laughter, but she found it did help to relax the muscles and take the pressure off the injured joint.

"Ever been in a swarm of locusts?" Tex asked. "Now that's a bug."

"Tasty?" McKaid asked.

"I don't rightly know. After the first crunch or two, I was too busy spittin' legs to taste."

"Oh, lordie," Elizabeth groaned. "Don't make me laugh."

"How's Straight Arrow doing?" McKaid asked Tex, directing his gaze to the Indian riding at the head of the caravan.

"Ah, you know. Those Apache boys can track a crow."

"Tell me again about Ramirez," Elizabeth requested. "Everything you know or have ever heard that could possibly help me."

"You won't be there that long," McKaid said, but for the next two hours McKaid and Tex Donner and eventually Biff Story talked to her about Hiraldo Ramirez.

At noon the lawmen, the Apache, the lady, and McKaid stopped to rest their horses and to stretch stiff and sore muscles.

"Eat as much as you can, sweetheart," McKaid said, giving

her his portion of fruit in lieu of the dried meat she couldn't chew. "Get some rest. I'm going to try to pinpoint our position on the survey map and see if I can locate where Ramirez might be hiding."

Straight Arrow and the three Rangers gathered around the map Biff had brought from the assay office and traced the route they had taken that morning.

"These marks are deserted claims," Biff said. "These were settlements what died out when the gold did."

"It looks as if there are three possible sites that Ramirez could use—this, this, and here," McKaid said, pointing out larger abandoned mining compounds.

"This no good," Straight Arrow said. "No way out. Walls of canyon very steep at this place. This other mark is in open valley." He shook his head.

"You've been through these hills?" Tex asked.

"I have traveled the little river, this marking on map."

"By crackey, we got us a guide here."

"What about this one?" McKaid asked, indicating the third possible site.

"This place has good water and can be defended. The way we go will take us through this canyon. His men wait here—and here to attack."

"We're walking into a trap? Is that what you're telling us?" Tex asked.

"The trail easy to follow. Corbett want McKaid to come, or he is fool."

"Can we get in there another way?" McKaid asked, studying the map. "What about where the river comes into the gorge?"

"We must go around mountains. Many days."

"And the second exit is a couple miles farther than that," McKaid observed. "We have to get past those guards then, if this is the only way in."

"Yup. Looks to me like this is the place," Tex agreed.

"What do you think?" McKaid asked his Indian friend.

Straight Arrow's steady gaze met McKaid's. "This game of chess I do not know, but battle is old friend to Apache. This place I would choose."

"That's good enough for me," McKaid said. "Now, how can we get into the gorge without being seen?"

"Apache are not seen or heard," Straight Arrow answered.

"McKaid," Biff said thoughtfully, "Corbett's heading in

290

this direction. We could go over this ridge and meet up with his trail at this point, close to where the gorge narrows. If there are guards along the trail watching for us, we can bypass them."

"That's good, Donner. Can it be done?"

All eyes turned again to Apache knowledge. "It can. It not easy trail," he said, his eyes turning to where Elizabeth slept. "She won't hold us back."

"She has pain," Straight Arrow said. "You have medicine?"

"What I have would make her sleep."

"She will drink Apache cure?"

"If you've got anything to help, she'll take it."

He nodded once. "We go. We travel many of your miles before night."

Lenore stood once more at the small window opening and looked out at the camp of Ramirez. She was in a hut, no more than rock walls and some wattle and dried mud for a roof, imprisoned with the other captives. They were guarded and allowed out only at certain times of the day, and only one at a time. She'd been there for a whole day. It seemed like a lifetime.

"Come, child. Sit down," the priest advised. "You will make yourself sick with worry."

"I can't, Father," she said, but she tried. She sat down beside the still priest and the quiet Indian woman and made an effort to calm her jumpy nerves. "The waiting is the worst. I know they'll come for us, but I'm afraid for them as much as I'm afraid for myself." The last admission was shameful in the face of the two brave prisoners who shared her cell.

"We all have fears, my child. Do not lose faith. We are in God's hands."

She shook her head in denial. "You don't know what he's like, Father," Lenore cried.

"Was I not abducted when he plundered my parish, killed my friends, raped good women of the Church?"

"You misunderstand," she said dejectedly. "I know Ramirez is all of that and worse, but I meant Corbett. He's the one who scares me."

"Ah, the young and foolish one. Ramirez has a fondness for the boy."

"He says he loves me and I'm going to be his woman. He

291

keeps saying it, over and over."

"He tries to convince himself. He has a desire to possess what he cannot obtain without force. That is why he brought you to this place."

"Partly. Ramirez thinks I'm McKaid's *amante*."

"I hear much of this McKaid. Is he the man you fear for, the one you love?"

Lenore was aware of the steady green eyes that watched from the corner. It was unusual for an Indian to have such eyes. She was Straight Arrow's wife, the one who was supposed to be traded for McKaid. What had happened, she wondered.

"No, Father. My heart belongs to another. We're going to be married. McKaid is my neighbor and my friend. He's also a Texas Ranger and a territorial marshal of New Mexico. He and Ramirez have been enemies for years." She stood again and paced agitatedly. "What will happen when Ramirez learns that I'm not the woman he wants? He's killed so many of McKaid's friends out of pure spite."

"Then you must prepare yourself for that, and for whatever else they want of you."

"How can you be so calm? Can't we do something? Are you going to simply sit here and wait for Ramirez to kill us?"

The Indian spoke for the first time. "The priest tried to protect me, and they cut him. We try to escape, and they break his leg. He has done enough."

Lenore gasped, staring in shock and mortification at first the Indian woman and then the priest. "Please forgive me," she said falteringly. "I'm such a fool." She broke down and cried.

"There, there," the padre consoled. "Don't go on so. We both fought the same battles of the spirit."

Lenore got herself under control and looked up into the Indian's sympathetic eyes. "You speak our language. I didn't know."

"My name is Mary Runningwater."

"I'm Lenore Beaumont."

"And I'm Father Francis. Now that we are acquainted, and more sure of each other, we will talk of other things or play a game to pass the time."

"Mary," Lenore said quietly, "Straight Arrow will come with McKaid and my fiancé. I know he will."

"You have seen my husband?"

"Oh, yes." She went on to tell them what Corbett had

demanded for her return. "As you're still here, I can only assume they meant only to cause conflict between your people and mine, and in so doing, to draw McKaid away so that they could more easily capture me."

"We have lived in peace there. My heart would be sorry to leave our valley."

"McKaid wouldn't let that happen, Mary. He went with your husband. He was willing to trade his life for yours. Apparently Corbett changed his mind."

"My people will be angered by this. If Straight Arrow thinks me dead, he will come with many warriors. He will fight even McKaid for Apache justice."

"They won't fight each other, and it doesn't matter which of them comes. They'll find us, that's all that matters," Lenore said.

"You must not deceive yourself, child," Father Francis said solemnly. "Ramirez will kill us if we are of no use to him. He will not let us return if he is to be denied his victory."

"But if he can't hope to win . . ."

"It is as you said. He will kill us for spite, to strike one last blow against his enemy."

"Then we're to accept this fate, accept that we're doomed to die? I'm sorry, Father. I have to hope for more, I have to believe we have a chance."

"Who has ever stood to win against a man as mad as Ramirez? There is no reason in him, no compassion, no fairness, only a fear and hatred that begets greed and lust for power and fame. Is that not why he hates this Texas Ranger? Does he not seek to destroy all men who defy his dominance? From such destruction he feels in control of his life, and his fears are temporarily forgotten."

"What fears?"

"He fears death."

"Most people do, but they don't kill others because of it."

"His is not an ordinary fear that comes and goes with his moods. His fear for his body and his soul stays with him always. Thrice a day he summons me to pray for his soul, and every hour of the day he surrounds himself with loyal protectors. He will tell you it is for other reasons he does this, but in my heart I know the truth of it."

"You sound as though you feel sorry for him."

"I feel compassion for all who are in distress, and I must

293

sincerely pray for them. And for you, that you can learn forgiveness."

She sighed. "Yes, I suppose you must."

"But that does not mean I cannot also pray for our deliverance or for the deliverance of all who would be injured in the future by his cruelty."

"Then pray for the men who will come for us. It is they who are in pain and danger and in need of your prayers."

That night her own faith, her own values, and principles were put to the test. They had retired, each in a single blanket on the hard earth, when Corbett stepped through the doorway.

"Lenore," he summoned. "Come."

"No," she refused in sudden, choking panic.

"I have given you a day to get used to the idea of being my woman and to accept it, but your time is up. Now come with me."

"No, I won't."

"I never wanted it to be this way. I wanted not to fight you, but I will have you one way or the other. You are mine."

"I'll never be yours. Never."

"You'll be mine, or Ramirez will take you for his own," Corbett snarled. "He wants you, and it's only because of me, because I want you, that he made you unavailable to the other men. She wouldn't like that, would she, squaw, being passed from man to man?"

Lenore, feeling sick and faint with fear, turned to Mary Runningwater. "Oh, sweet God, is it true?"

"It is better one than many," Mary answered stoically.

Lenore pressed herself to the cold wall and sank weakly to her knees. She wondered what Father Francis had thought he could do to protect Mary against men like this. They had both fought and both suffered for it. Hopeless despair settled on her shoulders. But still . . .

"I can't. Oh, please, I can't. If you feel anything for me, let me alone."

"Get up, Lenore," Corbett spat. "You will come with me, or I will take the squaw and give her to every man in the camp."

Lenore's eyes snapped up to his. How could he be so cruel? How could he make her responsible for the pain of another woman? She looked at the priest, and her eyes hardened.

"This is the kind of man you would have me forgive?" she raged, a wild creature fighting the snare of the hunter. "Either

294

I submit to his abuse or suffer knowing what I have caused Mary to endure. What is my choice to be?"

"I will go," Mary said, standing and placing a gentle hand on Lenore's bowed head.

"No." Lenore stood, too. "I couldn't live with myself if I let you go in my place. He knows that," she said, turning hate-filled eyes to Corbett. "Don't you?"

Corbett shrugged indifferently. His arrogant smirk enraged her further, choking the air from her lungs.

"I never thought I could hate this much. You may violate my body and force my compliance, but you will never have my submission. I will loathe you until I die. And I will pray to God with every breath I draw, to grant Elizabeth the power of her curse on you."

Corbett took one long stride and jerked Lenore against him, pulling sharply on her hair to tilt her face to his. "Curses! Do you think I believe that nonsense?"

"Even God believes in the power of devils. But you will believe only what your small mind pleases to believe, so what more is to be said."

"I'll show you what I believe," he growled, pulling her toward the door.

"Yes! Show me how virile you are that you must take by force what a *real* man is given freely in love."

Lenore did not return until dawn, when she was shoved roughly into the stone hut, her face swollen and discolored from abuse.

Mary Runningwater led her to her blanket and eased her down. Lenore began to cry, and once she started, couldn't stop.

The priest consoled her and pressed a cool, wet cloth, a piece from his long brown robe, to her bruised eye. "It is good to weep, my child. It cleanses the soul."

Lenore wondered why he called her child all the time. Probably for the same reason she addressed him as Father. She laughed through her tears and shook her head. They didn't understand.

"He hit me. He hit me often, but he didn't rape me. He couldn't." She did laugh, an hysterical sound that sent the priest's concerned eyes to Mary's.

"Calm yourself, Lenore," Father Francis advised. "It does no good to deny the truth, it only prolongs the agony."

"It is the truth. Her curse worked. Elizabeth cursed him,

and he couldn't do it. He tried once, then he was afraid to try again. That's when he began to hit me. He said again and again that it was my fault."

"Who is Elizabeth?" Mary asked gently, trying to make sense of Lenore's rantings. She wished she had gone in her place. Lenore was not strong enough in spirit for what she had endured.

"Elizabeth is McKaid's woman. She was there when Corbett abducted me. She tried to stop him," Lenore explained, needing to talk.

"My husband says McKaid has woman called Lizzie girl."

"That's Elizabeth. McKaid calls her Lizzie." She spent the next hour telling them stories about Elizabeth, why she had come to New Mexico, how she had met Mary's husband, how she had suspected before everyone else what would happen, how she had tried to stop Corbett from taking the wrong woman.

"He called her a witch," Lenore explained, recounting the incident. "She was saying anything, crazy and dangerous things, to gain enough time for someone to realize we were gone. She threw this ridiculous curse at his manhood. That's when he hit her. He hit her so hard."

"Is she a witch?" Mary asked.

"Elizabeth? No. She's clever and brave, but she's no witch."

"Did Corbett think her a witch?" the priest asked, finding her story intriguing.

"Not at the time. She confused him and made him very angry. He was calling her every vile name he could think of, and witch was one of them."

"So she used it to her advantage, or yours, it seems," he said, nodding his head. "There is much power in superstition and fear. I know of a man in Spain who repeatedly put himself in mortal danger until he died needlessly, all because a gypsy fortune-teller said he had not long to live. He was thrown from a horse while jumping a gate he could have opened. The horse was not trained to jump. He knew this, but a fear as deeply rooted and strongly believed as his has a way of making itself a reality."

"You mean because he believed he was going to die, he made it happen?"

"That is a simple way to say it, but yes, although I do not believe it was a deliberate or conscious act to take his own life. The part of the mind that seeks to preserve life was crippled in him."

"The fortune teller—she was proved right," Lenore said.

"Yes, but perhaps 'not long to live' meant five or ten years to her."

"You believe in gypsies and witches?" she asked the padre.

"I do not doubt the powers of good and evil, nor do I know from which the gypsy gained her vision. Only a fool would deny the existence of such abilities, especially when we cannot be certain what forces lie beyond our own limited experience. I can know only for certain that the power of God reigns supreme."

"The Apache have many gods," Mary Runningwater said.

The priest nodded. "Or perhaps you see many faces of the one God."

"You do not believe we are heathen savages as most white men say?"

"I believe God reveals Himself to all His people in His own way. We are all God's children."

"Does your God allow this to happen to his children?" Mary asked, encompassing their small stone hut with her sweeping hand.

"I do not blame God for the destruction and pain mankind brings down upon itself because it will not care for its own as He commanded us to do. God is not to blame that men like Ramirez exist. He suffers our pain with us and would lend us strength to endure."

"Must we endure what we could change if we fight? Do you say that Apache justice is wrong? Straight Arrow will seek to kill Ramirez and Corbett. He will battle to destroy his enemies."

"God helped His chosen people to destroy their enemies as well. Mine is not to judge. I don't have the answer to that. You must find it for yourself."

Mary nodded, seemingly satisfied. She turned to Lenore and stroked her arm soothingly. "I would meet this woman called Elizabeth if we are rescued."

"I'll introduce you personally. I think she'd like to meet you, too. She admires your husband. She also thinks he is stubborn and insulting because he'd rather speak with a man than talk to her."

Mary chuckled. "That is the Apache way. But when we are

alone, he can laugh and play as one of our young children."

"Mary," Lenore asked hesitatingly, "will Straight Arrow turn from you because of what happened? I mean with Corbett and the other men?"

"As I, he will seek to avenge himself and me, and then we will both put it from our minds. Now you must forget. You need to sleep. We do not want you to become sick."

Late that evening a man rode into camp, causing a stir of commotion outside the captives' window. Father Francis motioned Mary to help him to the window. Neither disturbed Lenore's deep sleep.

"What is it?" Mary asked, unable to understand the rapid Spanish being spoken.

"That man," he motioned to the rider, "is Uvaldo. He was in Santa Fe to spy, to glean information about McKaid. He says the town speaks of a grand wedding to come between Beaumont's daughter-in-law, Lenore, to McKaid's foreman."

"They know they have the wrong woman. What will they do with her now?"

"Shh. He also says McKaid has made plans to send Elizabeth east on tomorrow's stage. Ramirez is sending three of his men to stop the stage and bring her here."

"Do you think they will succeed?"

"I would not doubt it. Ramirez goes to great lengths to get what he wants."

"What did he want from you?"

"Absolution. He wants me to assure him passage into heaven."

"Can you do this?"

"No. Listen. Ramirez is demanding that Corbett, a man named Gonzales, and one of the Dawsons go for McKaid's woman."

"Corbett? It is good that he will be gone."

"I hope so. Perhaps they will decide to spare Lenore harm if they think they can extract money from her father-in-law for her safe return."

"Yes. I, too, hope she does not suffer their cruelty."

"You are very brave, Mary Runningwater. They have hurt you much. No woman should be treated in such a vile way. I will pray that you can forget in time."

"I know their faces. They will be punished." Her steady green eyes held determination and defiance. "It is Apache law. In spite of my French father, I am Apache. It is Corbett who will wish to forget."

Corbett rode beside his partners throughout the early morning hours to reach the south edge of Santa Fe before the stage departed. It wasn't difficult to find a place in Apache Canyon to lie in wait for a quick ambush. They would have the woman and be gone long before anyone in Santa Fe could be alerted.

Corbett was relieved to be away from camp. He dreaded having to face Lenore again after he'd made such a fool of himself with her. How she must be laughing at him. But it wasn't really his fault. It was that woman who'd thrown a curse on him. He hadn't been able to stop thinking about her hate-filled eyes. He was sure she'd given him the evil eye when she spat that curse at him. And when he'd been unable to do anything with Lenore, he knew it for a fact. He was happy in a way to be going after the witch. He remembered how excited she had made him, and in a way he still became excited when he thought of her, but now he only wanted to kill her. If she died, her curse would die with her. Or would it? Would he be cursed for the rest of his life? That thought made his blood run cold, and the more he thought about it, the more reluctant he became to tangle with her again. What if she did something even worse?

He had wanted to confide in Ramirez about her and suggest that they let her leave New Mexico, but he couldn't without explaining why. And he couldn't bear to tell the man he admired most in the whole world a thing like that, that he couldn't get his pecker hard because he had a curse on it. Besides, there was always the chance he could get the curse removed if he gave Lenore to the witch as she had wanted him to do in the first place.

The stage rumbled into view, and the three men waited until it was upon them before revealing themselves, firing several warning shots into the air.

"Easy," Bert said to his guard, pulling the team to a slow stop. "If you try to take 'em now, you'll be dead. Sit tight. You'll get your chance."

"Pull up," Dawson called, firing another shot over Amos and Bert.

"Okay, mister. Don't get your dander up. I'm doin' my best. I ain't 'bout to take you on when we ain't even carryin' no gold."

"It ain't gold we're after," Corbett said. "We want your passenger."

"Now boys, you don't want to get McKaid riled. I suggest you turn around and get on about your business somewhere else."

"You ain't in a position to make suggestions," Dawson warned. "Corbett, Gonzales, get the girl. And watch her. She's probably got a gun."

Corbett, pistol drawn, jerked open the stage door. He recognized the dress, it was the same one she'd worn at the ranch—the day she cursed him. A chill of apprehension raced up his spine, but he ignored it. "Get out," he ordered.

"Move, bitch," Gonzales rapped out. "Pull her out."

Corbett stepped up and grabbed the voluminous cape that was draped loosely around the passenger. It fell away, and Corbett gave a strangled cry and pushed his way past Gonzales, away from the ghastly image printed for eternity on his mind.

"Hey, *amigo,* what is it?" Gonzales cried in surprise.

Dawson looked back at the commotion, but he never saw what his two friends saw, for Bert took that second of distraction to pull a gun from beneath his leg and fire.

Gonzales saw the face at the same second his compadre was shot. He spun around, both from a need to be away from the distorted face and to protect himself from gunfire. His long-barreled pistol caught the door and slipped from his nerveless fingers.

For a split second he glanced at Corbett. Corbett's gray-green face, drawn and drained of color by shock and horror, was the last thing Gonzales ever saw as a bullet caught him in the chest.

Corbett lowered his gun and stared at Bert and Amos.

"Glad to see you show some sense, sonny," Amos said, removing the gun from Corbett's nerveless fingers. "McKaid don't take to havin' what's his stolen. It's a right smart move to leave Miss Elizabeth alone." He motioned Corbett into the stage.

Corbett, stunned, shocked, scared, backed away from the

stage and what was inside. He bolted and ran into the trees.

"Should we go after him?"

"Nah. He's so scared, he'll run hisself silly. Besides we're supposed to let one of 'em get away."

Down the road a few miles Bert and Amos dug a shallow grave and dumped the three dead men into it. Two bodies were still warm, one, who had been hanged the night before—the man the sheriff had draped in Miss Elizabeth's clothes—was already cold, stiff, and bore the ghastly effects of hanging.

"He does look a sorry sight," Bert said, looking at the grotesque passenger dressed in Miss Elizabeth's clothes. "Ain't no wonder the kid took off. Scared the piss out of him."

"Reckon that face'll give him nightmares for months to come."

"If he lives that long. Let's get these bodies covered up. They're givin' me the cold creeps."

Chapter Nineteen

Corbett was drunk and still pulling cork when he clumsily gave the signal and rode into Ramirez's camp.

"He's got a belly full o' whiskey," Biff said, watching with McKaid and Russ from the guard's position on the bluff. "Must've rattled him some when he saw what you left for them in the stage. You're gettin' downright nasty, pullin' that kind of trick, McKaid."

"It's justified," McKaid said, unconcerned. "Let's hope your ideas work as well. And if I may remind you, it was Lizzie who said to turn their own tactics on them."

"God help you if'n she ever decides to turn yours on you."

McKaid suppressed a grin. "She's full of surprises, that's a fact. When I think I've got her sized up, she throws me for a loop."

"You think we got a chance here?" Russ asked. "I wish we knew where Lenore was."

"I think Ramirez won't know what hit him. And once we've got him off balance, we'll keep him there. Here he comes. He's probably furious that Corbett doesn't have Lizzie. I wish I could hear."

"Your Injun pal can. That be good enough for me. He's some smart fella. Never thought I'd say that about no redskin."

"I only hope he doesn't catch sight of Mary Runningwater. He may revert to Apache ways in a hurry. Is the dynamite set?"

"Tex has it in hand," Russ said. "And I made sure none of the rocks will fall on the camp. We don't want anyone hurt, especially the women and the priest."

"Are you sure you want to send Elizabeth down there?" Biff asked.

"Hell no. I went along with it because I thought you all agreed it was the only way."

"We agreed because we thought you did," Russ said.

"Someone has to get in there and find out where the prisoners are and what shape they be in," Biff said. "I may not like it, but Elizabeth does seem to be the likely one to get in there without being shot on sight. As she said, the queen is the most versatile player on the board."

"They could do worse to her than shoot her on sight," Russ speculated.

"Nothin's worse than dead, friend," Biff said flatly.

McKaid's jaws clenched. "If they try, if she gets in a tight spot, the jig is up. We go in shooting."

"What are you gonna do with the two dead guards?"

"Send them to the Circle K with two of the deputies."

"What for?"

"If Elizabeth is right, as a present to Ramirez. She thinks eventually he'll go there for me. They'll be waiting for him when he does."

"What if he doesn't? What if this whole thing falls apart?" Russ asked.

"Then we fight, and some of us die."

"I'd almost rather risk that, than sit here waiting while Lenore is down there," Russ said.

"And what if it's Lenore what dies?" Biff asked.

"We'll give Elizabeth her chance. She thinks she can do it," McKaid said. "Let's get back to camp. It'll be dark soon."

Ramirez was indeed furious. "The woman, where is she?" he demanded, jerking Corbett from the saddle. "Where are the others?"

Corbett staggered and fell to his knees. He started laughing wildly. "Dead," he said between bursts of laughter. "They're dead."

"You are drunk," Ramirez accused, attracting a large audience, including Carmen, who pushed her way through the men to Ramirez and Corbett.

"Drunk? Why shouldn't I be drunk?" Corbett laughed. "Here, have some." He lifted his bottle to Ramirez, who took it and dashed it to the rocky ground.

"I should have shot you the day you came to me. You are trouble to me. Always trouble."

"Trouble?" He laughed again. "I saved you, *amigo*. I saved you from that witch."

"Kill him," Ramirez ordered. "He has had his chance to prove himself."

"Oh, yes. Kill him," Corbett mocked. "I'd rather be dead than face her again."

Ramirez raised his hand to stay the guns of his men. "Who?" he asked, his curiosity aroused by Corbett's crazy ravings.

"Her. The *bruja*. McKaid's woman. Ellsbeth, the Daughter of Michael, or something like that."

"What is this you say," demanded Ramirez, hauling Corbett to his feet. He slapped him sharply across the face. "Talk sense."

"Witches don't make sense. They put spells on you. She'll put one on you, too, if you don't do what she wants." His hold on his young and volatile emotions broke under the strain and the whiskey, and he began to cry.

"She told me she was McKaid's and that McKaid belonged to her. She told me not to take the Beaumont woman. She said Lenore would be hers, too, and so would I. She's a demon. She put a curse on me. She took away my manhood because I didn't bring *her* here instead of Lenore. I did what you said. I brought the woman you sent me for. It's your fault, Ramirez. It's your fault I ain't a man no more."

"What does this mean—you are not a man?"

"You should be the one with this curse," Corbett went on hysterically. "Not me. You!"

"He's *loco*," one of the men said. "You want us to shoot him?"

"No, wait. Did you stop the stage, Corbett? Was she on it? Was McKaid's woman on the stage?"

"She was there. Oh, God in heaven. She was there, but she had the face of the devil. It's true, Ramirez. I saw her. She put a spell on Dawson and Gonzales and they were killed. They never got a shot off. I couldn't shoot. I couldn't even move. I swear it. Let her go. You don't want her here."

The men around Ramirez shifted uneasily. They were uncomfortable with Corbett's tale; they were suspicious by

305

nature, having lived in a culture shot through with legends and fears of the unknown, and they were leery of getting involved with demons and dark forces of evil. Even Ramirez wasn't so confident anymore.

Carmen, seeing her chance to get back at Corbett for her disgrace and demoted rank among the women, took it. "It is true, Ramirez. The women talk. They say he is no good anymore. A cursed man could curse us all. If he has offended a *bruja*, we are all in danger. Give the woman back and get rid of Corbett."

"No," Ramirez said. "Without the Beaumont woman, I have no power over McKaid."

"Then keep her, but kill him."

The men around them grumbled their agreement with the woman. They wanted no part of the young man who had been contaminated by evil. Ramirez had been unlike himself with the boy. He coddled him, he took him under his wing, he forgave him transgressions for which anyone else would have been punished severely. They began to believe Ramirez was touched by a curse, too, that his mind had been turned, that he'd been possessed. They wanted the boy dead.

"Sure, kill me. Burn me at the stake," Corbett jeered. "But don't forget that the *bruja* wants my soul. How will she feel about you all when I'm dead before she can get it?"

"He is a fool and a danger to us," Carmen argued, grabbing his sleeve. "He brings an Apache squaw here, and now a *bruja*'s wrath. He will destroy us. He must die, or do you care for him so much that you would endanger us all? Have your interests turned from me, your woman, to the affections of a boy?"

"*Silencio!*" he snarled and shoved her away, sending her stumbling backwards to the hard, unforgiving ground. "I must think. Bring me the priest."

Carmen smiled spitefully to herself as Ramirez stalked off and the men dispersed, whispering and complaining among themselves. At one time she would have sworn allegiance to Ramirez. She had had prestige and power, fine clothes and jewels. She had been his queen and his alone. But Ramirez had cast her aside and made her no more than a common whore, one who didn't even get paid by all the men who used her nightly. Now she would gladly sell her soul to be away from this place and these hateful swine.

She turned to the young man who had sunk again to the ground. "You are a fool," she jeered. "You will be sorry for what you have done to me."

Lenore and Mary looked at the priest and grinned. He looked back and lifted a brow in silent reprimand. "Come away from the window."

"Oh, Father, you can't blame us for being amused," Lenore said.

"The work of the devil is rarely amusing."

"No, but the work of Ellsbeth, the Daughter of Micah, is."

"Who is this Micah? Aside from one of God's prophets."

"He's her father. Micah Hepplewhite, a professor at the College of William and Mary in Virginia." She twirled around in glee, laughing. "Don't you see, you were right. He cursed himself."

"And that incident with the stage, a young woman with the face of the devil?"

"They're up to something," she said, shrugging. "Elizabeth is not a witch. It's Russ and McKaid, and the other Rangers. They're out there, I know it."

Mary Runningwater's head snapped up, and she ran to the small window opening. She listened intently for a moment, her eyes scanning the compound. She glanced at Lenore, her green eyes alight, then cupped her mouth and gave a perfect imitation of a mountain quail. She listened for a return call, but when none was forthcoming, she turned and grinned smugly.

"What is it?" Lenore asked.

"A secret signal between Straight Arrow and me. We used it before we were married, when we were forbidden to be together, to find each other in the forest."

"He's here then," Lenore said, beaming with excitement. "They're all here."

"Yes."

A man shoved open the crude door and ordered the priest to follow. Father Francis rose and propped his crude crutches under his robed arms. He had expected the summons after the scene outside. Ramirez would seek comfort and counsel

307

from him yet again, especially in the face of the current threat. He knew he could never betray or demean his vows to the Church by deceit or lies, but he didn't think he'd have to face that situation. The Word of God would be his sword and shield. Father Francis was about to enter the battle.

Ramirez paced the narrow space in his own hut, agitated beyond any emotion Father Francis had ever seen in him.

"Leave us," Ramirez snapped at the man who had escorted the priest, and who waited curiously in the doorway to hear what would be said.

"Padre," Ramirez said when they were alone. "I must know. The tales of *brujas,* are they true?"

"The Bible speaks of casting out devils. I do not doubt God's Word."

"*Brujas.* What of *them?*"

"Evil is known by many names. Names are inventions of man. Evil is evil, whatever it is named."

Ramirez paced faster, not at all satisfied by that answer. "Corbett says he has met a witch who changed bodies. Can this be true?"

"Are you referring to the legends of spirits that take the forms of eagles or pumas?"

"No. Can a witch have beauty yet become ugly if she desires?"

"All evil is ugly, my son, but often evil can take the face of beauty and lure the heart to its wicked ways."

"Can a soul be possessed, can a man be cursed by evil? Can you protect me from such a curse?"

"Only God can protect the true believer. I can pray for you, but you must repent of your own evil ways. You have influence over your men and your women. If you do not cease the killing and stealing, the raping and debauchery, if you refuse to make restitution for your sins, my son, you will bear their guilt and find no peace for your soul. You must turn away from this life."

Ramirez bristled with resentment. "I do not bring you here time and again to listen to your preaching. You will not speak of it again. I grow weary of hearing it. I will go, you will remain here and say the prayers for me."

Father Francis shook his head in sorry resignation. He could not reach the man beneath the hatred and greed. Until Ramirez

308

sincerely wanted to change his life, all the prayers in the world would not help him.

As the time drew near for Elizabeth to move the queen into enemy territory, McKaid grew more and more apprehensive. He began to see flaws all through their plan. He knew Ramirez had heard Corbett's tale, and he knew all the men in the compound were uneasy about it, as Straight Arrow had reported as soon as he had returned to camp; but those initial reactions didn't guarantee that Ramirez or his men believed or would be intimidated by Elizabeth. They could easily kill her the minute they saw her, either out of fear or spite. They might realize it was a ruse. Ramirez could be an extremely clever man at times. There were so many pitfalls to their game. McKaid's stomach churned at the thought of Elizabeth having to deal with Ramirez in any way at all.

"Lizzie, could we go for a walk? I'd like to talk to you."

Elizabeth nodded and came to her feet, taking her place at McKaid's side as they walked. "If you're going to try to change my mind, you'll be wasting your time."

"I do want to change your mind. The more I think about this crazy scheme, the more I don't like it."

"That's the whole point. Biff says it has to be crazy. It has to be absolutely and totally unexpected. The more bizarre, the more unlike the predictable Ranger McKaid, the better. What happened to you when you found your dog hanging in your hotel room? Could you think straight? What did you feel when your partner was killed and mutilated?"

"I felt rage and horror, and I wanted to strike back. And that's what I'm afraid of. Ramirez may strike at me through you."

"Not if we can frighten him enough. And I'll have you to help, don't forget. This time he'll be the one attacked. He'll be on the defensive. We pull the strings. He'll flounder and get angry, and he'll come for you, and you won't be there. We'll have him chasing shadows just as he's done with you. He won't know what to do next."

"I don't know, Lizzie. It's all so uncertain."

"Yes, it's a gamble. But Mary and Lenore and the priest are the stakes. They won't have a chance if you attack full force.

309

Remember what happened to Rosanna when you took a posse to rescue her. Ramirez didn't have to kill her. He did it to prevent you from winning. But if all goes according to plan, we'll all be out of there before he realizes you're even involved. Give it a chance, hmm?" she implored.

"You don't know how difficult this is for me, sweetheart."

"I know what I felt when you left to trade your life for Mary's."

He stopped and turned her to face him. Very slowly and with infinite tenderness he cupped her face. "Maybe you do understand. I didn't realize until now what the wives and sweethearts and families go through each time they watch those they love ride into danger. It takes more courage for me to let you go than it would take to go myself."

She looked up at the sky where the first stars were just becoming visible. "I don't have to go just yet, McKaid."

He took her hand and pulled her after him with such haste that she was laughing and running to keep up with him. When he found a secluded spot far enough away from camp, he spun her around and into his arms. His lips fastened on hers unerringly.

He crushed her to him, holding her as if he'd never let her go, as if he meant to imprint the very shape of her slender body into his own.

With insistent demand his mouth moved against hers, drinking deeply of the sweet taste of her, thrilling as her tongue joined with his, soaring with love as the very breath they breathed they shared as one.

"Lizzie, my Lizzie, how I love you," he murmured, trailing kisses across her jaw to the sensitive and erotic softness below her ear. "Ah, no, did I hurt you?" he asked, realizing what he'd unthinkingly done. He moved back to her lips, much more gently this time.

"It doesn't hurt now. It doesn't hurt at all," she answered, pulling his head to hers. "I've missed you so much."

Passion flared to life swiftly and intensely between them. McKaid's hands roamed her back, pressing her breasts to his chest, her hips against his tumescent body.

She moved sinuously against him, teasing and tormenting with pleasures and the promises of pleasures to come. She felt so good, so safe and complete in McKaid's arms.

McKaid's lips went to her neck and sent shivers of delight through her body. She tilted her head back, opening herself to his possession, submitting to his dominance as he nipped, laved, and kissed her slender and vulnerable throat.

He was hampered by the collar of her blouse, and soon had the garment unbuttoned and released from the waist of her riding skirt. Slowly he pushed it aside, letting it fall at their feet, and covered the exposed satin of her shoulders with hot, burning kisses. With his thumbs he hooked the narrow straps of her camisole and slid them over her shoulders and down her arms, baring her rounded breasts to his view.

Shamelessly she stood before him, and hungrily he filled his eyes with the sight of her.

"Beautiful," he whispered thickly. His fingers rested softly on her shoulders, and he let them slide leisurely downward until his hands could lift and mold the soft shape of her breasts. The hard nubs of her nipples burned into his palms.

With trembling fingers she reached for the buttons of his shirt. He cupped her hands with his, stilling them.

"I want to see you. I want to look at you, all of you, as I did the first night we loved." His fingers worked swiftly yet with gentle care as he removed the rest of her clothing, and then he stood back to admire and adore his woman. His woman. A surge of pure love overwhelmed him, and he dragged her again into his arms to hold her possessively. His beautiful, wonderful Lizzie. How could he bear to risk her life?

"I love you so much," he said. "So much." He kissed her, a short hard kiss, and then his hands and his lips were everywhere on her body. He praised her shoulders, her arms, her fingers with kisses; he adored her breasts, giving both his ardent attention, prizing from her throat the cries and whimpers of pleasure he loved to hear. He knelt before her and buried his face in her soft abdomen, touching his tongue to the softly padded points of one hip and then the other, covering the softer flesh between, flesh that cradled her very feminity, with hot, moist kisses.

Lower he bent until his tongue dared to explore the soft bronze curls at the juncture of her thighs. His hands cupped her firm rounded buttocks and slid down and up the length of her long shapely thighs. He pulled her closer and touched his tongue to the heart of her desire.

311

In all her wildest dreams, all her fervent longing and desire for McKaid, never had she imagined anything like what he was making her feel. She clutched at his shoulders, she held his head to her, not to keep him there, but because she had no strength in her legs to support herself.

Waves of passion began to beat at her, she felt her body's response surging forward with each insistent touch of his hot tongue.

"McKaid, please stop," she cried. Still she couldn't make herself move from him. She couldn't release him from her grip. "I can't . . . I don't . . ." she floundered as radiant bursts of ecstasy began to throb through the core of her womanhood.

"Yes," he growled in masculine victory. "Yes."

Her knees gave way completely, but he caught her and cradled her against him as her body gently floated back to earth from its shattering heights.

She tilted her head to his, her eyes lustrous and dreamy. An impudent grin tilted the corners of her soft lips. "I didn't think that's how it was done," she said, bringing forth a deep gurgle of laughter from her world-wise, woman-wise lover.

He swung her up in his arms and spun around. "Do you know what a delight you are? Do you know how powerful you make me feel?"

"Powerful?"

"I could conquer the universe."

"But you didn't . . . You're not even undressed." A faint blush touched her cheeks at the realization.

He stood her to her feet. "I will be. Undress me, Lizzie."

"Then we're not finished yet?" she teased, deftly slipping buttons through buttonholes.

"That was to whet your appetite. The serious business is yet to come." He flicked his forefingers over the rosy tips of her nipples and watched them come to life for him. He bent his head toward one.

"Hold still," she scolded.

"The hell with it," he cursed and began tearing his own clothes off. "I'm too old to be patient."

As each piece of his clothing fell away, she marveled at the magnificence of his masculine form, his broad shoulders, narrow hips, long well-muscled limbs. The sight of his proud and fully aroused manhood filled her anew with a desire to take him into her body and hold him tightly imprisoned within her.

312

She laid her hands against his chest, slowly relearning the muscles that tensed at her touch, that rose and fell with his agitated breathing. As he had done with her, she let her lips and tongue trail a line of warm kisses down his chest, stopping to nip at his flat nipples and tug gently on the sparse springy hair that dusted his chest.

She became bolder. Driven by a natural instinct, she caressed the rippling and responsive skin that held the sensitive spheres of his male body. Slowly her fingers explored in small exciting motions. He groaned her name and tightened his grip on her shoulders. She let her fingers slide upward until she held the smooth, hot head of his shaft in her hands. Gently, she squeezed.

"I want you too much," he burst out and jerked her hands from his body. Something wild and primitive was released inside him, and in one motion he lifted her and lowered her to the pallet of their discarded clothing, covering her body with his own. His mouth took hers, heady with the taste of passion, and his hands beneath her shoulders and hips lifted her into his body.

She needed no prodding, no small nudge, to open her body to his, and when he found himself poised against the hot and ready brink of her depths, he took her in one strong and sure thrust.

There was no pain in the force of his possession, only surprise, delight, and an awesome wanton excitement that the man she loved so dearly should desire her so fiercely.

He did not spare her the full power of his masculine strength, but she met that strength with equal power of her own, binding him to her with long silken legs, moving as one with him, and losing herself with him in the glorious final explosion that shook their bodies and left them at once defeated and victorious.

"Sweet heaven," he groaned, rolling to her side, his breathing labored and his heart hammering. "How can I let you go now?"

She turned her head toward him and lazily opened her eyes. "You can, because you have to. Shh," she said and laid her fingertips across his lips when he would have argued. "Don't say anything more. Just hold me for another minute."

*　　　*　　　*

313

For the second time Straight Arrow went over the layout of the outlaw camp with Elizabeth. "Four tents are here," he explained, drawing a diagram for her in the dirt. "Ramirez sleeps here, Mary Runningwater and captives in this lodge. Guards here and here," he added, pointing to positions on either side of the camp.

"Here's your pack," Russ said. "I checked it again. Everything is in place. I don't have to tell you I appreciate this. You must know that. Stay alert, and be careful. If you need us, give the signal, and we'll be there in seconds."

"I know. Try not to worry, and . . . keep McKaid busy."

"Sure."

She checked the small knife strapped to her inner thigh, she tightened her loose moccasins, she retied her hair, secured her canvas pack to her back, and took a deep breath.

"I guess I'm ready," she said to Straight Arrow. "Let's go before McKaid can dream up some excuse to keep me here."

The route the Apache chose by which to enter the camp was steep and hazardous, but it was climbable, if only just. She watched every move Straight Arrow made on his way down the rocky gorge, placing her feet where he trod, using the same handholds he used, moving as noiselessly as he. She knew he slowed himself for her sake, nevertheless she became quickly exhausted and found keeping up with him an arduous task. The muscles of her arms, shoulders, and legs ached and burned from holding her own weight and clinging to the side of the cliff. Even her eyes ached from trying to see in the dark. Only Straight Arrow's occasional nods of approval buoyed her up and gave her the courage and strength to go on.

Their silent journey seemed endless, and she was depleted of strength when Straight Arrow came to a stop a furlong downstream from the enemy camp. They concealed themselves in a thicket by the water's edge, and only after the Indian was certain they were alone did he speak.

"Lizzie girl make good Apache," he said in hushed tones. He looked up at the sky. "Not long to wait. You must prepare."

Where did he get his stamina? She wanted to collapse onto the ground and not get up for a week, but she forced herself to keep moving. She opened her pack and took out Emma's long black cape, the one she'd worn at Clint's funeral. She checked the secret pockets Emma had sewn into the hemline. They were filled with small packets just as Russ had

314

said. The next garment she pulled out was a plain black dress, this she put on over her own buckskin riding skirt and brown blouse, turning so that her Indian friend could fasten the hooks at the back. He did so, although his big fingers were clumsy with the minuscule hooks. A sash the color of blood she tied at her waist, letting the long tails stream down the front of her dress.

She threw her head forward and, bending at the waist, fluffed out her thick hair until it was a snarled mane about her shoulders. She flung the weighty cape around her shoulders and, keeping her hair free of it, hooked the frog at her neck.

"How do I look?"

He raised his imperious brows.

"Evil. Do I look evil?"

He shook his head slowly. "No."

"Oh, never mind. Hold this." She gave him a small mirror to steady while she carefully lined her eyelids with kohl, tilting the outer corners upward, then painted her lips scarlet. She took a last look at her appearance when she finished. The mirror was jiggling suspiciously, and she looked up to see Straight Arrow's shoulders moving in silent laughter.

"This isn't supposed to be funny. It's supposed to do what your warpaint does—scare the living daylights out of them."

"Umm," he grunted, controlling his mirth admirably. "War paint did not scare Lizzie girl. It is time to go." He took the leather pouch from around his neck and put it over her head.

"What is this?" she asked, again freeing her long hair.

"It is for luck. Give to Mary. You stay in trees, wait for dynamite to blow, and for outlaws to leave camp. Be very silent, Lizzie girl. My braves close to you. You need help, you call out."

The night guards were dispatched to relieve the men presently on duty. Santiago and the younger Dawson boy drew duty. They rode to the mouth of the gorge, dismounted, and began to climb in opposite directions up the paths on either side of the narrow entrance. Dawson saw the deputy sitting where the guard should have been. He drew his gun to fire, but the shot never sounded. An Apache arrow caught him in the neck, another in the chest, and he crumpled like a puppet whose strings had been cut.

315

Santiago climbed the north side. He called out to his compadre, but before he could receive an answer, the ground rumbled and shook with a series of loud explosions. The sound came from deep in the canyon, and Santiago took several leaps down the hillside to investigate before he remembered his friend who hadn't answered his call. He yelled to Dawson, but Dawson didn't answer either.

"Juan, hey *amigo*." He clambered back up the hill. "*Amigo*, did you hear that?" He stopped and staggered backward when he saw his friend. Or what should have been his friend. A prickling sense of doom ran up his spine. The clothes on the ground were Juan's, but the body inside them was rubble and rock.

The first three sticks of dynamite exploded in the sky over the gorge in a flash of thunder and light. The next three sent a shower of rocks rumbling down the hillsides from three different directions.

McKaid lit three more sticks and waited until the fuses burned dangerously close to the explosives, then he pitched them high over the edge of the bluff. Three more startling and deafening explosions lit the sky and echoed resoundingly between the high rock walls of the canyon. Rumblings reverberated for long seconds after the blast, like hollow growlings of an angry earth, or the demons deep within the molten core.

"That's an easy way to lose your head, pal," Russ said to McKaid.

"Mine's not worth much if I didn't even have the sense to keep Lizzie out of that rat hole."

"Move your butt, McKaid," Russ answered, knowing he had to keep McKaid occupied or he would do something rash. "We've done all we can here. Let's be ready for the next move."

Chaos reigned in the outlaw camp. Men struggled into their pants and boots, grabbing their guns and racing toward the west end of the clearing. Some were torn from the arms of women, women who had grown apathetic and resentful of the misuse of their bodies. Others were disturbed from games of

316

cards and chance, some wakened from drunken sleep. All were taken by surprise, shaken from their security by the violent disturbance to their impregnable hideout.

Ramirez stumbled out of his hut, guns in hand, just in time for the second blast, and just as disconcerted and confused as the rest of the men.

"Earthquake! The rocks are crumbling. We'll be buried alive."

"Rockslide. It is only a rockslide."

"Lightning hit the earth."

"*Madre de Dios,* what is it?" another cried as the third blast lit the sky with a deafening crack.

"Get back to camp and take cover," Ramirez shouted above the noise of their voices. "If we are under attack, I want you prepared. Go, and hurry. Ramon, go to the entrance and see if they have spotted anyone."

"Do you think it's McKaid?" Corbett asked, coming to stand at Ramirez's side.

"I cannot say. It could be no more than aging blasting powder left by miners. But if it is McKaid, he will be dead before the sun rises."

"Don't forget I brought him to you. I got the woman for you. We made a deal, Ramirez."

"You brought him to me?" Ramirez sneered. "You led him here with your carelessness. If he is up there, he has a posse of lawmen with him. That is not what I wanted. I wanted him here alone to watch what I do to his woman. But I am not even certain I have his woman, am I? She is his neighbor, not his *chata.* You are an impatient fool. You do not take the time to think before you act. And now you make demands?"

In all the confusion, several minutes passed before the men saw the woman in black standing beside the campfire in the center of the compound. "Ramirez, *amigo,* we have company," one of the men shouted. "Come quickly."

"It's her," Corbett cried. "That's her, Ramirez, that's the one who cursed me. She's McKaid's woman. We have her now, and we have him."

How he changed when in the presence of Ramirez, Elizabeth thought. He was filled with bravado when someone stronger stood by his side to protect him. She looked at Ramirez for the first time, and her knees began to shake, whether from fear or plain exhaustion she didn't know. She clamped them together and stood taller, throwing her head back and pasting a mocking smirk on her lips. If she acted sure, maybe she'd feel more confident. Maybe her trembling would stop.

Ramirez looked at her, then turned to Corbett. "And if McKaid is up there for us to have, do you think she would be down here? I think not. How do you get here?" he asked Elizabeth. "Where do you come from?"

She didn't answer. She said instead, "I have come for the one you call Corbett."

By sheer force of will she met Ramirez's gaze and held it, unflinching. He had eyes as black and sinister as the night, eyes that glinted with malice. She knew he must never sense fear in her, even though she was quaking with it. Ramirez would disdain weakness. He would take it and use it against her. As she intended to do with him.

"Take her," Ramirez ordered his men. "Search her and bind her hands and feet."

Elizabeth's laughter was demonic. She whirled around, her cape billowing in a black arc behind her, and pinned the men with a challenging gaze.

"Which of you would lay hands on me? Which of you longs for the arms of death? Which will be first to offer me your eternal soul?" She turned again. "You," she stabbed a finger at Ramirez. "Will you dare to touch me? Will you stand in my way? Will you try in your simple mortal ways to prevent me from claiming what I must have? I have come only for Corbett. I will have him. Whether I also take you, is for you to decide."

Into the silence that followed, a rider galloped into camp, nearly getting himself shot for his haste. Santiago slid from his horse, panting for breath.

"Juan is gone," he said to his leader. "*Dios*, he is gone."

"He deserted me?" Ramirez demanded, his voice rising. "He took one of my horses?"

"I do not know. Ramirez . . ." he said, dropping his voice to a lower volume. He didn't want all the others to hear. He didn't want to be treated as Corbett was because of some crazy and unlikely story. "His gun was there, and his clothes and boots, but they were filled with rocks."

"Dawson?" Ramirez asked after the other guard.

"The same. It's like they were turned to stone."

"See, I told you," Corbett crowed. "She did it. That's how she got in here."

That brought the count up to four, Elizabeth thought. One by one, McKaid and the lawmen were picking off Ramirez's pawns. The grin that tilted her lips was not faked when she turned to look at Ramirez.

He was struck dumb. He was skeptical that she was what Corbett claimed, but he wasn't prepared to take the chance that she was and would do him harm. Corbett's stories of curses and demons, four men dead—two of them in a mysterious manner—earthquakes, her appearance from nowhere, the lingering smell of brimstone that surrounded her. It was too much to chance.

"Bring the padre," he commanded sharply, eyeing Elizabeth's reaction. Would she quail from a priest?

Elizabeth turned her attention to Corbett. She smiled seductively. "You have nothing to fear from me. Young men are my specialty. Why do you not leave this old one and come to me," she implored, holding out her arms to him. "It cannot be enjoyable to live without the carnal pleasures of the flesh. With me you will find such pleasure again."

"No. You see, Ramirez. I'm not crazy. Kill her." Corbett himself drew his gun with a clumsy quaking hand.

"Shall I turn your hands into claws," she asked fiercely to cover the terrible fear that she was soon to die. "Shall I cause your fingers to wither and curl into knots at the ends of your arms?"

The priest, already alerted by the mayhem in camp, had been standing at the window with his cellmates, watching the activity outside. He wasn't certain what was happening, but Mrs. Beaumont seemed to be, and she'd implored him to go along with this woman. There wasn't time for explanations before he was dragged from the hut and shoved forward to stand before Elizabeth. He took a breath. He hoped he would be as convincing as she was.

"Ellsbeth of Micah," he said aghast and crossed himself. He backed away. "This is the woman of whom you spoke?" he asked Ramirez, feigning alarm. He crossed himself and began to quietly recite a prayer, praying in earnest for forgiveness for his deception. But there were lives at stake, lives of decent people, people who looked to him for guidance and help. He had a responsibility to them before that of a hardened heart such as Ramirez had shown. God would understand.

"Hello, priest," she spat scornfully. "Do you still seek the

319

chaste path to God?" She turned to Ramirez. "One of my failures. I do not like to fail, but I had so little time with this one. He brought the bishop, you see, to fight against me. But he cannot call to a higher order now." She sauntered to where the priest stood leaning apprehensively against his crutches, as if he would use them if need be to ward her off. She also had to get away from the awful smell of the sulfur she'd thrown into the fire before she began to choke on it. "I have looked far for you. I have time, priest. This time I will win. Perhaps you will surrender to me now."

He crossed himself and prayed louder, chancing a glance at her face. There were questions in her eyes, but he couldn't answer them. Nor could he ask his own. Now was not the time, while the outlaws were watching.

"Where is McKaid?" Ramirez asked boldly, counting on the shock of the question to spark a revelation from her. He was shaken by the priest's response to the woman, but he couldn't let his men think he was afraid. If they thought he feared the woman, they would run. He'd have no one to protect him.

"He is out there," she said, waving a hand to the vast countryside. "Searching for one of your men, I believe."

"He is not here, with you? He did not bring you?"

"I have no need of McKaid to take me where I wish to go."

"What if I told you I plan to kill McKaid?" Ramirez asked, prodding further.

She shrugged negligently. "McKaid is mine already. His mortal flesh does not matter. Do you like to kill, human?" she questioned. "Perhaps I should summon my sister. She also finds death intriguing. Many have tried to kill her, men like you, Ramirez. But she's a clever one, my sister. She drives them mad, and when she is finished with them, they kill themselves."

The sound of horses interrupted her dramatic lie. The men around them turned to see three of the gang riding away.

"Stop them," Ramirez ordered. "Stop them."

The men raised their guns, but hesitated. Ramirez did not. He fired, and one of the three riders dropped to the ground, shot in the back. The other two leaned lower in their saddles and galloped out of camp.

Ramirez swore volubly. "You have done this," he snarled accusingly at Elizabeth.

"I have done nothing." She turned to Corbett and smiled

again. "Where is your tent? I will wait for you to come to me."

"You will not," Ramirez declared. "Put her with the priest. He will not use his prayers for me, now he can use them for his own soul. And put more guards at the entrance."

Elizabeth smiled, and followed the priest's slow progress to the stone hut. Three more men, one dead, two very soon to be in McKaid's hands. Ramirez was fast losing his notorious army. No one touched her, but no sooner had she stepped into the hut than the rough door was slammed and barred behind her.

Chapter Twenty

"Elizabeth," Lenore cried and rushed to throw her arms around her friend.

"Shh," Elizabeth warned. She steered Lenore away from the door and to the back of the hut where they could talk in private, when she saw Mary Runningwater's curious eyes trained on her. She let out a sigh of relief. "I'm shaking all over."

"You've taken an awful chance, coming here," Lenore said. "You could have been killed out there. What is that smell?"

"Brimstone. Come, we must talk," Elizabeth said, sitting beside the Indian woman. She was lovely, Elizabeth thought. No wonder Straight Arrow had been so hard to convince. "You are Mary," she said, removing the small bag suspended at her neck. "Your husband sent this for you."

"Straight Arrow," Mary whispered, taking the leather pouch.

"He said you would know what to do with it."

Mary opened the bag and emptied the contents onto her skirt. She smiled. "They are poison quills," she explained. "They have been painted with the venom of a deadly viper. Do not touch the black tips."

Elizabeth turned to the priest. "Ellsbeth of Micah?" she asked wryly. "You surprised me, but you gave me courage. I was terrified."

He shrugged and looked heavenward. "It seemed advisable to perpetuate the deception for your safety, though I wondered for a moment if I had not caused more harm than good. Mrs. Beaumont told us what you had done for her. You saved her much torment."

"I'm glad for that, but you must know that, if I did, it was by sheer chance. I would have said anything to stop Corbett from taking her. I would never have thought of casting a spell if he had not first called me a witch. And then it just popped out. I was very angry."

"But you knew of the superstitions and legends of these people?"

"McKaid did mention it once, but I didn't think much about it."

"Is McKaid here? How is Russ?" Lenore asked.

"McKaid is here, yes, and Russ is worried sick."

"What are they planning? Are they coming to rescue us?"

"If they attack, Ramirez will kill us, just as he killed McKaid's fiancé four years ago. No, we are going to disappear."

"Disappear?" Father Francis asked. "As if by witchcraft?"

"We have already turned the guards to stone. No doubt the two who rode out of here will also be found the same way."

The priest had to grin. "You turned them to stone?"

"In a manner of speaking. We stuffed their clothes with rocks. This won't work for long, I assure you. We must carry out our plans swiftly. Ramirez is no fool."

"What is this plan?" Mary Runningwater asked.

"We are leaving tonight. Straight Arrow is waiting by the stream for us and will guide us up the wall of the canyon. By sunrise we will be gone."

"But we are guarded day and night," Lenore said. "How can we escape?"

"Well, I plan to drug the guards, so somehow I'm going to have to get out of here for a few minutes."

"I cannot go," Father Francis said. "You must leave me here."

"No," Lenore said. "Don't let him stay. They've already hurt him."

"My leg is broken, Miss Hepplewhite. I will hold you back. You must go without me. Ramirez will not harm me further."

"Let me think a minute." She pressed her fingers to her temples and paced the small square of the hut. Her legs had started to tighten up in reaction to her strenuous exercise. Even with rest, it would be difficult for her to make the climb back to the top. It would be impossible for the priest with a broken leg. And he wouldn't get far on foot with the extra guards around camp. She looked at the three of them. "All right. The two women go. If Mary and Lenore don't show up, we'll have two impossibly irrational men to deal with on top of Ramirez. I'll stay with Father Francis. We should be able to keep this ruse going for one more day. Explain to McKaid," she said to Lenore, "and tell him to devise a way to get the padre out of the gorge. We'll wait for him tomorrow night at the same place you are to meet Straight Arrow tonight. And Lenore, keep McKaid calm. You know what he's like. If he comes storming down here, people will die unnecessarily."

The gorge fell quiet as the evening turned to night. The fire in the center of camp was kept alive by the two guards on patrol. Four guards had been dispatched to the entrance of camp, though none went willingly. The only other man awake was the one who stood outside the prisoners' hut.

Elizabeth knocked on the door from the inside. "Señor, I have need for some privacy."

He kicked the restraining prop away from the door and swung it open. "It's late, *gringa*. You should have thought of that earlier." He waved his gun, directing her back to the inside of the hut.

"The need to relieve this mortal body did not arise until now."

"Know this, woman," he retorted. "I am not fooled by your lies or your threats."

"Are you not? Why did you not speak your mind to Ramirez?"

"Ramirez believes all that nonsense. He does not listen when his soul is at stake."

"You care not for your soul?"

"I care about me and what I want. Heaven, hell, angels, and witches, they are for fools."

"You dare to call Ramirez a fool?"

"I'm smarter than that. Go to sleep."

"I cannot sleep. I must insist you let me out."

"*You* insist? Prisoners are taken out three times during the day. You will have to wait."

"I can make it worth your effort, señor," she said beguilingly. "If you care nothing for your soul, that is."

He looked her over from head to toe. "Perhaps you can, at that. Come out then, but no tricks or I'll shoot you."

She smiled her gratitude and stepped over the portal, waiting as he braced the board against the door again. She looked around, taking in every detail about the camp.

"You will not touch me," she warned as he reached to take her arm. "It is forbidden."

He paused, then dropped his hand, using his gun to direct her toward the campfire. She grinned, her face averted. He wasn't as sure of himself or her as he pretended.

"Who goes?" one of the guards, a young man, harked. He got to his feet and stepped forward. The other man threw down his cards, spat in the fire, and scratched his crotch.

"Paco," the guard said. "It's me, Paco. The woman needs to take a . . . to go for a walk."

The two guards walked over to them and looked Elizabeth over. "She don't look like a witch," the older man said.

"Ramirez said three times a day. He won't like this," the younger said.

"Ramirez is asleep, with my woman in his arms," Paco said grudgingly. "I plan to have a taste of this one. Don't expect us back for a while."

"Hey, *amigo*, let me have her when you're through, eh?" jeered the older man.

He was dirty, and smelled of his own sweat. He spat again, and Elizabeth shuddered at the brown and decayed teeth he showed when he grinned at her. Not for the first time she felt a sickening, crawling fear that something would go awry and she'd suffer at the hands of such men as these. As Rosanna must have. No wonder McKaid had nightmares. It would kill him if it happened all over again.

"Is that coffee?" Elizabeth asked divertingly. "Might I persuade you to share it? I haven't eaten all day."

The guards exchanged looks uncertainly, neither inclined to deny her. "Have a cup," the young one said.

She strolled to the side of the fire where the pot rested in the coals. She lifted the lid. "It smells wonderful," she said, pouring herself a cup. It smelled horrible, acrid and burnt. As strong as the brew was, they'd never taste the sleeping powder she covertly sprinkled into the pot. She sipped her coffee slowly, then stood to her feet. "Could I pour you a fresh cup," she asked, bending and wrapping the hem of her cape around the hot handle again. She held the pot out questioningly.

The men accepted her offer, and she swirled the pot a few times and poured each of them a refill. She hoped she hadn't overdosed them. She'd put two whole packets into the coffee.

326

"We go now," Paco said impatiently. "I do not want Ramirez to wake and find me gone from my post."

"Thank you, gentlemen," Elizabeth said, tossing the remainder of her vile-tasting drink away and setting the tin cup down. She pulled her cape around her and faced them. "I will not forget your kindness."

She allowed Paco to guide her into the cover of vegetation along the creek. He let her go and stepped away. "Get done with it," he said.

Elizabeth stepped behind a scrubby juniper and ducked down. She hoped Straight Arrow meant what he said. She stayed where she was and waited until Paco called out to her.

"You have had enough time, señorita."

When she rejoined him, Paco pulled her against the eager bulge in his pants and tried to cover her lips with his own. She pushed him back, glancing frantically for Straight Arrow. "Do not be in such a hurry," she purred.

The knife was quick, piercing the flesh between his shoulder blades. She pressed his head to her shoulder to muffle his cry of pain and sank to the ground under the weight of his unconscious body.

"What's going on down there?" Russ asked for the fifth time.

"Nothing that . . . Wait. There she is," McKaid said, peering intently through the extended spyglass. "She's walking toward the fire with one of the guards."

"Alone? Is Lenore with her?"

"No. She's alone. And she's having a goddamned cup of coffee. What the hell is she doing," he growled, "taking a stupid chance like that? Why didn't she stay in the hut? Doesn't she know what could happen? Those men are animals. Hell, she's pouring them coffee."

"Relax, McKaid. She's probably drugged them. Let me see. And will you please keep your voice down. These walls echo."

"Dammit, he's taking her into the woods. I'm going down there. No stinking bastard is laying his friggin' hands on my woman again."

"Hold on, McKaid," Russ urged, pulling McKaid back down to the ground. "She said she'd signal if she needed help."

"I'm not waiting. This was a mistake from the beginning. I

knew it."

"If you go riding in there with a posse, you'll really be making a mistake. They'll all be killed."

"I can't just stand by and watch . . ."

"How do you think I've been feeling? I've lived for days with the same nightmare. The only hope I have is the hope Elizabeth gave me. I have to believe in her."

One of the deputies moved up and positioned himself on the ledge with McKaid and Russ. "See anything?" he asked.

"Yeah. All bad," McKaid retorted.

"We got two more of the guards."

"That doesn't help Elizabeth," McKaid snapped. "That snake took her into the bushes."

"You think we should go in?" the deputy asked.

"You can't get there in time to save her anyway," Russ said. "If he's going to rape her, he won't waste time doing it. She was out in the open. If she needed us, she had every opportunity to tell us."

"Sure. Sure. Calm down, McKaid. She's a tough lady," the deputy encouraged.

McKaid inched away from the edge of the bluff and sat up, grabbing a stick and stabbing at the ground. "I can't bear this. I'm no good at waiting. She's down there in God knows what danger, and I'm . . ." The stick snapped with a loud, brittle crack.

"He's only got fourteen men left with him, McKaid," Russ said. "We could take 'em if you decide to."

McKaid moved back to his vantage point on the ledge. He raised the glass to his eyes and watched. "No. We'll wait. I just hope she knows what she's doing."

Elizabeth crawled from under the weight of Paco's fleshy body. Straight Arrow was nowhere to be seen, and the knife was gone. She felt for his pulse and breathed a sigh of relief when she felt the thready beat against her fingertips. This man was a murderer who deserved pain and suffering and even death, but Elizabeth knew by the extent of her relief that she'd never be able to take a man's life in a premeditated act. She'd have to be in jeopardy of losing her own before she could kill. That knowledge didn't give her much comfort in this den of thieves and murderers. "Be strong and quick," McKaid had said. She was neither.

She rolled Paco over and took his weapon. On hands and

knees she crept to the edge of the clearing and hid herself among the tall grasses, watching and waiting.

She knew that on the other side of the compound Lenore and Mary were waiting for her to return for them, and both carrying out more of her hastily devised plans. Hours seemed to pass in the minutes while she waited anxiously for the sleeping draught to do its work so she could get back to them.

"Pour me another cup of that coffee, *amigo*. I can't seem to stay awake."

His young friend picked up the pot, staggered, and fell to his knees. He dropped the pot and leaned on his hands as dizziness overtook him. One arm buckled under him and he rolled to the ground and curled up for a long nap. His friend never got his coffee, but he didn't care as he, too, slid into a deep sleep.

Elizabeth whistled noiselessly. When it worked, it worked with a vengeance. She looked from one end of the camp to the other. With her heart racing in her breast, she stood, wrapped her cape about her body, and walked sedately into camp. As she passed the sleeping guards, she took two more guns. She lifted the board propped against the door of their hut and opened it.

"Thank God. We were so worried. What took so long? You have guns!"

"I had to persuade the guards to have a cup of coffee with me. Are you ready?"

"Coffee? Elizabeth—"

"Not now. Your clothes?"

"We've done what we could with what rubble was in the hut." Lenore wrapped the rough blanket more securely around her slender shoulders, looking at her dress and petticoats filled with loose rocks and dirt.

"It's fine. Straight Arrow has spare clothes in my pack. You'll have to leave your shoes."

"You must keep the quills," Mary said. "Keep them with you at all times, but take care you don't prick yourself."

"Yes. Thank you, Mary. And thank Straight Arrow."

"Are you sure we can't take Father Francis?" Lenore asked.

"It's a treacherous climb. He couldn't do it with one leg. McKaid will think of something."

"You must not concern yourself with me, my child," the priest said. "Since Miss Hepplewhite insists on staying behind, you must get safely away from here and get her message to

329

Mr. McKaid."

"We will tell him," Mary said. "Come, Lenore, we must go."

Elizabeth opened the door and motioned for the women to follow. Mary stopped her.

"You have done enough. I will do this. Where is my husband?"

"Go across the camp and follow the creek downstream. He's waiting about . . . Why don't you use your special signals? I'm sure you can find each other."

Mary smiled, then sobered. "Ramirez will be angry that we are gone. His anger will fall on you."

Elizabeth nodded. "I know. Hurry now. And Mary, block the door when you leave."

McKaid and Russ waited anxiously for the captives and Straight Arrow to come into view, helping them up the last of their steep climb.

"Where's Elizabeth? What happened?" McKaid asked. "Why didn't Lizzie and the padre come with you?"

"Ramirez broke the padre's leg," Mary answered, first to catch her breath. Lenore was buried in Russ's arms, crying and too exhausted by the strenuous trek to respond.

"Elizabeth is staying with him. She believes he will be killed if he is the only one to remain. She hopes to prevent that. She instructed me to say that they will meet you tomorrow night and that you must find a different path for the priest to travel. He cannot climb this."

She sank to the ground, her knees weak. Straight Arrow knelt beside her and touched his hand to her long, tangled hair. He lifted his face to McKaid.

"I gave to you your life and that of your woman. Now you and your woman return to me my wife. I give my thanks. My men stay in canyon to protect Lizzie girl for you."

McKaid nodded. He felt sick. He didn't think he could stand another day of waiting. But Lizzie was down there still, and counting on him. "Let's get back to camp. The sun will soon rise, and we have to revise our plans before nightfall. Do you need help with her, Russ?"

Russ lifted Lenore easily and held her cradled to his chest. He didn't think he could ever put her down again. "She's not heavy," he said, her actual weight seeming light compared to the cumbersome burden of guilt and worry he'd carried over the past interminable days and nights. "Thank you, McKaid, Straight Arrow. I can't express . . ." His voice wavered with emotion, and he swallowed hard. "Thank you."

McKaid clapped Russ on the shoulder in understanding. "We're not out of this yet."

"McKaid, you will take Mary Runningwater to camp. I go back to scout for easier trail."

"The sun will be up soon."

Straight Arrow did not reply, only stood taller and lifted one brow uncomprehendingly.

McKaid grinned. "Sorry, friend. I forgot how invisible the Apache can be even in daylight."

Voices raised in anger tore Elizabeth from the arms of sleep and sent her shooting painfully to her feet with her heart pounding in her chest.

"No need for alarm, my child," Father Francis comforted her. "I regret your sleep was disturbed. You slept so little."

She rubbed her temples and brushed her tangled hair from her face. "I'm whipped."

"We cannot admit defeat yet."

"No, no. I mean I'm exhausted. And I ache all over."

"Ah. Then you are not giving up?"

A ghost of a smile hovered on her lips. "I still have some fight left in me." More angry words came from outside. "I think someone is reaping the whirlwind for my mischief."

"Ramirez found the two guards asleep at their posts, and one of the other men found Paco, alive but delirious and muttering some warning about touching you."

"Have they mentioned the missing guns?"

"No. They will fear to do so in front of Ramirez. I expect we'll have a visit from our notorious leader at any moment. If I might make a suggestion, I believe we should now become bitter adversaries and put the distance of the hut between us. And if you can utter a few incantations . . ."

"Incantations? Good heavens. I can't . . . Wait. Double, double, toil and trouble, you mean? Eye of newt, and toe of frog?"

He chuckled, shaking his head. "Trust you to come up with one. They come now. Quickly."

331

"By the pricking of my thumbs, something wicked this way comes." Elizabeth rushed to the opposite side of the hut and put on her cape. Excusing herself, the lifted her skirt and withdrew the slender knife. She pricked the end of her little finger. Using her own blood she painted a crimson mark on her forehead and the palms of her hands. She hid the knife in the dirt beside her.

"That's dedication," the priest said wryly, drawing a line in the dirt to separate them and adding crosses on his side of the divide. He knelt and began his prayers.

She followed his example. She sat cross-legged and began to rock back and forth, swaying her arms above her head and chanting Shakespeare.

The door was flung open and Ramirez, gun drawn, ammo belt slung across his chest, stepped through the low portal. He looked from the terrified priest to Elizabeth, adorned in blood. His gaze went to the mounds of rock and clothes which hid the three guns.

"Where are the others, Padre?" he demanded of the priest.

"Let me out of here, señor, please release me from this woman," Father Francis begged pitifully.

"I will know! Where are the women?"

"They are gone. I beg you in the blessed name of the Virgin, release me from this place of evil."

"Do your prayers not protect you?" he jeered.

"She is the daughter of Micah, I am but a mere man."

"Tell me of the women. I will have the truth."

The priest dropped his head and nodded. "The Indian woman is the wife of the chief, she knows the ways of the shaman. She knew Ellsbeth for who she is and offered up her own prayers for protection. Ellsbeth became angry. She looked at the Indian and spoke words, and then Mary Runningwater was gone. Please, *por favor*, put me in another hut."

"What of the Beaumont woman?"

"Mrs. Beaumont argued with Ellsbeth to spare my soul. She argued, and then she, too, was gone." He crossed himself and murmured a short prayer. "She was a kind woman, and she is at peace, this I know. She is safe from the shadow of death you have brought into this valley."

"I did not bring the witch. I would be rid of her, too. She brings destruction to my men. She bewitches them."

"You know why I have come, human," Elizabeth said

332

evenly. "Deliver the man to me and I will go. But I will take the priest as well. I have unfinished business with him."

"Do not heed her, Ramirez. She will turn your head, she will beguile you."

"But you will be saved from my wrath, human," Elizabeth said reasonably. "I was not sent for you."

"Who? Who sent you?"

She laughed malevolently. "One mightier than all your men, one who could destroy you with a flick of a finger, one who could bring the mountains down upon your head. He waits for you, mortal, but he is patient. He has no need of me to bring you to him, you will deliver yourself into the fiery jaws of hell. You fear this?" she asked, feigning surprise at his pallor. "Do not," she entreated kindly. "You will learn to love the taste of flames."

"Padre," he said, turning his fear-distorted face to his only hope of salvation.

"You must repent of your ways. You must seek God's help. You . . ."

"Silence!" Elizabeth commanded the priest. "You will speak not of this in my presence or I will take him while he is still mine to take. Go from me, human, before I forget who it is I have come for."

Ramirez wasted no time in taking himself from the hut. With one last glance at the inert mounds on the floor, he slammed and braced the door.

Elizabeth clutched at her hammering heart and sank to the dirt floor, drained of energy. She rested her forehead against her drawn up knees and tried to calm herself. How much longer could she keep this up? How many more times could she keep her own fears from her face and voice. She lifted her head to meet the priest's gentle eyes.

"I don't know how actresses do it," she said. "It's draining."

"You are very pale, but you were quite convincing. I'm almost afraid of you."

"And you, sir, speak from both sides of your mouth. Yet, you never once lied."

"I hope it does not occur to them to burn you at the stake."

"Tell them that only works when the moon is full." She unwrapped her arms from around her legs and leaned back. Her fingers encountered the knife she'd buried, and she picked it up. "Perhaps, since they have already searched you, you had

333

better keep it for me."

He took it and sat down beside her. "It would not do for them to find it in your possession."

"Do you think he'll be back before nightfall?"

"Ramirez is convinced you are who you claim. More correctly, he is afraid not to believe you. But the others, I would not depend on fooling them. We are in the ironic position of having to rely on Ramirez for our protection."

"Then we'll have to convince the others." She had no mind at the moment to think about how that could be done. She drew a long weary breath and massaged the sore muscles of her legs.

"You need to sleep, my child. I will watch at the window."

"I'm more hungry than tired right now."

"Go to sleep."

Lenore lay between McKaid and Russ on the edge of the cliff above the camp, looking down at the place she'd been held captive, the place where two of her friends remained imprisoned.

"How are we to get them out?" she asked.

"Straight Arrow has found a trail to the cliff which the priest can walk. From there we're going to bring them up the face of the rock by rope."

"Elizabeth, too?"

"Yes, if it's necessary. If my other plan fails. Are you sure about last night, Lenore? That man didn't hurt her?"

"I don't think so. She was gone a long time, but she came back alone, and she had guns."

"Guns? She's armed? That could be good or bad."

"Mary said she led that man to where Straight Arrow was waiting. He has Apaches all through the gorge. Did you know that?"

McKaid and Russ exchanged glances, and Russ gave a short chuckle. "No wonder she wasn't reluctant to go with him. She was right again, McKaid. They're too biased to think a woman can hurt them, and our little queen has crossed the board and is playing havoc with them. And they can't even see it happening."

"What are you talking about?" Lenore asked.

"Chess," McKaid answered. "We're using Lizzie's chess strategy."

334

Lenore knew the game well. "Ah. The queen. The most destructive piece on the board. And this witch business? Turning people to stone?"

"A diversionary tactic while we eliminate the pawns and reclaim our people."

Lenore laughed softly, her voice low and full of humor. "You'd have been proud of her. And the priest."

"He won't give her away, will he?"

"He acted as if she were the devil incarnate. He addressed her as Ellsbeth of Micah in front of the whole camp. He won't reveal her deception. He told us what fear can do to a man, and he said Ramirez is full of fear. Father Francis wanted us to leave him there, but Elizabeth wouldn't hear of it. He'll help her however he can, of that I am positive."

"Just to be on the safe side, I'm sending Tex and Biff in."

"The two knights?" Lenore asked.

"We've hit Ramirez hard with all this spirit stuff. Maybe too hard. I don't want him to start getting suspicious. Biff and Tex are my insurance."

Father Francis shook Elizabeth's shoulders. "Elizabeth, Miss Hepplewhite," he whispered. "Wake up. The woman is bringing our meal."

Elizabeth sat up and groaned at her protesting muscles. "How long did I sleep?"

"It is nearly noontime."

"Oh, you should have wakened me." She stood up, straightened her dress, and draped her cape around her shoulders again. "Hadn't you better get to your own side of the hut, Padre? It wouldn't do to be seen in such close proximity to me."

Carmen entered the hut and handed them each a tin of beans and meat spiced with hot peppers. She glanced uncertainly at Elizabeth as if she wanted to say something but wasn't entirely decided as to whether or not she dared.

"I'll bring you coffee," she said. She paused at the door and turned. "Would you like a pan of water? You must wish to freshen yourself? I have some over the fire."

"Thank you . . ." Elizabeth responded, raising her brows expectantly.

"I am Carmen. I will bring the water to you."

The woman left, and Elizabeth threw the priest a glance of surprise. "Hers is the first friendly face I've seen." She turned her attention to her meal.

"Do not be deceived. She thinks only of herself. She was Ramirez's woman before he disgraced her by giving her to his men."

"Why does she stay?"

"Where can she go? She is a prisoner as we are. She is more hopeful than the other women who have come to accept the wretchedness of their existence, but she fights a difficult battle. Ramirez will never give her the freedom she desires. He owns her, she is his to torment."

When Carmen returned with the promised coffee and water, she lingered, fidgeting nervously with the folds of her colorful skirt.

"You want something of me," Elizabeth said curtly. "Speak your mind."

"Are you truly a witch?"

Elizabeth grinned sardonically. "Have I ever said so?"

The priest intervened. "A witch cannot declare herself. Do you doubt your own eyes?"

"I . . . No." She braced herself and faced Elizabeth. "You put a curse on Corbett. I want you to put the same curse on all these men."

Elizabeth set aside her plate and rose to her feet. "You want me to curse all the men in your camp?"

"It is not my camp. I loathe this place and these people."

"And if I do this for you, what will you do in return for me?"

Carmen didn't even flinch at the question. "I will do anything you ask."

"Will you?" Elizabeth asked, throwing the priest a quick glance. "Will you give me Corbett?"

"Corbett? But he is at Ramirez's side at all times. How will I do this?"

"You must convince Ramirez that Corbett is mine and that I will not relent until I have him. His only hope to escape my wrath is to give me this man. And it would not distress me to see their loyalty to each other torn asunder in the process."

Carmen's lips curled cynically, and her black eyes glittered with hatred. "Loyalty? I thought him loyal to me at one time. It would please me to see them at each other's throats."

"Then we agree? You will do this? And you will bring

336

Corbett to me when I instruct you to do so?"

"Yes. Yes."

"Then come back in an hour. I will prepare a potion for you."

"A potion?" Father Francis asked when Carmen had gone.

"A potion," Elizabeth confirmed. "It may be chancy, but under the circumstances . . ."

"What happens when this potion doesn't work?"

"It will work. I'm only concerned that it might place us in worse trouble. I'll have to use belladonna. It's difficult to predict a reaction to that when the men drink so much whiskey and tequila. They may become dangerously irrational."

"More so than they are now?" he asked.

"Yes, I see your meaning," she responded, grinning wryly. "All right, then we will risk it."

On foot the two bedraggled miners entered the canyon. Ramirez had ceased to send his men in pairs to guard the mouth of the gorge, he now had five men who took positions at the eastern perimeter of camp, all within sight of each other. Biff and Tex exchanged a long look. Loaded with packs of camp supplies, they walked into their midst.

"You, stop there," one of the guards shouted.

The two Rangers stopped and looked around as the five men surrounded them.

"You are on our claim," Tex accused, not cowed by the long pistols trained on them.

"Your claim? This is our camp. You are the intruders here."

"I have a legal paper from Santa Fe that says different, sonny."

"We care nothing for your paper," the guard sneered. "It is nothing if you are dead." He cocked his pistol.

"One moment," one of the others said. "They may have information from Santa Fe that Ramirez could use. Take them to camp."

"Ramirez?" Biff said, stepping a pace backward. "We don't have no quarrel with Ramirez. We'll go. You can have the claim, ain't that right, Pard?"

"Yeah, sure. We'll just be on our way."

"You will come with me," the guard said, "to see Ramirez."

"Hey, pal, we don't want no trouble. We said—"

337

"Move!"

Shuffling at an arthritic pace, the two Texans preceded their captor into camp.

"Search them and their packs," Ramirez ordered when the old men had been presented to him. He took the affidavit of claim and examined it. "I do not read your language," he said and tossed the paper into the fire.

"Now, wait just a dad-burned minute," Biff protested.

"Sit down," Ramirez said smoothly. "We must talk."

"Talk? You just burned the proof to our claim here."

"Your claim is not important since this place belongs to me. You spoke of being in Santa Fe. When was this?"

"Why—ah—three, four days back," Biff answered, disgruntled.

"You were there when they hanged my man?"

"Don't know of no hangin'. We heard tell your man broke out of jail. The sheriff had a big posse and some high-powered marshal out after him."

"This marshal, it was McKaid, no?"

Biff and Tex looked at each other. "Yeah," Tex answered. "That was him. Heard he was a Texas Ranger or some such thing. We didn't hang around to find out."

"You run from the law?" Ramirez asked.

"We ain't runnin', we just ain't nosey," Tex answered.

"Did this Ranger have a woman with him in Santa Fe?"

"I didn't see no woman, but talk has it he's marryin' up with some rancher's daughter."

"Yeah. Widow Beaumont," Biff confirmed, nodding his grizzled head. "I 'member that, now you mention it. Weren't there talk he was sendin' her back East for fancy clothes?"

"You gettin' loco in your old age? That weren't his sweetheart, it was that other'n. The teacher. She got a touch of the green-eyed monster 'cause of the weddin', so he sent her packin'. Leastwise, that's the gossip we heard in the Cantina," he said to Ramirez.

Ramirez scratched his head, thoroughly perplexed. "You say it is the Beaumont woman he is marrying? Not the teacher?"

"Hey, we ain't been invited to no wedding? You asked what we heard. That's it."

"Did you see him put this teacher on the stage?"

"Nah, but Bert and Amos said the Ranger paid her fare and

338

paid them to put her on the train in Abilene."

"Bert? Amos?" Ramirez asked, becoming more and more confused.

"The stage drivers."

"Get Corbett," Ramirez said to his men.

With avid interest, Carmen inched closer to Ramirez and the miners. She'd heard what they said, and she was interested to see Corbett's reaction to it. Maybe this was her chance to discredit Corbett. Maybe the miners would do it for her.

Corbett sauntered over importantly. He stood, legs spread, defiant against the men sent to bring him to Ramirez. "You wanted to see me?" he asked.

"These men say McKaid was to wed the Beaumont woman. They also said the other woman, the teacher, was on that stage. I want an explanation."

The blood drained from Corbett's face. "What is to explain? You asked for the Beaumont woman, I brought her to you. I did as you asked. If you've lost her since then, that's not my fault."

"You swore to me that she was not McKaid's woman."

"Well, that witch claimed that *she* was McKaid's woman. Why shouldn't I believe her?"

"We would have McKaid by now if we had not listened to him," Carmen spoke up. "He has meant nothing to us but trouble since he came here and held a gun to your head. You should have shot him then. If he were not such a weak fool as to believe the rantings of a jealous woman, you would have your revenge on McKaid by now, and we would be gone from here. He brought the Apache squaw, and now a witch here," she spat, pointing a finger of accusation at Corbett. "We will suffer for all of that. Now when McKaid comes for his woman, we won't have her, and when the Apache come for the squaw, we won't have her either. Because he brought the witch. I would begin to think that *he* was sent to destroy us. Maybe he works for McKaid."

Corbett spun around and slapped her hard. "You lying whore." He turned to Ramirez. "She's been looking for ways to even the score with me ever since you threw her out of your hut," he said. "She blames me that you did that. She tries to make a fool of me. Can't you see that?"

"I don't have to make you look stupid. You do that for yourself," Carmen refuted from the ground where she'd fallen.

"What she says, it makes me think," Ramirez said. "Witches' curses, people disappearing." He shrugged eloquently.

"You'd listen to her over me?"

"Before you came, we had no problems like you bring with you."

"It's because of you that that witch came here, not me. You sent me to the ranch," Corbett defended angrily.

"We'll just be gittin'," Tex said, standing and stuffing his belongings back into his pack.

"I regret it, but I must insist you stay," Ramirez replied and signaled his guards, who drew their weapons.

"Okay, pal, don't get jumpy," Tex said. "We just don't like what we're hearing. We had one run-in with a witch. Once in a lifetime's enough."

"That's right," Biff agreed. "Witches ain't nothin' to mess with. No-siree."

"A friend of ours hired a gypsy witch once to get his wife back from the man she run off with. She came back, sure enough, when her lover died of a mysterious ailment, but she gave her husband such a beating when she learnt what he done that he decided he didn't want her no more. He refused to pay the witch, and the next morning he was found shot in the head with his own gun. His wife said he went crazy, locked hisself in the bedroom and pulled the trigger." Tex didn't mention that the wife had later been found guilty of murder, or that the gypsy had been a fraud, or that the mysterious ailment that had killed the lover had been a stroke.

"If you've a witch hauntin' you, you'd best do as she says," Biff added.

"You can't really believe that nonsense," Corbett chided.

"Are you not the man who begged us to believe you? Are you not the one who was castrated by a witch's curse?" Carmen asked. Corbett, flushed red with embarrassment and rage, turned murderous eyes to Carmen. "It is so," she continued, glaring back defiantly. "He is worthless as a man. The witch wants him, Ramirez, and she won't leave us in peace until she has him. Why take the chance? I know you have a fondness for the boy, but will you risk everything for him? I say we give him to her and be done with both of them."

"You'd like that, wouldn't you?" Corbett spat viciously. "You think with me gone he'll take you back again, after everyone else here has had you?"

"You haven't had me," she shot back. "Eunuch!"

"Pardon me," Biff drawled, "but do we have to listen to this? If you're hell-bent on keeping us here, at least put us somewheres away from these two. We'd be beholdin' if we could rest a spell in peace. We been walkin' since daybreak."

"Take them away. Lock them up with the priest and the witch."

"Hey, pal, we ain't goin' where there's a witch. You can shoot us right here. At least we won't burn in hell."

"Take them," Ramirez exploded, at his emotional end. "All of you, get about your business. Leave me."

"Ramirez . . ." Corbett pleaded.

"I go. I have heard enough. First I have the wrong woman, then I have the right woman, then I have no woman; first you claim she's a witch, then she isn't; she was on the stage, but she's here. Carmen is right. You are a fool, and I am a bigger fool for trusting in you. I will think on what I have been told."

"Surely, you can't believe—"

"Silence, I say. Your whining tires me."

"Don't cross me, Ramirez. I spared your life once. You owe me."

"You talk of sparing *my* life! Time after time I spare yours. One mistake after another you make. I would have killed another man for any one of them. But you, I spare. Why? So you can make more mistakes? It is time I stop being a fool. It is time I do what I know I must. Not you, not the Apache, and not some witch will stop me from getting McKaid."

"And how will you do that without his woman?" Corbett challenged to cover his own nervousness.

"I'll get his children. I'll get his housekeeper. I'll get everyone on that ranch if necessary. I will bring McKaid to his knees on my own."

Chapter Twenty-One

"Where is he going to wreak his havoc this time?" Father Francis asked, when late that afternoon they watched and listened as Ramirez organized his raiding party.

"Can't rightly say," Tex answered, "but at a guess, I'd say he's going for another of McKaid's people. We've took everyone from him so far."

"Miss Elizabeth is still here," the priest reasoned.

"He's convinced she ain't the right woman. 'Sides he's afraid to tangle with her. He'll go for them kids."

"Children? We can't permit that. It's intolerable," Father Francis said. "Can't you stop him, get word to McKaid, do something? You're Rangers, aren't you?"

"No need," Biff answered. "Miss Elizabeth guessed he might try that. Them kids is well and truly hid by now. There ain't nobody at the ranch. Shee-shucks, if we'd a had her on our side, we'd a won the war."

"We did win the war," Tex said.

"You call settling for statehood winning the war?"

"Oh, that war?"

"I was lookin' forward to bein' king."

"I would'a been the king," Tex declared. "You ain't even Texas born. But you could'a been my general."

"General what? General flapdoodler for you, you old fool."

"They go," the priest said.

"They're not taking Corbett. Carmen must have done her part well," Elizabeth observed. "Do we now have a divided camp?"

"Looks that way. Corbett is fit to kill."

"How many men remain here?" the priest asked, craning his

343

neck to see over the other three heads.

"Looks like only five plus the women."

"One of the women is comin' now."

A moment later Carmen let herself in the door. She turned to Elizabeth's side of the hut and lifted her face. Her eye was swollen nearly shut, her lip cut and bruised.

"I have done your bidding," she said.

"Corbett did not like what you had to say?"

"As you can see. Do you have the potion?"

"Yes. I have it, but why do you need it when the men leave?"

"Because Corbett stays here. He will rape me this night, if he can, because I mocked him openly. If he can't, he'll kill me. The other men will be too drunk to stop him, if they cared." She snorted disgustedly. "When Ramirez leaves, they turn to animals. The women suffer . . ."

"I'll get your potion. Put it in their coffee or their drink. Do not take it yourself. About the other women I care not. Do as you wish."

She twisted the folds of her bright skirt around her fingers. "Are we . . . do I owe you anything else?"

"We made a bargain. You fulfilled your part." She handed Carmen a cup of liquid.

"Except for bringing Corbett to you."

"I will take Corbett myself. You owe me nothing more."

The escape that night was less of an ordeal than anyone expected. Carmen drugged the coffee and saw that all the men drank a good measure of it. The sky was just beginning to turn a pale shade of purple when the two Rangers, armed and ready for a fight, managed to get the door open and to overpower the guard. The camp looked as if it had been hit by a plague. Bodies were lying about, some with plates of food in their laps, some with women in their arms. One fell dangerously close to the edge of the fire. Biff pulled him away and proceeded to tie his hands and feet as Tex did with the others. Those not overcome by the drug gave up without a struggle to the Texas Rangers. Only Carmen remained unaffected by the drug. She sat in stony silence as the four captives became her captors. Tex signaled McKaid, and within the hour the gorge was emptied of all traces of man's presence.

"This was all a trick, wasn't it?" Carmen asked, having lost her fear of Elizabeth.

344

"An elaborate hoax, yes," Elizabeth answered, helping the bound woman onto one of the horses. "Ramirez must be stopped. Surely you can see that."

"He will be furious when he returns. I wish I could see his face."

"I'm sure it will be a formidable sight. If he returns."

"The potion, what was it?"

"A drug."

"And the curse?"

"His conscience."

"Ramirez, he goes for McKaid's children. If he has them when he returns, he will kill them."

"He won't have them."

"You've thought of that, too. You are very devious, or you *are* a witch." Her lips curved admiringly.

"How did you get involved with Ramirez?"

"He saw me, he took me," she said with a shrug. "A girl learns to make the best of what she cannot change. What will your lawmen do with us?"

McKaid rode over just then. "They won't abuse you," he said. "But as to what happens to you, it depends on how much trouble you and the others are to us."

"We won't be any trouble. They," she nodded to the other women, "want out as much as I do. They will cooperate."

"Can we depend on you to see to that when the drug wears off?"

"*Sí.* I will scratch their eyes out if they do not do as they are told."

Biff came over and led her horse to the long line of other prisoners. He and the priest and three of the deputies led the drunk, groggy, hallucinating group, all tied to their horses, out of the canyon and toward Santa Fe where they would be incarcerated until their trials. Tex and the other lawmen rode back to camp. Corbett, as promised, was turned over to Straight Arrow. It was a bargain made, a bargain kept in the interest of justice and peace.

McKaid scouted the deserted compound one last time before he returned to where Elizabeth waited. He dismounted and drank in the sight of her. Gone were the black cape and dress, gone the wild mane of hair. Her face was scrubbed clean and her hair braided in one long plait that hung down her back. She was Elizabeth, his strong, brave Elizabeth. Unable to wait a moment longer, he pulled her into his embrace and buried his face in the crook of her neck.

His arms closed around her in a grip so fierce she thought her ribs would crack. She smiled at the evening sky. It felt good to be in his arms again. For half an hour she'd watched as he issued directions to the deputies, and oversaw the exodus from the hideout. She thought he'd never be finished with his duties.

"I was so worried about you," he murmured. "Russ'll probably tell you how many times I started down here to get you." He lifted his head and claimed her lips in a long and thorough kiss.

"Don't ever put me through that again," he said against her mouth, tracing her full lower lip with his tongue before kissing her again and again.

"McKaid," she said, pushing against his chest. "McKaid, we can't stay here." In another minute they would be unable to stop at a kiss.

He looked into her eyes, his own dark with passion. "They didn't hurt you?" he asked. His voice shook and his fingers tightened on her upper arms. She could see how he had worried.

She shook her head. "No. Nor Lenore. But poor Mary Runningwater . . ."

"I know. Straight Arrow will deal with Corbett for what he has done to Mary."

"What will he do?"

McKaid draped an arm around Elizabeth's shoulders and walked her to Lucky Lady. "Don't think about it. You don't really want to know."

"Aren't you supposed to take him in? Doesn't the law say that white men—"

"If the Apache ever captured a man who had raped you, I would want them to bend their laws in my favor, and I would show no mercy to the bastard. I promised Straight Arrow he could have Corbett. He has him. I don't intend to cause a war over the likes of Corbett."

He lifted Elizabeth into the saddle and mounted behind her, nudging the horse into motion. "You don't feel pity for Corbett, do you?"

"Not really, except that he's so young."

"He's not like any of those young men who died in the war,

Lizzie. He's been taught since boyhood to kill. He won't change. If he's turned loose, he'll go on killing. If he's taken to Santa Fe, he'll hang. It's unfortunate, I know, but it's frequently the way it is out here. I've had to shoot two men no older than Corbett because they thought they could outdraw Ranger McKaid. I was forced to kill them or die by their guns. It's lamentable, I agree, but the very young and impetuous of the gunslingers have no concept of their own mortality. They see only triumph, glory, and invincibility. The older ones, the men who have learned that they can be killed, are the dangerous ones."

"Men like Ramirez," she said. "Men who let others do their fighting and dying. What will happen to you if you let the Apache have Corbett?"

"It doesn't matter. I'm resigning from the Rangers. Besides, who will know but us?"

"That's not ethical, McKaid."

"Ethical? As in rape and murder?" He grinned. "As in curses and witchcraft?"

"Hmmph! Are you really resigning?"

"Yes. It's time I got on with my life, and let the younger men take over."

"Like Tex and Biff?"

He laughed. "Exactly."

"Why did you send them into camp? That wasn't part of the plan."

"Neither was your staying down there with the priest. So, I added a little insurance of my own. If I couldn't get you out, I wanted Ramirez out. And the Rangers in. I was worried that he'd get wise before you could be rescued."

"I was worried about that, as well, especially when Father Francis reminded me that people used to burn witches at the stake. How is Lenore?"

"She's fine. Russ stayed with her. He's not about to leave her side now. Not that I blame him. I'm of the same mind."

"What about Ramirez? Aren't you going after him?"

"There's no need. All his stolen loot is here. He'll come back here, and we'll be waiting."

"More changes? I thought we agreed you'd take him at the ranch. What makes you think he'll come back after he sees what's waiting for him at the Circle K?"

"You."

"Me?"

"When he starts thinking about all this, he'll realize he's riding into a trap. I don't want to do anything he expects. I've done too much of that already. So the ranch, if he does continue on to there, will be just another surprise that will leave him more confounded. But if he does go to the ranch, he will know I'm involved, and he'll be livid. He'll come back here for you, to kill you, because you'll be all he can reach that belongs to me. And because you made a fool of him."

"And when he comes back?"

"Then it will be over."

So sure of himself was he that Ramirez never questioned his own interpretation of the past events. All the way to the ranch his mind went over and over what he'd do to McKaid's people, and how he'd laugh at McKaid's pain. Wild, vindictive excitement surged through him, having the same effect as a beautiful woman in his bed.

McKaid wouldn't be there. He was hunting for the man who escaped from jail. Or was he? Not until the ranch came into view did he begin to ask himself those questions. What if McKaid was waiting at the ranch for him? He could be, but more likely he was looking for the Beaumont woman. What if a posse awaited him? McKaid didn't work with a posse anymore. He was a loner.

The scenes played over and over in his mind. With McKaid gone, the victory would be easy. Even if McKaid was there, he could send in his men to distract him, and he could go for the children and the woman. Ramirez was not stupid. He knew he couldn't take McKaid if McKaid was expecting him, but he could wait. The time had come to make McKaid pay again. Ramirez didn't plan to kidnap anyone this time. He intended to kill the woman and the two children McKaid had taken in, and he would kill as many of the vaqueros as he could in the process. If he could kill those children, he preferred to wait to kill McKaid. He preferred to let McKaid suffer. There would be another time for McKaid, when the witch and Corbett were gone, and when he'd recruited more men to strengthen his army, when he wasn't so distracted and confused. He would do as always and return to Mexico. But he would never forget. And neither would McKaid.

348

When he, Ramirez, was finished with this night's work, McKaid would know the bitter taste of utter defeat. And when McKaid returned home, when he learned of the death of his family, he would know that the battle was not over. He would know his life was to be spent alone with his guilt and remorse, always watching his back, always waiting for the next blow, never free.

The ranch was lit, but quiet when they approached it. At Ramirez's signal they rode at full speed down the hill behind the ranch and surrounded the house. Ramirez stormed the back door, kicking it open and shooting as he entered. Two others followed, both advancing in like fashion into the other rooms of the house.

"The house is empty," one shouted. "They are gone."

"No!" Ramirez growled, unwilling to see his dream crumble. He, too, raced from empty room to empty room. "Search the ranch. Kill anything that moves," he said, slamming out of the front door. He was the first to shoot as he walked into the dangling legs of two men hanging from the porch rafters.

"*Dios*," the man behind him swore. "That is young Dawson. And Rico."

"Turned to stone, were they?" Ramirez sneered, his lips twisting and his eyes burning with unholy rage.

"This is Apache arrow," one of the men said, removing the projectile from the dead man's neck. "You think Apache do this because Corbett does not return their squaw?"

The Apache. In all his plans, he hadn't considered the Apache. "I do not know," Ramirez bit out. He spun away and leaped down the stairs, away from the stench of death.

"Louis, take three men and search the barn and stables. The rest of you men come with me to the bunkhouse. We search the whole ranch."

"Ramirez, it is not safe here. We should go. If the Apaches . . ."

"You question my orders?" Ramirez demanded.

"No, señor," the man demurred, looking fearfully at his two dead friends. "We obey."

The bunkhouse was locked, but a light burned inside. Ramirez signaled two men to check around back. Both returned shaking their heads.

"I cannot see anyone, but I can hear a noise, someone moving around inside," one of them reported.

"Kick the door in," Ramirez ordered, standing to the side.

The door gave way with one kick. A thundering blast followed that sent the man at the door flying backwards, his shirt stained crimson around the gaping hole in his chest.

Without thought the other three opened fire on the two occupants of the ranch.

Only when the men were dead did Ramirez realize that they were tied to the bunks and that the gun that fired at the newcomers had been rigged to go off when the door was opened. One by one he lifted the heads of the dead men.

"Juan and Santiago," the man at his side said.

Ramirez cursed profanely. "It is McKaid. He makes me shoot my own men. He is behind all of this. That woman, she makes a fool of me. They will all die. The padre will wish he had not betrayed Ramirez with his lies. I will kill them all."

The other men came running at the gunfire. All stood stunned at yet another twist of fate. "We are cursed," one complained. Another added, "We go back to camp now? We let the witch have Corbett?"

"We go back," Ramirez stated, "to kill the priest and the woman. She is no witch."

Some of the men didn't agree with that plan. "If this is McKaid's work, how can we know he won't be waiting to ambush us? How do we know our camp is safe?"

"Corbett is there. He will protect what is mine." Ramirez strode toward his horse.

The men looked at each other, none of them confident in Corbett's ability to do anything right. Corbett was a child with a head full of nothing.

"Ramirez," one of them said, "if the miners spoke the truth, the woman who is to marry McKaid is only a few miles from here. McKaid's people might be at her ranch."

"And we could take a different trail to our camp from there and avoid an ambush."

Ramirez stopped and looked at his cohorts. "Beaumont's ranch? *Sí. Sí.* We go there. Lopez, cut those men down from the front of the house. Put them with the others in the bunkhouse and burn the place down. Burn the whole ranch to the ground."

The bunkhouse went up in swift towering flames. The men were moving toward the barn and stables when the first howl of a coyote met their ears. Another echoes. Several more followed.

"Apache. They watch from the hills. This is the work of those savages. Forget the rest, we go," Ramirez ordered. "Corbett must have succeeded in setting the Apache against McKaid. If the Apache want McKaid, they want us more."

They left the Circle K with haste and rode toward the Beaumont ranch. The call of the coyote followed them, tracking their progress, stalking them. The haunting howl raised the hairs on the back of Ramirez's neck, but he wanted those kids. And he wanted that woman. He wanted McKaid to suffer and to lie awake nights remembering his long-time enemy. So he rode on. He rode through the juniper and piñon, through rock-strewn arroyas, he forded the Rio Grande, and crested the hill behind the Beaumont Ranch. They pulled their reins back sharply when they saw what lay before them.

Three campfires burned in the front of the hacienda, all surrounded by towering lodges. Indian women tended to the evening meal. Children played at their mothers' sides. The Apache had taken possession of the ranch.

"*Madre de Dios!*" Ramirez exclaimed. "Let us go. Hurry!"

They swung their horses around. Behind them, astride their mounts, were ten braves, armed with long rifles. Straight Arrow rode forward as the Indians surrounded the Mexicans. Mary Runningwater sat behind her husband.

Ramirez glared at her. "So you escaped my camp," he said, seemingly unafraid. "That leads me to believe the Beaumont woman escaped with you, no? And is she also here with your people?"

Mary Runningwater did not respond. Her face was as empty of expression as that of her husband.

"You must believe I had no part in the raid on your settlement. I knew nothing of it until that fool Corbett brought your woman to my camp. I never touched her, I swear to you."

Straight Arrow said nothing, but led his horse past the row of Mexicans.

"This one," Mary said, pointing to one of the men. "And this one."

"Take them," Straight Arrow said quietly, just loudly enough for four of his men to hear and move at his command. "It would be foolish to interfere," he warned Ramirez.

351

The two Mexicans, easily disarmed, panicked, knowing exactly why the squaw had singled them out. They struggled and pleaded for Ramirez to save them, finally throwing curses at him as Ramirez sat without moving a muscle while they were dragged from their horses and led to sure and painful deaths.

"Be warned, Mexican. The Apache would see you dead. If you are a wise man, you will throw the guns down and wait silently here for McKaid to come for you. White man's law is more merciful than Apache law."

Sweat beaded on Ramirez's forehead. To die at the hands of the Apache was a terrifying thought. But to see McKaid win was worse.

He searched the blank eyes of the Apache chief. They had the men they wanted. Would they risk coming after him in the black of night? He didn't think so.

With a loud shout he kicked his horse and rode into the remaining Apaches. Bullets flew in both directions. One of his men screamed. Ramirez did not look back. Pressing himself to the back of the horse, he raced toward the river.

Ramirez was furious at being thwarted. His insides twisted and burned with rage that McKaid had evaded him yet again, and in doing so had left him with an Apache threat hanging over his head. Nothing was going right. Ever since Corbett, ever since that witch . . .

Gradually, as the miles lengthened between the five who escaped and the Apache, his head began to clear. He began to think more reasonably. Maybe McKaid wasn't involved. There had been no sign of McKaid. Maybe this was all Corbett's fault. In his youthful ignorance and eagerness, he'd brought the Apache into the fight. No one could fight the Apache. The Apache were ruthless and would do anything to avenge a wrong, as they apparently had. They'd taken both the Circle K and the Beaumont Ranch, probably because McKaid had resisted Corbett's ransom plan. And no one but the Apache could possibly sneak into *his* camp and kill *his* guards and take *his* prisoners. The Beaumont woman had probably been taken as a slave. The lame priest would be no good to them, so he'd been left behind.

But what of the other woman? Why had she come? Why wasn't she taken? Was she what she claimed? Was she a witch? Had she been conjured up by the Apache shaman? Maybe she was the witch doctor, a spirit, a spectre. She had permitted no one to touch her, and those who had had been afflicted. Hadn't the priest said that evil could take the form of beauty? He had Corbett to thank for that, too. None of this was his own fault, Ramirez thought. He was still Ramirez. And once he returned to camp and gave Corbett to the witch, his troubles would disappear. Everything would return to normal again.

They rode throughout the night, and it wasn't until nearly daybreak that Ramirez's thoughts began to shift and to wander in yet another direction. It was then that he knew. It was then that the last few days began to make sense to him. He pulled his horse to a stop and threw his head back and laughed, a great surge of admiration, albeit reluctant, growing for his new adversary. His laughter turned to an evil chuckle. His men stopped, too, and looked at him curiously.

Ramirez's eyes narrowed as he looked at his men, weak men, and his grin disappeared. For a long moment he stared at them, as his thoughts raced from one possibility to the next.

"I think, *amigos*, that you must go on to camp without me."

"Without you?"

"I will follow in a short time. Instruct everyone to prepare to return to Mexico."

"You have given up on McKaid?"

"For now," he lied. "Only for now."

"*Sí,*" one of the men said, nodding. "I can say this pleases me. Much has happened to make the men wary. They are loyal to you, but they want no more of this."

"Go, then, and prepare."

"You will return?"

"I will be there." But he knew he wouldn't. The camp, his people, were already gone.

Elizabeth turned in McKaid's arms and pressed her body into the curve of his, resting her cheek on the rise of his muscled shoulder. She inhaled the warm scent that was his alone and snuggled closer. A gentle smile formed on her lips, and she drifted again into a peaceful and secure sleep.

McKaid's lashes fluttered. He turned his head toward hers and peeked through his lashes. The sky was just beginning to brighten. The clouds had changed from moon-dusted iridescent forms in the indigo sky to dark shadows against the mauve sky. Another hour and everyone would be stirring.

He looked down at Elizabeth. Her face was relaxed, peaceful in sleep, and on her lips was a tiny grin. What was she dreaming about to put such a beautiful smile on her face?

His skin prickled when he recalled all that had happened in the last days with Lizzie right in the middle of it, and he had to forcefully restrain himself from tightening his arms around her lest he waken her. There had been times when he'd wondered if he'd ever hold her against him again.

He was relieved and very thankful that it was over, at least as far as she was concerned, and that she was safe. Only one more day and it would be over for good, and Ramirez would be dead. Then he could begin to think about the future. Their future. It didn't even matter to him that Ramirez had probably burned the ranch to the ground. He could start again. He could do anything now that he had Lizzie at his side.

She stirred, and without thinking he pulled her tighter into the warm strength of his body. Her hands slid around his chest, and a soft purring sound came from her throat.

"Are you awake?" he asked softly.

"Umm," she responded, pressing her lips against the bare flesh of his chest where his shirt had fallen open. Her tongue darted out and traced lazy patterns against his skin.

"What are you doing?" His voice was quiet, but still rumbled deep in his chest, vibrating against her lips.

"Tasting you."

"It's a dangerous pastime, young lady."

"Are you waking up now?" she asked seductively, sliding her hand down his chest and under the unfastened top of his trousers.

"Lizzie," he warned.

"I dreamed of you all night, McKaid, and I woke up wanting you again."

He could believe her. He'd wakened twice during the night in the same condition. It would have been funny if it weren't so dismayingly beyond his control. He had gone months on end in the past without giving women a thought. He'd never been plagued by physical needs other than hunger, thirst, and the need for rest. But since meeting Lizzie his body had been in a perpetual state of arousal. There had been times when he thought he'd go crazy if he didn't soon have her, and once he'd made love to her, his body had demanded more and more. She'd become a raging fever in his blood that couldn't be assuaged. And he couldn't help himself.

But he must control himself for Lizzie's sake. He didn't want to frighten her or disgust her with his greedy randiness. What would she think of him? He didn't even know what to make of it himself.

"We made love twice last night," he said reasonably.

"Is there a limit?" she asked, sliding her fingers lower, finding and grinning at the answer she sought.

"God, no," he groaned. "But, Lizzie . . ."

"Suit yourself, then," she said airily. "But don't blame me when I get cranky and irritable. For weeks after we met, I wanted to yell at you, or hit you, or pull your hair out, but we both know that wasn't really what I wanted. You showed me what I wanted. I needed you because I loved you. So if you want to risk my foul temper again . . ."

"I'm not hesitating for my sake, woman," he growled, turning her face so he could read her eyes.

"Oh? You think you're doing me a kindness? When all I want at this moment is to feel you inside me again? I need you there. Are you going to deny me?"

"Hell, no," he muttered, claiming her lips, pressing her into the hard earth with the weight of his body.

"Hurry, McKaid. I want you now," she said, tearing her lips from his, fumbling with fasteners on his clothes and hers.

Under the cover of the blankets they kicked their clothing aside, save for the shirts protecting their exposed arms and shoulders. Impatient, she wrapped her slender legs around his and drew him to her. With a low chuckle of delighted amusement he thrust the full length of himself into her.

"Ah, yes," she murmured, closing her eyes in ecstasy, tightening her legs to keep him imprisoned within her hungry body.

"What insatiable wanton have I turned loose on the world?" he teased.

Her lashes lifted, and she gave him a narrow reproving glare. "Not the world, McKaid. Just you. You've only yourself to blame. And I shall expect you to do right by all this delicious wantonness you've spawned in me."

"What if, in my aged condition, I can't keep up with your youthful appetite?"

"Are you suggesting I find a younger lover?"

"I'd kill anyone who touched you," he replied, and she

could see by the sudden savage darkening of his eyes that down deep he meant that.

"So possessive," she bantered, moving her body teasingly around his. His arms tensed beneath her shoulders and hips, and he pulled her hard into the powerful length of his body.

"Haven't you learned yet, my sweet seductress, that we humans, for all our pretense of civilization, are only a breath away from the savage beast. Right now I wouldn't bat an eye at tearing the throat out of anyone who tried to take you away from me."

"That sounds very dangerous. Can you be domesticated with time?" she asked, feeling her breasts swell and tingle, feeling her lower body begin to respond, knowing she'd never want him to change in any way. This untamed, unreasonable, unpredictable man suited her undeniably.

"You wouldn't like domesticated," he growled, moving within the hot recesses of her femininity. "We're two of a kind, Lizzie. We're two parts of one whole. What you need, I'll need, and my desires will give life to yours. That's how it will always be between us."

Two parts of one whole. His deep words penetrated to her very soul and wrapped her in a world of love and security, and an overwhelming passion for her mate. She couldn't answer, her body was taking control from her mind, demanding to show her love, to take the fulfillment it needed. She clutched at him, arching her body to be even closer, to take him more fully into her with each successive velvet stroke.

His deep melodious words of love were interspersed with kisses along her neck, across her jaw, on her open mouth. He nipped the sensitive skin of her lips, then soothed them with gentle strokes of his tongue.

"I am obsessed with holding your body in my arms, kissing you, possessing you completely. Knowing that you feel it, too, keeps me sane. You do feel it, don't you? I can see it in your eyes when we're near each other, in the way your breasts swell beneath your clothes, the way your breathing changes. And I can feel it in the air between us."

"McKaid," she cried desperately.

"You belong to me, Lizzie, I belong to you. Without you I'm incomplete, I'm nothing. I love you more than life."

Her body suffused with a radiant warmth and burst forth in a splendor of pulsing delight that tore a groan from McKaid as he joined her in climactic bliss.

"Oh, McKaid," she said in a rough whisper between gasps of breath, "I love you, too. So very much."

"One more day, just this one day," he said, rolling to her side and holding her close to his wildly beating heart, "and then we'll have a lifetime to love like this. We'll build a new ranch, we'll build a home with a dozen bedrooms, and we'll build a family to fill them. Would you like that, Lizzie love?"

"More than anything in the world, McKaid. I only wish Uncle Clint had lived. He would be so happy for us. He wanted this, you know?"

"Yes, he dropped enough hints. You're not doing this just to please him, are you?" he asked, rising up to challenge her with his piercing blue eyes.

She chuckled. "Doing what? Loving you? You can't will love to happen any more than you can stop it. Love just . . . is, that's all. I know I fell in love before we got to the Circle K, before Clint even had the chance to start getting ideas. He only prodded us in the direction we were already going, just to get some peace and quiet in the house again."

"I surely do miss him, Lizzie."

"I know." She ran her finger across his brow, brushing aside the dark lock that always seemed to prefer to curl in the opposite direction from the rest of his hair. She moved her finger away, and very stubbornly it fell back across his broad forehead. She smiled fondly and ran her finger over the downward slant of one dark brow to the bold line of his square jaw.

"You are perfect," she said softly. "I could look at you all day."

"I need a shave."

She scraped a fingernail along his rough cheek. "It's very appealing. Everything about you is so male and attractive to me."

He touched her own soft cheek. "It doesn't do you any good. Your face is rubbed red. But I know what you mean, it's the same with me." He grinned devilishly. "Our opposites fit together very nicely."

She thumped his shoulder, grinning with him though she felt her cheeks grow warm. "I didn't mean . . ."

He laughed. "We'd better get dressed then, or I'll show you that I did meant just that."

She gave a soft sign of resignation. "I suppose the others will be up soon. I wish we had more time together. When we get home, can we go back to your secret camp?"

"I'd like that." He pulled his pants on, throwing her a wink.

She grabbed her own clothes and began to dress. "And no one will know where we are. We'll have a long weekend together with no interruptions, nobody needing something, demanding our time, tearing us apart."

"You sound as if you've missed me."

"I did miss you, but I felt you with me, watching over me. I couldn't have done it, if I hadn't known you were there."

He pulled his boots on, then stood in front of her, buttoning the last of the buttons on her blouse. "I want you to stay here today while we go down after Ramirez. So far we've avoided any gunplay, just as you anticipated, but this will be different. Ramirez will fight to the death. And he'll take whoever he can with him. I want you out of the way where I don't have to worry about you."

"Yes, McKaid."

"I'm going to go one step further and make it an order. I can't function at my best if I have to consider where you are and if you're out of the line of fire."

"Yes, McKaid."

"Ramirez will know right away that I'm here, and if he gets even a glimpse of you, he'll go mad with fury. He won't stop until he makes every effort to kill us. So, you have to see . . . Did you just agree with me?"

"Yes, McKaid."

His eyes narrowed suspiciously. His chin went up, and he worried the inside of his cheek thoughtfully. "You're planning something, Elizabeth Hepplewhite, and I won't have it." She turned away to hide her grin, but he grabbed her and swung her back around to face him. "I'm serious, Lizzie. Never more so. You are not to leave this camp. And I don't see what's so funny."

"Oh, stop looking down your nose at me. I said I'd stay."

"But I want you to stay. You *never* do what I want you to do. What are you up to?"

"If I don't agree with you, I tell you about it. I don't lie. Have I ever said I'd do something and then not done it?" She threw up her hands. "You take umbrage when I disagree, and pick a fight when I agree. For the last time, I'm staying here.

358

I'm going to use the last of the water to wash my hair, and then I'll pack everything up so we'll be ready to go when you've finished your business. I may even take a nap. And if you suggest again that I'm plotting some devious action, then I'll do just that."

"Okay, okay. I'm sorry. But you have to admit you have given me cause to suspect."

"Oh, really? When?" she demanded. "Tell me when."

"Well there was that business with Russ, for one thing."

"What business?"

"Trying to make me jealous."

"Oh, for pity's sake. And what about you and Lenore?"

"And I come home to find the place swarming with Apaches, then I come back a second time to find you unconscious and the town having a party on my front yard. And then this crazy scheme. You have a way of landing yourself in the middle of everything. For once, just once, I want you to stay out of it."

"May I remind you, sir, that—"

"All right," he cut off her tirade. "It may not have been your intent to become involved, but . . . somehow . . . you . . . get there."

"That's very unfair, McKaid. This crazy scheme is the first thing that's gone *right*. But rest your mind. You're on your own this time. Consider me out, as of now." She grabbed up her belongings and her dignity, threw him a frosty smile, and strode back to the main camp to make some much needed coffee, crossing her fingers that he'd take care of Ramirez quickly before something else went wrong for the renowned Ranger Dash McKaid.

Chapter Twenty-Two

When the men had gone, Elizabeth and Lenore cleaned the cooking utensils and packed them away, save for the coffeepot.

"Will six men be able to take the whole gang?" Lenore asked.

"Only nine can be left if they all return, but I don't think they will. One was probably killed at the ranch, if Biff's plan worked, and two men with Ramirez were among those who raped Mary. Straight Arrow won't let them go unpunished. That leaves only five and Ramirez to return. The odds are even, with surprise on our side."

"I wish Russ hadn't gone. I don't like being without him after what happened. How can you bear to think about McKaid being a lawman? How can you stand watching him ride into danger time after time?"

"Right now I can do without his cocky arrogance. He had the colossal nerve to insinuate that I somehow instigated all the troubles in which we've found ourselves. Can you believe it?"

Lenore looked at her friend, snickered, then broke out in laughter. Elizabeth stood and placed indignant fists on her hips, a fierce scowl creasing her brow, turning her eyes a deep gold.

"I hope you're laughing because you agree with me."

"Actually, I can sympathize with McKaid."

"McKaid? What about me?"

"You have to admit that ever since you arrived, life has become rather unpredictable."

"Since I arrived?" Elizabeth squawked, incredulous. "I'll have you know, Miss Prim and Proper, that my life in Virginia was the next thing to a nun's life. *Nothing* ever happened to me!" Lenore sputtered with laughter again, which only added fuel to Elizabeth's pique. "The biggest excitement in my life was when I read *Pilgrim's Progress.* 'A young Woman, her name was Dull.'"

Lenore hooted. "You can't seriously expect me to believe you."

"Cross my heart. I was the most well raised and placid of young ladies."

"Placid," Lenore repeated humorously.

"Yes. The only time I ever got really angry and did something unspeakably rash was when Tyler Benson asked me to marry him because I was a suitably sensible girl, not given to frivolous adornments that would drain his bank balance, and because I was plain enough that he wouldn't have to worry about my being unfaithful."

"Good heavens. How despicable. Tell me you kicked him in the shin, the way you did to McKaid."

"That's my whole point. I would never have dreamed of doing something violent. I—ah—simply told Tyler that I'd have to check with my two secret lovers before I could accept his proposal, because I wasn't sure they'd be willing to share me with yet another man. I never saw him again. But don't you see? It was McKaid who changed all that. I came here to take care of two orphaned children. I gave up my boring life to become a boring nanny. He was the one who dove through the stage door, threw a few wild punches, some of which nearly hit me, shot a man dead, kicked him out the door, then kissed me—an absolute stranger. My life has been out of control ever since."

Lenore had dissolved into gales of laughter again, and tears of mirth were rolling down her face.

"I'm a hapless victim in all this," Elizabeth persisted, her voice rising.

Lenore held her sides and pleaded for Elizabeth to stop. "It is good to laugh again though," she admitted. "I feel better."

"Hmmph," Elizabeth grunted. "Let's get the rest of this gear packed up. I'd like to wash my hair."

By noontime the two women had completed their chores and sat on a blanket in the shade of a cluster of scrawny pines to wait for the men to return. So far they had heard no gunfire, so they could only assume Ramirez had not yet arrived, or else had surrendered peacefully, which was unlikely. Elizabeth tossed her brush onto the blanket and began to braid her damp hair.

"It's taking an awfully long time, isn't it?" Lenore asked.

"The Circle K is miles from here. Try to get some rest. We'll have a long ride when they do return."

Elizabeth was more than a little tired, herself. She tied the end of her braid with a blue ribbon to match her clean blouse and lay back on her elbows, letting her eyes scan the rugged terrain.

What she saw was a far cry from the rolling hills, neatly trimmed lawns, and delicate greens of the forests in Virginia, but the land of New Mexico that had looked stark to her at first now touched her with its raw, primitive beauty.

Maybe it was the land itself that turned its people into creatures of volatile passions, that filled them with sharp angles and edges and spiraling highs and lows. Maybe it was a permeating aura left from the mighty violence that erupted to create the peaked mountains and carve out the deep abrupt gorges. If the people were transplanted to a place like Virginia where streets were laid out to precise specifications, and lamps placed at measured intervals, where homes were built in neat rows, and the vegetation shaped and tamed for maximum effect, if they were moved to an environment where years of civilized men in all their accumulated wisdom had decided how to eat, sleep, drink, dress, talk, and think, and had laid a blanket of constraint over all people, would they be any different? She had to believe they would. That or suffocate. Or go mad from the chains of repression.

And what of herself? Could she go back now and control the temptations to lose her temper, to punch Arnold in the mouth, or dump her coffee in the lap of that insufferable bank president who'd given her position to a man. Hadn't she shed her own inhibiting bonds of propriety?

She closed her eyes and lay back, pillowing her head on her hands. She didn't want to go back. She loved this land and its people whose spirit was irresistible. And she had changed. She didn't think she'd conform to city life again. This land had drawn her in and worked its magic on her in the same way it had everyone else.

Her short stay had been a baptism of fire, to be sure, but she belonged here now. She couldn't imagine any land throwing more at her at once than this one had, but it hadn't been all bad. In fact, it had been wonderful, giving her the oppportunity to draw on her courage, intelligence, and spirit. So many emotions had been born in her, not the least of which was her love and passion for McKaid. Her sterile world of before held no appeal to her.

Every cloud has a silver lining. And all that had happened to her had a good side. Although she abhorred the circumstances that had brought her to New Mexico, she couldn't help but be grateful that she'd been given the opportunity to start a new life, to love those two children, and to share life with McKaid. If no one else benefitted from Corbett's destructive life, she had, selfish as that thought was.

Ramirez was another matter. No one benefitted where he was concerned. Pain, grief, and devastation followed in his wake. Whoever put an end to that man's reign of terror would be doing the world a great service.

Her lazy thoughts drifted to the last few days. She felt a warm sense of satisfaction that no one on the right side of the law had been hurt. Their plans had been thus far successful.

McKaid had given her credit for their strategy, but she knew it was undeserved. All she had done was suggest a reversal of roles and compare all that had happened in the past with a game of chess, analyzing each party's actions and the resulting effects. Biff and Tex were the ones who had come up with the idea of using scare tactics to throw Ramirez off the track, especially after she'd recounted what had happened when Corbett had abducted Lenore. They, knowing how fanatical Ramirez was about the Church, suggested witchcraft and came up with the idea of using dynamite, brimstone, drugs. Emma, in an outburst of temper, prompted them to turn people to stone.

"This is unforgivable," she had declared, slamming the pot onto the table. She'd been refilling the coffee cups around the table and listening to all the talk, and her restraint had snapped. "The poor lass was nearly killed today, and you're talking of sending her into a den of murderers. If I had the power, I'd turn you into stone, to match your hard hearts."

McKaid had gone gravely silent at that, then snapped his fingers and grinned. "We could do that! They wouldn't know what to make of it if they found their guards turned to stone, especially if we practically blow up the canyon before that. They'd think Elizabeth came from the deepest pits of hell, shaking the earth, causing human life to petrify at her will."

"Ramirez isn't going to be fooled by some sideshow," Emma protested.

"Don't be too sure of that," Tex had said. "Ramirez lost his whole family when he was a lad because of a *bruja's* curse. At least that's what he believes. He's so afraid that that curse has passed from his father to him that he keeps a priest at his hacienda to exorcise evil spirits. That's probably why he stole the padre from Las Vegas."

Emma was aghast. "He sounds demented."

"Oh, he is that," Biff agreed. "He's also very clever. That's what makes him so dangerous. Escaping lawmen, especially McKaid, has become a game with him, one he's got addicted to, and the worse the crime he can get away with, the better. So he turns his men loose to do any danged thing they feel like doing to their victims."

"And you're thinking of sending Elizabeth in there?"

"The problem is how to get Lenore *out*," Russ said, annoyed with everyone at the table. "Why don't we just go in there and get her?"

"I did that once, and it had disastrous results," McKaid said solemnly.

That had been the first time Elizabeth had realized to what extent McKaid blamed himself for Rosanna's death. That had also been when she had decided to go ahead with their plan. She wasn't going to let that happen to him again. It was her fault Lenore had been kidnapped, it was up to her to help get her back. After that she had been adamant about their plan, and no amount of arguing from either McKaid or Emma could dissuade her.

She had to admit, however smugly, that their strategy had paid off. Ramirez had been just as disconcerted as Tex had said he would be, he'd been all but paralyzed by his fears. It was easy to be amused now that it was over. Or almost over.

A few more hours. She closed her eyes and turned on her side, pillowing her head on one arm and blocking out the harsh light of day with the other. Very soon now her life would change in a different way. She would become Mrs. McKaid. Elizabeth McKaid. She tried the name out in her mind. No, it had to be Lizzie. Lizzie McKaid.

She wondered what her future husband was doing at that moment. She tried to picture him and the others surrounding Ramirez and his band of outlaws, taking their guns, tying their hands behind their backs to lead them to jail.

She tried very hard to picture it, but she couldn't. Ramirez's face wouldn't materialize in that scenario. And why should it, she thought, on the edge of sleep. He wasn't the type to ride into a trap. He would know by now, if he had any wits at all, that McKaid had been involved from the first.

Her stomach clenched at the thought, and she came wide-awake. Her heart leapt into her throat and she stared, wide-eyed, at her elbow propped on the gray blanket in front of her face. McKaid and the others were expecting to ambush Ramirez, but Ramirez would have guessed that by now. What would he do? Ride away? No. He'd want revenge on McKaid, he'd want it at any cost. And not only McKaid. What better way to hurt McKaid than . . .

"Lenore," she cried, and shot up. "Lenore," she called again, but already it was too late. Standing not ten feet from their blanket was Ramirez.

"Oh, my God," Lenore gasped, inching herself backwards.

Ramirez laughed malevolently. "The witch and the woman she turned to stone," he drawled. His sinister grin turned to an ugly scowl. "You have made a fool of Ramirez. You will suffer for that. Get up."

Elizabeth glanced at Lenore's ashen face, feeling all the same terror and dismay mirrored there. If she hadn't been so busy congratulating herself, she might have second-guessed him sooner. Now it was too late. Her heart cried for Russ and McKaid. And Lord, McKaid had demanded that she stay behind. He'd never recover from that. Damn Ramirez. He just never quit causing pain.

Her fear congealed in her stomach and transformed itself into a hard lump of anger. What right did he have to do this to them, or anyone? She stopped thinking of her own safety and accepted that she was going to suffer and probably die. But Lenore didn't have to lose her life, too.

"Get up!" Ramirez roared, "or I shoot you where you are."

Which told Elizabeth that he had some other idea in mind besides a quick death for them. More torment for McKaid, no doubt. She looked at Lenore, who was almost catatonic with fear.

"Come on, Lenore," she said, wrapping an arm around her friend's shoulders and helping her to her feet. With her other hand she pinched her arm hard.

The pain seemed to snap Lenore out of her panicked state, and Lenore winced and turned wide, questioning eyes to Elizabeth.

"Get yourself under control," Elizabeth said severely. "You don't want to be shot, do you? What would *Russ* do if he never saw you again? You wouldn't want that would you?" Elizabeth tried with every ounce of strength she had to project her thoughts to Lenore.

After a few seconds, Lenore's brow twitched and she nodded her head once. "I'm all right now," she answered evenly.

"Very sensible of you," Ramirez sneered. "You will come with me."

Elizabeth turned. "As you wish, señor." She took two sedate steps toward him and pretended to stumble. Her fight for balance took her headlong into Ramirez.

"Go!" she screamed to Lenore. With all her might she swung at the arm holding the deadly weapon. It went off, making her ears ring, but she felt no pain. "Run, Lenore," she screamed again to make certain her friend knew she was unhurt.

She couldn't think of Lenore's state of mind after that because all her concentration was directed at keeping Ramirez from shooting her friend in the back. Ramirez hit her, yanked at her hair, swore vilely at her, but still she clung to his gun arm, clamping it beneath her arm, wrenching in one direction then another, sinking her teeth into his wrist. At the same time she kicked at his shins with the sharp-edged heel of her boot.

"Damn you, *puta*," he growled when one particularly strong kick connected.

She jerked on his arm when he stumbled from the pain, and he lost his balance completely, taking her with him to the rocky ground. But Lenore was out of sight.

She knew she could never win in a battle of physical strength, so she didn't resist when he straddled her and pinned her arms to the ground.

"You bitch," he snarled and slapped her across the face, first with his open palm, then the back of his hand. Just like Corbett, she thought, only more vicious. Corbett hadn't been quite so brutal until he'd punched her with his fist. She

367

squeezed her eyes shut and waited for that, too, knowing Ramirez would certainly break her jaw if he hit her with his fist.

Instead, he jerked her to her feet and propelled her through the bushes, down a ravine, and through a maze of rocks to where he'd tethered his two horses.

Before he could stop her, she twisted free, loosed one of the horses and slapped it sharply on the rump, sending it racing off. He slapped her again and drew his gun, angry enough to shoot her there and then. She glared defiantly at him.

It took a good deal of control on his part, but finally he shoved her toward the remaining horse, ordered her into the saddle, and mounted behind her. She didn't know what he had in mind, but she was certain it wasn't going to be pleasant. Again she found herself in a position where she had to stall for time, so she bit back her resentment and curbed her desire to slam her elbow into his stomach. Riding double would slow them enough for McKaid to find them.

"Where are you taking me?"

"Into the mountains where not even McKaid will be able to find us."

"For what purpose?"

"A clever mind like yours can find that answer, no?"

"No doubt to cause McKaid anguish," she said airily. "He's not the same man you've known in the past. But then you've already realized that, haven't you? Doesn't that worry you? Oh, and those two old miners, they're Texas Rangers."

"You think I fear two old men?"

"How do you imagine they got to be old? They're very good. And don't forget the Apache. There's nowhere you can possibly go that they can't track. McKaid has quite a following now, whereas you have none. You're all alone this time. Eye to eye with McKaid. Are you ready for that? You might hurt me, rape me, you might even kill me. You might be able to cause McKaid further heartache, but you'll never live to see it. This was your final mistake, Ramirez. They won't let you live to hang. They'll give you to the Apache, and you can suffer with Corbett. But then you didn't know about Corbett, did you? He didn't even resist when we captured your camp. And Carmen, she was a great help to us."

Ramirez said nothing in response to her diatribe, but his body stiffened behind her. And at the mention of Carmen, his head jerked up. "You lie. Carmen would never betray me."

"Carmen is a proud woman, and a beautiful one. Did you think you could treat her as you did and keep her loyalty? You don't know women if you did. She's probably enjoying her new-found freedom in Santa Fe this very minute, and thanking us for it."

His temper seemed to snap. He whipped his horse into a gallop, nearly sending her out of the saddle. To make matters worse, he clamped his arm around her chest with one hand brazenly covering her breast to hold her against him.

McKaid knew the minute the three Mexican bandits rode through the narrow entrance to the gorge that Ramirez wasn't among them. And it was only a few seconds after the lawmen had surrounded the gang and disarmed them that the shot echoed through the mountains from somewhere frighteningly close to where the women were.

"Ramirez," he whispered. He knew then with a sickening sureness where the missing man was. Why hadn't he thought of that? Why had he insisted that the two women stay up there away from any protection? How stupid could he get?

"Russ," he yelled. "The women. Take over here, Tex."

"Sure thing. Don't go blazing your way up there and get your arse shot off. You take care."

"It's not me I'm worried about, Tex. I've got that old feeling again."

Russ and McKaid were out of the canyon and halfway up the slope of the hill when they spotted Lenore near the top. She stumbled and slid a few feet down the loose stones, then got up and started running again.

"She'll break her neck," Russ growled, chagrined yet relieved at the same time.

The men made their way up the hill to Lenore in dead silence. McKaid watched the blur of movement as Russ jumped off his horse and scooped her into his arms. But everything was a fuzzy blur to McKaid. Their voices weren't even clear. And he was going to be sick.

"McKaid," he heard Russ call as if from a long way off. "McKaid, buddy, get off that horse before you fall off."

"My God, he's as white as a ghost," Lenore said, as they got McKaid down to the ground.

369

McKaid struggled away from their hands and fell to his knees, wretching up the bitter contents of his stomach.

"Here, take a swig of this," Russ said, pressing a flask of brandy to McKaid's blanched lips.

McKaid shuddered violently. He pushed himself to his feet, fighting off their help, took a couple of blind steps, then collapsed again to his knees. He sagged back on his heels and covered his ears.

"Jesus Christ, I can't make myself ask. I don't want . . . to know."

Appalled, Lenore was propelled into action. She knelt in front of him and pulled his hands away. "McKaid, McKaid, I think she's still alive. Can you hear me? She's still alive."

He stopped breathing and stared at her. His brows were working as if he were having trouble making sense of her words. "The shot?" he asked.

"Ramirez crept up on us and took us by surprise. Elizabeth told me to go for Russ, and then she threw herself at Ramirez. I heard the shot, but she called out for me to keep going, so I did. I glanced back once before I climbed down the rocks, and she was still struggling with him. There haven't been any more shots."

"He won't kill her yet, McKaid," Russ reasoned. "He wants you. She's his bait. There's still time, man. Take another swallow of brandy and pull yourself together. She needs you."

Russ could see the life surging back into McKaid's lifeless features. His hand still trembled on the flask, but his color was returning and his mind seemed to be working again. He knew McKaid had been strung tighter than a bow string over this whole caper, but he had never realized until now just how much it was costing him.

McKaid had breezed in and out of the ranch over the last half-dozen years, always seeming bigger than life. The legendary Dash McKaid. He was tough, hard, formidable, unapproachable. It had only been during the last few months that he'd come to know him better and to see a more human side to his character. Even after Elizabeth had arrived, Russ had doubted the depths of McKaid's emotions. He had never appeared to be a man who cared for anything or anyone very deeply. He'd been worried for Elizabeth in case the heartless Ranger hurt her.

Maybe he just hadn't seen the obvious signs. A truly hard

man wouldn't have adopted two kids who were no blood relation to him. McKaid must have had some pretty deep feeling for them and their parents to do that. And what he thought was callousness when Clint was killed, now looked very different. And there was no question of how he felt about Elizabeth.

Russ wondered if he could put Lenore in danger to save Elizabeth as McKaid had done for him. Hell, he hoped he'd never be put to that test. His relief at seeing Lenore stumbling down the hill gave him grave doubts that he could. But McKaid had.

"Your hands are bleeding," McKaid said to Lenore.

"I fell. It's nothing."

"I'm coming with you," Russ stated as McKaid stood.

"No," McKaid said abruptly. "You take care of Lenore. I'm going alone."

"I can help," Russ argued. "I owe you."

"You don't owe me anything. This is all my fault. From beginning to end. Look, Russ, this is Ranger work. I can go faster on my own."

"Then at least take my rifle and the rest of my ammo. How much food do you have left? You don't even have a bedroll. Take mine."

Russ transferred most of his supplies to McKaid's saddlebags, adding the flask of brandy before buckling the flaps down. McKaid finished securing the bedroll, wrapped snugly around the extra rifle, to the back of the saddle, then mounted up.

"If you're not back by tomorrow, I'm sending Biff and Tex after you."

Ramirez drove the horse at a grueling pace for hours. Elizabeth thought that any moment now her spine would crumble and her body would simply give out on her. The horse was in no better shape. He was covered in a frothy lather.

"You're killing this animal," she yelled back to him, angry and exhausted.

For spite he urged the horse faster, but after a few minutes, he, too, could see he was jeopardizing their only means of transportation. When they stopped, it was Elizabeth who dragged the saddle to the ground and rubbed the horse

371

down with a shirt she'd found in the saddlebag.

"What are you doing?" Ramirez demanded, grabbing the shirt from her.

"Saving your horse," she spat back. "But it's all the same to me if we walk. In fact, it would serve me very well. And McKaid."

"As you say," he relented, throwing the shirt at her. "You may continue."

"I don't think so," she answered, dropping the shirt on his boots. She turned and stalked away.

His fingers bit into her arm, and he jerked her around, grabbing her braid and wrapping it around his hand until he'd forced her face up to his.

"If you care for your life, you will keep your mouth shut and do as you are told." He shoved her to the ground and kicked the soiled shirt at her. He exuded fury, and she knew she had better tread more lightly. She gritted her teeth and clenched her hands to keep from throwing a rock at him, but she brought her temper under control and wordlessly complied.

Through the whole night and well into the next day, Ramirez kept them on the go. Elizabeth slipped in and out of sleep at intervals during the long endless night. She had no idea how Ramirez kept going or how he knew where to lead his horse through the black shadows of night.

"Make a fire," he ordered brusquely when he dismounted at mid-day.

She sat in the saddle glaring at his black head. She wanted nothing more than to stretch out in the open and sleep while the warm rays of the sun heated the night's chill from her body. But he led them into a shadowy cavern cut out by time from the overhanging cliff. The least he could have done was allow her to bring her blanket. Now he wanted a fire. Next it would be cook his meals, wash his clothes, tend his horse.

Well, a fire and some hot coffee and food sounded good. And she wasn't doing it for him.

"How long are we staying here?" she asked when the coffee was brewing over the fire. She spoke to him now only as frequently as absolutely necessary, but she needed sleep badly, and she wanted to know his plans.

"We will stay until nightfall. Get some sleep. I do not wish to hold you in the saddle again tonight."

"Where are we going?"

372

"To Mexico."

Mexico. She should have guessed. He was too cowardly to face McKaid without help from his countrymen. Plus, he'd be safe in Mexico. The Mexican officials didn't care what Ramirez did, so long as he did it in another country. And Texas Rangers had no jurisdiction in Mexico. It was a new twist for Ramirez to take his victim out of the country, but not a bad move for him, all things considered. It would be hell for her, though, if he succeeded. She might be able to thwart the interest of one man, Ramirez, or physically fight him off as he wasn't a great deal larger than herself, but a whole hacienda full . . . She knew with absolute certainty that that was his plan for her. And McKaid would be made to watch. She had to find a way to slow their progress. She couldn't allow them to cross the border. It meant getting rid of the horse. How?

She was still thinking about it when Ramirez tossed a dried biscuit and chunk of greasy jerky in her lap. He sat down and began tearing at the meat with his teeth, his gold front tooth winking at her every now and again. Her appetite deserted her. She couldn't eat looking at him, and she couldn't eat anything that was as tough as the dried meat, or that smelled so rancid. She poured water in her cup, dropped the meat in, and set it on the fire to stew.

"Do you cook?" he asked.

"Yes." Here it comes, she thought.

He tossed the sack of provisions to the ground beside her and took out a beat-up tin pan. "Cook a meal for later. We will eat before we leave."

She snatched the pan away from his outstretched hand. "I'm just as tired as you are."

"Do you defy me again?" he spat at her.

Wearily she filled the pan with water, beans, and more dried meat.

"Put some pepper in that. I like my food to have flavor."

"Fine," she retorted, tossed a whole dried red pepper in the pot, and set the pot of beans on the coals to cook. He chuckled but said nothing more. She'd probably just ruined supper, at least for her, but she was beyond caring. She lifted her tin cup from the coals with the hem of her riding skirt and fished the softened meat out. Finally she could chew it.

When she'd finished eating, she stretched out on the hard rock floor and closed her eyes.

"Put your hands behind your back, señorita."

"You can't mean to tie me."

"I, too, wish to rest. I do not want my throat slit while I sleep." He bound her hands and feet, then moved uncaringly away and made himself comfortable.

There was no way she could get comfortable lying down, so she found a place where she could lean back against the rock wall. In spite of her churned-up emotions, she drifted into a fitful sleep and dreamed about McKaid, chained by the neck, being led by Ramirez through the streets of a dusty Mexican town, stoned by jeering women, blood dripping from where his ears had been.

Chapter Twenty-Three

The deck was stacked equally against both McKaid and Ramirez. They each had their problems. McKaid clung to that thought as to a lifeline when his doubts began. And he could win, he could find Lizzie if he kept his wits about him.

Ramirez had a good lead on him, but he was also riding double on a horse much less powerful and enduring than Lucky Lady. Ramirez didn't have to slow his pace to follow tracks, but then the tracks from riding double weren't hard to follow. Still McKaid was falling behind.

Ramirez wouldn't stop during the night and risk disclosing his position with a campfire. He'd keep going, knowing for one thing, that tracking them would be next to impossible. He'd put as much distance between them and him as he could before he chanced a stop.

So McKaid rode well into the evening, until finally the light deserted him completely. He could do nothing then but take a break to rest his horse and his own weary body. He did manage to nod off for short periods of time, but his thoughts, his nightmares, his overwrought nerves, his fear that he'd oversleep and lose precious light robbed him of real rest.

The night was an endless curse for McKaid, a time of forced and helpless inactivity, a time when touch, sight, taste, smell, even hearing had nothing much to offer his mind as a temporary distraction from his beleaguering worries about Lizzie. How was she? Had he hurt her, raped her? Was she hungry, was she cold, was she terribly frightened?

Of course she was frightened. Who wouldn't be? He tried to remember what her eyes looked like when she was scared. He couldn't recall very many occasions when he'd seen fear in her. The first time was probably on that damned stage, but he hadn't really seen fear—shocked disbelief, maybe, but not fear. She had been afraid of that rattler, though. Her eyes had been huge saucers of burnished gold in her paper white face. He didn't know what had happened after that brief second. His next memory was of waking up in bed with Lizzie standing over him.

Not much frightened Lizzie. She had a good head and steady composure. Anyone who could face the Apache, stand up to Corbett, and successfully pull off what she had with Ramirez wouldn't be easily intimidated. She had probably made life hell for Ramirez since he took her.

As amusing as that thought was, it gave him cause for concern. Lizzie could push a man to the end of his patience with her sassy remarks. Ramirez had a short fuse, especially when he was cornered. He might decide that he was better off without Lizzie. He could decide to kill her and escape to Mexico and safety, just as he'd done a dozen times before when he'd been running from the law.

However, the facts indicated that Ramirez had something else in mind this time. He could have killed Lizzie in camp, but he hadn't. So what was he planning?

At first light McKaid was in the saddle and back on the trail of his enemy and the woman he loved. If his spirit had flagged during the night from his doubts and fears, it was reborn in full strength with the dawn and the return of purpose. An entire day of light stretched ahead of him, and he intended to use every minute of it to close the gap between them.

Elizabeth struggled her way out of another nightmare only to open her eyes and remember the one she was living. She sat up and groaned at her aches and pains.

Ramirez was still asleep, snoring lightly. He looked harmless enough in sleep, it was only when he opened his eyes that the carrion of his soul became apparent. What was she to do about him? She knew McKaid was out there looking for her, but he'd never be able to reach her at the pace Ramirez was moving. She put her mind to work on the problem.

She could always give the horse a good slap and chase it off, as she'd done with the other one, but Ramirez would kill her for a stunt like that. Besides, where would the animal go?

Ramirez would find it easily enough. So that left what? Whatever it was, it had to look like an accident.

"You are awake," Ramirez stated and yawned. He sat up and stretched, then got up and walked out of the cavern.

"Wait a minute. Aren't you going to untie me?"

After a few minutes he returned and freed her. "You can serve my meal now," he ordered.

She bristled. On top of her disturbing dreams and aching muscles, his arrogant assumption that she would act his slave was more than her temper could tolerate. She stood and headed out of the cave.

"Where do you go?" he demanded, drawing his pistol.

She turned and glared at him. "It's no wonder you can't keep a woman except by force. I'm going outside, alone."

The hammer clicked back on his gun, and she stopped and turned again. "Go ahead. McKaid will know where you are then. He can't be far behind. It doesn't really matter what happens to me as long as McKaid kills you. Look at all these mountains. How many millions of years do you think they've stood there before we laid eyes on them? And they'll go on for a million more with or without you and me. We are nothing. We were given life to profit this world, not destroy it as you do. My life is fair exchange for your death. That will be my contribution to this world." She walked away. He said nothing, but neither did he shoot her.

When she returned she divided the beans between them. Ramirez spooned his greedily. Elizabeth was more circumspect, remembering the red pepper. As she suspected, the food was hotter than Mrs. Cerillo's pickles. But not for anything would she let Ramirez mock her. She ate every last bean, despite her flaming mouth and smouldering stomach. When she finished, beads of perspiration glistened beneath her eyes and across her upper lip. Ramirez was sweating, too.

One good thing came of her cooking. She required quite a few stops during the next two hours. For once she was thankful for the affliction.

Night fell quickly and completely in the mountains. Elizabeth still had not found a way to slow their pace. Except for a few minutes, Ramirez kept her in sight at all times when they stopped to rest. It was during one of those brief respites he allowed her for privacy that she struck upon an idea. She got lost.

As soundlessly as she could, she moved away from Ramirez into the thick brush. She slid down a shallow ravine and hid between two rocks. And she waited for him to find her.

"Señorita," he called. "You will come back now."

And then, "Come back now, or you will be permitted no more privacy."

He thrashed his way back and forth among the dense junipers, calling out and threatening her. Twice he came very near to where she hid, but she held her breath and waited for him to pass. She waited for nearly an hour, long enough for Ramirez to get murderously furious, then she covered her face and arms with dirt, inflicted a few scratches on her hands and face, tore the elbow of her blouse, then sprawled herself on the ground and gave a low moan.

She had never been very far from the place where they had stopped, and it took only one more moan for Ramirez to find her. She heard his feet dislodge a rock and send a small avalanche of stones and pebbles raining down on her. She moved an arm and groaned.

Ramirez holstered his gun and rolled her over. "*Estupida!*"

Elizabeth took her time regaining her senses. She tried to stand and fell again to the ground. Before he could launch an attack on her, she flew into him.

She swatted his hands away. "Why didn't you answer me when I called? You let me get lost intentionally. Do you get some sort of sick thrill knowing a helpless woman is wandering around in the dark alone? You knew it was dangerous out here. Did you have a good laugh knowing I was scared to death? Oh, God, my head." There. That should be enough. She dropped her head into her hands. He was speechless. How bitter it must be to have all that anger built up inside and no excuse to vent it.

She turned accusing eyes to his and continued shrewishly. "Well, aren't you going to help me up? I think I've twisted my ankle. I thought you were in such a hurry. How could you let this happen? What if I'd broken a leg?"

"I would have shot you."

"Damn, I tore my blouse. Shot me? Like a horse? Why don't you do it then? It would eliminate this headache."

"You hit your head when you fell," he explained unnecessarily. He took her arm and pulled her to her feet.

"Don't touch me," she snapped, then swayed into his body.

"We will get up the hill together. You can rest in the saddle. You have cost us more than an hour."

"You let me lie here for an *hour*? Why?" she screeched.

Totally exasperated and ignoring her feigned limp, he hauled her up the hill and towed her to his horse. He swung her roughly up into the saddle and mounted behind her.

She grinned into the night. She'd gained an hour, but she wasn't through yet. After another hour had passed, much of which she spent holding her head, she slumped to the side.

Ramirez jerked her upright. She grabbed at his arm, nearly unseating them both. The horse danced sideways beneath them.

"Fool woman," he shouted. "You would get us killed?"

"I'm sorry. But my head. I'm so dizzy. I can't keep my eyes open." She leaned heavily against his chest and let her head fall back against his shoulder, as limp as a rag doll.

He mumbled a curse, but he held on to her and continued on his trek. She stayed that way for a long time, until she was sure she felt his arm tremble from the strain of holding her dead weight upright in the saddle, until she feared he would dump her on the ground.

"Russ," she moaned and thrashed her head into his jaw. His teeth snapped together, and he swore. "Russ," she groaned again, and then fell silent. Let him wonder why she called for Russ and not McKaid. Let him wonder, after all that had happened, if he still had the wrong woman.

A few minutes later she secured her safety. "Gold," she murmured. ". . . find the gold."

Ramirez stiffened behind her. "Gold?" he asked quietly into her ear. "What of the gold?"

"Map," she whispered, then louder. "I found . . . map. Russ."

"What map?" he asked louder. He shook her awake. "What map?"

She jerked upright, swaying slightly. "Pardon me? Oh, I must have fallen asleep. What did you say?"

"You spoke of a map. And gold. How do you know of this gold?"

She leaned forward away from him. "Gold?" she asked lightly, and chuckled unconvincingly. "I must have been dreaming."

"I think not. You have seen this map?"

379

"Why, no. I mean, I don't know what you're talking about. I'm not feeling very well again. I think I'm going to be sick. Could we stop?"

He sighed and clucked his tongue, glancing impatiently over his shoulder. "We get nowhere. Very well. There is the sound of water ahead. We will stop there. And you will tell me of this map."

"But, I—"

"Enough. I agree to stop. You agree to talk."

Elizabeth bathed her face and arms in the cool mountain stream then found a comfortable place to sit down. For effect she removed her left boot and massaged her ankle.

"You are feeling recovered?" Ramirez asked, sitting beside her.

"A little better, thank you," she replied sweetly. "I hit my head harder than I thought. If we could rest here for a while, I'm sure I'll be fine."

Ramirez looked at her through narrowed eyes. She was an enchanting woman, a woman of spirit, but he didn't trust her. And he didn't like the feelings she engendered in him to protect her. She was McKaid's woman, and he meant to kill her eventually. After what she had done, he should kill her now. Protect her? Who would protect him from her wiles? No, she was not to be trusted.

"Where did you hit your head?" He took her chin in his hand and studied her eyes.

Her gaze did not waver. "Here," she lied, pressing her hand against the right side of her head.

His fingers probed the area, unconcerned by her winces of pain. "There is no lump."

"Well, there is pain," she snapped and pushed his hands away. Her heart thudded in her throat. What would he do if he learned she'd deceived him yet again?

"Tell me of this gold."

She sighed wearily. "Why? You are going to Mexico anyway."

"Who knows of it?"

"I don't know. No one."

"Where did you learn of it?"

"From Uncle Clint, when he was dying."

"He said there was a map?"

"Yes, but if you burned the ranch, it's gone, so what does

380

it matter?"

"The map is at the ranch? In the house?"

"I don't know where it is."

"I think you do. Also, we did not burn the house."

Her eyes flickered up to his. "You didn't?"

"Where is it?"

She shook her head. "Even if I did know, why should I tell you? You would only steal it."

"It belongs to me," he thundered. "This land belonged to my family. Our land was stolen from us."

"Is that why you spend your life causing pain and destruction?"

"Why should I not? It is only what you deserve."

"Because it's senseless to punish people who had nothing to do with a war that happened years ago."

"Do not preach to me. I have had enough of preaching from the priest. You will tell me where the gold is."

"I don't think so."

He jumped to his feet, paced away, then swung back to her, stabbing a finger in her direction. "You will tell me. Do not doubt it. Get on the horse. You delay me long enough."

She pulled on her boot and stood. She'd gained a little more time and given him a reason to keep her alive, but she'd made him angry in the process. She'd receive no more sympathetic concessions from him.

"I will never tell you," she said defiantly, hoisting herself into the saddle. "Because of you, my uncle is dead."

He swung up behind her and pulled her back against his chest. His hand forced its way past her arms until he held her breast in his hand. He squeezed painfully.

"We will see," he said. "We will see what is the price of your silence."

McKaid traveled through the next day and into the night until again the light betrayed him. He found a secluded clearing, concealed by rocks and brush, and lit a small fire. With coffee brewing and a tin of hash warming in the skillet, he unrolled the survey map and pinpointed his position. He'd gone through the procedure frequently since beginning the search. From the look of it Ramirez was skirting west of the mountains, heading south toward a tributary river of the Rio

Grande. But the canyons and mountains into which he was heading were a treacherous maze. A man could be lost for years in there. And why was Ramirez heading south, unless he planned to return to Mexico. And with Lizzie.

If Ramirez got Lizzie into Mexico . . . He shuddered to think about it. Neither his status as territorial marshal nor as Texas Ranger would carry any weight with the Mexican authorities. They were resistant and resentful of any interference by *gringo* lawmen in the way they handled matters in their own country. And Ramirez was influential enough to convince them to look the other way where his activities were concerned. And influential enough to have a Texas Ranger thrown into prison for the rest of his life for daring to cross the border. What a great revenge that would be, for him to rot in a stinking dungeon and spend the rest of his life wondering from day to day what torment they were forcing Lizzie to endure.

He ate his meal and studied the map again. It was the only answer. Ramirez had to be angling for the Rio Grande. And if that was the case . . .

He took a lead pencil from his breast pocket and marked his present position. Noting the contours of the land, he surmised that, unless Ramirez reversed his direction, he'd have to circle the next peaks by the western canyons, then swing back east to meet the river.

McKaid decided to play his hunch. He charted a path of his own to the east of the same jagged peaks. His course would bypass the deep canyons and ravines that Ramirez would have to contend with and cut hours off his time. With any luck at all he would intercept them at . . . He marked a bold x on the map.

McKaid no longer needed to wait until daylight. He broke camp and set off on a trail of his own, hoping and praying he was doing the right thing. Please God, for once in his life, for Lizzie's sake, let this not be another of his fool's errands.

If Elizabeth thought she'd seen a glimpse of humanity in Ramirez, it was gone by the next day. He found a campsite and jerked her from the horse, shoving her roughly to the ground. The food satchel landed in her lap.

"See if you can do better this time," he sneered and turned to unsaddle his horse.

"Cook your own damn dinner. I'm not hungry."

382

He dragged the saddle over the back of the lathered horse and dropped it quietly to the ground. He turned to her, reached out a hand, and lifted her to her feet. He slapped her again, and before she had recovered from that shock, he grabbed her by the back of the neck and dragged her face to his. His other hand clamped roughly around her jaw. With savage brute force he covered her mouth with his, grinding her lips against her teeth. Pain aside, she squeezed her eyes shut, her whole being rejecting the touch of his hands, the feel of his thick lips on hers, and his acrid tongue pushing against her mouth.

He released her suddenly and she stumbled backward and fell. She spat until the taste of him was gone from her mouth, and she scrubbed her bruised mouth raw with the sleeve of her shirt.

"Do not try my patience, or you will find more than the taste of my kiss to wipe from your body. Do as you are told to do. *Pronto!*"

She scrambled to her feet, grabbed up the satchel of provisions, and moved away from him. Tears of indignation, rage, and just plain fear sprang to her eyes. She swiped at them, disgusted that he could reduce her to such a weak response. She dare not let him undermine her courage. She had to remain strong until McKaid arrived. This was no time for weakness of any sort, no matter what the provocation.

Self-disgust gave way to pure loathing. She snatched up kindling and firewood and threw it into a pile before going in search of more. She took delight in snapping the dried wood into smaller pieces, imagining with every crack that it was Ramirez's neck she was breaking.

She cooked a decent meal that afternoon, not for Ramirez, but to preserve her own strength. She needed nourishment to compensate for the little sleep she was getting. But how could she be expected to sleep when she worried about what Ramirez was going to do next? With his twisted mind it could be anything. And any time.

It was a long night, made more arduous by the steep hills they were required to traverse on foot. At least the cloud cover had passed, allowing them a silvery light by which to see. Even with that, her face and arms were scratched by branches she hadn't seen in the shadowed forest.

She thought she was exhausted after climbing down the wall of the gorge into Ramirez's camp, but that was nothing to what

383

she felt by the time the first light of morning streaked across the sky. Her feet were blistered, her hips and back aching, her leg muscles screaming. Twice she had fallen and hadn't been able to make herself get up. Ramirez had dragged her to her feet and shoved her on ahead of him. "You will keep going. If you stop again, I will use the time you spend on the ground to take my pleasure from you." Remembering his repulsive lips, his dank, fetid breath, she'd forced her feet to move.

The terrain flattened by daybreak, and Ramirez again ordered her onto the horse. Her own strength was so depleted that she couldn't even manage a care that they were abusing the animal. But by mid-morning she couldn't ignore it any longer.

"Your horse needs to rest. Look at him."

She thought for a minute that he was actually going to heed her warning. He stopped, dismounted, and waited for her to slide to the ground, but it was only to tie her hands in front of her and mount up again.

"You, señorita, feel pity for the beast. You can then spare him your weight."

"You intend to make me walk while you ride?"

"It is my horse. You are the one who burdens him."

"Go ahead," she shouted. "It's all the same to me if you kill him."

He didn't reply, but tied the other end of the rope to the saddle horn and rode on.

Her arms were nearly jerked out of their sockets, but she soon learned to balance herself and let the horse pull her along.

"Are you ready now to tell me where the gold is, señorita?" he called back.

"I told you. I don't know where it is."

"Where is the map?"

"I don't know that, either."

"As you wish."

McKaid positioned himself on a high outcropping of rocks and searched the river gorge through the spyglass. The shallow but turbulent river fell over rocks and swirled madly in its impatience to get to the Rio Grande. Although Ramirez could have taken any of several routes to this river, the only way to the Rio Grande was past McKaid.

For an hour he searched the hills and the canyon below the sheer rock walls. With each passing minute his doubts grew, until he was certain he'd made yet another mistake where Ramirez was concerned. He should have continued tracking him, he should have stayed with a sure pair instead of drawing to an inside straight. Whatever made him think he was smart enough to outwit a fox like Ramirez? He had never succeeded in the past.

It was then that a scurry of movement at the far end of the canyon caught his eye. He snapped the glass up and searched. The vegetation was thick in the canyon, a dark green covering over the sandy red earth and rock, making it difficult to find anything that wasn't a contrasting color. Again movement caught his eye, but when three deer burst into the open and zigzagged their way into the cover of a thicket, his stomach plummeted. "Damn," he muttered. "Or should I be blessing your skittish hides?" Something or someone had sent them into flight. He moved the spyglass in the direction from which the deer had bolted. And there he was. Ramirez.

But where was Lizzie? Had Ramirez already . . . A flash of blue caught his eye. No. There she was. As he focused the glass, as he saw what that snake was putting Lizzie through, his rage boiled over.

"That goddamned bastard! That slimy, slinking son of a bitch. He'll pay for this."

Filled with murderous intent, McKaid stood up and snapped the telescoping glass together. "Now hold on, McKaid," he said aloud to himself. "You have to think this out." To go racing down there, to disclose his presence now, would defeat his purpose. He'd be exactly where Ramirez wanted him. Maybe not ultimately, but close enough. McKaid still believed Ramirez intended to use Lizzie to lure him across the border. But to force him to watch Lizzie suffer and die here would please him just as well.

"Hold on, Lizzie. Just a little bit longer, sweetheaert. Just a little longer."

Elizabeth, more exhausted than she'd ever been in her life, could only hold on to the rope and pray that her legs would continue to hold her upright. Perspiration ran down her face, stinging her eyes, matting her straggling hair to her face.

Rivulets ran down her neck, between her breasts, soaking her tattered blouse. Her lungs screamed from the efforts to drag enough air into her body, and her mouth felt as if it was full of sand.

Her wrists were raw and bleeding from the rough rope biting into her flesh, and her arms and chest were covered with abrasions from when she'd been pulled off her feet and dragged along the rocky ground.

She'd never in her short life rued anything she'd done more than mentioning that gold to Ramirez. It had turned him into a maniac. He wouldn't believe that she honestly didn't know where either the map or the gold was to be found, and her continual denials only enraged him more each time she uttered them.

"What's so important about the gold?" she'd raged at him the last time he'd badgered her about it. "You'd be arrested before you could mine enough of it out of the earth to do you any good."

"It does not need to be mined. The gold was smuggled from Mexico to buy weapons for Armijo, to fight against the Americans. It was to save this land for Mexico."

"So what happened?"

"It was stolen from us. As this land was stolen. I claim that gold for Mexico."

"Would Mexico get it, or would you?"

"McKaid will not. I will see to that."

"What makes you think it's the same gold?"

"The gold was destined for Sante Fe. It is here."

"If it is, it's spoils of war. With no one to prove who took it, or if it was even sent, as you claim, it seems to me that it belongs to whoever finds it. It must gall you that that man will be McKaid."

"It will not be McKaid."

"It will," she retorted defiantly, "and it is only right that it should, after all you've taken from him. You murdered a lovely, innocent young woman whom McKaid loved, and although no amount of wealth can compensate for that loss, it will do him good to know he took something of equal value from you."

"You will tell me where it is. Before I finish with you, you will tell me."

It was then that he'd kicked his horse into a canter and left her to struggle behind until she'd finally tripped and fallen. He hadn't stopped.

Ramirez rode to the creek and dismounted. He led his horse to the water and quenched his own thirst before he thought to untie Elizabeth. Elizabeth crawled to the water's edge and immersed her stinging arms into the cooling current. She cupped the cold clear water in her torn hands, splashing her face as she drank. Forcing her body to move, she pushed herself up onto the bank and collapsed, shading her eyes with her forearm. How could she go on like this? Nothing was left of her.

She rolled her head to the side and opened her eyes. The sun was bright, glinting off the rocks. No, only one rock. Only it wasn't a rock. She glanced at Ramirez. He had his back to her. She sat up and studied the rocky hillside. She caught the flash again, and then for only a second McKaid stood and waved his arms.

He disappeared from her view again, but the sight of him, just knowing he'd found her, gave her renewed strength. McKaid. His name rushed through her like a warm brandy, a reviving tonic, filling and warming the crevices of her mind and spirit that days of hardship and fear had eroded.

She must be ready, alert at all times. She must not betray with even a glance in his direction that McKaid was up there. And she must stay away from Ramirez. Even now McKaid could be taking aim, waiting for the perfect time, the perfect shot. She knew, as McKaid would, that if Ramirez did not die instantly, he would expend his last breath, his last heartbeat, killing her.

McKaid took cover behind the rocks, his heart beating thunderously. The time had come to finish with Ramirez, and he wasn't at all sorry to be doing the killing. After what Ramirez had put Lizzie through, shooting was too good for him, too quick, too painless.

But Lizzie was alive. Whatever had happened to her over the past few days, she was still alive. In time she would mend and forget. But for now, it was up to him to get her away from the source of her nightmare, it was in his hands to see that she was never exposed to this kind of danger and torment again. Nothing meant more to him than Lizzie's life, her safety, her happiness.

He put his mind to work. A shot from where he lay would be chancy. With the stealth of an Apache, he moved from cover to cover until he was in range for his aim to be accurate and his bullet true. He had one chance, one chance only. If he missed, Lizzie was as good as dead.

Crawling on his stomach, he moved into position, sighting down the long barrel of his rifle. "Move, Lizzie," he whispered, willing her to read his thoughts. She was too close, and he couldn't get a clear shot. Elizabeth moved off a short distance, stopping to collect firewood. "Come on, you bastard, step away from your horse. Give me one second."

He lowered his gun. He needed a different angle. Holding the rifle against his chest, he rolled his body over to take aim from the other side of the rock. There was no warning that he, himself, was in any danger, only the quickest of rustlings. And then the searing pain.

"*Stupid, stupid,*" he thought. "*Only you could do this to Lizzie.*" All his training, all his experience, what was it for? What was it worth when he couldn't even avoid a damned snake.

Pain was no stranger to McKaid. Still, it took all of his self-control not to cry out, not to let his finger tighten on the trigger. He clamped his teeth together, laid his rifle down, and loosened the jaws of the twining serpent from his left shoulder.

He drew his knive and sliced the head off, shoving the still curling, twisting remains away from him.

He couldn't reach the bite. How long did he have before the pain became delirium? Why his shoulder? Why not his leg? He took aim again, steadying the barrel with his injured arm. Pain like that of a red-hot branding iron spread over his shoulder and down his arm. Beads of perspiration formed on his forehead and trickled past his brows into his eyes. He wiped them clear and aimed again. The rifle shook in his hands. His vision blurred. Nausea rose in his throat, and he broke out in a cold sweat. Blackness edged in on him.

"No, dammit, no," he cursed uselessly.

Chapter Twenty-Four

Where was he? Why didn't he shoot? She'd given him every opportunity, staying as far away from Ramirez as he would allow. What was McKaid waiting for?

She'd prepared a hasty meal earlier from the little food left in the pack. They had both eaten, though she'd had to force the food down, and he'd already bound her hands and feet and had settled himself on the ground with his head propped against his saddle for his siesta.

He hadn't slowed their pace any that morning, neither had he constantly looked over his shoulder as if he expected to find the Ranger behind him. He seemed to feel they were safe now, that they'd lost McKaid.

She watched covertly as his breathing grew slow and steady, as his body relaxed, as his fingers loosened around the gun he slept with. His mouth sagged open, and his snoring began. *Now, McKaid,* her mind screamed. But still he didn't come for her. Something was dreadfully wrong.

She struggled desperately with the knots at her wrists, trying to cut them with a sharp stone, but all she managed to do was make her wrists bleed again. She twisted her body to try and reach her feet, but she was too stiff for that. But if she could get her feet out of her boots . . . She should have thought of that before, only what would she have done then? It took a few minutes of scraping and yanking against the corner of a rock, but she finally succeeded in sliding one foot out of its boot. Before long she had the rope off her feet and her stockinged foot back in her boot.

She couldn't risk trying for Ramirez's gun, or his knife. He slept lightly, and her hands were still tied. But disarm him she must. As silently as she could, she approached him.

"Be quick," McKaid had said. "Don't hesitate."

"Ramirez," she shouted.

Ramirez jumped, jerking forward from the saddle, and up came the gun. She slammed her booted foot into the side of his face as hard as she could. He slumped to the ground.

She twisted her body around and drew his long knife from the sheath on his belt. The rope at her wrists gave way under the razor-sharp blade. Free again, she wasted no time in completely disarming Ramirez.

She stood for a second over his inert body, holding his gun in her hands. She should shoot him. He deserved to be shot. It would save so much trouble if she'd just pull the trigger and be done with it. It would be over in a second. Over for her, over for McKaid. Just squeeze your finger.

She lowered the gun. "Dammit," she cursed vehemently. "You're weak." She forced herself to touch him, to see if he was still alive. He was. She used the same rope she'd been bound with to tie Ramirez's hands and feet, only she took his boots off first.

She led the horse into the clearing and slapped its rump, sending it off into the valley. Stuffing the canteen and knife into the food sack, she slung it over her shoulder. She took the pistol and rifle and both belts of ammunition Ramirez wore like armor across his chest, and began her climb up into the rocks to where she'd seen McKaid.

Dark pillars of clouds began to roll and churn overhead, forming themselves into dragons and two-headed beasts. Thunder rumbled in the distance, echoing ominously from the high rock walls. She looked up apprehensively and hurried her pace.

McKaid wasn't where she'd seen him. Where was he then? She dropped the rifle and heavy belts of bullets, deciding it was as good a place to hide them as anywhere. They were too heavy to carry. Standing up, she searched the area for any sign of McKaid.

McKaid moaned and lifted his head. His body was on fire. God, where was he? He tried to sit up, but the pain in his left shoulder sent him back to the ground and sparked his memory.

Ramirez. And Lizzie. He groaned again and tried to clear his head.

"McKaid," Lizzie cried, kneeling at his side. "Oh, McKaid, what happened?" She gripped his shoulders and tried to turn him over. He cried out in pain.

"My shoulder," he managed. "Snake bite."

"Snake bite?" she gasped, her eyes darting to the ground around them. She saw the headless remains of the snake and shuddered. She helped him sit up against the rock. He was flushed with fever. She unscrewed the canteen and pressed it to his lips.

"Drink some water. What can I do, McKaid? I don't know." She loosened his shirt from his pants, unbuttoned it, and slid it over his wounded shoulder. "It looks awful, McKaid. Am I supposed to cut it or something?"

"It's too late for that. Where's Ramirez? How did you get away?"

"I knocked him out."

"Did you kill him?"

"I couldn't." He winced, and she felt awful for being weak. "I tried, I really did, but I couldn't pull the trigger. But I tied him up, and I took his guns."

He was feeling worse, she could tell by his sudden pallor. "What can I do? Do you have anything for this?"

"In my saddlebag, but it's too far away."

"I can get it. Tell me where it is."

"No. Help me up. We have to find shelter. Thunder. A storm . . ."

She picked up McKaid's rifle. "Can you carry this?" Taking his good arm, she helped him to his feet. She wrapped his arm around her shoulders and supported him with an arm around his waist. His knees gave, and hers almost buckled under his weight.

"Which way? Where should we go? McKaid, don't pass out on me now."

He shook his head, then frowned down at her. "Lizzie, is that you?"

"McKaid," she barked. "Where should we go? Which way?"

He blinked and looked around. "That way."

"Okay. Let's go. Stay awake now."

391

They trudged on for what seemed like hours, but in actuality it was far less than that. When she turned to look behind them, she could still see the outcropping of rocks where she'd found McKaid. Her back ached and her legs burned, but she didn't mind. Her burden was precious. She tightened her grip on him and pushed on.

The light faded as they entered a narrow gorge whose vertical pink and gray walls shadowed the low canyon floor. Even in the fading light what she saw made her breath catch in her throat. The rock wall on one side was dotted with dark holes. Hundreds of dark holes. What whimsical force of nature had swept through the gorge poking its fingers into the forming rock? She noticed something else then that made her look again. The holes were randomly spaced, but in regular lines that followed narrow ledges along the face of the wall. And here and there were smaller structures with walls of rock, crumbling now, but definitely built at one time by men. She was standing on the site of one of the ruins McKaid had talked about. The ancient cave dwellings of the Old Ones.

McKaid slumped against her, and she helped him to the ground. He'd had enough for one day. He needed rest to fight off the poison. She left him for a few minutes and went to search out a cave they could use. The higher ones would be more easily defended if necessary, but she couldn't get McKaid up to them, so she found one not too difficult to reach, made certain it was free of snakes or other creatures, and stashed their gear. She went back for McKaid.

The cave had a low narrow opening, but inside it was roomy enough for her to stand and for them both to stretch out comfortably. Small niches had been carved out of the back wall, probably for storage, and at one side an open crevice led to the outside. She would build their fire there.

She helped McKaid get comfortable on the cave floor, then went in search of firewood. She was returning with her fourth heavy load when the rain began to fall. Now that she had McKaid tucked away, she hoped it poured. She hurried back to the cave, slightly damp, and dropped the logs on the pile. Lightning split the sky, and thunder cracked overhead, reverberating through the rock to her feet.

Emptying the contents of the food bag, she rummaged for the matches she knew were there. She built a fire and placed a pan of water beside it to heat. She slumped back against the

392

wall. Her day was beginning to catch up with her.

When the water was hot, she took off her blouse and tore a wide strip from the bottom where it was least dirty. She soaked it in the hot water, folded it into a hot compress, and placed it on McKaid's injury to draw out any poison left in the surface tissue. With another strip of material she tied it in place. It was all she could do. Which was nothing at all, she thought disconsolately.

She spent the night alternately sponging his fevered skin and wrapping her warmth around him to ward off his chills. She managed to get two cups of sweetened coffee down him as well as a little cooked rice. He never spoke, never really woke up to the point where he was lucid. He drank when she said, ate when she said, then fell asleep again.

Intermittently she sat in the low doorway and watched the storm, a storm unlike any she'd ever seen in the East. The lightning was relentless, flashing in long whiplike fingers across the black sky, almost too shockingly bright to watch. The violence of light and sound, the trembling and the shuddering of the earth, the rain that pelted in sheets from the heavens and cascaded in gushing rivers of power over rocks, through precipices, taking with it whatever dared get in its way, it fit the wildness, the untamed essence of this primordial land. It was magnificent.

Toward dawn McKaid's fever broke, and she knew that, though a long way from well, he'd won the battle. She placed the last of the wood on the fire and curled up beside him to sleep. For just a few hours, a few minutes, to close her eyes, feel McKaid beside her, and forget.

She woke with a start, her heart racing, but whatever dream had scared her was gone. Sun streamed into the doorway. The storm had passed, birds sang, the world went on as usual. She pushed the hair out of her eyes and stood up. The canteen was full again as well as two pans she'd set outside the doorway during the night to catch rainwater. She put fresh coffee in the pot and set it on the flickering embers, all that remained of the fire.

She checked McKaid's shirt, it was dry. She'd rinsed it out after his fever broke, when he'd soaked it through, and had draped it over a ledge by the fire to dry. She took the other pan of water and knelt by his side. When she laid the cool cloth against his forehead, his eyes blinked open and his hand shot up and grabbed her wrist, twisting her arm backward.

"McKaid. It's me. Stop it, McKaid."

"Lizzie," he said in astonishment. "What are you doing here?" He looked around, seeing his surroundings for the first time. "Where the hell are we?" He tried to sit up, though his head throbbed painfully. "Christ."

"Lie down, and stop cussing. We're in a cave in some ruins." She proceeded to bathe him, and he closed his eyes and let her.

"That feels good, Lizzie. How did we get here? The last thing I remember is that godda—darned snake."

As she wiped his arms and upper torso, she told him all that had happened. She cleaned his wound and helped him into his shirt. When she finished, he was strangely quiet. He wouldn't look at her, and when she laid her hand against his forehead, he turned away.

"Is that coffee I smell?" he asked, covering his eyes with his forearm.

"I'll get you a cup. Are you feeling worse?" She frowned worriedly.

"I don't think that's possible."

"McKaid, should I go and check on your horse? That was an awful storm last night. I could get your medicine, a blanket, food."

"Aren't you forgetting?" he asked wearily. "Ramirez is still out there. Besides, I don't need the remedy now. The worst is over."

"We do need food and blankets. And I could use one of your spare shirts."

"Where's yours? Did you wash it?"

"It was torn. I cut it up for bandages. You'll have to take me as I am," she said, pirouetting flirtatiously in her camisole. She got no response from him. Relax, she scolded herself. He's not feeling well. "I'll get your coffee."

McKaid was moody and uncommunicative for the whole of that morning. His fever returned from time to time, but never high enough to be concerned about.

"It's to be expected," he said flatly, when she mentioned it.

Finally she could stand no more. "What is it, McKaid? Are you still angry with me?"

"Why would I be angry with you?"

"You tell me. Because you think I deliberately got myself involved in all this, because I was kidnapped, because you had

394

to come after me, because you got bit by a snake. How would I know? But I can feel it."

"You're tired. Why don't you get some rest."

"Where's your horse? I'm going to get your gear. We need food and blankets for tonight. There's no dry firewood."

"No."

"If you won't tell me, I'll just go look for her."

"Elizabeth, you're to stay here."

"And listen to you sulk and clench your jaw muscles. Thank you, but I'd rather not."

"You pick the damnedest times to be obstinate."

"Why? Because I'm trying to prevent you from getting pneumonia on top of a snake bite? Because I'm trying to put a warm meal in your belly?"

"Then I'll go with you."

"I'm not strong enough to carry you back. McKaid, I've got a gun, if that's what you're worrying about. I've got—four guns to pick from," she counted. "You taught me how to shoot."

"A lot of good it did. You couldn't kill him once, what makes you think you could do it next time?"

"That was in cold blood. He was unconscious. You couldn't have done it either and be the man I know you to be."

"Maybe you don't know me as well as you think then."

"Look, I've been through agony. I don't need this from you."

He stood up and moved around the small cubicle, though he had to keep his head down. "I'm fine now, Lizzie. I just need to get my legs back."

"You're sick."

"And you're exhausted. You look like hell."

She felt like it, too, and his caustic criticism didn't make her feel any better. Tears stung at the back of her eyes, and she looked away, not wanting him to see her silly reaction to his rebuff.

He took her shoulders in his large hands and gently turned her. "Look at you. You're at the end of your strength, and no wonder. Your face and arms are scraped, your eyes are glazed over from lack of sleep, and you've dark circles under them that look as if your eyes have been blackened. You can't push yourself any further. And tears, Lizzie. Doesn't that tell you anything?"

He shoved aside his reservations, the dark and lonely thoughts he'd been thinking all morning, and pulled her into his arms. She leaned against him, unresisting but unresponsive, asleep on her feet.

"I'll tell you what," McKaid said, brushing her tangled hair with his lips. "You stay here and get some rest. I'll go and bring Lucky Lady back. I'm fine now."

Nausea churned in his stomach, his head was splitting open, but as sick as he felt, he had more strength than she did. Besides which, he wanted to check on Ramirez.

"Are you sure, McKaid?"

"Yes, Lizzie. I'm very sure." He took his shirt off and wrapped it around her shoulders. "Get some sleep while I'm gone."

He checked his guns, checked the pistol he left for Elizabeth, took his rifle, and moved to the small opening of the cave. "Stay inside, Lizzie, please. As long as Ramirez doesn't know where you are, you're safe." When she nodded, he checked the surrounding area and disappeared.

Elizabeth pushed her arms through the sleeves of McKaid's shirt, rolled up the cuffs, and fastened the buttons. It still held his warmth and his scent. She wrapped her arms around her midriff and sat down where McKaid had slept. Leaning back, she closed her eyes and tried to relax. He was right, she was exhausted. She wasn't even thinking straight. McKaid knew what he was doing. He would be all right. He was a Texas Ranger.

McKaid dodged from the entrance of the cave into the brush that had overgrown the valley floor. Keeping as much under cover as possible, he made his way to the eastern end of the canyon where he'd left his horse tied under a sheltering overhang. She was up to her fetlocks in mud, but otherwise dry.

"That's my girl," he said, untying her and leading her into the sunshine. "Sorry to have left you so long, but I was delayed." He put on one of his spare shirts, checked the saddle, and swung himself one-handed onto the horse.

Keeping to the trees, he rode through the valley back to where Ramirez had made camp. He didn't really expect to find him there, nor did he, but he did find his horse not far away, which meant Ramirez was on foot and close by. Leading the spare horse, McKaid headed back to the vicinity of the caves.

Nothing could be done until Ramirez decided to show himself. In the meantime he would take care of Lizzie for a change.

It seemed as if she'd just fallen asleep when a noise outside the cave wakened her. Thinking it was McKaid returning, she rushed to the doorway and stepped outside. The welcoming smile faded from her face along with all the color.

"You."

"So it is here you hide from me, señorita." His voice was light, friendly even, matching his smile, but his eyes told a different story.

She thought of the gun inside, but he had come too close for her to get past him. She stepped back from him. "Stay away from me."

He rubbed his bruised cheekbone. "No one kicks me in the face and gets away with it. I will have to show you now what it means to cross Ramirez."

She had no time to think. He lunged for her and she ran. "McKaid," she screamed in her headlong flight over brush and rubble, through branches and bushes that snatched at her clothes. "McKaid," she called again at the top of her straining lungs, giving one last scream as his hand caught her shirt and flung her to the ground.

He straddled her and his hands closed around her wrists. He laughed down at her fearful face. "You think McKaid can find you now? You are a dreamer. There are no tracks to follow after a storm."

"Help!" she screamed frantically. "Here! McKaid!"

"Enough of that, señorita. It is you and me now. And it is time for you to learn how to be my woman."

"Never," she spat at him, realizing he didn't know McKaid had already found them.

Ramirez began to paw at her clothes, tearing buttons off as he opened her shirt and pulled at her undergarment.

"You're wrong, Ramirez," she cried, twisting away as his hands began to explore her curves. "McKaid is here."

His hand stilled and he studied her face. His eyes flew to the oversized shirt she wore, and he knew she was telling the truth. Rage twisted his face into an ugly mask. His eyes seemed to bulge outward, his nostrils flared, and his thick lips rolled back baring his stained and uneven teeth. The glint of his gold tooth added that much more menace to his fury.

"How?" he snarled.

"He's smarter than you," she retorted.

"Is he? And yet I have his woman."

She screamed again, but he clamped his hand over her mouth, smothering the sound. "If I have nothing else, I will have you."

He tore at her clothes in earnest then, and she knew he meant to rape and kill her before McKaid could find them. Her desperation lent her the strength of the mad, and she fought wildly, kicking at him, scratching, and beating him when she could twist a hand free. He might take her, but he would suffer for doing it.

"Bitch," he snarled when he couldn't subdue her. Black rage shot from his eyes. He drew his arm back, and she knew he meant to kill her.

A shot rang out, and Ramirez reeled backward in pain, blood dripping into his hand. He looked down at it, incredulous. Elizabeth stumbled to her feet and ran. Ramirez ran also, but away from the sound of the approaching horse.

McKaid stopped when he reached Lizzie. He moved to dismount, but she stopped him. "I'm okay," she assured him. "Go after him, don't let him get away again."

"Stay here." McKaid wasted no time in turning his big horse and riding after Ramirez. Elizabeth's legs gave out, and she sank to the damp ground. It was over now. At last it was over, and she could breathe easy again.

She waited for the shot to sound, the shot that would signal the end, but none came. Long moments stretched into others, and she began to worry. At last she heard the sound of his horse. What had happened now? Why had she heard no gunfire? McKaid rode into view, and behind his horse walked Ramirez, bound and being towed, just as he had done to her. As she stood to watch, Ramirez fell to his knees. McKaid never looked back. He dragged the Mexican to Elizabeth's feet.

Ramirez rolled over and sat up, hatred and resentment sparking from his coal-black eyes. Elizabeth couldn't resist the jibe.

"How do you like being subjected to your own cruelty? Is it a bitter taste?"

McKaid grinned at her. Even at her lowest, she had spirit to spare. "It's time to go home, Lizzie," McKaid said. "Put your foot in the stirrup and get up here."

"Yes, sir," she answered saucily.

He swung her up and around so that she was sitting across the saddle in front of him, her right knee over the saddlehorn.

"It seems I can't leave you alone for a minute. Every time my back is turned you get into trouble. What am I to do with you?"

"Don't turn your back." She shrugged. "Why didn't you shoot him, McKaid?"

He grinned crookedly and urged Lucky Lady forward, leaving Ramirez to keep up or be dragged. "It appears, much to my regret, that I can't bring myself to shoot an unarmed man either."

"That was some shot earlier though. You're as good as your reputation boasts."

He snorted. "Not so you'd notice. I was aiming for his head."

Her eyes widened. "You missed by that far?"

"I have a headache."

As they prepared to leave the canyon, McKaid, though gentle in his concern for Elizabeth, was merciless with Ramirez. He jerked the Mexican's wrists behind his back and tied them so tightly that Ramirez cried out in protestation.

"It will save you from bleeding to death," McKaid answered. "I want to watch your eyes fall out onto your cheeks when they hang you."

He pushed Ramirez into the saddle and tied one boot to the stirrup. When he rounded the front of the horse to tie the other, Ramirez bolted. He kicked his heels sharply into the horse's side, sending it plowing into McKaid.

"McKaid, are you hurt?" Elizabeth cried.

McKaid pushed himself up and ran to his horse. "I knew he'd try something. I can't let him escape, Lizzie," he apologized, sliding his rifle from the boot.

"No."

McKaid braced his arms and took careful aim at the man galloping up into the hills toward freedom.

Fate had other plans. The horse, so badly abused by his owner, stumbled and veered sharply to the side, one knee buckling beneath it. The ground, loosened by the torrential rains slid away beneath his pawing hooves as he fought for purchase. Ramirez's guttural cries mingled with the high-pitched screams of the horse as they lost the fight and tumbled over each other to the bottom of the hill.

"Oh, my God," Elizabeth gasped, wide-eyed.

McKaid straightened and lowered his gun. "He can't have survived that, but let's check."

When they reached the foot of the hill, McKaid dismounted and helped Elizabeth down. Elizabeth could see that Ramirez was dead before McKaid bent to check his pulse. His body was twisted grotesquely and his head lay at an unnaturally odd angle.

She walked to the horse and knelt down, running a hand down his neck. His ears flicked, and his big brown eyes began to roll.

"Easy, boy," she crooned and stroked his velvet nose. "McKaid."

McKaid knelt beside her, resting the butt of his rifle on his bent knee. He shook his head. "His leg is broken, Lizzie."

Elizabeth walked Lucky Lady away, and held her muzzle against her shoulder while McKaid took care of the injured horse. The shot that she'd waited for earlier finally came. It was done. She began to cry.

McKaid slid the rifle into the boot and took her in his arms. He knew the feelings she was experiencing, the terrible letdown after living for days on raw nerve. It used to take him days to get over it when he first started with the Rangers, but he'd never had the luxury of tears as a release. For him it had been whiskey, women, and a few days alone out on the plains.

Feeling her body shake with sobs, feeling her hot tears burn into his chest, twisted at his heart and brought back his earlier resolve. His feelings were no longer important. Lizzie was.

He'd had no right to bring her to such a hostile land, a land which had almost killed her, he had no right to expect her to stay and risk it again. She belonged back East in her quiet college town with her quiet professor father and her quiet gentlemen callers. She belonged where there were sidewalks through flowered parks, carriages with cushions, tea rooms, concert halls, law and order and tranquility.

The picture of how she'd looked when he first met her flashed into his mind, all prim and starchy in her white ruffled blouse and brown skirt, with that gawd-awful bun, and those glasses sitting crooked on her uppity nose. And look at her now. Her hair was a rat's nest, her face sunburned, bruised, and scratched all to hell, her clothes torn to shreds and covered in mud. This is what he'd done to her. He'd got her uncle killed, he'd exposed her to the worst kind of vermin, shown her life at its lowest, and death at its ugliest.

He had taken everything and given nothing.

Her golden beauty bathed in moonlight, the touch of her hands on his body, the taste of her lips on his, her generous response to his lovemaking, these memories would be the hardest to bear, the hardest to die. But he would endure them, because it would assure Lizzie's safety, it would afford her a chance for a good life.

Yet sending her away was the most difficult task he would ever face.

Chapter Twenty-Five

"But you can't go," Lenore cried, pacing the bedroom as Elizabeth packed her trunk. "You can't!" The house and ranch were back in order again, and everyone was recovered from their adventure. And McKaid had made his decision.

"It seems I can."

"It will ruin everything. What about the children?" she asked. "How will they manage without you? And Emma, and Russ and me? We all need you."

"According to McKaid, you belong here. I don't. He has this nice little notion that I belong back in Virginia in a nice little house in a nice little town, swinging on a nice little swing in my nice little backyard, with nice little children at my feet and a nice . . ."

"And I'd like to give him a nice little kick in his nice little . . ."

"Lenore," Elizabeth cried, gaping at her friend's uncharacteristic audacity.

"Oh, it's all so monstrous. Why, if your father were here, if he knew what . . . that . . . well, you know what I mean, he'd insist that McKaid do the right thing."

Elizabeth blushed and turned away. "Yes. But he isn't here, and McKaid does think he's doing the right thing."

"Have you tried to talk to him?" Lenore asked, frantic that nothing be left undone to save the situation.

"Talk is a very civilized description of what we did. He's the most mule-headed man I've ever had the misfortune to know. I was this far, *this far*," she emphasized with her thumb and forefinger, "from begging him to marry me. It's more than my self-respect can tolerate, Lenore. I'll never beg any man to marry me."

"Of course you won't. Why should you have to? Oh, there must be something we can do."

"We?" She held up a restraining hand. "Now wait a minute, Lenore . . ."

"Elizabeth, you can't let him do this to you, to the both of you. You love him, and he loves you."

"Yes, I love him. I can't imagine what my life will be like without him. Does he really believe I'm going to forget him so easily, just pick up my life where I left off back there?"

"What will you do?"

Elizabeth folded her yellow dress, her one good dress, and placed it in the trunk. "I don't know. Try to find work, a place to live."

"You have no place to live?" Lenore asked, aghast.

"I'll stay with my father for a while, to be sure, but he remarried the week before I left. I can't intrude on them, not that they wouldn't welcome me. It's a small house. Though I suppose I could stay with my stepmother's sister. She's alone and often not well."

"I can't believe any of this. He's burying you alive."

"Perhaps I'll get off the train in St. Louis. That looked like an interesting city. I could probably find work there."

"You'd be all alone. Anything could happen, and who would you turn to? You must not think of doing that."

"Let's change the subject. I don't want to discuss this anymore. Have you finalized your wedding plans?"

"Yes." She sounded less than enthusiastic. "We'll be married in three weeks in Santa Fe. I wish you could be here. We wouldn't be getting married at all if not for you."

"Nonsense. It was only a matter of time."

"Russ and I both wanted you and McKaid to be there with us. We even thought about having a double ceremony."

"We're not Catholic, Lenore."

"Father Francis wouldn't care about that, and married is married."

"Father Francis is marrying you?"

She smiled. "He's staying in Santa Fe until his leg is healed. I thought, well, we became good friends while we were together. I wanted him to bless our marriage."

"I think it's a lovely idea. You'll have a beautiful wedding, Lenore, and a wonderful marriage. Russ loves you

404

very much."

"McKaid loves you, too, Elizabeth. You should have seen him when he thought you were dead. He was physically ill. I've never seen a man as devastated as he was."

Elizabeth was skeptical. "It's not apparent now."

"He'll change his mind. I know he will. He won't be able to let you leave."

But McKaid didn't change his mind. The next morning he waited silently by the wagon as Elizabeth bid Emma and the children a tearful farewell.

"Don't think badly of him, dear," Emma said softly to her. She dabbed at her eyes again. "He's doing it for you. He doesn't mean to be hurtful."

"I suppose not. Please don't worry about me, Emma. If you have to worry, worry about Ruthie. She's taking this very badly. She thinks I'm deserting her, and I couldn't tell her the truth. I didn't know what to tell her. Don't let her blame herself." Elizabeth knew from experience how miserable that was, blaming herself because prospective parents had passed her up in favor of someone else. Hating herself.

"I'll do what I can, dear," Emma said, looking worriedly at their bedroom window. Two very sad faces looked back.

Elizabeth looked up, and her heart tore in two. She took a steadying breath and faced McKaid. "I'm ready."

They didn't speak until they were on the outskirts of Santa Fe. Elizabeth had already said all she could think of to convince McKaid that she belonged with him, but he'd been unmovable. She didn't feel strong enough to put herself through it again, so she said nothing. But the tension between them grew thicker with each mile.

Finally McKaid withdrew an envelope from his shirt pocket and handed it to her.

"What is this?"

"It occurred to me that we had never agreed on a salary. It's not a large sum, but it will compensate for your time here."

She was furiously indignant and not a little hurt. "We never agreed on a salary because I am family. My sole purpose in coming out here was to help Uncle Clint and the children. Money was never discussed, and I won't discuss it now. I don't want your money. I have enough of my own, thank you."

"Then think of it as travel expenses."

"No."

"Elizabeth, you will take it. With Clint gone, I'm responsible for you, and you are not traveling across this country with no money in your pocket."

She had plenty of money, but she could see that to argue was to bang her head uselessly against that stone wall again. Ungraciously she snatched the envelope away and stuffed it in her satchel.

"I hope that salves your conscience. I'll have to take your word that it's adequate compensation since I don't know the going price for a mistress."

"Don't," he said wearily.

No other words were exchanged until her luggage had been stowed and the driver took his place on the high seat of the stage.

"This isn't Bert's stage?" she asked, dismayed that she'd have to travel without even Bert and Amos as company.

"No. This is Jake's. He's a good driver. You've no need to worry. Jakes will see you to the train in Abilene."

Having Bert and Amos with her would have delayed the feeling of being severed from New Mexico. They were part of her life here, they shared experiences and memories with her. With them she would have been able to hold on to hope a little longer. That was not to be the case, and she was disappointed, but she couldn't explain that to McKaid.

"Well, McKaid, I guess this is—"

"McKaid," a woman's voice boomed behind them. "Aren't you a stranger these days," the familiar voice went on, and Elizabeth turned to see Rosie, Mrs. Stanhope, bearing down on them.

"Rosie," McKaid greeted. "How's my favorite shopkeeper?"

"Good as ever. I hear congratulations are due."

Baffled, McKaid looked from Rosie to Elizabeth and back, his brow cocked questioningly.

"The Ramirez gang. A nice piece of work that was."

"Ah, that." He shrugged. "I had help, Rosie."

"Modesty? Are you ailing?"

McKaid laughed. "Maybe, Rosie. Maybe I am."

"On board, now," Jake called back. "Got a schedule to keep."

Rosie looked startled, only now realizing they were all standing by a departing stage. "Are you leaving?"

"I am," Elizabeth answered.

406

"Why dearie, I thought you'd be stayin' for good. But what with everything that's happened, I guess you got the right to change you mind. I'm sorry we didn't give you a better welcome."

"You goin' or stayin', lady?" Jake hollered.

"Keep your shirt on, Jake," Rosie yelled back. "You ain't goin' nowhere *that* important."

"Thank you, Rosie. I'm glad to have met you."

"Sure, sure. If you ever decide to give us another chance, you come back and see me. Hear?"

"I will. Good-bye, Rosie. Good-bye, McKaid."

The corners of his lips tightened and he nodded. He stood rigid, and she wondered for a second if he was afraid to move or to speak. She searched his face for any weakening, any sign that she could change his mind.

His chest was heaving as much as hers. "McKaid?" she asked.

His eyes met hers. They were surprisingly naked, full of pain, regret, indecision. He looked away for a second, and when his gaze returned she could see nothing of his inner soul, save his steely intent to have her gone. "Good-bye, Elizabeth." He turned and walked away, leaving her to climb into the stage alone.

She closed the door and took a seat in the corner. To her relief she was the only passenger. More would get on in Las Vegas, but by then she'd be able to face them without crying.

She glanced out the window. Rosie was still standing there, a deep scowl on her face as her bewildered gaze swung from her to McKaid's stiff back. The stage lurched forward. Elizabeth shut her eyes. She shut out the town, the people, the mountains that she had grown to love, but she couldn't shut out the pain.

Dinner that evening at the Circle K was a solemn affair. Emma's cooking was as good as ever, but it could have been stewed sawdust for all the interest the diners showed for it. Lenore and Russ had stayed on at the house, Russ having been given Clint's room in Elizabeth's absence.

"When is your father-in-law returning, Lenore?" Emma asked, trying to break through the brooding silence that hung over the table.

Lenore looked up from her untouched meal and laid her fork aside. "The day after tomorrow."

"Drink your milk, Ruthie," Emma said when Lenore again fell silent.

Ruthie looked up, and her blue eyes filled with tears. Her pixielike chin trembled.

McKaid's lips tightened as they moved from one to another around the table. "Take your sister upstairs, James, and read her a story. You might as well clear the table, Emma."

"I'll help," Lenore said quickly, wishing also to escape, before she said something she'd be sorry for.

McKaid excused himself and went outside. Russ, alone in the dining room, braced his elbows on the table and propped his chin on his fists. This had been the worst meal he'd ever sat through. The children were morose, and who could expect otherwise when yet another mother had been denied them. Lenore blamed him for not knocking sense into McKaid, something she wished heartily that she could have done herself. Emma tried feebly to inject some normalcy to the house, but it was useless without Elizabeth. How had one woman in such a short time come to be the mainstay of an entire household, so that her absence brought routine life to a grinding halt?

Because she was loved, she was important, she had become the steadying rudder in a floundering ship. Without her they were all adrift.

To the children, she had become a mother, the person they looked to for love and guidance in a world gone mad. For Emma she was daughter and mistress of the house who had taken the burden of responsibility from her tired shoulders. To Lenore she'd become sister, friend, confidante. Russ even found himself the possessor of a strong brotherly concern for her, and yes, love and an irrepressible desire to please her. To McKaid, if he'd only admit it, she was mate, the other half of him, the perfect complement, the perfect foil, his balance.

So where was she? Why wasn't she here where she belonged? Why was she sitting brokenhearted in some dismal stage destined for a place she didn't want to be? He pushed himself from the table and slammed out the front door.

He found McKaid leaning against the corral fence, smoking one of his infrequent cigarettes. Russ walked slowly but purposefully over and went directly for his throat.

"It's dark tonight. Where do you suppose she is now?"

McKaid grunted some response Russ couldn't hear and stamped out his cigarette.

"Did she have enough money?"

"Yeah."

"Did you give her that little gun of Clint's? I'd hate to think she was totally defenseless."

"She has it. She'll be all right," he snapped. "I'm sure of it."

"Who are you trying to convince?"

"Russ," he warned.

Russ was silent for a moment, peeling bark off the splitrail fence. "I understand why you sent her away."

"Do you?"

"Sure. The big Texas Ranger is a selfish, goddamned coward."

That earned him a punch on the jaw that sent him sprawling in the dirt. He sat up and rubbed his jaw.

"Hell, Russ, I'm sorry," McKaid apologized, offering Russ an arm up. "I don't know why I did that. Maybe because you're right." He raked his hand through his hair and rubbed the back of his neck. "I don't know anything anymore except that my guts are being ripped out."

"I was there when you thought she'd been shot, friend. I saw what that did to you. As hard as it is now, it's far easier than risking that again. Right?"

McKaid didn't respond.

"The trouble is she'll probably never find another man who can fill your boots."

"That's ridiculous."

"Is it? You took her, McKaid, and you taught her what it meant to be your woman, and she met every challenge head on. She met them because she *is* your woman. Look what she's gone through. You've stretched her so far beyond that narrow world she came from that she'll never be satisfied with it now."

"I'm trying to do what's best for her."

"Shouldn't she be the judge of that? At least be honest with yourself. You did it for *you*. If you don't honestly love her, if you sincerely want nothing more to do with her, then you did the right thing. But unless you can say that, don't claim you did it for her good."

McKaid turned away, unable to answer.

"Think about her for a minute. You brought a sparrow to

New Mexico. What you're sending back is an eagle. A very disillusioned eagle."

"But a safe one."

"A caged one. Not safe at all. She's learned to fight, and she's learned it from you. You're not saving her from trouble, you're just not going to be around to watch it."

"What's that supposed to mean?"

"You know how she thinks. She gets thoroughly disgusted with the world. Every injustice she sees is going to be another Ramirez for her. You didn't see her when she thought she lost you before. All that heartache and passion was buried beneath a bitter rock-hard shell of determination to see you spared any more pain. It was frightening to watch. She would have done anything for you, and no one stood in her way. We didn't dare.

"What I'm saying, McKaid, is that she'll go one of two ways. She'll fold her wings and give up entirely, and the Elizabeth you know will be as good as gone anyway. Or she'll spread her wings with a vengeance and beat herself to death on anyone she puts in the same category as Ramirez.

"You're very alike, you and Elizabeth. She's as much a renegade at heart as you are. You've sent her back to a world far more close-minded and unfair than this, and she won't accept it anymore. She'll take on one fight after another, big business, government, she won't care how powerful they are. She'll fight because that's all she has left. I've seen it in her. And keep in mind that under all their fine clothes and impeccable manners, there are men back there who are far more ruthless than Ramirez."

"You're wrong. You have to be wrong. She'll meet someone else, settle down, have a family . . ."

"If that's what you're determined to believe, there's not much more I can say, except that I don't think you know her very well. You've been trying to liken her to Rosanna ever since you fell in love with her, but she's not Rosanna. And you're not the man you were then either. Fate has given you another chance, with a woman your equal this time."

"I know she's not Rosanna. As much as I adored Rosanna, she was a child, a beautiful, spoiled child I wanted to pamper and protect. She wasn't half the woman Lizzie is, but she didn't deserve to die like she did. I couldn't save her, Russ."

"You made up for that. You saved Elizabeth. Don't throw her away now. Bring her back."

"I couldn't bear it if . . ." He swallowed convulsively.

"I feel the same way about Lenore. None of us knows when our time is up. Elizabeth could die next week in a train wreck. You could drop dead tomorrow. Why borrow trouble?" He picked up a stone and tossed it toward the barn. "I guess I've said all I wanted."

"She does have a temper, doesn't she," he said around a faraway smile

"And stubborn as hell."

"And sassy."

"She'll give you no peace."

"I knew that the first time I kissed her." He sighed heavily. "I need to be alone, Russ."

"Sure. See you in the morning."

By the time Elizabeth reached Las Vegas, she was furious. Who the hell did he think he was, ordering her out of New Mexico? Did he think he owned the place? She was just as angry with herself for letting him, but she could forgive *herself*, because she'd been in a delayed state of shock when he'd made his decision.

His decision. He had the most infuriating habit of issuing some edict then walking away without giving anyone a chance for rebuttal. And if anyone did try to argue, he turned a deaf ear.

Impossible. Domineering. Tyrannical. She was better off without him.

She told herself that over and over as she bought a quick meal and reboarded the stage for Fort Union. And she was doing fine until they met the stage coming the other way. The oncoming driver called them to a halt and got down to talk to Jake.

"Be just a minute, folks," he said, poking his head in the stage door as he passed.

Elizabeth's stomach constricted, and she felt tears threaten again. Bert.

"Miss Elizabeth," he said, surprised to see her. "Didn't expect you to be leavin' us so soon. Somethin' wrong back home?"

"No. Everything's fine." But it wasn't, and her tears told him so.

411

Bert eyed the two soldiers riding with her in the stage. "These men giving you a bad time?"

"No, not at all," she said, fighting for composure. "I'm all right, truly I am."

Bert could see she was embarrassed. He thumbed the two privates out of the carriage and sat down on the seat opposite her.

"I don't know why you're leaving, but I hope you ain't in no hurry."

She took a breath and let it out, back in control. "I'd rather not leave at all, Bert, but McKaid says . . . He thinks I'd be safer and happier back home."

"Safe? Who wants safe? Safe ain't no fun. But, heckfire, that's what I got to tell you. You'll have to go back to Las Vegas. If Jake and them soldiers want to chance it, that's their business, but you ain't going to."

"Bert, what are you talking about?"

"There's a bunch of wild bucks up ahead. They may be having a bit of fun, maybe drunk on likker, but they might take it to mind to really attack the next wagon what goes through there. It ain't safe for you. Not today anyway."

Jake poked his head in the door. "We talked it over, Bert, and we'd like to take her on through. The soldiers got to get back. You can come or not, as you wish, ma'am, but I suggest you wait till the army gets this under control."

"I'll go with Bert," she said, grabbing at the opportunity to delay her departure.

"Hey, Private, get the lady's trunk down, would ya. I hope to hell we don't have to start with military escorts again," he grumbled as he walked away.

Bert helped her down. "Wanna ride shotgun again? There ain't no room inside. I'll put Amos up top, that way you can sit beside me and tell me why you're letting McKaid run you out of town. Never thought I'd see the day he'd push you 'round."

"He's bigger than I am."

"Size don't mean nothin'. You just have to know where to hit. Ever seen a bluejay chase off a big crow? He gets up there and pecks at his head till the crow don't know what's up or down."

"You mean I should blacken his eye?"

Bert gave a hoot. "That sounds a good idea. Git on up there now, missy."

412

Elizabeth didn't get off in Las Vegas, but went with Bert and Amos all the way back to Santa Fe, determined to give McKaid what was due him. A good piece of her mind.

McKaid saddled Lucky Lady and made his way down the road to Santa Fe. He didn't care how late it was, he intended to telegraph Fort Union and have them put Lizzie on the next stage back. She was probably so angry by now that she'd fight the entire U.S. Army, but even if they had to tie her up and put her on the stage forcibly, he intended to get her back.

He wasn't deterred by the locked door. He pounded and demanded entrance until the telegraph operator woke up and stumbled to the door.

"Marshal McKaid," he said, recognizing the man outside. "Come in. What can I do for you?"

"I want to send a message to Fort Union."

"At this hour?"

"It's urgent. Please."

"Certainly. What do you wish it to say?" he asked, grabbing up his spectacles and a pad and pencil.

"Elizabeth Hepplewhite on stage from Santa Fe. Imperative she return to Santa Fe immediately. Sign it Marshal McKaid, and put whatever else is required to get a quick reply."

"Sure thing, Marshal, I'll have the answer in a minute."

"I'll wait then." He paced agitatedly at the front of the office while the telegraph chattered its message across the wire. This had to work. If it didn't . . . if it didn't, he'd have to go all the way to Virginia to get her, that's all. Russ was right. Damn him, he was always right. He made him feel a fool. Well, he was a fool.

He hoped once he married Lizzie, if she'd have him now, his sanity would return. It seemed as if he'd been walking in a fog ever since he'd met her. His mind, always so sharp before, wouldn't work, probably due to the shock of realizing he'd fallen in love again. Love, especially when it came unexpectedly and at an unfortunate time, could be a crippling emotion.

Although now that he was resigning from the Rangers, it didn't matter much if his mind was preoccupied with thoughts of Lizzie. Now that he had his priorities straight, now that he could forget about Ramirez, he could devote his thoughts

413

entirely to her. Not that he had much choice.

"Marshal," Harvey called.

He stepped quickly to the counter. "What is it? What did he say?"

"The operator is waiting. He asked if you're sure about a woman. It appears that the stage was attacked today, but there was no Elizabeth Hepplewhite on it."

Attacked? "Yes, I'm sure. I put her on it," McKaid shouted. Attacked by whom?

"Just a minute, sir." He went back to tapping, and McKaid took up his frantic pacing again. He stopped at the door and looked out. He couldn't lose her now. Not now. He slammed the heel of his hand into the door frame and spun around to glare at Harvey.

Harv held up his hand for McKaid to wait. After another few seconds he stood. "Sorry, Marshal. The two passengers on the stage went out on patrol, and Jake took the stage into town. All the operator knows is that no women arrived. He's sending someone to question Jake now. He'll send back a message as soon as he knows anything."

"Thanks, Harv. I'll be at the cantina."

His stomach felt like lead. His whole body felt heavy and utterly defeated as he dragged himself across the square to the street where the cantina was located. He'd put her on that stage. Where could she be? Kidnapped again? Maybe someone in the cantina had heard about the stage. Maybe . . .

The saloon door swung open and a rowdy group elbowed their way out. A high-pitched laugh came from their midst. McKaid's head snapped up, his body tensed. Was that who he thought it was?

Biff and Tex were there with Bert and Amos. Four old crusty buzzards and . . .

"Elizabeth!"

All five stopped in their tracks and turned their heads in McKaid's direction.

"Hey, McKaid," Tex drawled affably.

McKaid was in no humor for a friendly chat. "What the hell is going on here? What are you doing in there?" he barked at Elizabeth.

"Now, McKaid, my friend . . ." Bert tried.

"Keep out of this," he snapped. "I'm waiting for an explanation, young lady."

414

She lifted her chin. "I have every right to be in there," she answered defiantly, even if she did have to expend a great deal of thought and effort to get her words out distinctly. "If women can't go in there, then neither should men."

McKaid rolled his eyes and prayed for patience.

"That's tellin' him, girl," Bert preened.

A silly grin spread across her face, and her left knee buckled. She lurched, but Biff was at her elbow to steady her.

"My God," McKaid roared, furious. "You're drunk! I'm worried sick that your scalp is hanging on some buck's lodge pole, and all the time you're in a saloon going on a bust?"

She couldn't make sense of that. "What?"

"She weren't in the saloon," Amos came to her defense. "And we was with her all the time."

"Now that's comforting."

"Relax, McKaid. Consuela offered to fix her and Bert and Amos a meal since the café was closed. We was in the back room."

"Just the five of us," Bert added. "We took care of her real good for you."

"You call that . . ." he thundered to a halt. "I ought to shoot the lot of you. And you," he rounded on Elizabeth, "haven't you a sensible thought in your head? Of all the stupid things to do . . ."

Her lips tightened, her eyes flashed, and she pulled back her fist and swung.

McKaid easily dodged the wild arc of her small fist. He watched, stunned, as she lost her balance, spun in a continuing circle, and sat down heavily on her bottom.

She looked up at Bert and sputtered a giggle. "I missed."

"It takes practice," he said, pulling her to her feet.

"Marshal," Harv called, jogging across the green. "Got your answer," he said, coming to a halt by the tall lawman. "Jake said Bert Yingling took your woman off his stage. He took her back to . . ." His words died when he finally noticed the people with the marshal, one of whom was Bert. He looked at Elizabeth. "Is that her?" he asked, eyeing the weaving young lady on Biff Story's arm.

"Unfortunately. Thanks, Harv. Sorry I got you out of bed."

Harv grinned and shook his head. "Quite all right. Glad to see she didn't come to . . . too much harm."

McKaid stood like an avenging angel over the sorry group. It

415

would probably be funny in the morning. But right now . . . He turned his dark glare to Lizzie.

"Thank God it's late enough that no one is out and about. Your reputation may still be salvageable," he said. "No thanks to you men."

"I didn't do nothin'—anything to be ashamed of," she argued.

"Easy, lad. She's been on the stage all day, and not too happy to be there," Bert defended her. "You broke her poor heart."

"We was only liftin' her spirits," Tex said. "Couldn't believe it ourselves when she told us you sent her away. Thought you was a smart boy."

McKaid sighed and gave up. He couldn't fight them all. "A temporary lapse of good sense, I guess. At any rate, I've come to take her home. So if you gentlemen will excuse us . . ."

"Well, maybe I don't want to go with you," Elizabeth said, turning up her impudent nose.

"Yes, you do."

"No, I don't."

"Yes, you do." With one dark look McKaid dared the four men to interfere.

"How 'bout a game of cards, boys," Tex suggested.

"Good idea," Bert said, turning with his friends back toward the cantina. He gave McKaid and Elizabeth one last glance, and chuckled.

"You'll just send me away again," Elizabeth sulked.

"No, I won't."

"You won't?"

"No."

"I can stay for good?"

"Only as my wife."

Tears, never far from the surface that day, spilled over her lower lashes. "You came to get me?" her voice squeaked.

He grinned. No, he was never likely to see peace and quiet again with Lizzie around. But he'd never be bored.

"I came to get you," he answered gently.

"I came back to give you one last chance."

"And I'm taking it. Come here."